Also by Gary Slaughter

Cottonwood Winter: A Christmas Story
Cottonwood Fall
Cottonwood Summer

COTTONWOOD SPRING

COTTONWOOD SPRING

A Novel

by

GARY SLAUGHTER

Library of Congress Control Number: 2008934378
ISBN -13 978-0-9744206-4-6
ISBN -10 0-9744206-4-6

Manufactured in the United States of America
Cover and interior design and layout by Danita Meeks
Editing and proofreading by Joyce Wagner and Sharon Yake
Printing and binding by Falcon Press

Published by Fletcher House
P.O. Box 50979
Nashville, TN 37205-0979

For additional copies of *Cottonwood Spring*, contact Ingram Books, Inc. or www.fletcherhouse.com.

For Joanne –
With my everlasting gratitude
for her unwavering support,
encouragement, and plain hard work
during all four seasons
of Cottonwood.

CONTENTS

COTTONWOOD SPRING

1 RETURN TO RIVERTON

IN THE DIM LIGHT OF A BITTERLY COLD MICHIGAN
morning, Sergeant Jeff Tolna of the Riverton Police Department and
County Coroner Ray Black stood silently, staring down at a man's
body sprawled on the snow-covered bank of the Chippewa River.

Suddenly a fierce gust of wind swept across the still-frozen water
and slammed into them. Clutching their hats, they clamped their
coat collars tightly against their throats to protect against the frigid
March weather. To conserve their rapidly dissipating body heat, they
hunched over, as if to examine the frozen corpse more closely.

Unaware of the large man approaching them from behind, the
two were startled by his booming voice. "March's coming in like a
lion!"

The pair immediately recognized Chippewa County Sheriff
Connors, who greeted them with a raised mitten-covered hand
and a broad grin. In that wind, he realized they hadn't heard him
until he spoke.

"Darn it all, Roy! Where'd you come from? I nearly leaped out
of my skin," the sergeant mildly complained.

"I parked up on the street — other side of that stand of blue
spruce. Next time I'll wear my cowbell." Connors smiled again and
then turned serious. "Whatcha got, boys?"

"No sign of foul play — from outward appearances, Roy. I'd
guess he either froze to death or he drowned," the coroner replied,

relieved to share his initial findings. He was eager to return to the warmth and comfort of his tiny office, squeezed into the corner of the modest morgue in the courthouse basement.

"By the looks of his attire, I doubt he's from around here," added Sergeant Tolna. "Didn't have anything on him. No wallet — no ID. No personal items — rings, watch, or jackknife. Not even a hankie."

"What's he wearing anyway? Those are strange duds. Looks like a foreigner. Maybe he's a new German POW from out at the camp."

"Don't think so, Sheriff. Colonel Butler woulda called us if any of his POWs had wandered off."

"Who discovered the body, Jeff?"

"You'll never guess!" Sergeant Tolna said as he poked his thumb in our direction.

Wheeling his bulky body around, the sheriff stared at us in disbelief. "I might have known! Danny Tucker and Jase Addison! What brings you two *international heroes* out here so early and on a morning like this?"

Danny answered truthfully, "Dynamite, Sheriff Connors. Good old-fashioned dynamite! That's what brought us out here."

We hadn't meant for people to know our secret so soon. But when we discovered the body, we were forced to tell everything. The unbelievable chain of events that brought us to the riverbank that morning had started in the late winter of 1945. It was shortly after my best friend Danny and I had returned from the White House where President Roosevelt gave us our second *Medals of Courage*.

Let's see! Where should I begin?

WE HAD RISEN EARLY on that first Monday morning in March of 1945. As we sat around the breakfast table, Dad finished his coffee and caught up on the war news in the *Riverton Daily Press*. He would soon depart for the Burke Factory where he worked as a tool and die maker in the top secret bombsight department.

"What could be keeping Danny?" Mom wondered aloud as she leafed through her latest movie magazine. "He's never late for breakfast."

Since Danny had become my best friend the summer before, he had invited himself to share our breakfast on a daily basis. Not that he missed any meals at home, mind you. Wartime food rationing had seriously limited Danny's ability to maintain his king-sized eating habit. Though he was a slim and wiry 11-year-old, his appetite dwarfed that of any hardworking man in our blue-collar neighborhood. In Danny's case, partaking of a second breakfast at our house was not optional. It was an absolute necessity.

We were fortunate that my mother's parents, Grandpa and Grandma Compton, owned a farm where they raised cattle, pigs, and chickens. Unlike most American families, we enjoyed a sufficient supply of roast beef, ham, and eggs throughout the war years. Ever the opportunist, Danny joined the Addison breakfast table on his way to school each morning. We didn't mind because he entertained us with his agile mind and his bizarre observations about the world around him.

Danny was not unaware of the dent he made in our larder. Every other day, he supplemented our pantry with large commercial-sized tins of various food items from his family's basement. Their supply of thousands of cans was a result of the retirement of Danny's paternal grandfather. On that occasion, he liquidated his grocery business and took the profits in the form of a tax-free hoard of canned foodstuffs. But, after suffering pangs of patriotic guilt, he donated the entire inventory to his son. His generosity not only eased his conscience but delivered a substantial benefit to Danny's family.

Thump! Thump! THUMP!

The dramatic snow-stomping on our back porch announced Danny's arrival. He shoved open the back door and flew into our kitchen. Without so much as a word of greeting, he quickly peeled off his snow-flecked mackinaw, tossed it onto one of the hooks beside the door, and banged down into his regular chair at the table.

He was wearing his usual Monday morning uniform, a creative mix of Boy Scout and World War I doughboy attire. As usual, he also wore his favorite gray woolen sweater, sporting both of his *Medals of Courage.*

Because my parents were accustomed to Danny's dramatic entrances, they paid little attention. Instead, they continued to read and sip their coffee. But I felt my pulse quicken involuntarily as I observed Danny's expression. From experience, I guessed that he was about to announce yet another campaign. And I was right.

From his back pocket, he suddenly yanked out his *Handbook for Boys* and waved it at me. He turned to my mother and stuck the book under her nose. Finally he shook it at my father. Both ignored his theatrics.

Unperturbed, Dad gave us an update on the war. "Hey, folks. Great news from the Philippines. This past weekend, American airborne troops retook Corregidor — and a combined American and Filipino force has reoccupied Manila. Old General MacArthur's really got the Japs on the run. How about that?"

But Danny was having none of it.

"The war! The war! We're always talking about the war. This is just as important — right here, Mr. A," he proclaimed, slapping his scout handbook. "Do you realize that Jase and I are already way behind?"

"Behind what?" Dad replied innocently.

"Merit Badges! That's what."

"Merit Badges?"

"Sorry, Mr. A. You probably don't even know what they are."

"Yes, I do, Danny. I was a Sea Scout when I was about your age."

"A Sea Scout? What's that?"

"Like an Explorer Scout, but we had *ships* instead of *posts*. We focused on naval subjects but we also earned Merit Badges — just like you regular scouts. We could even become Eagles — if we got enough Merit Badges."

"So you know!"

"Know what, Danny?"

"Just how important Merit Badges are!" he nearly shouted, shaking his handbook.

With some trepidation, I decided to intervene. "Danny, you have to be a Second Class scout to work on Merit Badges. You haven't even finished your Tenderfoot requirements yet."

Mentioning this subject to him was entering dangerous territory. Danny simply did not approve of the *Tenderfoot* label on the initial rank in scouting. He considered the term to be demeaning. In fact, he had argued vigorously with Mel Carmody, our scoutmaster, to grant him a Tenderfoot waiver.

"Tenderfoot sounds too sissy," Danny insisted.

Dad tried to dissuade him. "Do you really think scouting is about turning boys into sissies? *Tenderfoot* simply means *novice, beginner* — the very first step. Like kindergarten comes before first grade and so on."

Using *kindergarten* as an example was a strategic blunder. Danny shook his head slowly and folded his arms. His body language shouted, *if that's the best you can come up with, I rest my case.*

I screwed up my courage and acquainted my best friend with some realities. "Even though you don't want to be *called* a Tenderfoot, you have to *be* a Tenderfoot before you become a Second Class scout. And you can't work on Merit Badges until you're a Second Class. So you might just as well get used to the idea."

Still Danny wouldn't concede the point. Instead he wondered, "Do they have Tenderfoot in the Girl Scouts?"

"Danny, you don't want to be a Girl Scout!" I scolded.

"At least, I wouldn't be a sissy there."

In an attempt to regain my composure, I read an article on the upcoming Academy Awards from the back of Dad's newspaper. The Bing Crosby movie, *Going My Way*, had been nominated for *Best Picture*. Mom and I had seen that film at Riverton's majestic Chippewa Theater. We invited Danny to join us, but oddly enough he declined. When pressed for his reason, he told us he didn't care much for *hitchhiking* movies.

After taking a huge bite of scrambled eggs, Danny turned back to me and continued, "I wonder if they have the Tenderfoot rank in the Marine Corps."

"Of course not! That's silly!"

"Exactly! They're much too macho."

Danny was THE most stubborn boy I'd ever met. Once he made up his mind, he wouldn't budge. I declared emotional bankruptcy. "Oh, forget about it. Let's go to school. It's getting late."

"Okay, Jase. Bye, Mr. A! Mrs. A! See you in the funny papers."

"Bye, Danny," Dad said, patting him on the shoulder.

Mom gave Danny a hug and kissed the top of his head. He looked into her face with glassy eyes and smiled. "Danny, if you were a Tenderfoot, I'd never think of you as a sissy. I know better. Don't you?"

"Sure I do, Mrs. A. I'll be a Tenderfoot — just for you."

Dad and I looked at each other and shook our heads.

"Hurry, Jase. I want to get to school early so I can study my Tenderfoot requirements."

The Conrad Hoffman Story
Milwaukee

"IS IT MY IMAGINATION or have I been talking to myself a lot lately?" Hoffman asked himself aloud as he admired his image in the full-length mirror.

He felt good to be in uniform again. Oh, how he missed the glory days back in New Jersey where he had been revered as a gifted protégé of his leader. And the crescendo at Madison Square Garden in 1939 had been ecstasy. He was somebody back in those days, on top of the world and free of any ties to Michigan.

But now he was heading back there. It seemed strange, even surreal perhaps. When he looked at himself, fully shaved and still trim enough to fit into his old outfit, he experienced a sense of peace and serenity that he hadn't felt since the war started.

The war had changed everything. That's when the organization he had worked so hard to build began to crumble. His colleagues and friends were rounded up like criminals. From time to time, he wondered what it would be like to be in prison with them. Sometimes, but not often, he even wondered what they thought about his abandoning them to protect himself.

Over the past five years, he continually reminded himself of how fortunate he was to have *obtained* the resources to finance his hurried departure. Oddly enough he had not felt an iota of guilt about running away. He had fled because he feared arrest and imprisonment. His former colleagues seemed to relish their collapse. As true zealots, they expected to be vindicated and rewarded in the end.

But Hoffman was no martyr. He was a pragmatist. An accountant by training, he relished order and control. His motivation for signing on was not religious fervor like the others. Hoffman sought wealth and power. He was convinced that the organization and its cause could help him meet his goals.

In truth, life had been hard for him since his departure. Like his old friends, he too was a prisoner of sorts. He had constructed his prison from fear and paranoia. Running from town to town. Working wretched jobs. Constantly looking over his shoulder in fear of discovery and arrest.

Shaking away those unpleasant thoughts, he pulled in his stomach, pushed back his shoulders, and saluted himself. It was just like the old days. He felt an overwhelming sense of pride and self-satisfaction.

He focused on the grand purpose that had reactivated his enthusiasm. But suddenly he was brought back to earth.

"Conrad, do you have time for breakfast before you go?"

"Yes, Aunt Greta. I'll take time. It's a long drive so I'll need my strength. Yes, it's a very long drive."

The Conrad Hoffman Story
On the Road to Chicago

AFTER LEAVING MILWAUKEE, HOFFMAN drove south on U.S. 41 toward Chicago. He relaxed and allowed his mind to wander. Naturally he thought of Aunt Greta. He had always been fond of his mother's younger sister. After all, he had lived with her since his mother's death when he was only a freshman in high school.

As the youngest daughter in a large German family, she had been expected to nurse the older family members until they passed away. Never questioning her obligation, she set aside her personal wants and needs to serve her family.

Only one of her three brothers had married, but that ended when he returned from the Great War with his lungs partially destroyed by mustard gas and with a strong dependence on schnapps to ease the pain. She had nursed him until his death nearly 10 years later.

Her only sister, Conrad's mother, had been so frail that she was among the thousands of fatalities resulting from the influenza pandemic in 1918. No one knew what had become of her errant husband who left her just before Conrad's birth.

Not that it mattered much to her but Greta had been well-rewarded. She was the sole heir to the wealth created and then hoarded by her frugal parents and siblings. In the end, there were just the two of them, Greta and Conrad. Because of that, they shared a special bond. She had always been there for him like a doting mother, forgiving his youthful whims and foibles.

She dutifully paid his tuition so he could earn his degree in accounting. She supported him fully while he studied and finally passed his CPA exams. She never inquired about his political activities or what happened to his prestigious position with the organization in New Jersey.

She had been very fond of Conrad's former wife. But out of respect, she had never questioned him about what happened to his marriage or to his children. Not that he knew much about their current situation either. Soon after he joined the organization in 1930, he was divorced. His wife never understood why he was drawn to its cause. At first, it had angered him. But that subsided as he devoted himself to his work. But when the war came, he lost both his cause and his comrades, some of whom he considered friends.

But, thank God, he had never lost Aunt Greta. She was the only constant in his life. She was the only person he could count on, the only one he ever truly trusted.

As usual, her breakfast had been complete, nourishing, and tasty. He packed his uniform, the incriminating papers he had hidden in Greta's basement in case they were needed to blackmail his former colleagues, and his cache of money, the result of years of skimming off his share just as his leader Kuhn had done with Hoffman's help.

With this money, he would change his identity when he arrived in Chicago. He'd return to Michigan to settle some old grievances and visit some people, before disappearing for the last time.

Of course for her own protection, his dear Aunt Greta would know nothing about this. In fact, she hadn't even asked where he was going in her car or how long he would be away. That's what he liked about her.

Why couldn't his wife have been more like Aunt Greta?

BY THE TIME WE reached the canning factory parking lot, Danny was his old self again. We saw the army truck that transported our friends, Otto Klump and his squad of German POWs, from Camp Riverton to their jobs at the canning factory each morning.

It always gave me a warm feeling to recall how Otto and the other POWs had rescued Butch Matlock's mother from their burning house the summer before. I remembered fondly how the U.S. Army had given permission for the POWs to rebuild the Matlock house with money donated during the fund-raiser that Danny and I had organized.

During that period, Butch Matlock became our good friend and a member of our secret neighborhood organization, the Forrest Street Guards. We FSG members maintained a close watch on our section of town, always alert for spies, saboteurs, and other enemies who sought to harm America by infiltrating our neighborhood.

Undoubtedly Danny's recovery could be attributed to our anticipation of starting a new week with Miss Sparks, our extremely beautiful sixth-grade teacher at Hamilton School. After all, there wasn't a single boy in our class who didn't have a raging crush on the lovely Miss Sparks. In fact, Danny and I ranked very high on her list of passionate admirers. We were downright irrational when it came to our favorite teacher. In our eyes, she could do no wrong. But little did we know that very morning our affection for Miss Sparks would be challenged by a stranger in our midst.

We also looked forward to seeing our close friends, Butch and Dilbert Dinkins. Dilbert was also invited to join FSG, but only after surgery cured his disgusting nose-picking habit. I mustn't forget Danny's heartthrob, Millie Zack, who lived across from Butch on Milford Street. This cunning girl with her freckled face and strawberry-blond hair possessed the power to turn Danny into a puddle of melted butter by simply batting her eyes. Seeing Danny, when he was afflicted with Millie's charms, was not a pretty sight. However, because he was my best friend, I accepted this minor character flaw.

When Danny and I walked into class that morning, we were confronted by a new face staring up at us from the first desk in the first row, the closest desk to where Miss Sparks stood when she addressed our class. After the morning rituals that included the Pledge of Allegiance, the Lord's Prayer, a Bible reading, and the class roll call, Miss Sparks turned her attention to the new boy whose name, I expected, we were about to learn.

We already knew quite a bit about him. First of all, this was no ordinary boy. He was very well-dressed and equally well-mannered.

He wore shiny black leather shoes, charcoal flannel slacks, and a navy-blue blazer with an intricate gold crest on its left breast pocket. I couldn't read the wording or decipher the forms depicted on the crest, but I have to admit it looked very classy. He also wore a starched white dress shirt and a blue and red striped necktie. The tie was snuggly held in place by a double Windsor knot.

His hair was slicked down by what Danny and I would call *brilliantine*, the oily hair tonic used by movie stars to keep their hair in place and look glossy. Even from my desk, a dozen feet away, the scent from his hair tonic was noxious. It smelled like almonds and cherries or some other sickeningly syrupy blend.

When I turned around to ascertain Danny's assessment of the new boy, I had no trouble reading his lips. After all, I had heard that same word about two thousand times at the breakfast table just that morning. Without a doubt, Danny's one-word descriptor was "SISSY!"

"Class, today we have a new student who has just moved here from Nashville, Tennessee. I know you'll give him a warm welcome. I'd like to introduce Johnson Bradford. Would you please stand so your new classmates can greet you, Johnson?"

"Yes, ma'am," the new boy replied politely, in a foreign-sounding Southern accent. Didn't he know that Riverton, Michigan, was the center of the universe and, as such, no Rivertonian ever spoke with a hint of an accent? How would he ever fit in here?

As he stood, I have to admit I was impressed by how tall and handsome he was. I was also impressed by his slightly tanned face and bright white teeth. He reminded me of Tyrone Power.

I had mixed emotions about Johnson Bradford. At first, I had felt revulsion but now I was feeling admiration. This was most confusing. I certainly knew what Danny thought. So I shook the warm feelings out of my head and returned to my initial impression. I didn't want to lose sight of the basics. This poor sucker didn't stand a chance. He dressed and looked like a prissy sissy. He smelled like a rose geranium. He had two names instead of one. And both of them were last names, for cripes sake. His parents must have been pretty dopey to make a mistake like that. He also spoke with that strange-sounding Southern accent. Finally he had the audacity to call Miss Sparks, *ma'am*.

Ma'am?

What a loser!!!

During the morning recess, Danny, Butch, Dilbert, and I met on the back steps of the school to compare notes. My fellow FSG members shared my perceptions to a tee. Danny was particularly firm in his negative impression of *JB* as he had dubbed him.

As the day wore on, we also realized that the new sissy was a world-class know-it-all. Whenever Miss Sparks was halfway through asking a question, up would go his hand. And when no other hands were showing, each time she called on him, old JB knew the answer. To top it off, he stood at attention and answered her question so politely that we wanted to throw up. Whoever this goober was, he was in deep trouble with us, the *elite* boys, in Miss Sparks' class. I promised to make a man out of this sissy-boy.

When the final bell rang, signaling the end of the school day, Miss Sparks asked, "Danny and Jase, would you stay a few minutes after school, please? I have a favor to ask of you."

When I found out what Miss Sparks had in mind, I for one was stunned. "Jase, Johnson's your new neighbor. So I thought you and Danny could walk home with him. You boys have a lot in common and I'm sure you'll become good friends."

JB stuck out his hand. "Johnson Bradford. Delighted to know you, I'm sure," he drawled in a dignified Southern accent. Still suffering from shock, I took his hand and shook it. He had a remarkably strong grip for a certified sissy. I failed to tell him my name or how I felt about making *his* acquaintance.

Turning to Danny, he smiled. But Danny beat him to the punch. Sticking out his hand, Danny declared in a mock-Southern accent, "I ahm Daniel Tuck-ah, and I ahm dee-lighted to make y'alls acquaintance, I ahm very sur-ah."

JB smiled and shook Danny's hand. While he did so, Danny winked at me and drawled, "Jase, ahren't you gla-ad to meet yo-ah new next do-ah neighbah?"

You could have knocked me over with a *feath-ah!*

AS WE MADE OUR way home from school that day, a thin coating of snow still covered the ground. In our part of Michigan, we could expect March weather to range from blizzard to balmy. That day was closer to the blizzard end of the continuum. The stiff north wind buffeted us as we crossed New Albany Avenue and trekked up Forrest Street toward my house.

Carrying out Miss Sparks' request, Danny and I escorted JB to his new home, that of our next-door neighbors, the Reillys. Naturally I wondered how JB came to live with the Reillys, but in keeping with the social mores of that time, I didn't ask. We walked up the wooden front steps and onto the broad covered porch. In warm weather, this was home to several pieces of wicker furniture and an inviting glider from which Mr. and Mrs. Reilly greeted neighbors sauntering by on an evening stroll about the neighborhood.

"You fellas want to come in for a while?"

I looked at Danny, who shrugged his shoulders. We both nodded our heads and entered the front door. I had only been in the Reilly house on a few occasions, usually to pick up or deliver something that Mrs. Reilly or my mother had borrowed from the other. Once it was a cup of sugar. Another time, my mother's movie magazine, featuring an article on Spencer Tracy, one of Mrs. Reilly's favorite Hollywood personalities. On my previous visits, I had always used the back door. Entering through the front door was a new experience.

I hadn't realized that the expansive first floor of the Reilly house was divided into two halves by a wide hallway, running adjacent to the staircase and extending from the front door back to the kitchen. As my eyes adjusted to the dimly lighted interior, at the end of the hallway, I saw Mrs. Reilly sitting at the kitchen table where I had always found her when I called. From what I could gather, she apparently spent much of her day there, reading newspapers and magazines, preparing meals, or working on various projects involving fabrics or yarn.

"Hello, Jase — and Danny! Welcome. Glad to see you've met Johnson, my favorite nephew. I was hoping it'd happen soon. Johnson, these two boys are very special neighbors. But, as you become acquainted, you'll discover that for yourself." Apparently aware of Danny's reputation for being perpetually famished, Mrs. Reilly directed her question to him. "Danny, how about some cookies and hot chocolate?"

Danny's hunger-induced smile propelled Mrs. Reilly into action. Soon we three boys were sitting at the kitchen table, surrounded by stacks of peanut-butter cookies and steaming mugs of cocoa.

"How about these peanut-butter cookies, Jase? Your favorite. Right?" Danny pressed, with an evil grin. Under normal circumstances, I wouldn't touch a peanut-butter cookie. And Danny knew exactly how I felt about the dreadful things.

After kicking Danny under the table, I met my social obligations by delivering a rave review, "These are the best peanut-butter cookies I can ever remember eating."

"Boy! That's the truth!" Danny added. I wasn't sure if he was confirming the fact that he had never seen me eat one or whether he genuinely liked them.

"Would you like to see my room?" JB inquired hopefully.

"Great!" Danny and I replied simultaneously.

The three of us bounded up the carpeted stairs to the second floor. By the number of doors surrounding the landing, I concluded this floor contained three relatively large bedrooms and a bathroom. JB's room was located in the rear, overlooking our backyard.

When we entered the room, Danny and I stopped dead in our tracks. We looked around in amazement and then at each other. This was a virtual trophy room, a shrine to the athletic accomplishments of Johnson Bradford.

Trophies covered the dresser and bedside tables. Blue ribbons, framed team and individual photographs, awards, and certificates of achievement covered the walls. Sports equipment was everywhere. Baseball bats and gloves, footballs and spiked shoes, tennis racquets and balls, and track shoes covered the floor around the perimeter of the sizeable bedroom. Jerseys and warm-up suits hung neatly in the large closet next to his spare blue blazers, flannel slacks, and white shirts and ties. A half-dozen pair of spit-shined dress shoes were arranged neatly in shoe trees under his blazers and other school attire.

Perhaps the most impressive feature of his bedroom was the striking navy-blue spread covering his double bed. In its center, the school crest, comprising elaborate embroidered images of bay laurels and noble Greek athletes hurtling through space, boldly proclaimed him a loyal son of *Stony River Academy.*

"Wow!" was about as much as I could muster.

Danny said nothing but his black eyes were as big as saucers. He glanced at me and shook his head. I knew what he was thinking. *This JB's some kind of sissy all right!*

After regaining our composure, we asked JB how he could have participated in so many organized sports. In Riverton, few were offered to boys before junior high, nearly a year away for us sixth graders.

"In Southern private schools, many sports are open to boys who're younger. For example, I was on the academy rifle team and the equestrian team when I was in fourth grade. If I'd stayed at Stony River, I'm pretty sure I would have made the fencing team this year."

Rifle, equestrian, and fencing teams?

This was too much for boys from a small-town Midwest public school to comprehend. We were clearly in awe of all JB represented and it must have shown on our faces. Quickly he set the record straight.

"But that's all in my past. I no longer go to Stony River. Nope, I'm just like you two. Hamilton School is where I belong. I'll miss Stony River, but I'm glad to be here with Aunt Mary and Uncle Patrick. And I hope the three of us can be friends too."

What were Danny and I going to say after that?

We assured him we were glad to have him in the neighborhood. To prove our point, we invited him to join us that evening for our Boy Scout meeting. We told JB we were on close terms with Mel Carmody, our Scoutmaster. This inside track all but guaranteed he could join our Wolverine Patrol.

But he had other plans. "I'm sorry. We're going to St.Thomas Church tonight for a charity dinner followed by bingo. Maybe I could come to Boy Scouts next Monday. All right?"

"You bet!" we chimed.

Before we departed, Danny turned to JB and gave him some heartfelt advice. "I think maybe you ought to go a little easy on the hair tonic and leave the fancy clothes at home from now on. They were all right for the first day. But I think you should wear some normal clothes to Hamilton School. Might help you fit in — know what I mean?"

As Danny's advice sank in, JB nodded his head slowly. Next he reached over and turned Danny around and around again. JB looked at me and winked. I could barely keep a straight face. "Thanks, Danny. That's good advice. But let me ask you a question. Where can I pick up a pair of combat boots and doughboy leggings like you wear to school?"

Danny looked at me and broke into laughter. Doffing his Boy Scout campaign hat, he bowed to JB from the waist. Then we locked arms and whistled our way down the stairs. After thanking Mrs. Reilly profusely, we hastily headed for the Addison house. When we arrived, Mom was just putting dinner on the table.

She looked up and suggested, "I thought you boys might like to eat early so you can ride over with Dad to the scout meeting. There's a short committee meeting tonight before your meeting. Would you like to eat with us, Danny? Your father's coming by in a while to go to the meeting too."

Without hesitating, Danny immediately took his seat at the table. "What're we having, Mrs. A?"

When I frowned at Danny, he caught my meaning.

"I mean — I'd love to eat with you tonight, Mrs. A. Whatever we're having will be dee-licious."

"Hi, everybody!" Dad exclaimed as he came through the kitchen door. "Sorry I'm late. We had a line down this afternoon. I stayed a bit to give Don Paulus a hand getting it back up."

He looked at Mom. "What's for supper, Marie?"

Danny looked at me and smirked.

"Did I say something wrong?"

We all laughed.

While we were finishing supper, Mom inquired, "What do you boys think of Johnson Bradford?"

Without checking with Danny, I replied, "He's a great guy. You should see his room — with all his trophies and sports awards — and equipment. He went to Stony River Academy, you know."

"Yes, I know."

"But, Mrs. A, why's he here in Riverton, living with the Reillys?"

Looking at the kitchen clock, Mom promised, "That's a long story. If you'll help me clear the table, I'll give you the *Reader's Digest* version while you're having dessert."

After clearing the dishes, we sat back down to listen to Mom.

"First of all, Johnson's mother is Mrs. Reilly's younger — and only — sister. She was a nurse in Nashville, Tennessee, at Vanderbilt University Hospital. She met and married Johnson's father who was a doctor there. Just before the war, wanting to do his part, he joined the navy and was assigned to the medical staff on the *USS Arizona.*"

When Mom mentioned the name of that battleship, we all stopped eating and stared at her.

"He was on duty when the Japanese attacked Pearl Harbor. Of course, the *Arizona* was sunk and he was killed. Mercifully his remains were recovered and sent home to his family. He only had an elderly aunt in addition to his wife and son. The navy made arrangements for him to be buried in Arlington National Cemetery in Washington."

"Oh, my gosh, Marie. How do you know all this?"

Even without a telephone, my mother knew everything going on in the neighborhood. Because she usually was the first in the family to know, this was not surprising to me.

"From Mary Reilly," Mom explained simply.

"After her husband's death, Johnson's mother suffered from severe depression. She lost her nursing job, and her illness consumed the money set aside for Johnson's private school. That's when Mary invited them to live with her and Mr. Reilly here in Riverton. Johnson's mother is in a psychiatric hospital near Detroit. To be honest, I don't know if she's a nurse there — or a patient. I didn't want to press Mary any further."

None of us said a word. Slowly we left the table and put on our coats. As we were going out the door, Danny surmised, "Looks like JB could use a couple of good friends."

DANNY AND I HOPPED out of the Tucker station wagon and ran into the First Methodist Church where we expected to find other scouts who had also come early with their fathers. When we reached the basement Sunday school area where Troop 46 met each Monday evening, we were delighted to see Freddie Holland. Not only was he our patrol leader but also the talented captain of our troop's Winter Camporee championship hockey team. But more importantly, like Danny and me, he too had received a *Medal of Courage* at the White House just a few weeks earlier. So he was a fellow international hero as well.

"Hey, Freddie!"

"Hey, boys. You're just in time to help me set up for the meeting while Scoutmaster Carmody meets with the committee in the office. What's new?"

While Freddie and I carried scouting paraphernalia including equipment, literature, flags, and patrol pennants from the storage closet, Danny delivered an uninterrupted report on the many commendable attributes of our new friend and neighbor, Johnson Bradford. Of course, Danny couldn't carry anything because he needed both hands for gesturing.

As Freddie positioned the flags and pennants and readied the stage for the meeting, he listened politely. When Danny ran out of steam, Freddie stopped what he was doing to ask, "Tell me, Danny. You kinda like this guy — is that it?"

While Danny sputtered, Freddie and I laughed. Pretending to be hurt, Danny stuffed his hands into his pants' pockets and stared at his shoes. Then he glanced up and replied, "You guys got me. Huh?"

By the end of the committee meeting, the basement was filled with scouts. As usual, our dress was a mixed bag, ranging from a full official scout uniform, worn by Scoutmaster Mel and patrol leaders, to that of ordinary scouts like me, who only wore one or two pieces of the official uniform. The most common combination included an official scout shirt and neckerchief atop civilian trousers, shoes, and socks. The official Boy Scout overseas cap was optional, especially during the winter months when heavy flannel hunting caps with built-in earflaps were much more practical.

Scoutmaster Mel took his place at the podium in front of the stage. Members of the troop committee lined up behind him. We stood on the stage in ranks facing them. Each patrol had assembled next to its patrol staff and pennant. Our pennant depicted a snarling wolverine.

Scoutmaster Mel held the three-finger scout attention sign above his head. Immediately we sealed our lips and answered his attention sign with one of our own. When all was quiet, he opened the meeting in our traditional manner. Following an appropriate patriotic rendition of the *Pledge of Allegiance,* we recited all the sacred elements of the Boy Scout credo including the *Scout Oath, Scout Law, Scout Motto,* and finally the *Scout Slogan.*

With the formalities out of the way, Scoutmaster Mel quickly got down to business.

"The Chippewa Council has announced two events in upcoming months which'll affect our troop. Your fathers and I have discussed these events and will lay out a detailed plan for the troop's participation."

Upon hearing Scoutmaster Mel's news, Danny jabbed my ribs with his elbow. I leaned his way and he whispered, "Merit Badges!"

Oh, no! He was back on that subject.

Trying to focus on what Scoutmaster Mel was saying, I ignored Danny.

"The first event is a Council-wide Court of Honor to be held in Lansing on May 17th. For you new boys, a Court of Honor is a public awards ceremony where scouts who've earned ranks of Tenderfoot, Second Class, and First Class are officially presented their badges. On very special occasions, the ranks of Star, Life, and Eagle Scout are presented to those who've earned the requisite number and kind of Merit Badges."

Danny's second jab nearly knocked the breath out of me. I clenched my teeth as the sharp pain shot through my rib cage.

"See I told you!" he whispered, loud enough for everyone to hear.

Scoutmaster Mel stopped and stared at Danny before continuing. "The second event is the Council's annual Camporee to be held in the last weekend of May in Courthouse Park in New Albany. Because we'll be one of three host troops, our campsite must be a perfect model for the other troops to emulate.

"These two events are closely related. If every scout in Troop 46 is well-versed in scouting skills and practices, we can produce a campsite to be proud of. To ensure you're familiar with these skills, we need each of you to master the requirements for your next rank. As a result, the great majority of you will receive badges at the Court of Honor.

"What do you think, scouts?"

At first, no one answered. And then without prompting, the entire troop inexplicably let out a roar that could have been heard all the way to New Albany and back again.

"All right, boys. Here's what we'll do tonight. Those of you working on Tenderfoot stay in your patrols. Patrol leaders please review the Tenderfoot requirements and what the new fellas need to pass them.

"Those working on Second Class and First Class will meet with me in my office. I'll do the same thing for you.

"For those working on Merit Badges, these fathers have agreed to act as official counselors for the following Merit Badges —."

Scoutmaster Mel waved the committee forward and introduced each one by his Merit Badge area of expertise.

Mr. Loomis agreed to counsel for *Surveying*. This was no surprise because he was a surveyor for the Riverton's public works department. The surprise came when Scoutmaster Mel announced *Stamp Collecting*. Who knew he was a philatelist?

No one was taken aback when Mr. Holland chose *Home Repairs* and *Gardening*. One look at the Holland house made that assignment a logical one. And it was expected that Mr. Studebaker, Riverton High's premier government and civics teacher, would agree to counsel scouts on *Citizenship in the Home, Citizenship in the Community,* and *Citizenship in the Nation*.

Dad's considerable expertise as a tool and die maker, coupled with the skills required for his second occupation as a sewing-machine repairman, made *Metalwork* an obvious choice. But I hadn't expected his second assignment. Dad agreed to counsel scouts in how to earn the *Fishing* Merit Badge. Naturally Mr. Tucker opted for the *Automobiling* and *Machinery* Merit Badges.

When Scoutmaster Mel dismissed us, I headed for Freddie and his guidance on passing my Tenderfoot requirements. When I joined the other new scouts grouped around him, I looked for Danny but he was not among us.

From across the room, I heard my best friend's loud voice. "Stay right where you are, Mr. A! We gotta have ourselves a little *fish* talk."

AS WE DROVE HOME from the meeting, the subject naturally turned to fishing. It started when Mr. Tucker wondered, "John, isn't it about time for Saginaw Bay perch to start running?"

"You're right. About this time last year, Jase and I went up perch fishing from the bridge over the Quanicassee River. Remember that, Jase?"

How could I ever forget that wonderful experience?

Each year in February or March, depending on the water temperature, yellow perch launch their annual spawning run. That year, Dad had heard from his friend, Don Paulus, that the run was on. By going up early on a Sunday morning, we would be able to fish for a few hours and still be back by midafternoon for Grandma Compton's obligatory Sunday family dinner.

We stopped at Homer Lyle's Bait Shop for three dozen shiners. While this number of baitfish would produce sufficient perch to make the trip worthwhile, it was a small enough number to ensure we would run out with plenty of time left to return home before the dinner. Since Homer only had a dozen, we took what he had and left for Quanicassee, thinking we could purchase more when we got there. We were wrong.

When we arrived, the bridge was jammed with fishermen, all busily lifting plump, ready-to-spawn yellow perch out of the dark-brown, fast-running waters of the river below. The small bait shack on the riverbank next to the bridge had posted a large handwritten sign that read:

NO BAIT
TRY AGAIN NEXT TIME

Not wanting to return home without using the few minnows we had, we parked the car about a quarter of a mile down the road and carried our equipment back to the bridge. Finding a spot at the railing was another matter. We stood in the middle of the bridge for 15 minutes, waiting our turn to take the place of a departing fisherman. A father with two small boys spotted us and thoughtfully waved us over.

"We're about fished out. Why don't you take our place?"

We thanked him as he scooped up his pail of perch and herded his sons toward their car. The boys playfully engaged in a tug-of-war over who would carry their father's fishing rod.

The instant we lowered our wiggling minnow-baited hooks into the water, we each had a perch. Then another. And another. By rebaiting our hooks with less than whole shiners, we stretched our bait into a catch of 20 plump perch. Predictably, after less than a half-hour's fishing, we ran out of minnows. And we still had a couple of hours before we had to leave for home.

"What're we going to use for bait now, Dad?"

"Got me, Jase. I could have bought some of Homer's corn borers, maggots, or wax worms. But they're so expensive I —." Dad seemed embarrassed to admit his concern over the cost of these more esoteric fish baits.

Earlier I had noticed the man fishing next to me closely resembled Bronko Nagurski, the star fullback for the Chicago Bears in the 1930s. Without our asking, the huge man offered a solution. Turning to us, he pointed to our lard pail and suggested, "Use der eyes."

"Their eyes?" Dad wanted to make sure he had heard correctly.

"I'll show yahs. Can I use yer hook, son?"

He snatched a perch from the pail and showed us how to bait a hook using perch eyes. It was disgusting. But I have come to learn this bait is used by perch fishermen even today. In fact, there are only three game-fish by-products that legally may be used for bait.

Salmon eggs, trout eggs, and perch eyes. For some reason, they work like a charm.

"And if yahs wanta have some real fun, put an extra leader and hook on your line. When dey really get ta bitin' here in ah hour or so, yahs can catch 'em two at a time."

"Really?" Dad was incredulous.

The man leaned toward us and whispered conspiratorially, "When da feedin' frenzy starts, yahs ken bait yer hooks with a shirt button. Dat won't stop dem perch from bitin'."

Following his advice, we tied a second leader on our lines. We positioned it far enough above our first leader to prevent the two from becoming entangled when we pulled them out of the water. After baiting each hook, we dropped them into the roiling river below.

Even before the arrival of the fabled feeding frenzy, my first catch with my two-hook rig was a double one. When I reeled in my line, I saw two dazzling yellow bodies flapping in midair. My *whoop* of joy caused all the fishermen around me to laugh. Our gigantic new friend slapped me on the back with his ham-sized paw and smiled a missing front-teeth grin at Dad.

After regaining my breath, I whispered, "Dad, maybe he *is* Bronko Nagurski!"

BEFORE THE SCOUT MEETING ended, Danny had relentlessly pestered Scoutmaster Mel until he agreed to allow Danny and me to work on Merit Badges before completing our requirements for Tenderfoot and Second Class. The plan depended on the cooperation of Freddie Holland, as well as Danny's father and mine.

Under Freddie's close supervision, we would work diligently to complete the requirements for both ranks in time for the upcoming Court of Honor. If our progress with Freddie remained satisfactory, we could work on the four Merit Badges, whose counselors were Mr. Tucker (*Automobiling* and *Machinery*) and my father (*Metal Work* and *Fishing*).

At the breakfast table that morning, his victory over Scoutmaster Mel in the Battle of the Merit Badges was Danny's only topic of conversation. By the time he had devoured his sixth piece of cinnamon toast, we Addisons had heard just about enough. Fortunately we were saved by JB's knock on our back door.

After introducing JB to Mom and Dad, I suggested we boys depart for school immediately to show JB the school gymnasium and locker room before class started. When Danny got up to leave, I noticed a look of relief in Dad's eyes.

As soon as we were out the door, JB wondered, "Danny, do you always eat breakfast at Jase's house?"

"Sure," Danny answered matter-of-factly. "I come early to make sure he's up in time for school. He doesn't have any brothers or sisters to get him up like I do. Anyway he did have a little brother — I mean a little cousin — for a while. But since Uncle Van got the *Medal of Honor* for winning the Battle of the Bulge, he's been stationed at the *Pentagram* in Washington, D.J. That's where he lives now, with Aunt Maude and Little Johnnie."

"Danny, it's *D.C.*," I gently reminded him.

He shot me a puzzled look.

"You said 'Washington, *D.J.*'. It's *D.C.*"

"I did? I must have been thinking about disk jockeys — on our radio. JB, did you hear about the radio Jase and I won last fall. It's a —."

"Come on, Danny. Let JB talk too."

"Anyway it's a good radio."

Although JB was not a chatterbox, like someone else I knew, he did reveal a lot about Stony River Academy. For one thing, all the boys were required to live in dormitories on the school's campus.

After his father died, JB worked at odd jobs to contribute to his school expenses. He even shined shoes for his friends, the sons of wealthier families, who liked him and were eager to help. That news struck me funny. My first impression was that JB was very rich. Now he was telling us he was actually a shoe-shine boy. He also revealed that his mother had become so ill she was no longer able to work. At that point, Stony River Academy was no longer a viable option for him.

Like me, I'm sure Danny was curious about the current state of his mother's health, but neither of us mentioned it. Instead, Danny changed the subject. "Did Mrs. Reilly tell you about our night-crawler business, JB?"

"Yes! She mentioned that last summer she and Uncle Patrick helped Jase and you catch night crawlers in your backyard. Is that right?"

My mind went back to that night with all our neighbors, including Mrs. Mikas, the gregarious and generous Hungarian bubba, who lived next door to us. Two Gold Stars hung in her front window to honor her two sons, Ivan and Theo. They were among a growing number of young men from our neighborhood who were killed in action during the war.

"Yep," Danny confirmed. "Last summer, the Reillys came to a number of our neighborhood night-crawler parties. We try to have them a couple times a week. Don't we, Jase?"

When Danny required me to validate his fibs, it infuriated me. And this fib was clearly off the charts. As far as I could remember, the *party* involving the Reillys was the *only* party that occurred over the relatively short course of our night-crawler career.

I ignored the fib and simply stated, "Danny and I are the sole suppliers of night crawlers — and other baits — to Homer Lyle's Bait Shop. He's an older man, who's pretty crippled up with arthritis so he needs our help. Fortunately we're able to make some pretty good money in the process."

"And we have some news for you, JB," Danny interjected. "We're thinking of giving up the bait-supply business. This could be perfect timing for all of us. If you're interested in taking it over, we could put in a good word to Old Homer. How about it?"

I couldn't believe my ears. This was the first I'd heard of *our* idea.

"Why would you and Jase want to give up that business? It sounds like a good deal to me."

Good question, I thought. I was eager to hear Danny's answer. Truthfully I wanted to watch Danny squirm, at least a bit.

But Danny wiggled out of the trap by telling another whopper. "Jase and I need to give it up because we're international heroes. There're a lot of demands on our time, you see."

And Danny didn't stop there.

"The bait business is so good that the whole Reilly family could be involved. You could make enough money to go to the University of Michigan where Jase and I are going. We got a scholarship from the Craddock sisters because I saved the life of old Nate Craddock. After that, Jase rescued me. That's how we got our first *Medals of Courage.*"

"Aunt Mary told me you fellas were recognized as heroes on several occasions. Tell me all about this. I really would like to know."

Holding his hand over his heart where, under his mackinaw, the two medals were pinned to his sweater, Danny stated soberly, "I'm sorry but I'm not the kind of person who brags about his accomplishments."

Right!

Finally Danny topped it off by unbuttoning his coat and asking, "JB, have you had a chance to see these beauties up close?"

"Danny!" I yelled, startling both JB and Mr. Modesty. I just couldn't help myself!

Feeling embarrassed by my forceful intervention, I changed the subject. "How was the charity dinner and the bingo at St. Thomas Church last night, JB?"

"Actually I really enjoyed it. And I won — twice. Fifty cents each time!"

Evidently Danny wasn't finished talking. "I used to be Catholic but now I'm a Baptist — I mean — I was baptized at a church camp where Jase and I go all the time. We're going again this coming summer. Do you want to come too? You don't have to be a Catholic any more if you come to our camp."

JB frowned and tilted his head toward Danny. I suspected JB was wondering if Danny were crazy.

"I didn't really mean that, JB. I like Catholics. Everyone in my family is Catholic. Well, except me I guess. You know what I mean?"

At that precise second, the school bell rang, summoning us to class. As we headed inside, JB seemed relieved not having to answer Danny's last question.

Danny sidled up to me and observed, "JB's a very *understanding* person. Don't you think so, Jase?"

And patient. And charitable. And tolerant. And...

After all, he's a friend of Danny Tucker.

2 THE BASKETBALL WUNDERKIND

The Conrad Hoffman Story
Chicago

IN CHICAGO, HOFFMAN MET A MAN WITH WHOM HE
had done business for years. Ulrich was the quintessential procurer.
Since his sources were so diverse and his prices so reasonable, the
organization had used him exclusively. When illicit merchandise of
any kind was required, he provided it in a timely manner. No
questions asked.

Ulrich was a particularly reliable source for firearms. False
identification documents including visas, passports, and drivers'
licenses. Unmarked currency from countries without extradition
treaties with the United States. Highly valuable and easily
transportable assets without traceable histories, including
diamonds and rare coins.

Because Hoffman was the organization's money man, he had
dealt directly with Ulrich on many occasions. Their relationship
was cordial but businesslike. As always, the terms were cash only
in unmarked hundred-dollar bills, unless advance arrangements
had been made for wire transfers. Today's transaction would be no
different. But Hoffman would not be acquiring Ulrich's
merchandise for the organization. On this occasion, Hoffman was
buying for himself.

Using established code words as a means of communicating safely, he had inventoried his needs over the phone. As he had dozens of times in the past, Ulrich had taken the order coolly and efficiently. Above all else, Ulrich was a businessman and Hoffman was a good customer.

As usual, Ulrich had booked Hoffman accommodations in a nearby hotel. After checking his luggage at the door, Hoffman parked his aunt's car in the hotel garage. Dropping the parking ticket and car keys into his briefcase, he reminded himself to give both to Ulrich, who would arrange for the car's return to Aunt Greta.

Using the false name Ulrich had provided, Hoffman checked in and followed the bellman to his room. After hanging his clothes in the closet, he relaxed in an overstuffed chair until the prearranged time to call Ulrich.

After the first ring, Ulrich answered curtly, "Hello."

"May I speak to Mr. Damien?"

"You have the wrong number."

"Sorry," Hoffman responded and hung up the phone.

A few minutes later, Ulrich answered the knock on the unmarked door to his office. Hoffman entered, carrying his briefcase and a leather valise containing Ulrich's cash. The men greeted each other warmly and shook hands. Then both sat down on comfortable chairs at a small oak conference table. In a third chair, Hoffman was pleased to see the tidy stack of parcels which he assumed was his order.

"Shall we get down to business, Mr. Ulrich?"

"Yes. Why don't we, Mr. Hoffman?"

"Before I forget, here's the key to the Milwaukee car and the hotel parking check."

"Your new car is parked in front of the building. Exactly what you ordered. A black '36 Ford four-door sedan." Ulrich handed the car keys, registration, and title to Hoffman. "The tank's full of gas. Oh, yes! You have a 'C' sticker on the car. I thought you deserved it."

Hoffman smiled. Since gasoline rationing, ordinary citizens were issued "A" stickers for their car windshields that entitled them to the least amount of gas. War plant workers and those working in other essential jobs rated "B" stickers. Doctors and ministers received "C" stickers, meaning that their gas supply was virtually unlimited.

"That's a pleasant surprise," Hoffman affirmed. "How much extra did it cost me?"

Ulrich dismissed his question with the wave of a hand. "Consider it a going-away present, my old friend."

Hoffman smiled again and nodded in gratitude.

Their business was conducted very efficiently. Ulrich opened each parcel, placing its contents on the table for Hoffman's inspection. Driver's license. Passport with new photo. Birth certificate. Draft card (4-F). Ration book. Traveler's checks. Entrance visa for Panama, his ultimate destination. And $30 thousand worth of Panamanian currency, in large bills.

When Hoffman was satisfied, he opened the valise for Ulrich's inspection. Ulrich rose to examine the cash but he stopped himself. "I almost forgot your last-minute request. Please forgive me. It's locked in my drawer." He left the table and went to his desk. "Here we are! Your Walther PPK with a box of .38 rounds. You'll love this little gem."

"Yes, I may need it when I reach my next destination. Thank you, Mr. Ulrich."

"And thank you, Mr. Hoffman."

The two men shook hands and parted.

Carrying his briefcase and the valise containing the parcels, Hoffman walked briskly back to his hotel. Overcome by a feeling of self-satisfaction, he whistled a march tune that he associated with his boyhood. The cadence of his walk kept perfect time to the music.

"What's the name of that march?" he asked himself aloud.

Surprisingly it came to him.

"*Unter dem Doppeladler!* Yes! That's it! *Under the Double Eagle!*"

The Conrad Hoffman Story
Chicago

BECAUSE HIS FIRST APPOINTMENT in Michigan was not until the following afternoon, Hoffman decided to spend the night in Chicago. This way he could enjoy dining at a nearby restaurant known for its traditional German food. And he could enjoy a good night's sleep before setting off early in the morning. The newspaper he had bought in the hotel lobby predicted colder temperatures but no precipitation. Weather would not impede the five-hour drive to his first stop.

Sipping a lager at dinner, he imaged himself arriving at his destination. He would wear his new dark-gray wool herringbone suit. Not only was it handsome and expensive but it was extremely warm. He would drape his new black overcoat over his arm. A white shirt and a gray and black striped tie would add a touch of elegance to his outfit. He was determined to look as prosperous, successful, and handsome as a man of his 44 years possibly could.

For his second stop, he had decided on a change of clothes. This stop required his uniform. Yes, he must be seen as a man of authority, rank, and prestige. The uniform would accomplish that quite nicely. Before arriving at this destination, he would stop at a gas station to change. If all went well in Michigan, he would spend the night in Fort Wayne, Indiana. After that, he was southward bound, without a care in the world.

According to plan, he was in bed early. Just before he drifted off, his old comrades, Kuhn and Otterman, came to mind. While they were serving prison terms, he enjoyed his freedom, gourmet food and drink, expensive clothing, new car, and dreams of a financially secure future in sunny Panama where, with his new identity, he would be safe from arrest. What would they think of him now? He relished the opportunity to confront them. To see the look on their faces when they saw their old accountant, who always followed orders and performed his job dutifully, carefully, and *honestly*.

If they only knew!

With delicious visions of vindication and retribution dancing in his head, he drifted off to sleep.

DUE TO DANNY'S LENGTHY LECTURES that morning, there was no time to give JB a tour of Hamilton School's newly-constructed gymnasium and locker room. Only those in junior high, the two upper grades, took official gym class. Like the lower grades, we sixth graders were sent outside twice daily for recess where we played games closely resembling organized sports. But this was child's play compared to the junior-high students who were teamed and trained by their popular gym teacher, Coach Clark.

Earlier Danny and I had explored the new facilities and wanted to show them to JB. After school on Thursday, we finally kept our promise by leading JB down the stairs into the well-built and impeccably maintained Boys Locker Room.

In one corner, Coach Clark's small office, with its wide glass windows, allowed him to keep an eye on his students while conducting business behind his closed office door. Next to the office, the shiny, tiled shower area was equipped with a dozen shower heads and soap dishes. On the opposite wall stood a long, double stack of small lockers where the boys stored their gym clothes. In front of the lockers, a polished oak bench extended from the front door of the locker room to a back door that led upward into the gymnasium itself.

"Wow! This is impressive. At Stony River Academy, our locker room wasn't close to being as new and well-equipped as this one," JB declared.

Danny smiled proudly. "Come on," he urged. "Let's go up to the gymnasium."

Before walking onto the highly polished hardwood floor, we removed our street shoes. The gymnasium was even more impressive than the locker room. On the wall opposite the large all-purpose stage, the retractable bleachers were open and fully extended. This configuration displayed the large seating capacity available for sports events and stage shows in our flashy new gymnasium.

"Boy! This is something," JB exclaimed. "I can't wait for seventh-grade gym classes."

A single basketball had been left on the floor near the locker-room door. JB bent over and tapped the ball lightly. Miraculously it bounced up into his hands. From about twenty feet, he arched a set shot that swished through the net without even touching the rim.

I was speechless. Danny was astonished. "Holy Smokes!"

From behind us, a voice called, "Hey, son. That was quite a shot. Can you do it again?"

We turned to see Coach Clark, dressed in his familiar *Hamilton School* sweat suit and holding a second basketball. The coach snapped a brisk pass to JB who snatched the ball from the air, pivoted, and sank another set shot just like the first one.

At that, the coach registered his own "Holy Smokes!"

After the introductions, I told Coach Clark that JB had just moved here from Tennessee and was in Miss Sparks' sixth-grade class. Danny informed him that like us, JB was 11 years old.

The coach took over the drill. "All right, son! Give me a few lay-ups. I wanta see you dribble."

JB effortlessly put down another half-dozen baskets.

"Okay! Take a few foul shots, please."

Swish! Swish! Swish!

After a dozen attempts, JB had yet to miss.

"Let's see how good you are on defense. Toss me the ball, JB."

With JB in position at the top of the key, Coach Clark began dribbling toward the basket. When he pivoted and bounced the ball between his legs, JB held his ground with his arms extended, moving alternately high and low, depending on the coach's moves. After a head-fake to the right, the coach quickly moved left and set up to launch a shot at the basket. With a perfectly aimed swat, JB batted the ball out of his hands. The ball bounced harmlessly down the floor and hit the wall under the basket at the other end of the court.

Coach Clark bent over and put his hands on his knees. After catching his breath, he announced, "Okay! Okay! I'm convinced. You're a *natural*, son."

"You should see him play with gym shoes on!" Danny exclaimed. He was right. JB had performed his extraordinary exhibition on the slippery gymnasium floor in his socks without the benefit of rubber-soled shoes.

"Man! If only you were in the seventh grade," Coach Clark professed. "Have you ever played organized basketball?"

"Yes, I have. I attended Stony River Academy. It was in a private school league where teams were organized by age groups rather than grade levels," JB explained.

"What age group was your team?"

"I played on my school's 14-and-under basketball team, starting when I was 10. And I did the same with a number of other sports."

Having seen JB's collection of trophies and ribbons, I knew he was telling the truth.

Coach Clark believed him too. "Around here, the only place that happens is the YMCA league. Danny and Jase, are you guys members of the Y?"

We shook our heads. The Y was one Riverton organization we had not explored.

"The season's nearly over. However, if you're interested in playing organized basketball for a couple of weeks, I'd be happy to call Mr. Temple, the Y director and coach. I'll tell him he needs you on his team."

"That'd be swell, Coach Clark. We'll go down there right away. Okay, guys?"

We decided to check in at home before setting off for the YMCA. After all, this was a school night. With three family cars in play, chances of getting a ride downtown were pretty good.

As it turned out, this was a wise decision.

COACH CLARK WAS NOT prone to bestow excessive praise on his gym students, even those who starred on the various teams he coached. In fact, his student-athletes complained he was downright stingy in that regard. So his effusive reaction to JB's basketball talents was quite extraordinary. On our way home from school, Danny and I discussed this unusual occurrence extensively. While I was certain JB was pleased with the results of his tryout, he was careful not to brag about it.

When we reached New Albany Avenue, a car pulled up beside us. "Hop in, boys. I'll give you a ride home."

The driver was Coach Jim Comstock who had the rare distinction of being the winner of the state football championship as Riverton High School's first-year coach. In his former role as our neighborhood bum, he was affectionately known as Gentleman Jim. In both roles, he was a respected friend of Danny and me.

As we got into the car, I asked, "Whose car is this, Mr. Jim?" Out of habit, I had used his old neighborhood title instead of *Coach Comstock*. But he didn't seem to mind.

"This is our new car. Well, not really new. It's a new used car. Louise Libby and I traded both of our old clunkers for it. Thought we'd need a better one after we're married."

I started to tell JB about the upcoming wedding when I realized that I hadn't introduced him yet. "Coach Comstock, this is our new friend, Johnson Bradford. He lives next door with the Reillys."

"I've heard about you, Johnson. I just dropped off some equipment at Hamilton School. Coach Clark wouldn't stop talking about this talented sixth-grade basketball player named Johnson Bradford. You must be very good indeed to generate that kind of enthusiasm from Coach Clark."

By this time, JB's face was beet-red. He choked, "Thank you, Coach Comstock."

"Did Coach Clark tell you JB might play on the YMCA basketball team?" Danny asked excitedly.

"Sure did. While I was there, he called Mr. Temple. After his conversation with Coach Clark, I'm sure he's eagerly awaiting your visit."

"I just remembered," JB told us. "It's a good thing we're going tonight. If not, we'd have to wait until next week. Right after school tomorrow, we're driving down to Detroit to see my mother. And we're not coming back until Sunday evening."

"Your mother's in Detroit?"

"She's in a hospital down there. Actually it's really kind of a rest home. Since my father was killed at Pearl Harbor, she's been —. She's not well."

Now we know for sure.

"Gee, that's tough, Johnson. I'm terribly sorry to hear about your father — and your mother. I hope she's better soon."

JB nodded without speaking. I wondered whether he meant to tell us about his mother quite yet. But perhaps by saying something it would be easier for him to talk about it with Danny and me whenever the subject came up. I hoped so.

"Look, fellas, if you need a ride, Louise and I could take you down and back. We're looking for an excuse to take the new car out for a test drive. Louise hasn't driven it yet. We could do that while you guys are visiting with Mr. Temple."

"Sounds good to me," Danny barked.

That was no surprise. Everything sounded good to Danny.

"Do you want to go now? Or after supper?"

"After we eat!" Danny ordered.

That was no surprise either. Nothing was ever allowed to come between Danny and his next meal. Nonetheless, within an hour, the five of us were on our way downtown.

By every standard, the Riverton YMCA was modest. It was housed in a small two-story brick building. The first floor was home to Jones' Auto Parts. The second floor had once been divided into two residential apartments, each containing fewer than 1,500 square feet. Just before the war, the apartments were converted into commercial property. The two occupants were Miss Millie's Dance and Ballet Studio and the YMCA.

To reach the Y, we climbed a long and narrow staircase. At the top of the stairs, by turning right you could enter the dance studio, which was perpetually populated by little girls in white tutus. By turning left, you entered the steaming hot, sweat-smelly, boisterous world of *young men.*

The Y consisted of two rooms approximately equal in size. The front room had enough space for a tiny office, containing one small desk, a chair, a file cabinet, and a black telephone. This was Mr. Temple's refuge into which he escaped several times a day, just to hear himself think and to open his window to breathe some cool and fresh air. The remaining area of the front room contained a pool table, a Ping-Pong table, a soft-drink machine that *sometimes* ate your nickel, and a candy-bar machine that *always* ate your nickel. These four attractions were constantly in use. Because of its refusal to function properly, the candy-bar machine kept Mr. Temple running back and forth from his office with a pocketful of nickels all day long.

Located in the back room, the *gymnasium* was only large enough for one-half of a basketball court. And that was it. Unless you count the two grayish, spotted and stained wrestling mats that lay on the gymnasium floor next to the wall. By removing the suspended ceiling and pushing the ducts, pipes, and wiring up as high as possible, Mr. Temple was able to place the basket hoop at the regulation height. But it was impossible to shoot an arching shot without the ball hitting some overhead obstruction and bouncing right back at you.

Having just visited the Hamilton School gymnasium, the YMCA was really quite a letdown for the three of us. But Mr.

Temple welcomed us warmly and did his very best to paint JB a rosy picture, by emphasizing the fact that the Riverton YMCA team played on some of the finest basketball courts in the area.

"We just don't happen to have one of them," he confessed, as if we hadn't noticed.

"You don't play your home games here, do you, Mr. Temple?" JB asked.

"Oh, I thought Coach Clark told you. We play all our home games at Hamilton School."

"In that case, I'd love to play on your team, Mr. Temple."

With that, Mr. Temple grasped JB's hand and pumped it round and round as though he were cranking a Model T Ford.

"Easy there, Mr. T. You'll damage the merchandise," Danny warned.

Mr. Temple came to his senses, bid us goodbye, and hurried off to prevent a small boy from kicking the candy-bar machine to death.

"SO MRS. LIBBY AND Coach Comstock are getting married. Huh?" JB confirmed as we waited for the couple to pick us up in front of the YMCA. "When's the wedding?"

"When they announced their engagement last Thanksgiving, they mentioned spring. I'm not sure exactly when," I responded.

"Coach Comstock's busy with Riverton High baseball until school's out. It'll probably be after that," Danny surmised. "Besides they'll want Anne and Barb Libby to be there. They'll probably wait until the girls get out of prison. Right, Jase?"

"Did you say *prison?*"

"It's a long story but here's the gist of it," I told JB. "Mrs. Libby's daughters worked with POWs from Camp Riverton at the canning factory. On a lark, the girls decided to help two prisoners escape. Danny and I discovered the four of them at Granville Park. That's a campground north of Riverton. They'd spent the night there with several bottles of wine. The girls were arrested and charged with treason."

"Treason!"

"Yep, a *hanging* offense in wartime!" Danny added dramatically.

"But the federal judge in Bay City thought the girls' motives were not to commit treason," I continued. "So he ordered them to be tried on a lesser charge of conspiracy. The girls decided to throw themselves on the mercy of the court. They both pleaded guilty.

"They could've been sentenced to several years in prison, but Gentleman Jim Comstock shaved his beard and wore a borrowed suit from Harry Chambers, the lawyer who was his old friend and who represented the Libby girls. He told the judge the girls had saved his life. Mrs. Libby testified how hard it'd been to raise the girls alone during the Depression. She and her first husband were divorced."

"But the judge still sentenced the girls to one year and a day in prison. They're in the federal prison for women in Parkersburg — down by Detroit," Danny interjected.

"Wow! That's still pretty stiff punishment for a lark! When'll they get out?"

"They were sentenced last summer. On June 30th."

"If Mrs. Libby wants her daughters there, maybe they'll have the wedding in July?" JB speculated.

"Nah, they'll get out early — on *patrol*," Danny declared confidently.

"You mean a *parole?*"

"That's what I just said — on parole," Danny insisted.

Before I could provide Danny with a much-needed Dutch Rub, Jim and Louise pulled up in their new car. When we hopped in, the couple looked like they were about to burst.

"We just heard some very great news, boys," Mrs. Libby announced. "We dropped by Harry Chambers' office. He told us that the girls are going before the parole board next week. And they're likely to get time off for good behavior. So they'll be home early — just in time for our wedding."

JB and I stared at Danny. In response, Danny polished his fingernails on his medal covered sweater and gave us his patented smirk.

Crystal-Ball Danny had done it again!

3 THE PAST IS PRESENT

ON FRIDAY MORNING, THE FOUR REGULARS HAD assembled early at our breakfast table. I was the only one not preoccupied by perusing something. Because I had no reading material in front of me, I was the recipient of factual *gifts* from all sides.

On the previous evening, the Oscars had been presented so Mom was totally absorbed with the Academy Awards. "I'm thrilled that *Going My Way* did so well. Aren't you, Jase? Oscars for *Best Picture* plus *Best Actor* for Bing Crosby and *Best Supporting Actor* for Barry Fitzgerald. Didn't you just love him in this movie?"

I didn't know whether to respond or just listen so I smiled and nodded politely. To be completely honest, at that particular moment, I was more interested in pancakes than Oscars.

"Listen to this, Jase," Dad reported. "According to yesterday's paper, 279 Boeing *Superfortress* bombers, B-29s, firebombed Tokyo. Can you believe that? 279 B-29s! The damage reported was *massive*. How about that?"

DURING WORLD WAR II, three bombing raids on Japan garnered extensive press coverage, particularly in the *Riverton Daily Press*.

The first was Colonel Jimmy Doolittle's daring raid on Tokyo in April 1942. While this raid did little material damage, its uplifting effect on American morale was significant. Just a few months earlier, American spirits had plummeted after the devastating Japanese attack on Pearl Harbor.

Doolittle's raid used only 16 B-25 *Mitchells*, courageously and cleverly launched from the aircraft carrier, the *USS Hornet*. All 16 of the planes were lost, along with a number of crew members. But this was not unexpected. After dropping their bombs, the crews continued flying until they reached Japanese-occupied China. There they bailed out, allowing their aircraft to crash. Some were killed by enemy ground fire. Others were captured and subsequently executed by the Japanese. The raid was depicted by the 1944 film, *Thirty Seconds over Tokyo*.

In early 1945, the B-29 incendiary bombing raids on Tokyo, launched from China and Guam, seriously crippled the will of the Japanese government to continue fighting. Of more than a dozen large-scale raids, the March 9th raid that Dad mentioned inflicted the most damage. That single raid resulted in the obliteration of 267 thousand buildings (nearly 25% of Tokyo's standing structures), 100 thousand deaths, and the destruction of 50% of Tokyo's industrial capacity.

Of course, the most notable raids occurred when devastating atomic bombs were dropped on Hiroshima and Nagasaki in early August 1945. In total, those two bombs killed an estimated 220 thousand people, mostly civilians. Fifteen days after the Nagasaki bomb was dropped, Japan surrendered unconditionally. This sooner-than-expected surrender is credited with saving the lives of one million American fighting men, the estimated price of executing a full-scale invasion of the Japanese home islands.

"BUT YOU KNOW, JASE," Mom continued. "I was really happy Ingrid Bergman won the *Best Actress* award for *Gaslight*. Weren't you?"

From behind his *Handbook for Boys*, Danny mumbled something about *artificial lures*. Since his arrival that morning, he had been studying requirements for the *Fishing* Merit Badge. Of the four badges he was allowed to pursue, evidently he had chosen to tackle *Fishing* first.

"Hey, Jase! Know how many fishes you need to catch to get this badge? Only three! That's how many. We could do that after school today."

I wondered where Danny was planning to fish. Because they had determined by the first of March the ice was not safe, Sergeant Tolna and Dad had removed their ice-fishing shanty from the backwaters of the Chippewa Town Dam. In Riverton, ice on the Chippewa was beginning to melt and break up as it did every spring. Mr. Frank, the Michigan Conservation Officer assigned to Chippewa County, had declared ice fishing unsafe throughout his jurisdiction.

"Now that I think of it, I'm disappointed that Claudette Colbert didn't win *Best Actress* for *Since You Went Away*. You and Danny saw that one. What a tearjerker! Wasn't it, Jase?"

After taking all this incoming factual fire, I still had not returned a single shot in response. Suddenly I remembered two gems of information from the evening before.

"Mom and Dad, we heard a couple of interesting pieces of news last night. Know what they were?" I hoped for an immediate reaction.

After several seconds of silence, Danny replied, "Oh, my dear Jase, we would love to know what you and that brilliant boy, Daniel Tucker, learned last night. Pray tell us."

He had used his Ronald Coleman accent again. While it was wearing very thin, I didn't let on because I appreciated what he was trying to accomplish.

With still no response, I decided just to transmit my two gems *in the blind* without performing a radio check with Mom or Dad before doing so.

"JB's mother is a patient in a rest home in Detroit. And Barb and Anne Libby go before the parole board next week. Mr. Chambers thinks they'll be home well before the wedding."

Still no response!

"Why, that's simply marvelous news, Jase, my boy. Tell me more!" Danny replied, exuding sarcasm.

I crossed my eyes and shrugged my shoulders. After returning my *salute*, the two of us excused ourselves from the table. As we grabbed our coats and were about to leave, my mother announced, "Mrs. Reilly told me that JB's mother is — in fact — a patient in a nursing home near Detroit. They're going down there to visit her this weekend. And also — really good news — the Libby girls are getting a parole and will be able to come home in plenty of time for the wedding. Isn't that great?"

"Why, that's marvelous news, Mrs. A. Tell me more!" Danny exclaimed. This time without the sarcasm.

Then he turned to me and ordered, "Let's leave early I need to stop at the canning factory and talk to Mr. Paulus."

"What for?" I was dying of curiosity.

Danny locked his lips with his imaginary key and stuffed it into his pocket.

I WAS HARD-PRESSED TO keep pace with Danny as we marched quick time to the Chippewa Canning Corporation, otherwise known as the canning factory. From past experience, I knew he was a man with a mission, and he would not reveal his purpose until he was good and ready. This was just another idiosyncrasy I chose to tolerate as Danny's best friend and admirer.

We circled behind the canning factory, jumped up onto the loading dock, and headed for the door that led into the can-storage area. Since the summer before, we had made this trip numerous times. Because the army truck from Camp Riverton was parked in the lot, I expected to see Otto Klump. His squad of German POWs was part of the scaled-back crew retained to can potatoes and beets over the winter. This activity kept canning lines operating productively between the major canning seasons of summer and fall.

I also expected to see Sergeant Rick Prella, the military policeman, who acted as the POWs' armed guard and truck driver. Over the course of the past year, Sergeant Rick's presence had evolved from guarding to pitching in on the canning line and keeping his POW friends company.

Don Paulus was a part-time security guard. He made his rounds and kept tabs on the condition of the refrigeration and canning equipment, as well as the general security of the huge building that housed the factory. Don's full-time job was head of maintenance at the Burke Factory where my father worked.

While he excelled in both jobs, Danny and I admired him most for his accomplishments while serving in the army in North Africa earlier in the war. There he survived brutal attacks by Rommel's Afrika Korps as he fought to maintain communication by radio between his unit and headquarters.

For his valor on the field of battle, Don was awarded the Silver Star. But he had brought home something else from North Africa. Danny and I viewed the awkward gait, caused by his artificial leg, as a reminder of Don's bravery and courage under fire.

"Good morning, fellas," Don said cheerfully. "To what do we owe the honor of your visit this morning?"

"Dynamite!"

I didn't know why Danny had uttered that word. But apparently Don had some idea of what was on Danny's mind.

"What about dynamite, Danny?"

"We heard you're going to be dynamiting the ice in the river tomorrow morning to prevent flooding. Like you do every spring. And you're starting down by the Ann Arbor Street Bridge. We'd like to be there."

We would?

Danny finished his explanation. "We're working on our *Fishing* Merit Badge. We need to catch three fishes. At least, one of them has to be with an artificial lure."

Because Don looked a bit confused, I took charge of the interrogation. "Danny, what does that have to do with *dynamite?*"

"Well, Jase," he explained, with noticeable impatience. "When Mr. Paulus dynamites the ice, fish come flying out of the water and land on the ice and on the shore. All we have to do is pick up three different kinds. Bingo! We've got our Merit Badge. Simple as pie."

Then he turned to Don. "Isn't that right, Mr. Paulus?"

"Let me see — I — yes. I'd have to say you're correct. When we dynamite the ice, some fish are stunned and float to the top of the water. And others end up flopping around on the ice or on the riverbank. A few of the old boys, like Bohunk Joe and Buddy Roe Bibs, show up and carry them off by the gunnysack. They don't mind eating carp, bullheads, and redhorse suckers."

"But, Danny! We're supposed to catch three fish with a hook and line — not by dynamiting them!"

Danny reached into his back pocket and hauled out his *Handbook for Boys*. He began reading, "— *catch three different kinds of fish by any legal, sportsmanlike method.* Mr. Paulus, is dynamiting the river legal?"

"Sure, Danny, but —."

"Okay then," he nodded and continued to read. *"At least one of the fish must be taken by an artificial lure.* So there you have it."

"Danny, *artificial lure* means something like a fly, a jig, or a spoon. Not dynamite, for gosh sakes!"

Danny shook his head and explained, "Night crawlers, crickets, and minnows — they're all alive. So they're *live* bait. Everything else is dead — including dynamite — so it's *artificial.*"

Turning to Mr. Paulus, Danny inquired, "Do you have any extra gunnysacks here at the canning factory?"

Seeing the handwriting on the wall, I quickly decided on my best course of action. "What time will you start dynamiting, Mr. Paulus?"

The Conrad Hoffman Story
Michigan

HIS DRIVE TO THE prison was uneventful. As predicted, the weather was cold and the sky blue and cloudless. There was little traffic or road construction. Under normal circumstances, he may have even deemed the trip pleasurable. To while away an hour before his scheduled visit, he stopped at a small coffee shop in the nearby village.

As the appointed hour drew near, he suffered a mild case of anticipatory anxiety. Quickly finishing his coffee, he returned to his car. In the invigorating, cold fresh air, he felt his confidence slowly return. At the precise time, he pulled his Ford up to the prison entrance as he had been instructed. He turned off the ignition and went inside.

When he entered the small gate house, he observed two armed guards behind the front desk, separated from him by heavy wire mesh. The anteroom was painted an institutional green. The drab paint reminded him of the Milwaukee bus station where he had waited for buses to carry him to his college accounting classes.

A tall muscular guard inquired, "How may I help you, sir?"

When arranging the visit, Hoffman was tempted to use his new identity to introduce himself. But he had no choice. Those he planned to see only knew him by his given name.

"My name is Hoffman. I called on Wednesday and spoke with Corporal Moore. I believe I'm here at the right time to visit with two of your inmates."

"Oh, yes. I'm Corporal Moore. This is the time we arranged. But I'm afraid I have some very bad news for you, sir. If I'd known how to reach you —."

"What do you mean, Corporal? Is there a problem with my seeing them?"

"Frankly I hate having to tell you, sir. But they've refused to see you. In fact, they were very emphatic about that. I even went to their cellblock personally and urged them to reconsider."

"My God! I'm shocked! What explanation did they give?"

"I was afraid you'd ask me that, sir. They wanted me to tell it to you — straight. So there'd be no misunderstanding about their reasons. They feel you abandoned them — left them in the lurch. And that you're a traitor. I'm sorry I have to tell you that, sir. But there you are."

Hoffman felt pressure building inside his head. His temples throbbed with anger and bitter disappointment. He really needed to see them. To apologize and wish them well before he left the country.

How could they deny him that right?

"You don't look well, sir. Can I get you a glass of water?"

"No, I'll be all right. Thank you for leveling with me — and for your kindness. I must leave now. Goodbye."

He forced himself to maintain his composure as he left the gatehouse. After reaching his car, he sat and stared at the steering wheel. He lost all track of time. Finally emerging from the initial shock, he found himself enraged by the rejection. He vowed to make the person responsible pay dearly. Dearly, indeed!

Energized by anger, he started his car and tromped on the gas. The wheels spun violently in the slushy snow and loose gravel in front of the guardhouse as he fishtailed out onto the tarmac road and sped away.

In just under two hours, he would resolve this intense feeling of anger. Reaching into his briefcase, he felt the comfort of the cold steel grip of his Walther PPK.

Ah, sweet revenge!

HAVING COMPLETED OUR DYNAMITE business with Don Paulus, Danny and I hurried to school. We had hoped to spend some time with JB before he left for the weekend. When we arrived at the playground, we soon discovered our hopes were in vain.

News of JB's sterling qualities had spread rapidly. His athletic good looks, classy clothes, and gentile southern manners made him particularly attractive to the Hamilton School girls. In fact, at that very moment, JB was completely surrounded by Queenie, Danny's older sister, and five of her eighth-grade classmates, all pretty girls. On the periphery, we saw Butch Matlock, Dilbert Dinkins, Sherm Tolna, and Danny's younger brother Chub, mesmerized by the bizarre behavior of JB's female admirers.

"If it weren't for Queenie's girlfriends, you'd swear it was a meeting of the Forrest Street Guards," Danny observed.

After quickly inventorying those present, I reported, "You're right. Counting us, every FSG member is here."

"There's only one way to fix this problem. JB has to be an FSG member. I'll call a meeting to vote on it at your house right after school. Agreed, Jase?"

Because I was eager to assemble all FSG members to discuss JB's membership, the day seemed to drag. Even before convening the meeting, one by one, each FSG member had approached me to vote for JB. By the end of the morning, there was only one holdout.

Surprise! Surprise! It was Queenie. At lunch hour, she cornered Danny and me in the hallway to give us her reason for opposing JB's membership.

"I really have nothing against JB. In fact, I think he's a doll. But it's not *fair* to make him a member of FSG."

"Why on earth not?" I demanded, bracing myself for her answer.

"Because my girlfriends aren't members. That's why."

"So, if we made all your girlfriends members, you'd vote for JB?"

"Sure. So why don't we?"

Danny had heard about as much of Queenie's rationale as he could stand. So he gave her some logic of his own. "Queenie, I gotta better idea. Seeing you're the only girl member of FSG, why don't you drop out? That way you could form your own secret organization. You could call it the CGC."

"CGC? What does that stand for?"

"Crazy Girls Club," Danny replied quickly. Being wise to her ways, he ducked just before Queenie's haymaker rendered him a head shorter.

"Okay! Okay! Tell you what," I pleaded. "Let's meet at my house after school and discuss this with all the members. Whatever we all vote for, we'll do. All right?"

After inspecting her nail polish for a minute, Queenie disdainfully agreed. Danny and I wandered back to our classroom to check out Miss Sparks and Millie Zack. Not for any special reason, just out of habit.

After school, we stood in the driveway, chatting with JB. When the Reillys pulled up, he waved goodbye, and off he went to see his mother. I hoped he'd have a pleasant visit.

As we headed for home, every male FSG member joined us. Butch, Dilbert, Danny, and I were the older members and Chub and Sherm, the younger set. Even without Queenie, we had a quorum. To save time, I convened a *walking* meeting. With some trepidation, I raised the issue of opening our membership to the gaggle of eighth-grade girls. Without the immediate threat of physical violence from Queenie, every boy quickly voted that idea down, down, and *down*.

"What about JB?" I asked.

That question was immediately voted up, up, and *up!*

"Good," Chub sighed with relief. "We already voted. Now we don't need a meeting with Queenie there. But she'll really be mad. Won't she, Danny?"

"No, I'll tell her, Chub. She won't be mad. I promise."

When we arrived, Queenie and her five girlfriends were standing on our front sidewalk. The idea of passing through that mob made me feel like a scab truck driver about to breach a Teamsters' picket line.

Accordingly I chickened out. "Come on, guys. Let's use the back door."

When we boys were situated in our front room, Danny invited Queenie to join us by going to the front door and curling his finger at her. As she entered, Danny stopped her and whispered something in her ear. The two of them left the room and went into my bedroom. After less than a minute, they emerged. Queenie was grinning from ear to ear.

Queenie's remarkable transformation confused me. But at Danny's urging, I continued the meeting. It was short and sweet. When I called for a vote on JB's membership, every member, including Her Queenship, voted in favor!

Following FSG tradition, we adjourned to the neighborhood cottonwood tree to sanctify the vote. Our cottonwood, the sacred FSG symbol of unity and truth, was no ordinary tree. First of all, it was huge. To make an unbroken circle around the tree, we four older boys had to lock hands to create a chain and then wrap ourselves around it. Second, our cottonwood stood right in the middle of the sidewalk, just beyond the Reillys' house.

When we arrived, Danny took charge of the ceremony. "Okay, everybody. Place your right hand on the old cottonwood."

"Sherm! The other one!"

"Okay. Now, repeat after me. 'I — and state your name'."

"I-and-state-your-name," Chub repeated as usual.

"Do solemnly swear to offer JB a membership in the Forrest Street Guards."

"Amen."

"Amen," everyone repeated. And that was that.

The Conrad Hoffman Story
Michigan

BY THE TIME HOFFMAN stopped at a gas station, his anger had subsided. After topping off his tank, he pulled around to the side and parked. Carrying his briefcase and the hanging bag holding his uniform, he entered the men's room. There he carefully removed his wallet containing his new identity papers, new watch, ration book, and loose pocket change from the herringbone-suit pockets. After placing these items carefully into an inside pocket of his briefcase, he zipped it shut. He wouldn't risk having his new identity discovered while he wore his uniform, which he planned to discard forever before heading south.

After changing, he hung his civilian clothing in the hanging bag. Reaching inside the briefcase, he extracted the Walther and slipped it into the custom-made, black-leather holster at his side. Looking into the mirror, he adjusted the combination cap to give himself the look of authority. Satisfied, he clicked his heels, buckled the straps of his leather briefcase, donned his black overcoat, and headed back to the Ford. After locking the briefcase in the trunk, he took his place behind the wheel.

Once again, Hoffman felt the comfort of the Walther at his side. His confidence soared. While driving to his next stop, he whistled *Under the Double Eagle* with a vengeance.

Vengeance? What a fitting term to describe his mood!

By the time he reached the city limits, it was dark. The skies were clear but there was no moon. He shivered and turned the heater up one more notch. It had been many years since he had left this town. He had the address, but he wasn't familiar with the street on which the house was located. Shortly after entering the street from the main road, he parked his car and turned off the lights and ignition. He buttoned his overcoat and adjusted his cap one more time. Then he opened the car door and stepped out onto the frozen gravel.

Wanting curious residents to think he belonged there, he whistled the march once more and took on an air of detached indifference. In the dim light of a street lamp, he saw that odd numbered addresses were on the right side of the street. Walking slowly north, he carefully checked the street numbers of each small house. By his calculations, the house he sought was just past the large dark house on his right. When he saw light shining brightly from the small windows of his intended destination, he experienced a surge of exhilaration.

Turning up the sidewalk, he double-checked the address and mounted the front stoop. Confidently he knocked twice on the front door.

He heard footsteps approaching and then the door opened. Through the storm door, an attractive woman with blond hair flecked with gray, shielded her eyes to see him. She opened the door slightly and stuck out her head to improve her view.

Recognizing the man, she screamed, "Oh, my God! Conrad! What're you doing here?"

"I've come to say goodbye, Louise. I've come to say goodbye."

AS WE STROLLED BACK down the middle of Forrest Street after the cottonwood ceremony, a black sedan pulled up and stopped under the box elder tree in front of my house. A man emerged and walked up the sidewalk toward us. By this time, it was too dark to determine who he was. But he was striding along, whistling the *Under the Double Eagle* march.

"Doesn't he know that song's one of Hitler's favorites?" Danny hissed.

Hans Zeyer, our friend and neighbor, had informed us of this shocking fact after observing Danny and me marching about the neighborhood, professing to be young American patriots while whistling Nazi marching music. This knowledge immediately put an end to *that* unpatriotic behavior.

By the time the man reached us, we had stopped walking. We just stood in the street without moving or making a sound. When he passed by us, we were stunned. He was wearing a uniform that looked exactly like those worn by German storm troopers, the nasty German Brown Shirts. Because the man was focusing on the houses to his right, he walked by without even noticing us.

When he had passed, we instinctively formed a huddle. I took charge.

"All right, you guys. I don't like the looks of this fellow. Did you see his uniform?"

Everybody nodded.

"Let's follow him and see where he's headed. Slow and quiet, everybody."

Without making a sound, we hunched over and floated down the middle of the street, following the dark form on the sidewalk ahead of us. House by house, he picked his way up Forrest Street.

Past the Reillys. Then the Zeyers. When he arrived at the Libby house, he turned and walked to the front porch.

We stopped dead in our tracks.

After knocking on the door, the sinister uniformed stranger waited as Mrs. Libby opened the door. When she saw who it was, she screamed a name. The man replied but we couldn't make out his words.

In the light of the Libby's open door, we saw clearly what happened next. The German Brown Shirt reached into a holster at his side and drew what looked like a small Luger. He pointed the gun at Louise Libby and waved her inside. The door closed with a bang.

We were astonished. I wasn't sure what to do next. Sherm's father, Riverton Police Sergeant Jeff Tolna, was the first source of help that came to mind. Conveniently the Tolnas lived right across the street from the Libbys.

"Sherm, is your father home? His patrol car's parked in your driveway."

"Nope. He's patrolling with another policeman tonight. My mother's not here either. She's downtown shopping because the stores are open on Friday night."

Since most neighborhood adults would be shopping, the sinister-stranger problem would have to be solved by FSG without any help from parents.

Suddenly we heard Louise Libby's voice again. She sounded very angry. The man's voice was loud and angry as well.

"We've got to do something, guys!" I exclaimed desperately. "Who's got an idea?"

"I got one," Sherm offered quietly.

We all stared at him. When he finished outlining his plan, we were truly impressed. It was amazingly uncomplicated.

"Let's do it!" Danny ordered.

The Conrad Hoffman Story
Riverton

"LOUISE, I MUST TALK to you. I'm leaving the country. We won't have another chance. There're things I need to say. Can't we be civil — just this once?" he begged.

"Are you insane? I haven't laid eyes on you for over 12 years. Not a bit of help raising the girls. Not one red cent of financial support. And you want *me* to be *civil?*"

"Yes, please. I —."

"I read in the paper about you and your German buddies. How your leaders were arrested for embezzlement and imprisoned in enemy-alien camps. The FBI was here trying to track you down. You're a fugitive from justice for Pete's sake! And worse — you're a traitor to your country. Why should I care one wit about anything you have to say now?"

"Louise, you don't understand. You never have. I've got to make you see —."

"I see all right. You force yourself into my house. All dressed up in your storm-trooper soldier suit. Point a gun at me. I see all right. You're an idiot!!! Just like all those other nuts in your club — the wonderful German American Bund. All you are is a bunch of Hitler-loving thugs. What am I missing, Conrad? I understand one thing pretty clearly. You disgust me."

Hoffman was becoming desperate. She had to understand.

"But Louise, I'm here to make it up to you — and the girls. I have money now. You can have it. I — just came from Parkersburg. I tried to visit the girls today, but they wouldn't see me. It was embarrassing. I was angry and hurt. But I'm not like that now. Really! I *do* want to help you. And them."

Louise stared at him and shook her head. Why would he think she would welcome him after all these years? The story of the girls' arrest, trial, and imprisonment was all over the newspapers. He must have read about it. And he must have known how difficult it was for her to raise them without any help from him or his family. He was *crazy*. She was sure of it.

"Conrad, give me that gun!" she demanded, holding out her hand. "Give it to me!"

"If I do, can we talk? Please! I need to talk."

"I *said* give it to me!" she shouted.

"All right, Louise! All right. Here — take it. I'm sorry I frightened you."

She took his Walther and stuffed it into her apron pocket.

"Let's get one thing straight. You and your German buddies have never frightened me. You don't frighten anybody. There isn't a person in America who thinks you are any more than schoolyard tyrants and no one — NO ONE — has ever had an ounce of respect for you.

"Good and loyal American boys — even from this neighborhood — have given their lives in Europe and in the Pacific because of your dear Nazi idols. But now where're your goose-stepping heroes. In a few short months, your glorious Third Reich will be nothing but a pile of rubble.

"And what's Conrad Hoffman doing about that? Running away like a scared rabbit! You're detestable! I've no respect for you and I never will. I'm ashamed to ever have been married to you."

Dabbing her nose with her hankie, she cried, "Why don't you just leave?"

"Louise, you promised to hear me out."

"I did no such thing. I want you to go. Go now or I'll call the police! Then you can spend the rest of your life in prison like your Bund brothers."

Hoffman's knees wobbled. Feeling dizzy, he collapsed on the couch. This was not going well, not well at all. He put his face in his hands and sobbed. He couldn't stop the tears. His life was in shambles. How had he ended up like this? What should he do next?

Suddenly it happened!

SHERM'S PLAN WAS SIMPLE. He ran into his house and returned with the keys to the patrol car, which he promptly placed in my hand. I crawled in and turned on the ignition, but I had no intention of starting this powerful machine.

It wasn't that I couldn't drive. Since I was eight, Grandma Compton had allowed me to practice driving her Terraplane round and round her circular driveway at the farm. But, in this situation, I decided it was safer not to depend on my driving skills. Besides, if I started the engine, I might alert our adversary just across the street in Mrs. Libby's house.

After putting the gearshift lever in neutral, I quietly instructed my FSG friends to push the front bumper to move the car from the Tolna driveway into the street. While they pushed me backwards, I turned the wheel, until the car faced the direction of the Libby house. When it was in position, I put my foot on the brake. My pushers shifted to the back of the car. As they moved me forward, I turned the wheel to the left so the car was aimed directly at the Libby front door. When the front wheels reached the sidewalk, I stopped the car. The house was only about 20 feet away. I set the emergency brake and prepared for our big show.

Because we agreed Butch Matlock had the deepest and loudest voice of us all, he sat in the front seat next to me. Sherm sat in the back to coach us on operating the three special police-car capabilities we would need. When we were set to launch, I whispered out my window, advising the rest of the FSG crew to take cover. Quickly they all ducked out of sight behind the car.

"Okay. Let's hit it, Sherm!"

Without hesitating, he reached up over my head and turned on the rotating dome light mounted on the roof. Suddenly the front of the Libby house was totally illuminated by blinding, moving swaths of alternating red and blue light.

Next he pointed at the siren switch. He had explained that it had two modes, constant and short burst. I touched the *constant* button first. After about 15 seconds of the earsplitting siren scream, I pointed at Butch who picked up his microphone and nodded his head. He was ready!

I stopped the siren momentarily. "You're on, Butch!"

Butch pressed the button on top of the microphone and bellowed his booming message:

THIS IS THE POLICE!
DROP YOUR GUN!
COME OUT WITH YOUR HANDS UP!

When he finished, I punctuated Butch's broadcast with a *short burst* of siren. Then I nodded at Butch who repeated his lines with gusto.

The Conrad Hoffman Story
Riverton — The Libby House

AN EXPLOSION OF FLASHING red and blue light flooded the room. The deafening blast of the police siren reverberated around Hoffman. He was totally confused! Panic nearly choked him.

Slamming his hands over his ears, he stood and faced the front of the house, trying to fathom what was happening.

THIS IS THE POLICE!
DROP YOUR GUN!
COME OUT WITH YOUR HANDS UP!

The loudspeaker message crashed into the room and nearly knocked him senseless. Terrified, he glanced at Louise and then ran toward the rear of the house. Banging out the back door, he ran like a madman from the noise and flashing lights.

When he reached the Ford, he jumped in, turned on the engine, and raced down Forrest Street toward the flashing lights. Swerving around the patrol car, he sped northward toward the river. After the Ford made a skidding turn onto Liberty Street, Hoffman gunned the engine. The car streaked past the waterworks and the foundry, flew over the mound where the railroad tracks intersected Liberty Street, and sped toward the entrance ramp to the Ann Arbor Street Bridge.

Hoffman was obsessed with leaving his likely pursuers behind him. The speedometer hit 70 miles-per-hour as he approached the bridge, his escape route to freedom. While cramping his steering wheel sharply to the right to bring the Ford in line with the bridge, he glanced over his shoulder to see if anyone was following him.

A split-second later, the Ford crashed through the guardrail and plummeted into the half-frozen river below. As the car slowly broke through the ice and sank into the icy water, he tried desperately to open the door.

It won't budge!

Exhausted and beaten, he sobbed, "I'm free! No matter what Louise says — I'm free!"

"WELL, I GUESS HE'S gone. I wonder if Mrs. Libby's all right."

In answer to my question, she opened the front door and smiled. When we told her that her visitor had escaped at a high rate of speed, she seemed instantly relieved. Then a quizzical look came over her face. "But where're the police?"

We laughed and told her how we had managed to fool the Brown Shirt. She broke into a fit of hysterical laughter. I assumed it was a well-deserved release of nervous tension.

When she regained her composure, she advised, "You better push that car back to the Tolna driveway before someone asks questions. By the way, I'm amazed and very happy you did that. And I'll never tell a soul about it."

After returning the patrol car to the driveway, we stood around speculating about the identity of the man and why he was visiting Mrs. Libby. We couldn't come up with an answer. But I promised I would speak with her and let everybody know the facts. On that note, we called it a night.

As Danny and I were walking home, Mrs. Libby opened her door again and hollered, "Boys, may I speak to you? Please?"

When we were settled on her couch, she told us she wanted to tell us about her mysterious visitor. But first, she pledged us to secrecy. We both crossed our hearts and promised never to mention the incident to anyone.

Whether some of our fellow FSG members will keep their lips zipped is another question.

"I'll get right to the point," she said bluntly, "The man's name is Conrad Hoffman. At one time, he was my husband. He's Barb and Anne's father. I haven't seen or heard from him for over 12 years, just after our divorce. We were divorced mainly because he joined a fanatical pro-German organization back in the 1930s. It was called the German American Bund. When the war began, many of the Bund leaders were arrested and sent to prison for subversive activities against America.

"Conrad was the organization's chief accountant. He worked closely with its leader, a man named Kuhn, who was arrested and prosecuted for embezzling funds from the organization. I assume he did so with the assistance of my ex-husband. By the way, the

man who prosecuted Kuhn was your old friend, Thomas E.
Dewey, when he was New York's District Attorney.

"For the last four years or so, Conrad has been a fugitive from
justice. The FBI visited me a couple of years ago to ask if I had any
knowledge of his whereabouts. Of course, I hadn't heard from him
in years."

Danny and I could hardly believe what Mrs. Libby was telling
us. We sat quietly and absorbed all she was saying.

The American German Bund

DURING THE 1930s, A number of pro-German groups existed in
America. These nationalistic organizations were commonly organized
and led by Germans who immigrated to America after World War I.
Nominally they claimed as their purpose, such lofty ideals as
encouragement of friendship and trade between Germany and
America or the preservation of Germanic culture in America through
the study and exhibition of history, art, music, and literature.

Like the National Socialist (Nazi) party in Germany, these
American-German organizations sought to gain political power.
They created semi-military branches to intimidate and strong-arm
their political foes. Many such groups were fervently pro-Nazi and
anti-Semitic in their beliefs and practices. As such, they became
fronts for espionage and other subversive activity against America
before and during World War II.

At the insistence of Hitler himself, these disparate organizations
were consolidated as the American German Bund. Their Hitler-
appointed leader and self-proclaimed *American Fuhrer*, was Fritz
Julius Kuhn. During World War I, like Hitler himself, Kuhn earned
the *Iron Cross* as an infantry lieutenant. This medal is the German
equivalent to our *Congressional Medal of Honor*. Unlike Hitler, after
the first war, Kuhn graduated from the University of Munich with
a Masters Degree in Chemical Engineering and moved to America
where he became a naturalized citizen in 1934.

In 1939, at the height of its popularity, the Bund held a rally
in Madison Square Garden, attended by some 20 thousand people.
They listened to speeches by Kuhn in which he referred to FDR as

"Frank D. Rosenfeld" and called Roosevelt's *New Deal,* the "Jew Deal." Predictably violence broke out between Jewish protestors and Bund storm troopers, who wore uniforms to emulate their German counterparts, the *Sturmabteilung* (SA), also known as *Brown Shirts* because of the color of their uniforms.

Seeking to topple the leadership of the Bund, New York City Mayor Fiorello La Guardia launched an investigation of the Bund's taxes. It revealed that Kuhn had embezzled thousands of dollars from the Bund, much of which was spent on his mistress. District Attorney Thomas E. Dewey indicted Kuhn and won a conviction against him. Of course, Dewey went on to be Governor of New York and was the twice-nominated Republican candidate for President of the United States.

When World War II broke out, Kuhn was arrested as an enemy agent and held in captivity until the war ended. Subsequently he was transported to Ellis Island and deported to Germany. Most Bund members were similarly interned during the war and deported afterward.

During World War II, most Americans are aware that 127 thousand Japanese-Americans were interned in relocation camps in the western states. A lesser known fact is that nearly 11 thousand German-Americans were also interned as enemy aliens and some of them were not released until as late as 1948, four years later than their Japanese counterparts. Serious abuses of civil liberties were proven in the cases involving both groups of internees.

MRS. LIBBY CONTINUED HER story. "Conrad came here because he's planning to leave the country. For some reason, he wanted to talk to me — and to Barb and Anne — before he left. This afternoon, he stopped at Parkersburg to visit them. To their credit, they refused to see him."

Mrs. Libby paused. "I should ask if you boys have any questions."

I certainly did. I was glad she stopped. Apparently Danny was too.

"We thought we saw a gun? Weren't you frightened?"

"Oh, I almost forgot. Here it is," she said, removing it from her apron pocket. "I made him give it to me. He's a lot of things, but I never thought for a minute that he'd harm me. Jim's stopping by in a while. I'll go down to the police station and make a statement. And give them this gun."

"Does Coach Comstock know about this man?"

"Yes. They met many years ago. It was just before we were divorced and when Jim was married. You remember that back in the 1930s his wife and two daughters died in an automobile accident."

We nodded. We had both heard that story from Dad and from Gentleman Jim when he testified in court.

"If you were married, how come your name's Libby and not Hoffman?"

"I was so determined to be rid of his memory that I requested the divorce judge to allow us — the girls and me — to change our names to Libby. That was my maiden name."

We posed several more questions before running dry. But before we left, Mrs. Libby returned to the subject of secrecy.

"I'd appreciate your not mentioning this incident to anyone — except your parents. Of course, Jim will have to know. But I want to protect my good name and not be associated with anyone belonging to an anti-American group like the Bund. And I also want to protect the girls from additional disgrace. They'll have a hard enough time living down their role in the POW escape, the trial, and spending time in prison. I hope you understand."

"We do — perfectly," Danny replied for both of us.

After saying good night, we sauntered home. On the way, Danny confessed, "I'm sure glad we're going fishing in the morning. I'd like to forget Conrad Hoffman — and fishing will be a perfect way to do just that."

"I agree. Let's dynamite old Conrad right out of our minds!"

We both chuckled at the image. But the image we would confront in the morning was no laughing matter.

EACH SPRING, WHEN THE ice in the Chippewa River began to melt and break off in thick floating sheets, Riverton city officials retained Don Paulus. His job was to dynamite any existing ice jams and still-intact ice in areas where, unless it was blasted, flooding was likely to occur. Because of his training as an army demolition specialist, Don knew far more about explosives and how to use them safely and effectively than anyone else in town.

Of course, there were a number of other Riverton men who considered themselves experts. You could hear their boastful claims on winter nights in the town's bars and taverns. They were easily recognized by the inordinate number of eye patches they wore and the foreshortened digits they raised into the air to make their points. They apparently failed to heed Alexander Pope's cautionary advice, *A little knowledge is a dangerous thing.*

But Don Paulus was the Real McCoy. When we told Dad we planned to go *fishing* with Don on Saturday morning, he readily gave us his blessing. Dad knew Don was extremely cautious in his work. He trusted him to ensure we were out of harm's way when the explosions were detonated and to restrain us from retrieving flopping fish from ice that would not support our weight.

Long before my parents were awake, Danny and I assembled a stack of peanut-butter, pickle, and mayonnaise sandwiches on white bread and stuck them down into one of the gunnysacks Don had rustled up from the materials storage room at the canning factory. Admittedly while the sack smelled a bit musty for use as a sandwich bag, we figured the musty odor would soon be offset by the strong scent of Mom's dill pickles. Besides, if things worked out, fish would soon join our sandwiches in the sack, and fish were not exactly odorless.

At Dad's suggestion, we drew ourselves a short, stout stick of firewood from the stack next to the outside basement door. He recommended a piece about the size of a hatchet handle. We would use them as bludgeons to subdue the flopping fish we were likely to confront that day.

With our gunnysacks slung over our shoulders and our sections of firewood stuck in our belts, we set off for the river and a morning of Merit Badge fulfillment. Starting at the Ann Arbor Street Bridge at daybreak, Don would work his way downstream toward the center of town.

Knowing his pace depended on the nature of the ice conditions he discovered as he drove his pickup along the shoreline, we decided to head directly for a spot well downstream from his starting point. That way we could work our way back upstream until we met Don. Our plan had the advantage of allowing us to walk comfortably on shoveled sidewalks instead of the snow, mud, and broken ice-covered shoreline of the river.

Our destination was the Addison Street Bridge, which spanned the Chippewa River near the center of town. When we arrived, we dropped down to the north riverbank. The frigid morning wind whipped against our coats. Our eyes watered. We hunched over and began our trek upstream toward the section of the river where we knew Don would be working.

"Of course, we'll know exactly where he is when he sets off his first charge," I assured Danny.

"Yeah, but how'll we know it's him?"

I was always wary of responding to Danny's illogical non sequiturs. But this morning I was still fresh so I bit.

"Who else could it be?"

"Maybe bank robbers blowing open a safe. Or guys out at the airport testing fireworks for the Fourth of July. Or —."

"Danny!"

He grinned smugly. "Gotcha!"

As we walked along, I noticed the ice had begun to break up, especially where the water ran over rocky patches, causing rapids during the hot-and-dry months of the summer when the river was lower. Even in early March, there were numerous openings in the ice, which had totally covered the river just a few days earlier.

When we reached the stretch where the river curved around the site of the Riverton Ice & Coal Company, we couldn't see much of the shoreline because of the bend. As we worked our way along, I noticed something ahead of us that looked like a large bundle of rags.

Danny had seen it too. "What do you think that is?"

"Don't know. Maybe it's a big carp."

"Or a walrus?" Danny quipped.

When we got closer, we were shocked to realize it was neither carp nor walrus. It was the body of a man. Because of his unusual attire, both of us recognized him immediately.

"Conrad Hoffman!"

"Yep," Danny confirmed. "Looks like he didn't get very far last night."

"We better go back to the ice and coal company and call the police. There's somebody working there all night. And they'll have a telephone."

"I'll go, Jase. You stay here." Mimicking the standard admonishment from detective mysteries on the radio, he added, "And don't touch a thing."

As Danny ran off, I looked down on the poor dead father of Barb and Anne Libby. *Why would anyone want to touch him now?*

Before Danny returned, I heard sirens, heading my way from police headquarters at the Riverton City Hall. But the first police car on the scene had sounded no siren. And it had come from the direction of our Forrest Street neighborhood.

When the car stopped, as I expected, Sergeant Tolna got out. Immediately I felt guilty about *operating* his patrol car without his permission. As he approached, he wore a reassuring smile. I assumed he had not heard about our adventures of the night before.

"Hello, Jase. Not a very pleasant way to start the day. Is it?"

"No, sir," I answered truthfully.

Before long, the key players required at the scene of a homicide were standing on the riverbank, staring down at the body. In addition to Sergeant Tolna, Chippewa County Sheriff Roy Connors was there and so was County Coroner Ray Black.

Danny and I watched the three men from a distance. They were speculating about the dead man's identity and cause of death. We knew the answers to most of their questions but neither of us offered our assistance. When they got around to us, we could straighten them out. Until then, we decided to bide our time.

"Who discovered the body, Jeff?"

"You'll never guess!" Sergeant Tolna said as he poked his thumb in our direction.

Wheeling his bulky body around, the sheriff stared at us in disbelief. "I might have known! Danny Tucker and Jase Addison! What brings you two *international heroes* out here so early and on a morning like this?"

Ignoring the sheriff's friendly tease, Danny answered truthfully, "Dynamite, Sheriff Connors. Good old-fashioned dynamite! That's what brought us out here."

The three men were understandably puzzled by Danny's response. But an unusual form of clarification arrived that very instant. We heard the sound of Don Paulus' first dynamite blast of the morning.

"That's what I'm talking about, Sheriff. We should be there scooping up fishes for our *Fishing* Merit Badge. But we'll help you clear up this criminal matter before we take off. Right, Jase?"

"Criminal matter!" the sheriff exclaimed. "Who's talkin' about a crime?"

"If you don't want our help, I guess we can always call G. Edward Hoover. Or Thomas E. Dewey."

"What?" The bewildered sheriff stared at Danny.

"This man is wanted by the FBI, Sheriff Connors. Jase and I captured — or almost captured — him last night. But he got away. That's okay though. Because now he's — you know — not going to get away again."

The three men stared at Danny incredulously.

"What's Danny talking about, Jase? Who is this man?"

Before I could tell all, Don Paulus pulled up in his pickup truck and yelled from the road, "Hey, Sheriff. You need to come see what that last blast of mine exposed."

"What is it, Don?"

"A shiny black '36 Ford sedan. Looks like it busted through the Ann Arbor Bridge guardrail — just recently. There's nobody in the car that I can see. It's got Illinois plates. Anyone know who it belongs to?"

"Conrad Hoffman, Sheriff," I told him calmly. "He's the man Danny was talking about — the dead man — there on the riverbank."

All three men stared at me in disbelief.

Sergeant Tolna declared, "I'll be dipped in sugar!"

DANNY AND I WERE determined to keep our vow to Mrs. Libby and not reveal her family's relationship with the dead man. However, given the number of law-enforcement officers, members of FSG, and curious neighbors who were disturbed by howling sirens, blaring loudspeakers, and flashing police lights, maintaining secrecy was impossible.

Within hours after we discovered Hoffman's body, members of the press had the details concerning his visit with Mrs. Libby, the nature of the uniform he wore, and his true identity. Later in the day when the police revealed the contents of his Chippewa-soaked Ford, a hodgepodge of rumor and fact swirled around Riverton like a Michigan tornado.

Of course, this entire process was hastened by the notoriously loose-lipped, younger members of FSG. Our fraternal bonds of loyalty prohibit me from mentioning their names, but their initials are *Sherm* and *Chub*. The Allies were lucky these boys never fell into enemy hands. Whenever the slightest adult attention came their way, they instantly became blabbermouths.

On Saturday afternoon, unaware of the brewing storm, male members of the Tucker and Addison families plus Sherm formed a production line in our kitchen. There we cleaned several gunnysacks of sundry fish, bagged by the skillful application of several megatons of Don's *artificial bait.*

Up to that point, neither of our fathers had even heard of Conrad Hoffman. They were totally unaware of our caper involving the unauthorized use of Sergeant Tolna's patrol car. And neither knew of his son's discovery of the man's body.

Truthfully, when Mom answered the knock on our door, I was not surprised to hear Chuck Nichols' voice. Danny and I enjoyed a mutually beneficial relationship with Chuck who was Riverton's leading newsman. During our brief, but intense, periods of celebrity over the previous months, Chuck had protected us from overly aggressive news hounds, and, in exchange, we gladly granted him exclusive rights to our stories.

We welcomed Chuck into our kitchen. He immediately pitched in by grabbing a fish scaler and a large bluegill and going to work. After a couple of Chuck's friendly but probing questions, the fish cleaning came to a complete stop when Mr. Tucker and Dad demanded a full explanation.

Our claims of privilege, stemming from our promises to Mrs. Libby, only stood, as long as it took Sherm and Chub to spill every last bean. When Danny and I came clean, all three men were flabbergasted by what they had heard.

We strongly urged that Chuck Nichols take all necessary precautions to protect the reputations of Mrs. Libby and her daughters. Since we were unable to keep our promise to her, it was the least we could do. Chuck gave us his word that he would do everything he could to deflect attention from the Libby family.

Just as we were finishing our long tale, there was another knock on our door. We recognized the voices. Danny and I glanced nervously at each other. When Louise Libby and Jim Comstock squeezed into our already overcrowded kitchen, our uneasy feelings reached a crescendo. Mrs. Tucker and Mom stood just outside the kitchen door so they wouldn't miss a word.

To our relief, Mrs. Libby immediately released us from our vow of silence. I didn't have the heart to tell her she was too late. Under relentless parental pressure, Danny and I had sung like two yellow canaries. She reported that Jim and she had just returned from the police station where she had filed a complete report.

"Danny and Jase, when you promised not to discuss this incident with anyone, you were so honorable and understanding. But that's behind us. The story is now a matter of public record. I've realized it wasn't fair for me to put you in that position in the first place. This is especially true when so many of your friends were involved. I imagine some of them were just bursting to tell what had happened."

Danny and I scowled at Sherm and Chub who fidgeted with their half-cleaned fish and tried to hide their crimson faces.

"Sheriff Connors has contacted the Detroit Field Office of the FBI and told them about my — about Conrad Hoffman. They were extremely pleased to hear of yet another case closed by — the two young Riverton *crime stoppers* — as they called Danny and Jase.

"The FBI's been searching for Conrad for years. They plan to issue a press release announcing his — I was going to say *capture* — but I suppose it'll simply state that he's dead and the case is closed. When the full story's known, I hope everyone will realize how brave all of you were last night."

At that point, Chuck Nichols offered to write the unabridged version of the story, just to set the record straight. Immediately we all agreed. For the rest of the afternoon, our front room became a press briefing with all of us involved, sharing everything we could remember about the incident.

Afterward Chuck went across the street to the Shurtleifs to phone Artie, the press photographer who took photos for the *Riverton Daily Press'* big stories. Taking advantage of the break, we dispatched Chub and Sherm to summon Queenie, Butch, and Dilbert so we all could have our pictures taken.

When Chuck had finished his last interview and Artie had snapped his last shot, they left with a gunnysack of newspaper-wrapped fish for their Sunday dinners. We breathed a collective sigh of relief, vowing to enjoy a good night's sleep and a quiet Sunday.

4 SPRINGING AHEAD

HAVING EXPERIENCED SUCH AN EVENTFUL FRIDAY
and Saturday, Danny and I were tempted to follow our parents'
example and sleep in on Sunday morning. But old habits die hard.
Sometime before dawn, I awoke when he entered my bedroom
and prodded me with his index finger.

"Get up! We're late."

Since Danny and I had become best friends, we spent Sunday
mornings visiting as many churches as possible. Customarily we
attended at least two or three different services. Our parents, none
of whom were regular churchgoers, usually slept in that day so we
were free to roam the city. We generously dropped our pennies
into collection plates of churches offering the best food. This
selection criterion satisfied Danny's extraordinary appetite.

For several very good reasons, we always kicked off our round
of churchgoing with the Good Mission Church. First, it was only
a half-block away, situated directly across the street from Pete's
Grocery-Hardware-Liquor store. That's where Danny and I
shopped for life's necessities as defined by 11-year-old boys. Comic
books. Strawberry pop. Candy bars.

The Mission provided a temporary residence for what today
would be called *homeless* men. Back in those days, if they were local
and known to us, we called them *bums*. And, if they arrived in
Riverton on one of the many freight trains that transited our fair
city each day, they were *hobos*.

In the minds of Reverend and Mrs. Squires, who owned and operated the establishment, these poor souls were more likely to change their ways and accept the Almighty if they were provided a warm bed and breakfast on a daily basis. Their only fee for these basic creature comforts was to endure one of the Good Reverend's fiery sermons.

On Sunday mornings, Danny and I worked *meal jobs* at the Mission. That is, we acted as busboys to the hungry congregation and enjoyed a hearty breakfast in exchange for our efforts. Of course, we endured the sermon and were the only attendees trusted enough to pass the collection plates after the Reverend finished his Sabbath scorcher.

Perhaps the Mission's greatest drawing card was its music. Edith Squires played a hot piano. Her rendition of each hymn was a lively blend of ragtime and boogie-woogie. Our favorite was Edith's *Rock of Ages*, which she frequently played just for us.

Our second stop was usually the First Methodist Church because it too was relatively close by. The cookies and donuts, served between the first and second services, provided an excellent dessert after an entrée of sausages and stacks of syrupy pancakes at the Mission.

We also were fond of Miss Bundy, the church secretary, and Mel Carmody. He filled two essential roles in our lives, head usher of the church and trusted scoutmaster of Troop 46.

Depending on the times of their services and the quality of their menus, we attended a half-dozen other churches whenever the fancy struck us. These included the Congregational, Baptist, Church of Christ, Evangelical, and two Catholic churches.

The Catholic churches were easiest for us to work into our schedules. During the war, they said mass practically around the clock. Because Riverton war plants ran their production lines on a 24/7 basis, these churches needed to provide services to coincide with the odd working hours of their members.

This theory was reinforced by the fact that attendees at the Catholic churches were often dressed in coveralls and sat in their pews with lunch-buckets at their sides. On occasion, some attendees did not go directly to mass after their shifts ended. Instead they took time to visit with friends at one of Riverton's many taverns, which were also open for business at odd hours. I can still recall the unusual aroma that characterized Sunday mornings at these churches. It was a blend of burning candles, incense, and *hops.*

ON THAT PARTICULAR SUNDAY morning when we returned home, Mom and Dad were preparing to leave for our usual Sunday family dinner at the farm. While my father had no relatives living in Riverton, my mother's entire immediate family, including her parents and three married siblings with children, lived in the area. All family members were expected to *come home* each Sunday. Although the hour was never specified, by one o'clock in the afternoon, every Compton, not serving in the armed forces, assembled at the farm.

"You boys ready to go?" Mom included Danny in her question. She knew that he and Grandma Compton shared a special relationship based on mutual admiration and a shared passion for food.

Danny smiled and nodded enthusiastically. "Could we stop at my house for a second before we go?"

Naturally I assumed Danny wanted to tell his parents he was going to the farm with us.

However, as I thought more about it, that would have been very unusual. Long ago, his parents had abandoned all hope of keeping tabs on Danny. His mother never worried, as long as he was home when the streetlights came on.

"Sure, Danny. That'd be fine." Dad told him. "Let's go!"

"I have to get something first."

We all watched with curiosity as Danny walked to my bedroom and emerged seconds later, carrying the portable radio that he and I had won in a contest the fall before. As co-owner of the radio, Danny was entitled to use it at his house half the time. But he had always insisted that it remain in my bedroom. In the Tucker house attic, he shared a large bedroom with Chub and Queenie, who was nuts about big band music, which Danny and I abhorred. Keeping our radio in my bedroom eliminated the possibility of Queenie inflicting *big band* on his sensitive ears.

"What're you doing with the radio?"

"Giving it to Queenie for six months."

"Why would you ever do that?"

"For a friend."

Blink! The light bulb above my head clicked on. "Is that how you convinced her to vote for JB?"

Danny smiled and winked.

While Danny went inside to deliver Queenie's bribe, we waited in the car. Soon the front door burst open and Queenie, pulling on her loafers, ran down the porch steps and across the yard toward us.

Throwing open the back door, she hugged me and kissed my cheek. Needless to say, I was surprised. No! Shocked! And then embarrassed.

If Queenie said "Thank you, Jase!" once, she said it a thousand times.

Her enthusiasm was amazing! She had been depressed since Glenn Miller, the father of big band music, had been assumed dead when his airplane disappeared in the fog over the English Channel. Miller had flown from London to meet with military officials in Paris to plan his next USO tour to entertain the troops on the European front lines.

As we drove away, I looked back. Queenie was still waving at us. Danny summed it up in one word. "Girls!"

We were the first family members to arrive. "We got here kinda early today. Didn't we, Dad?"

"Before dinner, Grandpa and I thought we'd run up to Ft. Lewis to see if the Indians are netting any lake suckers. Walt Williams, who works at Burke's with me, told me their run started early. They're actually running under the ice this year."

Decades earlier, the Chippewa Indians and the U.S. Government had signed a treaty, spelling out special Indian fishing rights in the area around Ft. Lewis. Each spring, when the lake suckers launched their spawning run, the Indians were allowed to dip them from the Chippewa River, using huge square nets hung from birch-tree frames mounted on the riverbank.

"You boys like to go?"

"You bet we would, Mr. A!" Danny answered, before I could open my mouth.

OVER THE YEARS, DAD and I fished for almost every species that inhabited Michigan waters. We always agreed that fish fell into two categories, good-to-catch and good-to-eat. The Big Ones including muskies, pike, and bass, fell into the first category. We fished for these just for the sheer joy and excitement of landing them.

Like everyone we knew, we believed muskies and pike had far too many bones to be considered edible. While bass were not *bad* eating, they would hardly be classified as *good-to-eat.* Top winners in this category were walleye, yellow perch, bluegill, sunfish, and trout including native brook, speckled, and brown. There was another in our good-to-eat category. Smelt!

But smelt were different because they were not normally caught by hook and line. In early spring, these fish were netted or *dipped* from shore or by wading out into the rivers where they traveled en masse to their spawning grounds. The real sports purists would never say they were going smelt *fishing* but rather that they were going smelt *dipping.* Since Dad and I weren't purists, we used these terms interchangeably.

On one occasion, a few months before Danny moved to Riverton, Dad and I did catch a quantity of a fish that didn't fit into either category. The white sucker, or *lake* sucker as we called it in Riverton, was not much fun to catch, at least when you used nets. And it was not all that good to eat. That's not quite accurate. While the lake sucker's flesh actually has a sweet flavor, dealing with all those bones made it almost impossible to enjoy.

As Homer Lyle, who owned our favorite bait shop, often advised, "The only way ta make a lake sucker et-able is to smoke him. Or pickle and can him. Just too durn many bones. Yah gotta soften them bones somehow so yah can eat 'em suckers down — bones and all. Smoke or pickle, that's the tickit. Or I guess you kin jest boil 'em up fer soups and chowders."

Homer was one of Riverton's few true fishing authorities. But the thought of having to process our catch by smoking or pickling was daunting to me. To enjoy fish at their very best, we usually cleaned freshly caught fish, dusted the resultant pieces with flour and pepper, and popped them into a frying pan coated with melted butter. Smoking or pickling seemed unduly burdensome.

"With this streak of warm weather we're havin', I'm sure they're a-running up there. When they spawns, great schools of 'em rushes outta Lake Huron. Up the Saginaw River. Then up the Titabawassee and the Chippewa. From there, they fan out ta lay their eggs in the upper reaches of hundreds ah tiny cricks and ditches that's carried the runoff ah melted snow into the Chippewa. They'll be in them places so thick yah kin pluck 'em out with a dull pitchfork."

When it came to fishing, Homer was never wrong. Accordingly he was held in high esteem by every Riverton angler. We were no exceptions. So the insider's tip he gave us that day was extremely difficult to ignore.

As we drove back from Homer's, Dad was unusually quiet, but I was pretty sure I knew what he was thinking. So I broached the subject. "Smoking or canning suckers sounds like a lot of work, Dad."

"Yeah, not something I want to take on. That's for sure."

Since I was right about the first half, I went for it all.

"What time are we leaving in the morning?"

"Let's shoot for six o'clock."

I knew it! We just had to see for ourselves.

We followed the route that Homer had given us. Upon arriving at our destination, we slowed down and scanned from side to side to spot our objective. There it was! A string of dead cattails running diagonally across the fallow hayfield.

"Looks like a drainage ditch. Let's take a look, Jase."

After removing our two smelt nets and a pair of five-gallon lard pails from the trunk, we carried them across the field toward the cattails. Other than our waders, this was the equipment we used for smelt fishing so we figured it would work just fine for lake suckers too.

Our smelt nets were fabricated from woven-wire mesh. To hold it open, the mouth of the cone-shaped net was double-wire sewn onto a circular metal frame. A sturdy, ash-wood shovel handle was driven into a holder, welded onto the frame. The handle was secured in the holder by two strong woodscrews.

"Wow! Look at 'em! They're packed in there like sardines, Jase."

Sure enough, just as Homer had predicted, the lake suckers were packed together and fighting their way up a farmer's drain ditch to some mythical headwaters where they could deposit their eggs and sperm.

To understand what we saw in that two-foot-wide ditch, you first have to realize that the lake sucker and sardines are not in the same ballpark. On average, suckers mature enough to spawn are between 14 and 18 inches in length. Their substantial, trout-shaped bodies are heavy and powerful.

"Might as well get to work," Dad affirmed, taking his first scoop.

I followed his lead, scooping and dumping my catch into the lard pail.

"They're a bit heavier than a scoopful of smelt. Wouldn't you say, Dad?"

"That's for sure. I think we've already got all we can carry."

This was far easier than the proverbial shooting fish in a barrel. After three scoops, we had each filled our lard pails to capacity. After sliding the two net handles under the bails, we lugged our catch back to the car. We must have looked like two medics carrying a fat man on a stretcher. Because of the weight of our load, on two occasions we had to stop to catch our breath. When we reached the car, we lifted the lard pails into the trunk and braced them in place with the smelt nets. They weren't about to move.

On the way home, we discussed what to do with our catch. We knew we couldn't just fry them up like other fish we caught. And smoking or pickling was definitely out of the question. We had to identify another disposition for our lake suckers.

"Dad, maybe we can give them to Danny's grandfather. He raises foxes on his farm out south of town. If foxes eat horse meat, maybe a fat sucker would be a welcome change."

"Hmm. Maybe so," Dad mused, sounding unconvinced.

"I guess we could take them out to Grandpa's neighbor, Mr. Henry. Maybe he could smoke them in his smokehouse."

"Gee, Jase. I don't know. We don't have all that many. Firing up his smokehouse is a lot of work."

I was running out of ideas. "I wonder if Grandpa's pigs would eat them. They eat everything else."

"I'd rather bet on the foxes."

"Yeah, me too."

We drove in silence for a few miles. I was wondering why we had come on this trip in the first place. I was beginning to feel, as if we had simply gone on a lark. When we entered Riverton, I had yet to sort this out. Time was short and we had to decide what to do with our lake suckers.

"Jase, let's face it. These fish are going to be as hard to get rid of as a load of carp."

"Carp! Why didn't I think of that?"

I shared my plan with Dad.

When we pulled up in front of the small white shack, Dad announced our presence by tapping the horn gently. Without waiting for a response, we got out and opened the trunk. We set the lard pails of lake suckers on the ground, slipped the net handles under the bails, and carried the pails to the door. Dad knocked loudly.

"Hullow — whoos dat?"

"Mr. Joe — it's us. John and Jase Addison. We have something for you."

Bohunk Joe, our revered neighborhood bum, stuck his head out of the door and vacantly stared at us. No doubt he was feeling the effects of Pete's finest fortified red wine.

"For you, Mr. Joe," I said, pointing at the pails.

When he realized what we had brought him, his face brightened. He smiled at us, as if we'd just given him gold bullion.

"Fur Joe — datz fur Joe?" he sobbed.

I'd seen Joe's tears many times before. He was an extremely emotional man.

Bending down, he caressed the top fish in the pail. Then he picked it up and smelled it. I thought he might kiss it. But he smiled broadly and nodded at us. My guess about the value Bohunk Joe would place on our lake suckers proved to be correct. But I may be taking too much credit. After all, he was the only man I knew who preferred a bony chunk of carp to a filet mignon.

"Tanks youz! Masur Adhasun. Jaze. Tanks youz."

He picked up the first pail, opened the door to his shack, and unceremoniously dumped it inside. After repeating the process with the second pail, he proudly handed back our two empty pails. At that point, he was so overcome with gratitude that he could not speak.

As we were backing out of his driveway, I looked at Bohunk Joe. Tears were pouring from his eyes and down his cheeks. His shoulders were shaking with sobs. Whenever Joe had broken into tears in the past, I always had difficulty deciding how I felt about that. But, in this case, I knew I felt good.

Once we were under way, Dad proclaimed, "This was a great day, Jase! Yep, a great day all the way around, I'd say."

Who could disagree?

"WHAT'RE YOU DOING BACK so soon, John?" Mom asked when we walked into Grandma's kitchen.

"We got skunked! By now, I figured the ice would be out of the river up where the Indians net lake suckers, but it hasn't broken up yet. They hadn't even set up their nets," Dad answered. "Maybe we'll go back next weekend." Then he turned to Danny. "I guess they don't have any scouts in Ft. Lewis who're working on their *Fishing* Merit Badge so they haven't done any dynamiting up there."

Mom and I smiled. Danny smirked.

"Dynamiting? Who's dynamiting?" Grandma sputtered, looking up from the sink where she was washing the fish we had brought in the gunnysack. "Boys, promise me now you'll stay clear of those men when they dynamite the ice in the river. Okay?" Not waiting for our response, Grandma asked Dad, "John, these fish you brought look great. Where do you catch fish like these this time a year?"

At that, laughter *exploded* from us all, including Grandpa.

"Mercy, I don't know why that was so funny. Maybe I should send it off to Bob Hope to use on his next radio show. Oh, mercy me."

On our way to Ft. Lewis, we had told Grandpa Compton about our Saturday activities, including both the story of Conrad Hoffman and how Don Paulus' dynamiting resulted in enough fish to fill our gunnysacks.

After the laughter subsided, Grandpa was wise enough to change the subject. "Boys, we gotta new litter of pigs — and a new calf — that's been born since you were here last. That heifer you like came in, Jase. You ought to go out and take a look at 'em."

"Wanta go, Danny? How about you, Mick?"

From his cozy box behind the cooking stove in the kitchen, my fox terrier friend opened one eye, yawned, and then slouched back to his nap.

As we were leaving the kitchen, Grandma observed, "Funny thing, we do have a new calf but we also lost one. Born dead. That hasn't happened in a long time. Dad was out clearing some brush along the lane when he heard the heifer let out a bellow. Guess it was breeched."

When we got outside, Danny wondered, "What's *breech* mean?"

"Don't ask, Danny. You don't want to know."

He nodded solemnly.

When we arrived at the pigpen, the huge white sow was lying on her side feeding her litter. Being a city boy, Danny had never seen anything like it.

"Wow! How many are there?"

I counted quickly. "I see nine."

"Do they all belong to that — that one mother pig?"

"Yep! Sometimes a sow will have more than nine."

Danny was mesmerized. "How long will they be eating like that?"

"You mean how many weeks?"

"No, I mean how long does it take for them to get their — eat their dinner?"

"Oh, as long as the sow lets them. That's never very long. When she starts to get up, they'll get real mad. You should hear them squeal."

"I don't blame them," Danny empathized.

It struck me that he was particularly capable of identifying with the baby pigs. He too was short-tempered when cut off abruptly from his normal food supply.

We watched the pigs for a total of about five minutes, which apparently was Danny's limit. He looked at me kind of funny.

"Wanta go see the calf?"

Without answering, he dashed out of the pigpen and raced ahead of me, right past the cow barn. Turning left, he streaked past the granary, speeding toward the horse barn. For an instant, I wondered if he really knew the difference between a cow and a horse.

"Danny! This one!" I yelled, pointing at the cow barn.

Glancing over his shoulder at me, he immediately changed course. Instead of stopping at the horse barn, he stayed on the driveway which turned and headed for the road. There, he turned right and headed north, reentering the circular driveway near the front yard. Finally he raced up the driveway in my direction.

Our paths merged right in front of the cow-barn door. In all, he had run about a hundred yards when the cow barn was only 20 yards from the pigpen.

"Did you forget which was the cow barn?"

"Nope!"

"Why did you run past it and around the driveway?"

"Just getting a little exercise, Jase," he puffed. "Okay?"

"Okay, Danny." I granted him the benefit of the doubt.

I guess it's better to be winded than wrong.

When we entered the cow barn, it took a few seconds for our eyes to adjust to the dim light. Grandpa kept new calves tethered to a steel ring mounted on the wall opposite the last stanchion. The calf was bedded down with straw on which he slept a good portion of his day. When the calf was taken to his mother for feeding, the soiled straw was forked into the gutter that ran behind the row of cows, and fresh straw was added to his bed.

When the calf saw us come through the door, he stood immediately and prepared to be led to his next meal. I hated to disappoint him and gave him a good rub under his chin instead.

"Wow, he's big! Isn't he, Jase?"

Danny's question caught me off guard. I was thinking a week-old calf should be larger than he was. Then I remembered what Grandpa had told us. This was the first calf of a heifer, a young female cow. In that case, he normally would be a bit smaller.

I humored Danny. "He's a good size all right."

"Why isn't he with his mother, like the pigs?"

Before answering, I had to think a minute. I had never really given that much thought. I just knew that Grandpa always separated the calf from its mother, except for nursing time.

"I guess Grandpa doesn't want the other cows to step on him. Or doesn't want the calf to take milk from the other cows. I —."

To be honest, I ran out of credible guesses.

"Then how come he keeps the mother pig and the little ones together? Won't the mother step on the little pigs?"

Danny had a good point. I knew that Grandpa lost a number of piglets when the sows rolled over on their own litters. But I truthfully didn't know the answer to Danny's question about the calf and cow.

"Danny, I really don't know. Why don't you ask Grandpa when we go in for dinner?"

That seemed to satisfy him, at least temporarily.

"Speaking of dinner, let's go up to see how it's coming along. All right with you, Jase?"

When we returned to the house, the driveway was filled with Compton family cars. The kitchen was filled with Compton women, assembling dinner. The front room was filled with Compton men, playing Set-Back. And, within an hour, the entire Compton clan and one ravenous Tucker were filled with mouth-watering country food.

On our way home, I wondered if Grandpa had answered the calf-cow question. Danny assured me that he had.

"Well, what was his answer, Danny?"

"Grandpa doesn't know, but he promised to tell me when he finds out."

I looked at Danny who wore a mischievous look on his face.

"Are you kidding me?"

"What do *you* think?"

I didn't know *what* to think. And I didn't know the answer to the calf-cow question either. But somehow I was sure Danny had the answer.

WHEN WE PULLED INTO the driveway, JB was sitting on our front porch. Smiling broadly, he waved at us wildly. He jumped up and waited patiently as we came to a stop.

"Gee, I hope that enthusiasm means his mother's better," Mom said.

The first thing I wanted to know was "How was the trip, JB?"

"Wonderful! My mother's doing really well. She may be coming here soon. We'll know in a week or two. Her doctors think it might be good for her to be here with family."

"That's wonderful news, JB. I'm so happy for you. Wouldn't it be great to have her here? We'd sure like to meet her," Mom assured him.

Mom and Dad went into the house to put away the frozen beefsteaks and chicken breasts that Grandma had sent home with us. We three boys stayed out on the porch steps to talk.

"Anything happen around here while we were in Detroit?"

Boy, if only he knew!

While I was attempting to organize all that had transpired in my mind, Danny beat me to the punch.

"Not a thing happened, JB. Nothing. Nada. Nil. Naught. Zilch. Zip. Zero. Zero minus a million — minus a billion — minus a —."

He was possessed.

"Danny! Please stop," I begged. "What's gotten into you?"

Quickly I reviewed the events JB had missed. I covered the Conrad Hoffman visit with Mrs. Libby. FSG's commandeering the Tolna patrol car to scare him off. Our discovery of Hoffman's body on the riverbank the next morning. How Don's dynamiting had revealed the sunken Ford. The money and false documents the police found inside the car. How the FBI had described us as *crime stoppers*. Finally I told him about all the fish we had gathered after each of Don's blasts.

JB's mouth had fallen open. His eyes were as big as saucers.

Turning to Danny, I asked, "Have I left anything out?"

"Nada. Nil. Naught. Zilch. Zip. Zer —." He caught himself, just before I lowered the boom.

"You'll be able to read all about it in tomorrow's *Riverton Daily Press* too," I added in conclusion.

"Wow!" was all JB could say.

"Just another average day in the neighborhood," Danny quipped.

Then it struck me. I had left out one very important event.

"JB, how would you like to join the Forrest Street Guards?"

Danny and I filled him in on the history of FSG. We inventoried the members, explaining how each one had earned the right to be considered for membership. We told him the vote was unanimous to make him a member, without mentioning Queenie's bribe. Before we were halfway through our sales pitch, JB bought our whole line of goods. We had ourselves another proud and capable FSG member.

JB could not wipe the grin off his face. Danny and I were amused and pleased that he was one of us. We sat quietly for a minute reviewing all that had happened since we had seen each other.

Out of the blue, Danny proposed a great idea.

"I was just thinking, JB. Why doesn't the YMCA basketball team practice at the Hamilton School gymnasium instead of that shoebox gymnasium at the Y? If you'd ask Coach Clark personally, I bet he'd let Mr. Temple do it. Heck, the YMCA already plays their home games there. Besides, if you practiced there — say after school, Jase and I could come and watch you. In fact, all the kids in school could come, especially Queenie and her girlfriends."

JB and I thought Danny's idea was excellent. I suggested that the three of us stop by the gymnasium first thing in the morning so JB could ask the coach if Danny's idea was feasible.

We were sitting, smugly thinking how brilliant we all were, when Mom opened the door behind us. "Who's up for some hot chocolate?"

"Got any of those oatmeal cookies left, Mrs. A?" Danny inquired, wearing his winning smile.

"You didn't think I'd forget those. Did you, Danny, my sweet?"

Mom's term of endearment caused Danny to squirm just a bit, but he bounced right back.

"Anythahng you say, mah'am," he drawled.

A perfect imitation of our new friend, *Colonel Johnson Bradford, F.S.G.*

WHEN WE ARRIVED AT Hamilton School, it was too early to go inside. Before the bell, entry was limited to teachers and staff. We hoped Coach Clark would arrive soon. After he heard our proposed agenda, we knew he would invite us in to talk. As it turned out, he was the first teacher there.

JB got right to the point. "Morning, Coach. We came early to talk about the possibility of moving the YMCA basketball team's practices to the Hamilton gymnasium. Could you spare us a few minutes before the bell rings?"

A strange look appeared on his face. "Are you guys pulling my leg?"

It was our turn for strange looks.

"I've been thinking the same thing since last Thursday — the day JB shot those hoops for me. In fact, yesterday I called Mr. Temple to discuss this idea — again. Wait. Why don't we go inside where we'll be more comfortable?"

After reassembling in his office, Coach Clark related his earlier conversation with Mr. Temple. "We talked about this way last fall, before the season even opened. Mr. Temple gave me two reasons for *not* moving his team practices here. First, he was the Y's basketball coach and its director. He couldn't be in two places at once. His gymnasium's not ideal, but it's where he had to be during practice times.

"Second, some of his players go to parochial schools — like the Catholic and the Lutheran schools. He wasn't sure parents would approve of their kids coming to a public school to practice."

"What difference would that make?" I reacted without thinking.

The coach agreed with me. "Exactly! I belong to St. Thomas so I spoke with the parents whose sons play on the Y team. They couldn't care less. They thought the advantages of practicing and playing home games in this facility far outweighed all other considerations."

"No disrespect intended, Coach, but why didn't you ask Mr. Temple to reconsider?"

"No disrespect taken, JB. I figured, as long as he was stuck there at the Y after school and in the evening, there was no chance of his coming here to hold your Y team practices. But that changed recently.

"Did you meet Rudy Rosewood when you went down there? He's the new assistant director. He was hired so Mr. Temple can concentrate his efforts on fund-raising for a new building to house an expanded and improved Riverton YMCA."

"Boy, that's good news. That place is a dump," Danny observed, without hesitation.

"You're absolutely right, Danny. The place is *definitely* a dump. That's why the area YMCA leadership authorized the fund-raiser.

So that's it!" the coach said, looking at his watch. "That bell will be ringing in a minute."

"But what about moving the practices here?" Danny demanded.

"Sorry! I forgot to say — it's a done deal. Just have to run it by our new principal at lunchtime today. Are you boys available? I want to introduce JB as a Hamilton student who'll benefit by having Y practices here. Of course, if JB improves, Hamilton will have a better junior-high player next year. See the logic?"

"Everybody benefits," JB declared.

"Exactly!" the coach agreed. "I believe it will even help Mr. Temple's fund-raising too." Then turning to us, he added. "The principal wanted me to bring you two along to the meeting."

"Why us?"

"I honestly don't know. Please eat your lunches fast and meet me in the principal's office at 12:30 sharp. See you there, guys."

We were unable to concentrate on anything Miss Sparks taught that morning. We were dying to know why the principal wanted us there. By the morning recess, we were downright paranoid.

Danny fretted. "We didn't do anything wrong. Did we?"

I considered Danny's question for a second. My conscience was clear. Nonetheless, by meeting time, we were both nervous wrecks. In contrast, JB was cool as a cucumber.

As we all shook hands with Mr. Lund, his friendly manner immediately put us at ease. We sat in the chairs grouped around his small conference table and relaxed. The coach outlined the advantages of moving the YMCA team practices to Hamilton. JB added his ideas. Danny and I even chimed in a few times.

Evidently we were most convincing. About 10 minutes into the meeting, Mr. Lund announced, "Now then, Coach Clark, I see no need for further discussion. It sounds like a good decision. I'll let you take care of all the details."

When we stood to leave, Mr. Lund asked, "Could you boys stay a little longer? I have something to tell you. There's nothing secret about this. Coach, why don't you and JB stay as well?"

We all sat back down.

"You may not know this but I'm from Owosso. In fact, I grew up there. After the University of Michigan, I returned to teach at Owosso High."

At that, Danny and I both smiled. We sensed where this was heading.

"This past weekend I had a phone call from an old friend. You boys know him. You helped him last fall when he ran for President. I'm talking about your friend and mine, Thomas E. Dewey, the Governor of the State of New York."

JB practically leaped out of his seat. "Wow! Thomas E. Dewey!"

Mr. Lund continued, "Governor Dewey wants me to make arrangements for an event here at Hamilton School next week. Because he'll be visiting his mother in Owosso, he'd like to present you boys with a token of appreciation from the people of New York — for what you did this past weekend."

This is where Coach Clark nearly came out of his chair. "Gee, how exciting! What did you do? What'd I miss?"

"The full story will be in the *Riverton Daily Press* this afternoon, according to the reporter who called me about an hour ago. In short, Danny and Jase played key roles in bringing to ground —. Oh, my! I wasn't trying to be funny. Anyway they helped close the FBI case on Conrad Hoffman, a dangerous and long-hunted German operative who was indicted and tried in absentia by none other than Thomas E. Dewey.

"So that's about it! Tom says to give his best to you and your families. And he'll see you next week."

On our return to class, JB confided, "Sometimes when I play basketball, I go through streaks when I can't miss a shot. I can knock down one shot after another — all afternoon. You guys are like that. Time after time, you effortlessly knock down the bad guys. Boy, I admire that."

We two ardent JB fans couldn't have asked for more.

THE DECISION TO MOVE the YMCA basketball practice to Hamilton gymnasium was enthusiastically endorsed by the faculty and the student body, especially the junior-high girls. Because the practices began immediately after school, the time was very agreeable for students, particularly those who sought an excuse to socialize with their friends rather than go straight home to start their homework and chores.

Since practices were open to the public, parents or even students from other schools could attend. When the school janitor opened all the bleachers on that first afternoon, no one expected them to be filled with observers. But that was the case, right from the start.

The practice-session format and the constituency of the players contributed significantly to the popularity of the sessions. Because the public-school basketball season was over, Coach Clark offered to help coach the Y team. *Coach* Temple, as everyone now called him, knew a good thing when he saw it. He immediately accepted Coach Clark's generous offer and proposed a division of labor. The Hamilton coach was renowned for his offensive coaching abilities, while defense had always been Coach Temple's long suit. They agreed to split the coaching duties along those lines and launched their joint venture.

More importantly, they received valuable help from an unexpected source. Knowing the strength of his Hamilton junior-high squad, Coach Clark invited those players to attend practices as well. Without exception, each player volunteered to come.

This worked perfectly. The two coaches divided the YMCA team into two squads. When Coach Clark coached offense to the A Squad, he used Hamilton's best defensive players as his practice team. And when Coach Temple was running defense with the B Squad, he used Hamilton's best offensive players to create more realistic drills. When both coaches were satisfied, they swapped squads and started over. This provided both squads a good workout in offense and defense each day.

The first half of the practice session followed that format. The spectators, watching these two talented coaches do their stuff, were both entertained and educated, especially parents of players who practiced on their own at home. Soon a cadre of educated fathers, and even some mothers, could competently run drills with their sons on their driveways in front of garage-mounted baskets.

But as attractive as they were, the first-half activities didn't keep people in their seats for the entire practice. In the second half, a full-blown scrimmage game between the YMCA and Hamilton School teams provided the pièce de résistance. Even though some of its players had yet to matriculate to junior high, the YMCA team was very talented. And the Hamilton team had won the junior-high championship each year since Coach Clark became the coach.

Despite the fact that he was three years younger than some of his teammates, right from the start JB proved himself to be the most gifted player on the YMCA team. Not only was he the team's top scorer, but he led in assists. His willingness to share the ball with others, even those who didn't always make their shots, endeared him to members of both teams. His unselfishness was recognized by his coaches and by the fans who watched from the bleachers.

During the week, different people were credited with having conceived the brilliant plan that moved the practices to Hamilton. Those most often cited were Mr. Lund, Coach Temple, Coach Clark, JB, and Danny. Normally Danny might have claimed full credit for himself. Among the three of us, he was the one who first suggested it. But oddly he wanted none of the credit.

As we walked home from practice on Friday, JB wondered why Danny was reticent to reveal that it was his idea.

He pointed an index finger upward and declared, "*Success has a thousand fathers, but failure is an orphan.*"

Both of us looked at Danny, expecting more. But apparently that was all he wanted to share on the subject.

After saying goodbye to JB, I joked, "Danny, did Queenie get some more fortune cookies?"

"Nope!"

"Then where did you get that *success* saying?"

"From Grandpa Compton's *Farmer's Almanac.*"

I should have known.

5 | GYPSY MUSIC

TYPICALLY BY EIGHT O'CLOCK ON A SATURDAY morning, Danny and I would have been off on one of our weekend adventures. Dad had already left to deliver Mrs. Smalley's sewing machine that he had repaired the evening before. Mom was singing her favorite hymn, *In the Garden*, while she cleaned the winter's accumulation of soot and mold off the back-porch steps with a bucket of soapy lye water and her new scrub brush.

The warm sunshine and balmy southern breezes were signaling, in no uncertain terms, that spring had finally arrived. As proof, a member of the advanced contingent of black-headed male robins was chirping stridently from the crab apple tree in the backyard. His call warned competitors to stay away from the nesting site he had selected for his mate who was due to arrive with the other ladies any day now.

Despite the flurry of activity surrounding us, we boys were still glued to our chairs at the breakfast table. Not that we weren't spending our time productively, mind you. Danny was busily rearranging his silverware while I concentrated intently on the pink-red, hand-painted strawberries, adorning our family sugar bowl.

Neither of us anticipated the surge of adrenaline-generated energy that was about to engulf us.

The squealing of brakes and skidding of tires in front of our house announced what was coming. This was followed by the violent slamming of a car door and the *slap-tap, slap-tap* of farm-woman shoes scurrying up our front sidewalk.

Bam!

Bursting through the front door, she announced her arrival, "Marie — Jase! They're back! Where are you? Hello!"

Danny's eyes sparkled as Grandma Compton, his favorite admirer, entered the kitchen.

"There you are! And Danny too. How wonderful!" she declared, giving us both a huge hug. She glanced around the kitchen and asked urgently, "Jase, where *is* your mother?" She glanced around again. "Marie! Where on earth are you?"

Still clasping her scrub brush, Mom opened the screen door with one finger. "Hello, Ma! What brings you into town so early?"

"I've seen them — Lorant and Gisella. They're here early this year. Well before Easter. Camped at the stockyard's parking lot. They'll work around here until after the stockyard on Thursday. Then they'll come out our way and work around there. Isn't that wonderful?"

"Is the baby with them?"

"Oh, yes. Little Jenci looks just fine. Fit as a fiddle. And how he's grown! Old Vidor and Ema look pretty good too," she chuckled.

Danny looked at me and shrugged his shoulders.

"Grandma's Gypsies."

"Gypsies!" Danny gasped.

"Marie, I can't stay. I have to get over to the Tuckers and pick up some spark plugs for the Craddock sisters' old car. I'll talk to you tomorrow when you come out for dinner. You boys come too. Bye now."

We heard her Terraplane roar to life. Within seconds, the green rocket hit full speed and disappeared into the clouds. Or, at least, that's how it always seemed to me.

"Wow! That was quick — even for Grandma," I observed.

"Tell me about Grandma's Gypsies!" Danny demanded.

Putting aside her bucket and brush, Mom sat down at the table.

"That's a long story, Danny. A long, long story."

He folded his hands and beamed at her. "I have nothing but time, Mrs. A."

GRANDMA COMPTON'S AFFECTION FOR the Nyari family would have been hard to comprehend, let alone accept, by almost everyone living in America during the 1940s. Most people believed that Gypsies were deceptive, dangerous, and only marginally useful as a race. After all, what did they do besides tell fortunes, play Gypsy music, sharpen knives, or sell horses, tin pots, and beads?

For as long as I can remember, the colorfully painted Gypsy wagons drawn by the handsome breed of Gypsy horses were a common sight, slowly trudging along country roads around Riverton. Like every Riverton boy, I had been warned that these people, as fascinating and attractive as they were, could not be trusted. They would just as soon pick your pocket or steal your chickens as they would look at you. They were tricky and wicked. And you didn't dare leave them alone with your valuables including your jewelry, your livestock, or even your children, whom Gypsies were rumored to steal without the slightest hesitation.

Of course, Gypsies were accustomed to this perception. Their genesis as an Indo-Aryan race from Northern India had spelled trouble for them right from the beginning. Centuries ago, when Muslim invaders conquered their homelands, the Gypsies were enslaved, uprooted, and condemned to a millennium of wandering.

Everywhere they roamed, Gypsies were ostracized and forced to fend for themselves in foreign lands and cultures throughout the Mideast, Europe, and ultimately North America. They were persecuted and massacred, marginalized, and shunned by the people of every land to which they fled.

As recent as the 1930s and '40s, Nazi Germany erroneously declared Gypsies to be non-Aryans. Accordingly they were stripped of their citizenship, imprisoned, and later exterminated in the same death camps that killed six million Jews. Although opinions vary, as many as a half-million European Gypsies may have perished in the Holocaust.

Riverton was an ethnic melting pot where Germans, Poles, Czechs, Slavs, English, Irish, French, and Dutch all co-existed relatively harmoniously. Still there prevailed a natural xenophobic aversion to any ethnicity not among the relatively restricted number of nationalities and races present in the Riverton caldron.

Like most Midwest farming communities, there were Indians and Mexicans present in and around Riverton. We had Christians of all stripes and a handful of Jewish families, but there were no Muslims or Buddhists. And no people having dark-brown or black skin lived in Riverton back then.

So Rivertonian suspicions about Gypsies came honestly. These people were truly different, well outside the ethnic range of experience of the average Rivertonian. They were dark. They dressed exotically. They spoke a strange language. Their culture was alien to that known by any of us.

If you could get them to admit it, Gypsies knew that some of their mores and ethics were not in keeping with the acceptable code of conduct prevalent in mid-20th century America. In other words, they did lift an occasional chicken and perhaps pick a pocket or two. To many of them, stealing was how they made a passable living. But stealing somebody's child? Any Gypsy worth his salt would have drawn the line there.

But getting back to Grandma Compton, she was not a person without fears or phobias. For a lifelong farm woman, she was extremely skittish about snakes, mice, and spiders, for example. Once while working in her vegetable garden, I came across a small garter snake. I picked it up with my rake and showed it to Grandma, who was doing laundry on the back porch overlooking the garden. Truthfully I did a bit more than just *show* her the snake. Actually I *thrust* the reptile right into Grandma's unsuspecting face. I did it to scare her. And, boy, did it work!

Her reaction was so severe that I vowed never to scare her again. The price I paid for my uncivilized behavior was my assignment to terminate the poor snake. There was no mercy for this creature. Even as a boy, I considered snakes a boon to any garden. But, feeling fully contrite, I dispatched the snake with a single swat of my rake. That was the first and last time that I have ever knowingly taken a snake's life. And this is the first time, after a lifetime of feeling guilty about it, I have ever confessed to doing so.

As phobic as Grandma was about certain fauna, she wasn't like that at all with human beings. Her beliefs about people stemmed from her strongly-held Christian principle that everyone was basically good. As a Christian, it was her job to offer an opportunity for every person she met to prove it. Not just to her but to themselves as well.

Please don't misunderstand. Grandma never proselytized or preached at people about her beliefs. She felt strongly that people learned Christianity, at least the form she practiced, more effectively when she simply allowed them to observe her example.

Two summers before, when the Nyaris, a young family of Hungarian Gypsies, knocked on Grandma's door, she extended the hand of friendship and treated them with respect and Christian kindness. Her small investment paid off handsomely for all concerned.

SEVERAL DAYS BEFORE WE met the Nyaris, Grandma and I were in Riverton completing a series of urgent errands before heading back to the farm. An *urgent errand* was defined as any excuse to hop aboard the magical Terraplane for a high-speed flight to any corner of Chippewa County. Our last stop was the Riverton stockyard, where Grandma hoped to purchase some jam-worthy strawberries from her favorite vendor at the open-air produce market in the parking lot.

The Terraplane's tires squealed as Grandma turned sharply off New Albany Avenue and headed for an empty parking slot. Having decided she was properly situated, she stood on the brakes and removed her foot from the clutch. Her loyal steed chugged to a *stall-stop,* and we hopped out.

When Mr. Soldani saw us, he patted the shoulder of his current customer, wiped his hands on his white apron, and walked over to greet us. He shook our hands vigorously and bowed over and over again. He was fawning over Grandma to a degree that I had not seen before. She was a good customer, but I sensed there was something else going on.

"Hey, you. Get back here and wait on me," the other customer snarled. He was a wiry, angry-looking man. "What do you mean by leaving me standing here? You dirty greaser."

Mr. Soldani looked sadly into Grandma's eyes and shrugged his shoulders. He turned back to the man and tried one more time to explain his pricing policy. "Excusa, sir. But lika I tolda you, price-a isa mark on dat sign." He pointed at the sign so the man could see. "It say thesa berry sella atta tena cent a quarta. Zata's it — for everybodez. Take her or leave her."

"Look, you little guinea, you can't charge 10 cents a quart for these crappy berries. It's highway robbery. I'll give you a dollar for 15 quarts. You take it or leave *her!*"

"Mizza Compatone. Canna you helpa me — tella zat manz a —."

At that suggestion, the grumpy man took a step toward Grandma and yelled at her. "Back off, lady. This ain't none of yer business. Wait yer turn — or I'll see to it that ya don't get outta this parking lot without your tires punctured."

Grandma's jaw dropped, and she stood up on the tips of her toes. I could see her knuckles whiten as she tightened her grip on the straps of her huge, black leather purse.

Just as the man was about to push her back with his straight arm, a familiar face suddenly loomed over his shoulder. It was Sheriff Connors.

"Hold on there, bub!" Taking a firm grip on the man's left shoulder with his powerful ham-sized paw, he continued in a remarkably soft voice, "I been standing back there watching — and listening to — you, mister. I don't like the way you treat my friends and neighbors."

At that, the man twisted around and took a wild swing at the sheriff, who perhaps wasn't expecting the relatively small man to put up much of a fight. The punch missed, but the sheriff's sharp left jab to the man's chin did not.

Crack!

The man stumbled back and fell into Grandma. His thinking seriously impaired, he unwisely gave Grandma a strong shove.

Thump!

During the last microsecond of his consciousness, the poor man felt the pain of the full weight of Grandma's heavy purse connect solidly with the side of his head.

The sheriff, Mr. Soldani, and I stared in amazement at Grandma, who casually brushed off her purse, straightened her hair a bit, and nodded her head at us. Looking down at the unconscious man, she proclaimed emphatically, "Take that, you bully!"

We all cheered. Grandma feigned embarrassment, but I knew her well enough to know she was proud of herself.

While the man was still lying on the ground, the sheriff extracted his wallet from his coveralls. He removed the driver's license and read the man's name.

"George C. Larson. Has a Fenton address."

"Oh, laws!" Grandma sputtered. "What have I done?"

"You know this man, Mrs. Compton?"

"Not by sight, but I do recognize the name. He's the new manager of the Brown farm on South Barrington Road — just on the other side of Elmer Hagen's place from us."

"He certainly isn't off to a very neighborly start. Is he? I think maybe a few hours in the cooler over at the county jail might bring down his temperature a bit."

At that, Sheriff Connors grabbed the back of the man's collar and dragged him away from Mr. Soldani's stand over to his patrol car, which was parked about 50 feet away. He opened the backseat door, lifted the man by that same collar, and tossed him into the car like a rag doll. He slammed the door. Finally he turned to us and tipped his hat.

As the sheriff drove off toward New Albany to deposit his prisoner, Grandma looked at Mr. Soldani. "Now then, how much *are* your berries, Mr. Soldani?"

At that, we all laughed for a solid five minutes.

WHEN GRANDPA SAW US pull into the driveway, he slammed the barnyard gate closed and walked briskly in our direction. He did not look happy. Neither did Mick, the fox terrier, who was trailing along behind him.

"What's going on, Dad?"

"It's that son of — that bull. He busted down the barn door again and went inside to nurse. If he weren't so darn valuable, I think I'd shoot him."

That bull was nearly full-grown. But he couldn't adjust to adult life and wanted to cling to his childhood. More specifically, he wanted to cling to his mother, who by this time was dwarfed by her calf. His drive to reconnect with her for yet another meal was so intense that, on three occasions, he had broken down the cow-barn door to reach her.

For a number of reasons, this was not acceptable. First, the bull was becoming too big for Grandpa to control easily. Second, his mother was no longer producing *nursing* milk. Assuming her calf was weaned, Grandpa had put her back into production. Her milk was now a cash crop, not to be squandered on her delinquent offspring who was supposed to be taking his meals by grazing with the rest of the herd. Third, having to repair that barn door constantly had become downright tiresome.

"What're you going to do with him, Dad?"

"Now that you're back, I want to hook up the trailer and move him out of the barnyard, away from his mother."

"Where to?"

"I thought we'd put him in the orchard."

"With the water in the crick being as high as it is?"

That year the spring rains were record-setters. And the creek that flowed through the north end of the orchard was still running fast and deep, much too dangerous for cattle. Though Grandpa regularly used the orchard as an alternative grazing area for his milk cows, he hadn't done that yet this year. He didn't want to risk having a thirsty cow misstep and then be swept away by the creek and drown.

"We hafta take that chance. Water's still awful high, but I doubt that bull's crazy enough to get down in that crick."

"Whatever you think best, Dad."

"Back your car over to the trailer and I'll hook you up. Then you and Jase can help me muscle him into the trailer. Knowing him, he's not going to like it much."

It took us nearly two hours to get the young bull into the trailer and moved into the orchard. And the bull wasn't at all happy. He bawled and bellowed the entire time. The bull's mother was no help either. She encouraged his protest by answering his pleas for help with a chorus of bellows and wails of her own. Once released into the orchard, he was even more belligerent, taking out his frustrations by head-butting the largest apple tree there. While the tree showed no signs of wear and tear, I was certain young Mr. Bullhead was in for a splitting headache later on.

The three of us piled into the Terraplane and headed back to the house. When we arrived, we found a magnificently painted Gypsy wagon parked under the massive elm tree in the center of the circular drive. A Jersey cow, tethered to the back of the wagon, munched casually on the grass under the tree.

Perched atop the wagon in the driver's seat, holding the reins to a muscular, black and white Gypsy horse, sat a young Gypsy woman. When we drove in, she waved at us. Her friendly smile revealed ivory teeth that contrasted dramatically with her amber-brown skin. Long, jet-black hair flowed over her shoulders to her waist and a red babushka covered her head. Heavy gold earrings shimmered in the sunshine. Ankle-length, colorful woolen skirts layered with multiple petticoats swirled about her feet. Her luxurious shawl had been knitted from soft, azure-blue virgin wool.

On the front sidewalk, stood a tall and handsome Gypsy man. He sported deep-purple pantaloons tied at the waist with a swath of crimson silk and a full pale-yellow silk shirt that undulated as he moved. He wore a broad brimmed hat, similar to those worn by the Three Musketeers.

Grandma pulled the car under the pear tree so Grandpa could unhitch the trailer. As soon as we were stopped, she immediately walked over to the man and extended her hand. He bowed politely and shook it. I couldn't hear the few words they exchanged.

After that, they both nodded and parted. Grandma entered the kitchen and the man went to the back of the wagon. Soon he emerged with a large stone wheel mounted on a stand with bicycle pedals and a drive chain that turned the wheel. Seating himself in the built-in seat, he waited patiently for Grandma to return.

Soon she appeared with a basket filled with every butcher, carving, and paring knife in the house. She set the basket at his feet and he immediately began to work. I walked over to watch. When he pedaled, the wheel turned round and round. To set the angle of the edge, his first pass of the knife caused sparks to fly in every direction. As he honed the blade to a finer and finer edge, the sparks stopped. Near the end, the blade was barely touching the surface of the stone.

Grandpa approached and watched for a while too. Then he nodded at the man, giving his approval. The man pulled a shiny black hair from his own head to demonstrate the sharpness of the knife. The hair severed neatly at a mere touch of the blade. Carefully he wrapped the finished knife in an oil-soaked cloth and reached for another. Obviously he took great pride in his work.

While the knives were being sharpened, the woman showed Grandma the strands of colorful beads that hung around her neck. I really couldn't visualize Grandma wearing them, but I had to admit they were truly beautiful. The woman explained that the strings contained every type of bead that she carried in her inventory. If desired, she could tailor a string using any combination of beads.

When Grandma inquired about the cost, her response amused me. "One chicken iss all!" she answered, pointing at the fat Rhode Island Red rooster, pecking away inside a wooden cage strapped to the side of the wagon. I was enamored with her mysterious accent.

By the time Grandma's knives were sharpened to a tee, it was late afternoon. I was beginning to get hungry. Grandma must have read my mind.

"Won't you folks have supper with us? We have plenty for all."

Very politely the couple declined. But in doing so, they asked permission to spend the night where they were parked. Grandma readily agreed and offered the use of the pump for drinking, laundry, or bathing. Grandpa offered hay and oats for their horse. And ground feed for the cow that trailed behind the wagon. He suggested the man lead his animals to the trough next to the cow barn to water them down for the night.

That must have reminded Grandma of another need.

"And feel free to use either of those," she added, pointing at the farm's *His* and *Her* outhouses.

After supper, I peeked out at the wagon. The couple was seated around a tiny campfire. She was sipping what looked like a cup of tea. He was smoking a thin-stemmed clay pipe. They looked very peaceful.

By this time, the farm was very quiet. I was just turning away from the window when I noticed a movement inside the wagon. Instantly the woman rose and climbed up to the opening behind the driver's seat.

She reached in and removed a small baby, presumably from its cradle, which was situated immediately behind her driver's seat for easy access as she drove. She opened her blouse and offered the baby dinner. Not wanting to invade their privacy, I looked away.

Before I went to bed, I told Grandma and Grandpa what I had seen.

Grandpa wondered, "Why do you suppose they didn't show us that baby earlier?"

I couldn't help but imagine the very worst.

I wonder who the baby belongs to.

THE GYPSIES PLANNED TO be under way just after sunup. So it was no surprise to us when we arose to hear them pulling out of the driveway and heading north. When I looked out, I saw the two Leghorn hens that Grandma had exchanged for the knife sharpening. The two birds shared a wooden cage strapped next to the one holding the fat red rooster.

We were just having a second cup of coffee when there was a frantic knock on the door of the screened-in porch. I was the first one to look out.

"It's the Gypsy lady! She's got the baby — and the cow."

"Something's happened! Dad, come with me. Let's see what's going on."

I glanced down the road in the direction the wagon had headed. "Hey, the wagon's stopped down by the bridge. They didn't get very far."

The woman was nearly out of breath from running back to the house, carrying her baby, and dragging the cow on a rope behind her. At first, she rattled off her story so quickly we couldn't understand what she was trying to tell us. We slowed her down and she started over.

After leaving the farm, they had driven to the bridge over the flood-swollen creek. When they looked upstream, they were amazed to see a young bull being swept downstream toward the bridge. Assuming the bull belonged to their generous hosts, the man grabbed a length of rope he carried for emergencies. Since the rope was very strong, he assumed it would do the trick.

His plan was simply to attach one end of the rope securely to the wagon's front axle. After tying a slipknot in the other end, if he were lucky, he could lasso the bull as it floated by. He figured the weight of the wagon would hold the animal until he could go back to the farm for help.

Fortunately he got the lasso around the bull's neck. That was the good news. The bad news was that he seriously underestimated the bull's size and weight, not to mention the force of the water propelling the animal toward the bridge.

Instead of the weight of the wagon holding the bull, the force of the stream jerked the front axle sideways, causing it to snap under the pressure. But there was more good news. The broken end of the axle had dug into the surface of the road and, for the time being, was holding against the strain of the roaring stream and heavy bull. This situation was, by no means, certain to continue. At any time, the axle could snap again, putting the wagon in serious jeopardy once more.

The Gypsy man stayed with the wagon to watch the situation until Grandpa could arrive with help, preferably in the form of a strong team of horses and another heavy rope to pull the bull from the water, thereby releasing the tension on the remaining segment of the axle.

If the situation worsened, he would have no choice but to cut the rope and save the wagon, even if it meant losing the bull.

"Jase, tie up that cow. Ma, you load the woman and baby in the car — and get on down there. Tell the man we're coming with a team of heavy horses and a stone boat. And tell him not to worry about that darned bull. If he has to cut that rope, so be it!"

Grandma settled her passengers in the Terraplane and tore off for the bridge.

"Come on, Jase. Let's hitch up Jim and Fanny and get on down there."

We ran to the horse barn, harnessed the team of heavyweight horses, and hitched them to the stone boat, a huge sled-like plane. While Grandpa retrieved the coil of towing rope, I held the reins. This heavy rope was used during haying to lift automobile-sized fork loads of hay into the loft.

As soon as Grandpa jumped on the stone boat, I flicked the reins and gave the team their head. In less than a minute, we were at the bridge. After unhitching the team, we tied a large loop in one end of the towing rope and placed it over the collars of both horses. After tying a slipknot in the other end, we lassoed the bull.

Despite having been rescued from drowning, the bull was still feisty. I was tempted to remind him that his only other option would involve a complete makeover, from young bull to filet mignons and hamburger. But I didn't say a word.

When we cut the Gypsy's rope, Jim and Fanny effortlessly dragged the bull out of the creek. Using the towing rope, we tied the shivering bull to the oak tree in the corner of the north field. Over his bellowed objections, we left him there while we inspected the damage.

"That axle's broken, all right. We might be able to repair it — by welding, I mean. Or maybe we'll have to replace it. One way or the other, we gotta move this wagon over to Nate Craddock's farm. See it? Just over the hill. Nate's a master welder — got a full set of equipment in his barn."

The Gypsy quickly agreed.

"Grandpa, how can we possibly get the wagon over there with a broken axle?"

Grandpa had an enormous amount of common sense, with experience to boot. After thinking a second, he informed us, "That front axle's broken. So we probably can't do too much more damage to it. We'll just take off the front wheels, hitch up those heavyweights, and drag it over to Nate's."

Grandpa turned to the Gypsy man. "What do you think?"

"Iss good! Iss very good idea!" he told Grandpa confidently.

"If I'm right, we should have you on your way in no time."

We didn't know that Grandma was standing behind us until she spoke. "Dad, don't be so sure about that. That baby is too sick to travel anytime soon," she announced, pointing at the Terraplane. "As soon as you can get this wagon out of the way, I'm taking this mother and baby over to the Henrys to call Doctor Moran. If he's in his New Albany office, I'll take them there. If not, I'll go straight to Riverton Memorial."

At first, there was panic in the Gypsy man's eyes. But soon he accepted the situation and thanked Grandma profusely. "I know baby iss sick. Not good at all. Thank you, missus."

We jacked up one wheel and removed it. And then removed the other. After stacking the wheels on the stone boat for transportation to Nate's a little later, we unhitched the Gypsy horse and tied him to the back of the wagon. Next we lifted up the wagon tongue and tied it back to keep it out of the way.

Finally we hitched Jim and Fanny to the outside ends of the broken axle and slowly dragged the wagon off the bridge onto the shoulder of the road. After squeezing by, Grandma raced off to the Henrys with the mother and ailing baby.

Once we determined the load in the wagon was fairly balanced, we were able to increase the speed of the horses. When we reached the intersection of Barrington and Henry roads, not surprisingly, we looked up to see Grandma heading our way.

She stopped briefly to report. "Dr. Moran says it's best to meet him at Riverton Memorial, as soon as we can. I'll call the Henrys with any news."

Then she was gone.

I had forgotten people's revulsion to Nate Craddock when they first met him. Putting it plainly, Nate was a very dirty man. Despite some valiant effort on Grandma's part, his personal hygiene was still practically nonexistent. The Gypsy man took one look at Nate and immediately stepped back. Nate's clothing was in terrible shape. His current set had rotted away and barely hung to him by threads. The richly dressed Gypsy looked as though he had just met the Devil himself.

But you couldn't deny Nate this, he really knew his stuff. He took one look at the broken axle and shook his head. There was no doubt in Grandpa's or my mind that Nate was absolutely right when he announced, "There's no way to weld that axle. It's done for."

Grandpa and the Gypsy man looked despondent.

"Now, now! Don't be discouraged," Nate advised, with a twinkle in his eye. "Look over there against the wall. Know what that is? That, my friends, is a perfectly good axle that I been wondering what to do with. By my reckoning that should cut down to just about the right size. I'll get my torch set up. I'll need to do a little burning."

Nate was in his element. In charge and burning something.

"Tell you what you do, Bill. You and Jase take that team and get them wheels. The two of us will stay here and get this axle ready so we can install them the minute you get back," he promised.

I, for one, believed him. And he was right. Within an hour, the wagon was back in better shape than ever. With a brand new axle and wheels fully reinstalled.

After we thanked Nate profusely for all he had done, the Gypsy man asked Nate how much he owed him.

But Grandpa immediately intervened. "This one's on me. You broke that axle saving my bull. How much, Nate?"

"My usual for you, Bill — one crisp dollar bill."

"Now, wait a minute, Nate. That's not right. What's that axle worth — and how about your time?"

"That axle wasn't worth two cents laying there rusting in my barn. So that's a null. And all's I'm ever going to charge you for my time is one dollar. You know that."

There was no arguing with Nate Craddock.

So we followed the wagon back to the Compton farm to await news from the hospital.

While I fixed a makeshift dinner, Grandpa and the Gypsy man sat and talked on the screened-in porch. It had been hours since breakfast. While the coffee perked, I made ham sandwiches, using Grandma's freshly baked bread that miraculously was still warm. Some oatmeal cookies to dip in our coffee completed the meal. Not too bad, if I don't say so myself.

As we were finishing, Mrs. Henry arrived with some news, "Gentlemen, the baby's fine. They gave him some intravenous liquids. And the doctor recommended a special diet to get him back on track. The ladies will be home shortly with the baby. They can give you all the details."

As she was leaving, she noticed the Gypsy wagon looking as good as new. "Say, I thought that wagon had a broken axle."

"Not after the magic touch of Nate Craddock!" Grandpa declared.

You can say that again!

WE DIDN'T HAVE LONG to wait before Grandma returned with the mother and baby. We men watched from the porch as Grandma helped her two *patients* out of the Terraplane. Obviously Grandma had taken quite a liking to the two. This time, she wouldn't take no for an answer. The Gypsy family would simply have to share supper with us.

"But before that happens, we don't know what to call each other. We need to introduce ourselves properly. We're the Comptons. My name is Jane. This is my husband Bill. And our grandson, Jase Addison."

After the Gypsy man and woman each repeated our names a few times, they told us theirs. The family name was *Nyari*. The father's first name was *Lorant*. The mother, *Gisella*. They were Hungarian *Roma* or Gypsies.

"And the baby's name is *Jenci*. I remember that from the hospital."

Gisella smiled proudly and thanked Grandma again for her help. Lorant pressed the women to tell him about the baby's health. Gisella and Grandma explained that the boy was not tolerating his mother's milk. For some reason, it was causing him to suffer from severe colic. Because he wasn't consuming enough milk, he had become malnourished and dehydrated.

"What about Ema?" Lorant inquired.

"No, Ema iss no good," Gisella answered. "Still makes colic."

"Who's Ema?" I wanted to know.

"Ema iss our cow. And Vidor iss our horse," Gisella added. "We must find goat — a doe. What you call doe?"

"A nanny goat?" I suggested.

She nodded her head. "Nanny goat."

"Dad, I thought we'd run over to the Rau's after supper. They've got a sizeable goat herd. Maybe they can spare one of their females. If not, at least, we can get some goat's milk until we can find a nanny goat. That reminds me. What did you do with that bull?"

"The way he butted that spy-apple tree in the orchard, I figured he liked it. So he's tied to it until we can take him to the stockyard. I'm tired a dealing with him."

"Good!" Grandma pronounced. "Dad, could you and Jase finish your chores before supper so you could come with us to the Raus? As a matter-of-fact, we could just hitch up our wagon. That way we can all go."

Turning to the Nyaris, she suggested, "I'm sure you want to wash up before supper. If you like, you can go out to your wagon and *freshen up* while I put some things on the table."

Grandpa and I set off to do the evening chores while the Nyaris returned to the wagon. I looked back to see Lorant point under the driver's seat to show Gisella their new axle. Just as I was about to enter the barn, I saw a pickup truck speeding up Barrington Road. Without slowing enough, it skidded into our driveway and screeched to a dusty stop.

Grandpa ran back out of the barn to see a man hurriedly slam the truck door and stomp toward the Gypsy wagon. The woman with him cowered in the truck.

"Now who could that be?" Grandpa wondered.

"Who's that, Dad?" Grandma yelled from the porch. Suddenly she recognized the man. "Oh, for crying all night! What's he doing here?"

It was George Larson from Mr. Soldani's produce stand at the stockyard.

Larson ignored us. He seemed intent on confronting Lorant. Approaching the wagon, he yelled, "Give me back my rooster, you thief!"

Grandma grabbed her broom and stomped off the porch toward the wagon. Grandpa was confused by her aggressive behavior. It wasn't like Grandma at all.

"What's gotten into her, Jase?"

"It's the man from the stockyard — the man the sheriff took to jail. Name's Larson. He manages the Brown farm."

"So that's him — is it?" Grandpa ducked back into the barn. He emerged, carrying his pitchfork. "Let's see him try to bully me."

We Comptons joined Lorant just in time to hear another Larson tirade.

"You came to my farm yesterday when I wasn't there — and stole that rooster. It's got my leg band. Right there. I'm takin' it back with me. Right now! And you better skedaddle — or I'm calling the sheriff — and he'll lock you up."

"You're an expert on that aren't you, Mr. Larson?" Grandma quipped sarcastically.

Larson turned around and stared at her. "It's you!"

"You bet it's me! What's the meaning of this?" she demanded.

"They stole my rooster. He's got my tag on his leg." Larson pointed at the red rooster in the wooden cage. "See it! Right there — on his leg. It's mine."

Grandpa didn't say a word. He stood next to Lorant and remained remarkably patient. On the other hand, he was holding his pitchfork at the ready. He reminded me of a Detroit Red Wing, standing between his goal and the opposition's oncoming power play.

Turning to Lorant, Grandma asked, "What did you do for Mr. Larson to earn that bird?"

Before Lorant could answer, Gisella spoke.

Pointing at the woman in the pickup, she stated calmly, "I sell lady beautiful — custom-made — two-strand blue lapis and red garnet beads. Most time iss cost two chickens — but I feel sorry for her. Only take one chicken."

We all turned and looked at the woman. Small and haggard, she nervously clutched at the collar of her house dress.

When he saw his wife's reaction to the accusation, Larson immediately became enraged. He stomped to the truck, threw open the passenger door, and dragged the woman from her seat. She fell to the ground and attempted to regain her footing as Larson continued to drag her toward the wagon. When he reached us, he threw his wife to the ground.

"Tell me! Is what she said true?" he yelled. "Well, is it?"

The woman was shaking with fear, still clutching at her throat.

Larson bent down and tore open her collar. There it was. Just as Gisella had described. A beautiful double strand of sparkling blue and red beads.

"I'll teach you to lie to me!" Larson spit as he unsnapped the heavy buckle of his thick leather belt and pulled it from his trousers. "You ungrateful —."

Raising the belt above his head, Larson was about to bring the heavy buckle down on his wife. That's exactly when Grandpa made his move.

Thunk!

Time seemed to stop. The belt, buckle, and Larson's arm were all suspended in air.

"Ahwwee!"

Larson screamed as the tines of Grandpa's pitchfork nailed the shirtsleeve of his whipping arm to the wagon. Finally Grandpa reached up and jerked the belt out of Larson's hand. Then he flung it back toward the pickup truck.

Hanging there by his shirtsleeve, Larson reminded me of a pathetic scarecrow. He hung his head and cried in anguish. At that particular moment, I don't believe any of us had a modicum of sympathy for the man.

Grandma bent down and helped the sobbing Larson woman to her feet. Then she half-carried the woman into the house.

The sound of another car coming up Barrington Road hardly registered until it pulled into the drive. Sheriff Connors emerged from his patrol car, walked toward us, and surveyed the scene, including his former inmate Larson hanging forlornly from Grandpa's pitchfork.

He turned to Grandpa. "This your handiwork, Bill?"

"Afraid so, Roy."

"I appreciate it. You saved me the trouble of tracking this scoundrel down. I gotta warrant in my car for his arrest. In addition to his very disagreeable personality, he's an embezzler. Harry Chambers is the trustee of the Brown estate. He just had Judge Parker issue the warrant. Because I just let this rat outta jail, I figured he might want to make a call on Jane. They're old friends, you know."

The sheriff removed Grandpa's pitchfork and handed it to him. He gave Larson's arm a cursory examination and quickly released it.

"Nothing to worry about, Bill. Just a little scratch!"

Once again, he dragged Larson to the backseat of the patrol car and deposited him unceremoniously.

"Cuppa coffee, Roy?"

"No, Bill. I'll take a rain check. I got to do a lot of paperwork on this bird. Tomorrow, I officially evict them from the Brown farm. I'll send some men to help his wife load up and get outta there. You might pass that along to her when you go in the house."

"I'll do it, Sheriff."

"Can you see she gets home all right, Bill?"

Grandpa nodded, and we all watched as the sheriff's car slowly pulled out of the driveway.

"All right then, what do you folks say? About supper time, isn't it?"

Grandpa has always been my hero!

6 THE FRUITS OF FAME

CHUCK NICHOLS' SERIES OF ARTICLES IN THE *Riverton Daily Press* and his news commentaries on WRDP relating to the Conrad Hoffman case exceeded our expectations. His coverage was a masterful blend of objectivity and comprehensiveness. As Danny and I requested, he had given credit for our success to all FSG members. Following JB's basketball example, Danny and I were trying to score fewer points ourselves and chalk up more assists by sharing the credit with our friends.

But we were not naïve.

As we feared, the minute Chuck's story hit the wire services, Danny and I found ourselves in the spotlight once again. We rejected a flood of interview requests. Our family members and neighbors were subjected to aggressive confrontations by out-of-town reporters. As before, we were inundated by an avalanche of telegrams from people we didn't even know, promising great rewards for our doing various things for them.

In fairness, we did receive a number of congratulatory telegrams from people in high places with whom we had become acquainted during the previous year. While modesty prevents me from mentioning their names, we appreciated hearing from them again. However, experience had taught us that congratulations, no matter how well-meant and flattering, could never compensate for the high costs of fame. Our perspective enabled us to maintain a calm attitude in the midst of the inevitable maelstrom of adulation.

That was our state of mind on Tuesday, the day before Governor Dewey was scheduled to award us the *New York Medals of Recognition* in the Hamilton School gymnasium. The state of mind of the staff, teachers, and students was quite a different matter.

Since the Governor's visit was announced, with the exception of JB, Danny, and me, the entire school seemed to have gone crazy. Even people known for their coolness under fire, like Butch Matlock, were virtually dysfunctional. And those who were already a bit flighty, like Queenie, had departed from Planet Earth.

We sane people spent our time simply trying to figure out the others.

"Did you hear what Sherm told me?" Danny laughed.

I shook my head.

"He wondered if we could ask Governor Dewey to give him a medal for knowing where to push the siren button in his father's police car. I told him if he asked any more stupid questions, I'd punch *his* button — and see how *his* siren was working."

"You won't believe this! Coach Clark insisted that we put on a basketball demonstration for Governor Dewey," JB informed us.

"Think that's weird? This weekend, Queenie and her cheerleader friends met at our house. They planned to put together a special cheer for Thomas E. Dewey. But it was a total disaster."

"Why?"

"Because all the words that rhyme with *Dewey* — like *phooey, gooey, gluey, chewy* — made them giggle. And giggle! Every time somebody suggested another word, they'd start giggling all over again. They must have giggled for six hours."

"I'll sure be glad when this is all over!"

In the afternoon, Mr. Lund's secretary came to Miss Sparks' classroom for Danny and me. I was overjoyed to escape from the sixth-grade insane asylum. The level of emotional energy in the room was causing my teeth to ache.

"What's this about, Mrs. Pergola?"

"Mr. Lund wants to talk to you about a phone call he received from Governor Dewey."

We were immediately escorted into Mr. Lund's inner office. When we were seated in front of his desk, he informed us, "Boys, Governor Dewey just telephoned. He needs your advice."

Those were heady words.

"As you know, he went to college with Harry Chambers and Jim Comstock. They were fraternity brothers at Michigan."

We nodded yes.

"You may not know this, but I too was one of their Michigan fraternity brothers," he said smugly. "But that doesn't matter. Tom knows you boys are close to Jim Comstock. He'd like to invite Jim to the awards ceremony. And Harry Chambers and his wife, if you boys agree."

"That's fine. Danny and I haven't seen Mrs. Libby since the day we found Hoffman's body. I look forward to seeing her."

"Me too," added Danny.

"So you'd be totally comfortable having Mrs. Libby here — even though she was once married to Conrad Hoffman?"

Danny looked as puzzled as I was. "She hasn't been married to Hoffman for years. When he joined the German Bund, she divorced him and changed her name. She'd like to be at the ceremony because she's thankful we saved her life. At least, that's what she told us. Besides we want her there too."

"Exactly how I feel," I affirmed. "She should be there."

"That's just what Governor Dewey hoped you'd say. He's waiting for our call."

Mr. Lund had the long-distance operator place his call. Within minutes, Governor Dewey was on the line.

"The boys are highly in favor of Mrs. Libby being there with Jim. In fact, the boys would have been very disappointed if she'd missed it."

Mr. Lund listened intently. "You bet. Who first?"

Then he handed the receiver to Danny. "Say hello to the Governor!"

"Hello!" was all Danny could muster. But he nodded a dozen times. Then he handed the phone to me.

"Hello, Governor. It's me, Jase."

"Hello, Jase. I'm relieved to hear you speak. I put a slew of questions to Danny and didn't get a single answer out of him. Is he all right?"

"He nodded about a dozen times. He hasn't used a telephone very much. I guess he forgot you couldn't see him."

"Oh, I see. Don't want anything to happen to that one. Do we? First, I wanted to tell you both how very proud I am of each of you. And to tell you how much I look forward to being with you and your families tomorrow. I'm glad you both want Mrs. Libby there. From what I hear from Jim Comstock, she's a gem!

"I know this is a bit last minute, but I was wondering if you two would like to come over to Owosso on Saturday. There're some people here who'd like to meet you. And I have some things I'd like to tell you about and show you. If your folks are all right with that, you can ride over with George Lund who's coming here for a family visit. We'll have an early supper so he can have you back home at a decent hour that evening. What do you think?"

First, I told him how proud we were to receive the *New York Medals of Recognition*. And providing our parents approved, which I was sure they would, we would be delighted to come on Saturday.

"Well, good! I'll see you tomorrow afternoon then."

Still nodding his head, Danny was grinning from ear to ear.

ON THE MORNING OF the awards ceremony, Danny seemed preoccupied. At breakfast, he fidgeted with the pair of *Medals of Courage* pinned to his sweater. He hardly touched his food. He just wasn't himself.

"What's on your mind, Danny?" Mom inquired.

"Medals and badges," he responded.

"What about them?"

"We passed our requirements for *Tenderfoot* and for the *Fishing* Merit Badge. Right? And we're working on our *Second Class* and on the *Automobiling, Metal Work,* and *Machinery* Merit Badges. Right?"

"Yes. But I'm afraid I don't —."

"And today we're getting *New York Medals of Recognition*. Right?"

"So what's the problem, Danny?" I felt myself becoming impatient.

"I'm gonna need a bigger sweater."

Dad and Mom looked at each other and smiled. My first thought was that Danny must have been bitten by the Hamilton

School insanity bug. Before I could share my diagnosis with him, he was spared by JB's knock at the back door.

"Hello, JB. Come on in," Dad said, opening the door. "What's new?"

"Coach Temple told me I'll be the starting shooting guard on Friday night," he reported, with a grin. "And another thing. The team voted. I'm now the captain."

"Wow! That's wonderful news! You've only been on the team a short while. That's a real tribute to your leadership and hard work, JB. Congratulations. We're coming to the game. As a matter-of-fact, the Reillys, Addisons, and Tuckers all plan to sit together."

"It should be a good game. So far this year, the East Lansing YMCA's 14-and-under team is undefeated. But we think we can take them. We've got some good starters and strong backups on the bench. Our depth is our secret weapon."

"Not to change the subject, but have you heard any more about your mother, JB?"

"We're going down again on Saturday, Mrs. Addison. I'm hoping the doctor says she can come home with us."

We all told him that we hoped so too.

Dad excused himself, picked up his lunch-bucket, and pulled his jacket off the hook. After he opened the kitchen door, he paused and speculated, "If this weather keeps up, we're going to have an early spring. You boys will want to break out your bicycles soon."

"Do you have a bike, JB?" I asked.

"I did but we sold it for —. We sold it."

"In that case, we'll just have to see about remedying that situation. Won't we, boys?" Dad declared optimistically.

At Christmas, Danny and I had received bicycles as gifts of appreciation from E.F. Graham, owner of the Graham Markets. In the previous fall, we had rescued his Cadillac sedan and all its valuable contents after they were stolen by two Nazi POWs from Camp Riverton. That was when I rescued Danny, who had been kidnapped by the pair, and Nate Craddock, who had been held hostage and seriously beaten by them.

I had mixed emotions about our bicycles. While they enabled us to reach our destinations more quickly, they lessened our ability to converse with each other. On balance, I preferred to walk.

"Boys, this is your big day. You better shove off for school pretty soon. I'll leave work in time to pick up your mother. We'll see you at the awards ceremony later," Dad promised, before departing for work.

On our way to school, we told JB about Governor Dewey's invitation to visit him in Owosso. He was very impressed but wondered, "Where's Owosso?"

"It's about 20 miles west of Flint. Down toward Lansing," I informed him.

"Wonder if they have a YMCA?"

"Not that I know of," I admitted honestly.

Danny added, "If they do, it's got to be better than the Riverton Y."

"Yeah, but not better than the Riverton Y basketball team," JB reminded us.

IN ADDITION TO OPENING every section of bleachers, the Hamilton School janitors had completely covered the gymnasium floor with folding chairs. On the stage, they had arranged a row of chairs behind the podium for the dignitaries who would be attending. Chairs and music stands were placed at the far left of the podium to accommodate a small contingent from the Riverton High School band, who would perform the *Star Spangled Banner.*

Danny and I marched to the gymnasium with the rest of Miss Sparks' class. Because our class would be seated front-and-center, the janitors had placed *Reserved* signs on these chairs. And, since the two of us were the honored recipients, our class entered last. The members of the military police color guard, led by our friend Sergeant Rick Prella, who led the squad of MPs assigned to the canning factory, were standing at parade rest just inside the door.

By the time we arrived, students, teachers, family, newspaper reporters, friends, and neighbors had filled every seat. Latecomers were forced to stand in the back on either side of the bleachers. A dozen dignitaries, including Governor Dewey, were sitting on the stage waiting for our arrival.

While our classmates took their seats, Danny and I remained standing. Sergeant Prella brought his color guard to attention. They marched toward us and came to a halt right in front of us. The sergeant gave us a smart salute and whispered our instructions. After we side-stepped into place, the color guard escorted us up onto the stage and to our seats right next to Governor Dewey. They did a crisp about-face and marched to their positions near the American and State of Michigan flags. Before sitting down, we shook hands with the Governor and with the dignitaries on either side of us. I didn't recognize a number of them.

Reverend Squires gave the invocation and in doing so told everyone how honored he was to be our friend. And how grateful he was for our generous contribution to his ministry. Danny touched my arm with his elbow, and we both smiled when the Reverend cited our unselfish service at mealtimes at the Mission. After his unusually brief prayer, he concluded with a robust "Amen."

The band had been waiting for that word. It was their cue to begin playing. When they struck the first note, every person in the gymnasium rose and faced the flag. Those in uniform saluted. The rest of us placed our hats and hands over our hearts as we sang the National Anthem with feeling.

When we were seated, Mr. Lund took the podium to welcome everyone to Hamilton School. Next Harry Chambers stepped up to introduce his friend and fraternity brother, Governor Thomas E. Dewey.

He told us he had known Governor Dewey since their college days when they were members of the same fraternity, along with George Lund and Jim Comstock. He thought it was a remarkable coincidence that George was now the principal of the school where Danny and I were enrolled.

Next he focused on Dewey's career after Michigan. How he had graduated with honors from Columbia School of Law and later became a New York City prosecutor. In that job, Dewey had convicted mobster Lucky Luciano, head of the largest Mafia family in America. Later in 1939, as District Attorney, he had prosecuted the leadership of the American German Bund for embezzlement. This destroyed the ability of that subversive organization to support Nazi Germany from its American base during the war.

He told of Dewey's election to Governor of the State of New York as a young 41-year-old man. How he won the Republican nomination for President of the United States when he was only 42. And, despite his loss to Franklin Roosevelt, he had won the respect of every American for refusing to attack FDR's foreign or war policies for cheap political gain.

"It gives me great pleasure to introduce the Governor of New York, The Honorable Thomas E. Dewey."

The gymnasium exploded with applause.

"Thank you, Harry. I truly appreciate your kind words. I'm honored to be introduced by such a distinguished member of the Michigan bar. Moreover, you've been my trusted friend and supporter for many years.

"But this ceremony is not about Harry Chambers or Tom Dewey. It's about two exceptional boys from Riverton — Jase Addison and Danny Tucker. These boys have set a new standard for citizenship. Over this past year, they've taught the rest of us what it means to be a truly great American."

He turned and smiled at us.

"I'm not here in the capacity of Governor. I'm here as a humble representative of the people of New York to acknowledge and honor these brave boys. And to deliver our profound gratitude for all they've done to make their parents and family, their friends and schoolmates, their city and state, and their country extremely proud of them."

Governor Dewey went on in this vein for about two weeks. Or at least it seemed that long. It was all very flattering, but it was also exceedingly enervating. Danny managed to stay awake by tapping his toe on his chair rung in time with the cadence of Governor Dewey's delivery. Because we were seated just a short distance from the podium, the Governor must have thought the fillings in his teeth were picking up radio signals from the *Bongo Music* program on WRDP. I elbowed Danny a couple of times, but the magnitude of his tapping only increased.

Having already entered the dream state, I was barely awake when the Governor said, "Come on up here, boys."

Leaving me for dead, Danny set off for the podium without me. In the midst of my eerie out-of-body experience, I saw myself floating out of my chair and across the stage toward the podium. When I collided with Danny's back, I came to.

I was stunned to see hundreds of eyes from the audience focused right on me. But I did what any other international hero would have done under these circumstances. I tried to look cool and nonchalant.

But Danny saw through me. "How was the nap?" he whispered.

My pinning ceremony was uneventful. The Governor bent over, pinned the *New York Medal of Recognition* on my sweater, shook my hand, and moved on to Danny. However, as usual, Danny's case was different. Remembering Danny's *bigger sweater* comment at breakfast, I began to feel very sorry for Governor Dewey.

"A little to the right, Governor D. No. The other way. That's it. Pin it right there. No. That's not quite it. Try a little to the left. And up a bit. Be sure it's on the same level as my *Medals of Courage.*"

"Did we get it that time, Danny?" Governor Dewey asked hopefully.

"Nope! But that's okay. My mother'll straighten it out when I get home."

"I'm sure she will. Yes, I'm sure of it."

If Governor Dewey was shaken by any of this, he surely didn't show it. Talk about *cool and nonchalant.*

"Before you boys leave the stage to show your medals to your family, there's one remaining piece of business to attend to." He reached into his suit-coat pocket and pulled out a piece of paper. "Boys, I want to read this wire from another of your devoted fans."

Special Dispatch
The White House
March 21, 1945

Dear Jase and Danny,

Congratulations! Being a New Yorker myself, I'm delighted that my Great State has chosen you boys to receive this wonderful honor. You more than deserve it. Hearing of

> *your latest success against the American German Bund warmed the cockles of my heart. They were a bad bunch. And it's gratifying to see the last of their leaders brought down. It didn't surprise me a bit to learn that you played key roles in this operation.*
>
> *I'm not alone in this opinion. I'm pleased to send along the congratulations and warm regards of a certain cigar-smoking fellow whom you met when we were together in Washington a few months back. He's back home in England now, supervising the job of knocking the stuffing out of those Nazi rascals.*
>
> *Jase, Mrs. Roosevelt and I've become well-acquainted with your wonderful Aunt Maude and little cousin Johnnie since they moved to Washington to be with your Uncle Van. We've had them here at the White House for dinner on several occasions. They are a breath of fresh air. Just what this old boy can use now and then.*
>
> *Finally I'm not sure I'll be running for President again, but if I do I want you both with me during the campaign. Don't get too chummy with my loyal opposition and good friend, Tom Dewey. He's a very nice fellow but he's not a Democrat. So keep your eye on him!*
>
> *Please, do me one last favor. Thank Governor Dewey for allowing me to be a small part of your very special celebration. My best wishes to your families.*
>
> *Yours very truly,*
> *Franklin Roosevelt*

When he finished reading President Roosevelt's telegram, an explosion of applause arose from those in attendance. I had to admit this was a very special surprise.

We thanked Governor Dewey and the other dignitaries once again. After saying goodbye to the Governor, we told him we looked forward to seeing him in Owosso.

We slowly worked our way through scores of well-wishers to the spot where our families had been seated. Along the way, we saw

Jim Comstock and Mrs. Libby. They were talking to an older woman I didn't know.

Queenie was the first family member to touch our new medals. "Is it heavy?"

"Naw! Not at all," Danny assured her. "Besides this is an old sweater."

"No. It's not, silly. You just got it for your birthday."

"Anyway it must have shrunk. It's too small."

Thankfully we were saved by Chub. "Can I wear this medal to school someday?"

That ridiculous question earned him a Danny-applied *Dutch Rub*. Danny and I always believed it was good for the minds of small boys to have their heads stimulated in this manner at least once a month.

While we accepted the congratulations of our friends and neighbors, the Tucker and the Addison families lingered until the gymnasium was nearly empty. As we were leaving, I was very curious when I saw that Jim Comstock and Louise Libby were still chatting with the older woman.

"Mom, who's that lady?"

"Her name is Greta Frantz. She's visiting Louise Libby from Milwaukee. Conrad Hoffman was her nephew. Louise hasn't seen her for years but told me she always liked the woman. In the way of amends, Miss Frantz has generously offered to put the Libby girls through college after they come home from prison."

"Wow! That's great, Mom. They're pretty bright. College would give them a fresh start. Something to look forward to after they get out."

"It's a wonderful gift — but I was wondering about something, Marie. After so many years, Miss Frantz just drops back into Louise's life out of the blue and — the first thing she says is — she wants to pay for Anne and Barb to go through college. How did she ever come up with that idea?"

"Miss Frantz told Louise — sometime in the past — she'd helped someone else go to college."

"OH, MY. THIS IS exciting! I've never been to a basketball game before," Mrs. Reilly exclaimed. "When I went to school, we didn't have any kind of a gymnasium, let alone something as fancy as this."

We'd invited the Reillys to sit with us to watch JB play his first game for the YMCA. We'd come early to ensure we had good seats. Located in the third row at center court, our seats were perfect. The two teams had just emerged from the locker room. When they began to warm up, I could tell that JB was really hot.

Nudging Danny, I predicted, "Look how JB's shooting. I'll bet he's Riverton's leading scorer tonight."

"Did you two future Wolverines take note of the East Lansing team colors?"

Green and white. The same as Michigan State College also located in East Lansing. Of course, the Riverton colors were those of the University of Michigan, blue and gold.

Coach Temple and Coach Clark called the team together for a huddle in front of the Riverton bench. They both crouched low, dispensing last minute instructions and motivating words to the excited players surrounding them.

I turned to Danny, who had a smirk on his face. "What's so funny?"

"Oh, I'm just glad I thought about moving those practices here."

"I think everybody's happy about that. Good going!"

After a short cheer, both huddles broke and the starting teams took the floor. The tallest boys for each team stood in the center of the court, awaiting the tip-off. Before play started, each boy shook hands with his opposite number.

When the referee tossed the ball high for the tip, our center appeared to have jumped about a foot higher than theirs and skillfully tapped the ball to JB. With grace and ease, JB dribbled down the court toward the East Lansing basket. Using a head-fake, he darted around the defender and laid up his shot. The first points scored were ours. More specifically, they were JB's.

The sound in the gymnasium was deafening. Instead of inbounding the ball right away, the East Lansing team members and coach just stared at the crowd. They were awestruck. The home-field advantage of Hamilton School was something the boys from MSC town had never experienced before. I had a feeling this was going to be a long night for the visitors.

By halftime, Riverton had a solid lead of 24 to 13. JB accounted for half of Riverton's scoring. We stretched our legs and left the gymnasium. The line at the popcorn machine was incredibly long. I saw Danny gazing longingly in that direction. Dad noticed too.

"How about I treat you boys to a bag of popcorn?"

We spent the entire halftime break standing in line. By the time we reached the front of the line, people were flooding back to the bleachers.

"How do you folks like it so far?" Dad asked the Reillys.

"It's amazing! I'd no idea that Johnson - er - *JB* was such a good player. Every time he throws that ball, it goes through that basket thing — even from a long distance. It's amazing!"

While Mrs. Reilly didn't bother to hide her pride, Mr. Reilly was a bit more reserved. I wasn't surprised because he was the chief accountant at Michigan Electrical Motors. According to Grandma Compton, accountants are supposed to be reserved.

"Well, I wouldn't want our boys to be overconfident. They have a nice lead now. But things have a way of changing," Mr. Reilly cautioned.

Not wanting to be impolite, I didn't tell him what I thought of his reserve in this case. Much to our chagrin, before the end of the third quarter, his caution proved to be well-advised.

When the teams took the floor for the second 12-minute half, I was shocked to see JB sitting on the bench. Instead, the boy JB had beaten out for his starting position was on the floor.

Mrs. Reilly was very upset, "Well, for crying out loud! What's wrong with those coaches? Why's JB sitting instead of playing?"

Everyone in the gymnasium seemed to agree with her. Instead of cheering when Riverton won another opening tip-off, the crowd was silent. Shocked, I imagined, that JB wasn't on the floor, providing the spark he had generated both in the practice scrimmages and in the first half of this game.

I turned to Dad. "Why do you think JB's on the bench, Dad?"

"You got me, Jase. But I have a feeling we'll know before long."

Dad was probably right. He was saying I had to be patient. But it was tough when the green-and-white was outscoring the blue-and-gold, with two of their points for every one of ours.

I thought about the boy who had taken JB's place. His name was Ted Koshinsky, a good fellow and a student at St. Thomas Junior High. But this was a basketball game and, I reminded myself, nice guys don't always win ball games.

General George Patton stated something along those lines during his tussle with Field Marshall Rommel when they tried to outwit each other in North Africa. At least that's what I had read in the *Riverton Daily Press.*

Objectively speaking, the boy taking JB's place was about two inches shorter and at least a step slower. He possessed nothing close to JB's shooting accuracy. I couldn't imagine why the coaches had that boy, instead of JB, on the floor.

When the referee blew his whistle signaling the end of the third quarter, the teams were deadlocked at 30 points apiece. Riverton was cold and East Lansing was sizzling. The visitors were enjoying the great benefits of not having to double-team JB and not having to contend with the roaring home-crowd noise that had all but disappeared after the first half.

During the brief break between periods, Ted Koshinsky ran to the bench and bent over JB. Their exchange was brief but intense. JB pointed toward the court. Ted shook his head and returned to the floor. Before long, East Lansing was enjoying a six-point lead. Riverton's boys were flagging, standing midcourt with their hands on their knees, watching their opponents run past them and score basket after basket.

With two minutes left in the game, Ted Koshinsky called a time-out. It was Riverton's last. Then he called for the team to *huddle up* around him. The two coaches stood on the sidelines wondering what was going on. But to their credit, they didn't interfere. They allowed the impromptu *team meeting* to proceed without them.

When the time-out ended, Riverton inbounded the ball and moved methodically downcourt. Their entire demeanor had changed. Their exhaustion had disappeared. Their passing was crisp. They dribbled and darted with abandon. Their shooting was deadly. In short, they had regained control of the game. Sensing this, the crowd rose to its feet and gave the team the home-field advantage it had not enjoyed since halftime.

The effect on the East Lansing team was dramatic. The wind came out of their sails as they watched their six-point lead vanish in a series of unanswered points scored by their opponents. With two seconds to go, they took their last time-out and ran to their bench for solace from their coach. Instead, the coach screamed at them, shook his finger, and pulled at the jerseys of those whom he thought were most responsible for their collapse. Parents and other supporters sitting behind the East Lansing bench were visibly upset by their coach's abusive behavior. It was not a pretty picture.

When play resumed, it was Riverton's ball. The inbound pass to Ted Koshinsky was picture-perfect. He raced toward East Lansing's basket. There was only one defender between him and his goal. Suddenly he stopped and launched a set shot at the basket. The defender swiped madly at the ball and managed to deflect the shot, which struck the backboard and fell to the floor as the whistle signaled the end of the game.

"Can this game end in a tie?" Mr. Reilly wondered.

"In high school and college, they would play an overtime period — but I'm not sure of the rule in the YMCA league."

No one in the gymnasium had made a move toward the doors. Instead, everyone was staring at the three coaches and the referee, huddling in the center of the court. When the meeting broke up, the East Lansing coach stomped back to his bench, threw down his clipboard, and sat down with a *bang.*

The referee raised his hand to make an announcement.

"In this league, we do not play overtime periods. A game can end in a tie. However, —."

We and the rest of the crowd moaned and started for the doors.

"However!" the referee yelled.

We stopped to listen.

"However, despite having run out of time on the clock — the game is *not* over."

We were stunned.

"What's he talking about?" I asked no one in particular.

"On the last play," the referee continued, "the Riverton shooter was fouled. Number six please come to the foul line. You have two attempts to make one point. If you hit either shot, the game is over and Riverton wins."

The home crowd roared once again as Ted Koshinsky walked to the foul line. When he took the ball from the referee's hands, silence fell over the court. You could have heard a pin drop.

Instead, we heard the *bump, bump, bump* as Ted nervously bounced the ball before lofting his first foul shot.

The ball looked good all the way to the rim, where sadly it banged, rattled around, and finally fell to the floor.

Someone behind us stated the obvious. "He missed it!"

The crowd moaned and then cheered to urge Ted on.

The referee handed Ted the ball for his last attempt.

Bump, bump, bump!

The ball arched through the air. It looked like a perfect throw. Time stood still as it descended toward the basket.

Swish!

Roar!

"We won! We won! We won!" Mrs. Reilly screamed as she hugged her husband.

Riverton had won after all.

While we waited with the Reillys for JB to emerge from the locker room, Mr. Reilly offered his comments. "You know, when I mentioned things have a way of changing, I had nothing like this in mind. I'm not sure my old ticker can take many more games like this one. Goodness gracious."

This time I fully agreed with him.

On our way to the car, I posed the question that was on everyone's mind. "JB, why did the coaches take you out of the game for the second half?"

"They didn't. I took myself out," he answered curtly.

"I don't understand. You mean you *wanted* to sit on the bench instead of playing?" Mrs. Reilly was incredulous.

"In the first half, we weren't playing like a team. The guys were depending too much on one player — me. So I spoke to the coaches, and they agreed I could exercise my authority as team captain and pull myself out of the game."

"Unbelievable!" Dad exclaimed, shaking his head.

"Maybe so, Mr. Addison, but it worked. The guys finally started playing as a *team* and we won. From now on, whether I'm in the game or not, we'll play like a team. And I predict we won't lose another game."

For some reason, I had a feeling that this was one prediction you could take to the bank.

7 OWOSSO'S FINEST

SATURDAY MORNING ON THE WAY TO OWOSSO, MR.
Lund was still basking in the glory of our *marvelous* awards
ceremony. He talked of nothing else. Because the ceremony was his
first big event since becoming Hamilton School's principal, he was
understandably enormously pleased by its success. Danny and I
did not have the heart to inform him that we'd put this subject to
rest days earlier. There was another reason we were less effusive
than he. After receiving our third or fourth medal, it just
happened. We had become jaded!

Moreover, by Saturday morning, our memories of the awards
ceremony had been completely eclipsed by the thrilling experience
of watching the Riverton YMCA basketball team pull out a
squeaker against East Lansing. To us, winning with a foul shot in
postregulation far exceeded the importance of merely winning one
more medal.

During our initial meeting with Mr. Lund, I formed the
impression that, in Mr. Lund's mind, basketball didn't hold a
candle to any subject relating to Governor Dewey. Still
unconvinced, Danny gave it another try. "You should have been at
the basketball game last night, Mr. Lund."

"What basketball game was that, Danny?"

Forever the pragmatist, Danny immediately surrendered.

"So you and Governor Dewey have been friends for a long
time. Huh?"

"Yes, Danny. I've known Governor Dewey since I was five years old."

"You don't say? Tell me more."

At that point, I was extremely thankful that I had volunteered to sit in the backseat. I rested my head on the seat and closed my eyes, hoping to enjoy another sweet visit to my dream state. My wish was granted.

"Jase, wake up!"

"Where are we?"

My question set off an automatic response from Mr. Lund. As we drove, he directed our attention to points of interest along the way. Obviously he had given this tour many times before.

"This is Corunna — the county seat. There's the Shiawassee County Courthouse. Owosso's three miles from here, by way of Corunna Avenue. There's McCurdy Park. The Shiawassee County Fair is held there every summer. That's the Owosso stockyard. On Thursdays, farmers from all over the county bring produce of every description to sell — there in the parking lot.

"And here's the city limits. We're officially in Owosso now. If you go down Frazier Street — right there — you'll find the Owosso City Waterworks and the foundry. And there's the canning factory."

"Look, Danny! They have POWs here too."

"Yes. Camp Owosso has about 800 German POWs. It's out west of town. The POWs work at the canning factory and on farms in the area."

We turned onto Washington Street and crossed over a bridge. "That's the old Shiawassee River. See how it winds lazily through town before heading north to Saginaw Bay?"

"Just like the Chippewa," I noted.

Then we turned onto Water Street. "That's Sam's Barbershop. When I was a kid, I used to get my hair cut there. Here's the Owosso Fire Department and Owosso City Hall."

We merged onto Main Street and crossed over another bridge. "That's the old Comstock cabin. Elias Comstock, who was Owosso's first settler, built that cabin back in 1836. There's the Owosso Public Library. A beautiful Frieseke painting hangs on the wall there."

"Fri —. Who?" Danny sputtered.

"Frederick Frieseke was a famous artist who was born here in Owosso. When it comes to art, I'm not very knowledgeable. I'm sure Tom will tell you more about him later. At the end of this street, you'll find Curwood Castle."

"A castle! What's that doing here?"

"It was built in 1922 by Owosso's most famous author, James Oliver Curwood. Tom plans to take you there so I won't steal his thunder."

We stopped in front of a little white house, carefully painted and trimmed. The property was covered with flower gardens and well-pruned shrubs. After its winter sleep, the lawn was just beginning to display its lush greenness. A perfect house for a widowed lady of a certain age.

In the driveway was the old Chevrolet, belonging to Governor Dewey's mother. After losing to FDR in the 1944 Presidential election, Governor Dewey had returned to Owosso to seek solace from old friends and family. As usual, he stayed at his mother's home. On that trip, as he promised, he visited Danny and me in Riverton. Instead of using the chauffeured limousine that usually transported him, he drove himself to Riverton in the old Chevy.

I will never forget our conversation that day about how political parties were not as important as people. Even after losing the election, he spoke highly of FDR, praising his leadership through the Depression and the War. He told us that good leadership was far better for America than good politics. To his credit, he held fast to that philosophy throughout his years of public service. In the end, history would show that Thomas E. Dewey was not burdened by an unforgiving ideology. As a result, he was considered an extraordinarily capable and honorable man by members of both political parties.

"I'll come in to say hello, but I won't stay," Mr. Lund told us. "This evening, I'll pick you up at the City Club at seven o'clock as arranged. That'll get us back in Riverton well before nine."

Mrs. Dewey was just as friendly and outgoing as her son. She doted on Danny as all older women seemed inclined to do. "Danny, I see from your sweater that you're very proud of the medals you've been awarded. Am I right?"

"Yes, you are, Mrs. D. And that reminds me of something I wanted to ask you. Do you happen to have any old sweaters lying around the house that Governor D. has outgrown?"

Danny!

AFTER WAVING GOODBYE TO Mr. Lund, we joined Governor Dewey and Mrs. Dewey on the south-facing glassed-in back porch. Even though the porch wasn't heated, the leafless trees allowed the midday sun to warm us. Come summer, the porch windows would be replaced by screens to provide a perfect place to sit in the white wicker furniture and enjoy the cool summer breezes wafting upward from the nearby Shiawassee River.

Set just for the four of us, the lunch table was covered with an off-white linen tablecloth, probably imported from Europe before the war. The matching napkins were tightly rolled and inserted into sterling napkin rings that matched the silverware beside our plates. The peach-colored dishes contrasted softly with the tablecloth. Our cut-glass goblets sparkled like crystals in the sunlight.

Placed conveniently near the door to Mrs. Dewey's kitchen, a large serving table was covered with luncheon offerings. A platter heaped with thick slices of turkey breast and smoked ham. Large bowls of homemade potato salad and coleslaw. A basket containing an assortment of rolls and freshly sliced white and dark breads. A pair of identical pitchers, containing iced tea and lemonade, had just been removed from the icebox. Tiny beads of condensation ran down their sides, delicately etching the frost-covered glass.

In the center of the lunch table, a round lazy Susan offered a variety of accompaniments. Sliced pickles, both sweet and dill. Mustard, mayonnaise, and ground horseradish. Salt, pepper, sugar, and toothpicks rounded out the selection.

After serving ourselves, Mrs. Dewey advised, "Before the Governor takes you on your tour, he wants to tell you some things about Owosso, but don't let that keep you from enjoying your lunch."

Turning to Danny, she continued. "I've been told you have a king-sized appetite. Nothing makes a cook — like me — feel loved and appreciated more than to watch a young man eating heartily at my table."

"Mrs. Dewey, before lunch is over, you're gonna feel *really* loved by Danny," I predicted, winking at the Governor. "Seriously, Mrs. Dewey, this lunch looks delicious. Thank you for having us."

She smiled and rocked back and forth in her wicker chair. Obviously she enjoyed grateful luncheon guests, especially young men like Danny and me.

Governor Dewey then shared his plan for the day. During lunch, he planned to tell us about three famous men. Having grown up in Owosso, he had met two of them when he was a boy. The third man moved to Owosso a few years before, bringing his fame with him.

This all sounded intriguing. Even Danny listened intently, which wasn't always the case when presented with such appetizing alternatives like ours that day.

"After that, I thought we'd borrow Mother's car for a tour of the city. Hopefully what I'll tell you at lunch will make the tour more interesting. This evening I've invited a couple of people, who've wanted to meet you, to have dinner with us at the Owosso City Club. J. Edwin Ellis is Owosso's mayor and an old friend of mine. The other is a young fellow who's a Foreign Service Officer, visiting home from Colombia where he's currently posted. His family is one of Owosso's finest. His name is Alvin Bentley."

"Will you be coming with us to dinner, Mrs. Dewey?" I inquired hopefully. I really admired this lady.

"No. Unfortunately I have another engagement. Saturday is dinner and bridge at Christ Episcopal Church. It's a long-standing obligation. My bridge partner forbids me to miss it. You'll be dropping me off on your way to the City Club."

After taking a large bite from his mighty sandwich, the Governor realized he had forgotten to tell us something. After he chewed and swallowed, he added, "Through George Lund, I checked something with your parents before you left home.

"You see, the City Club requires gentlemen to wear coat and tie for lunch and dinner. I didn't know whether you boys had them. Your folks informed us you didn't. But don't worry about that. Before dinner, we'll stop by the tailor shop, located in the same building as the City Club. There we'll fix you right up. Afterwards, you can take those new duds along home with you as a souvenir of Owosso."

"Coat and tie. Wow, Danny!" I gasped. "Thank you, Governor. We can really use a nice coat and tie. Can't we, Danny?"

I was trying to get Danny to express just a little gratitude. *Silly me!*

"Too bad they don't allow men in uniform to eat there. We could've worn our scout uniforms."

"I didn't think to ask the manager about that, Danny. Good point," the Governor replied, with a twinkle in his eye.

All I could imagine was Danny trying to enter the Owosso City Club wearing what *he* called his scout uniform. What would Danny's response be when the headwaiter asked him where he preferred to be seated, in the *Scout* or in the *Doughboy* section?

As soon as he finished his sandwich, Governor Dewey surprised us. "Do either of you boys have a nickel on you?"

Spontaneously we both patted our pockets, knowing full well that neither of us had a nickel to our name.

"Why? Should we leave a tip?" Danny quipped, smiling at Mrs. D.

"No, I wanted to —. Oh, here! I have one." Extracting a Jefferson nickel from his pocket, he held the coin in the air. "Have you ever wondered who designed this coin? That is, who drew the artwork and sculpted the dies to stamp it out?

"That person is Felix Schlag, who's lived in Owosso since 1943. His wife's a teacher and —."

"And she's a very fine lady. I've met her and like her very much," Mrs. Dewey interrupted.

"What I was going to say is that, in addition to his design skills, Felix is a gifted professional photographer. I thought it would be a grand idea for him to take a picture of the three of us, all dolled up in our dinner wear tonight. We have an appointment at 5:30, right after we finish at the tailor's."

I picked up the nickel from the table and inspected it. I'd never really examined it closely before. On one side was Thomas Jefferson's portrait. On the other, an engraved depiction of Monticello, Jefferson's stately home in Virginia.

"Jefferson's head is on what's called the *obverse* side of the coin. And his home is on the *reverse* side," the Governor told us.

"Where'd Mr. Schlag learn how to do this kind of work?" I really hadn't appreciated what I was holding in my hand until now. Our coins were miniature works of art.

"After the first war, in which he fought on the German side by the way, he studied classical art at the Royal Academy of Art in Munich, Germany. During the 1920s, while he still lived in Germany, he won a number of awards in design. In 1929, he moved to America and took a job as an auto stylist for General Motors down in Detroit. He worked in that profession until he moved to Owosso. After he arrived here, he started his photography studio."

"When did he design the Jefferson nickel?"

"His design was selected by the U.S. Mint in 1938. Apparently he was among nearly four hundred designers who submitted their work for consideration. This was the very first time the design of a coin was selected in this manner. As the winner of the competition, his prize was one thousand dollars. He's very proud of this, and he should be."

"Think about it, Jase. Every guy in the world who has a nickel in his pocket is carrying a little statue made by the man who's going to take our picture tonight. How about that?"

Danny nailed it. This was pretty impressive all right.

MRS. DEWEY REFUSED OUR offers to help clear the table. "You boys relax. I'll take care of these things while you listen to Governor Dewey's next lecture," she told us, topping off our lemonade. "I'll eavesdrop from the kitchen."

"Mother, I may need your help with this first — ah — *lecture*."

"Don't worry, son. I'll add my two-cents' worth if needed."

"Frankly I'm not much of an art expert, but I do enjoy the paintings of Owosso's most famous artist. His name is Frederick Carl Frieseke. I'm a bit biased because Frieseke grew up just a few blocks from here. Since he was born in 1874, he was quite a bit older than I. However, I met him when I was a boy. He certainly was a very impressive man."

"Tom, did you know his father was a brick maker? And that the boy's poor mother died when he was just six," Mrs. Dewey chimed in. "Because he always wanted to be an artist, he left Owosso after high school to study at the Art Institute of Chicago. Then he went off to New York for more study at the Art Students' League."

When Mrs. Dewey returned, carrying a plate of chocolate cookies, she continued. "His mentors encouraged him to study in France. In 1898, I believe, he moved to Paris to enroll at the Académie Julian where he was influenced by another American artist, James McNeill Whistler. During that period, Frieseke began to establish his reputation as a gifted painter. For nearly, twenty years he maintained an apartment and studio in the Montparnasse Quarter. Many other famous artists lived there as well."

While I had expected Governor Dewey to do all the talking, he seemed content to defer to his mother.

"In 1905, Frieseke married Sarah Ann O'Bryan. Later, their daughter Frances was born. He used both women as models, especially for his paintings set in nature."

When Mrs. Dewey returned to the kitchen, she spoke louder, "The real turning point in Frieseke's career came in 1906 when he rented a summer cottage in Giverny that adjoined the property of Claude Monet. By this time, Monet was recognized as the founder of French Impressionism. His followers believed an artist should express his perceptions of nature, rather than simply record nature.

"By the way, many of Frieseke's paintings were set in his colorfully painted summer cottage or in its sun-drenched gardens. During his 14 summers there, he emulated Monet. His style evolved until he too became recognized as a leading impressionist painter. After the First World War ended, he and his wife bought a summer home in Normandy where he continued to hone his skills and deepen his understanding of his medium."

As the afternoon sun warmed the porch, I was having difficulty staying awake. While I didn't want to be rude, I wasn't sure that I could absorb any more information about Frederick Carl Frieseke. Across the table, Danny's eyes were at half-mast. His huge lunch, coupled with the warm sun, had rendered him downright indolent. I could see he was dangerously close to departing for a visit of his own with Morpheus.

From the kitchen, Mrs. Dewey was not aware of our struggle to stay awake. But Governor Dewey was. He saved us by concluding *her* lecture just in time. "In short, Owosso is very proud to be the birthplace of one of the world's most renowned impressionist painters. On our drive, we'll stop by the public library to see one of his paintings that I like very much. And I bet you boys will like it too."

At the sound of the Governor's voice, Danny's eyes popped open. He turned toward the kitchen and inquired, "Tell me, Mrs. Dewey. Weren't Frieseke's *plein air* nudes considered his best works?"

At first, you could have heard a pin drop!

Suddenly an explosive *guffaw* erupted from the kitchen and filled the porch. We all broke into laughter.

It was just what the doctor ordered. By the time we recovered, I was reenergized and ready for the next event. Governor Dewey rightly suggested that movement was in order. So we decided to launch our afternoon tour by piling in the car and heading for the library. We wanted Mrs. Dewey to join us, but she declined, saying she had a bit of gardening to do. After a few hours with Danny, she was probably in need of a nap herself.

We reached the library in no time. Upon entering, Governor Dewey pointed at the wall. There it was! Prominently displayed high on the east wall of the library's main room. When we moved closer, I observed that the subject was a young woman, dressed in white, holding a parasol. She was seated on what looked like a park bench. These key elements had been rendered in a blend of muted pinks and purples. The background of tiny blossoms and leaves had been created by hundreds of individual brush strokes of darker hues of blues and grays from Frieseke's palette.

As we were leaving, Danny confirmed the name of the painting with Governor Dewey, "So that was *Lady with the Sunshade*, 1910. Right, Governor?"

"Why — that's right, Danny. How did —?"

"Don't get me wrong, Governor. That's a very fine painting, but I personally prefer *The Garden Pool*, circa 1913. Don't you?"

Governor Dewey looked at me and then back at Danny. "How do you know all these things, Danny?"

Danny glanced at me and winked, "You know, Jase. *Success has a thousand fathers —.*"

Grandpa Compton's Farmer's Almanac?

Danny's first choice paid off handsomely for the owners of *The Garden Pool.* In 2006, this oil-on-canvas painting sold for $2.368 million, setting a new world auction record for the Owosso-born artist, Frederick Carl Frieseke (1874 - 1939).

WE PARKED THE CAR on the street in front of a brick building. Next to the heavy glass entrance door with brass hardware, a small engraved plate told us where we were.

> **Owosso City Club**
> **Members & Guests Only**

I was confused. "Governor, I thought we were going to the tailor shop first."

"Don't worry! The shop's just inside the door."

When we stepped inside, sure enough, there was a quaint little shop with two tiny display windows on either side of the entrance. Each display area only had room for one half-body mannequin. One wore a black suit jacket, white shirt, and red silk tie. And the other, a dark-gray glen-plaid sport coat with a black turtleneck sweater. On the floor of each window were neatly arranged rows of overlapping socks and ties, as well as assorted accessories.

On the glass transom above the door, the name of the shop was painted in crisp gold letters. *Andre's Quality Menswear.*

Once inside, I sensed this was a very special place. The ambience was elegant, and the whole shop smelled like the inside of a new wallet. It was no larger than our small front room at home. Shelving, covering what little wall space was available, contained a modest inventory of sweaters and dress shirts. The only fixture in the store was a glass case that displayed leather goods like gloves, belts, and wallets and accessories like key chains, watch fobs, and cuff links. It also served as the counter. I saw no cash register. Through a door behind the counter, I observed a tiny draped fitting room and a treadle sewing machine. Suits, sports coats, trousers, and overcoats hung on racks that lined the back wall of the store. And that was it.

"Welcome, Governor. We've been expecting you. We're fully prepared to meet your needs."

"Wonderful, Andre! I'll let you take charge."

"We'll be delighted. We'll start with the measurements. Who'd like to be first, young gentlemen?"

Because there were no other people working in the store, I thought it odd that this well-dressed man, with a measuring tape around his neck, continually referred to himself as *we*. I was under the impression that this appellation was reserved for royalty or the editorial page.

Apparently I wasn't the only one who noticed. Tapping his chest, Danny responded, "We'll go first!"

Like birds on an electric wire, Andre's eyelids flew up and then came back to roost in a mild scowl. Danny whistled through his teeth as the man measured him from stem to stern.

"You're next, young sir." Andre waved me over. Figuring Danny had inflicted enough damage on the poor man, I played it straight. My tailor seemed relieved.

The entire process took fewer than 15 minutes. I noticed the man hadn't recorded our dimensions. Instead he had committed them to memory. Now that was impressive.

"Thank you, Andre. We'll return around five o'clock," the Governor told him as we were leaving.

"We'll be back too," Danny told him, tapping his chest again.

After closing the door, I looked back to see Andre with his head back, inspecting his ceiling.

I *wonder* why?

"WELL, BOYS. THERE SHE is. Curwood Castle. What do you think?"

We were speechless. It was magical!

Built in the style of an 18ᵗʰ century Norman château, this miniature castle was not a large structure. While it sported three turrets, the tallest was only two stories high. Its exterior was yellow-buff stucco, dotted with carefully embedded fieldstones for added interest. The roof, slate with copper trim, reminded me of those I'd seen on gingerbread houses at Weinstcin's department store the Christmas before.

"Who built this castle? Why was it built?"

"Who was Curwood? What's it used for?"

"Let's sit over there on that bench, and I'll answer all your questions."

"James Oliver Curwood was born in Owosso in 1878," he began. "Curwood never completed high school, but he was bright enough to pass the entrance exams of the University of Michigan where he studied journalism.

"In 1900, he sold his first story. Back in those days, he was working as a reporter for the *Detroit News-Tribune.* Nine years later, he'd saved enough money to travel to the Canadian Northwest. This trip and many others provided him inspiration for his novels. Many of these were wilderness adventures set in the Yukon and Alaska. His personal experiences in the wild contributed to his lifelong commitment to conservationism.

"Between 1908 and his death in 1927, he wrote over 30 novels, some of which were published after he died. I remember how much you boys like movies. Almost half of his novels were made into films for which he wrote most of the screenplays.

"By the 1920s, he was one of the most popular American novelists and a very wealthy man. But he'd always dreamed of building a castle overlooking the Shiawassee River. In 1922, his dream came true. The castle became his private studio where he could retreat from his nearby home to create his much-loved stories.

"He also used the castle to entertain visiting dignitaries from the publishing industry and Hollywood, including William Randolph Hearst and Louis B. Mayer. After his untimely death in 1927 at the age of only 49, the castle was willed to the City of Owosso. Since the war started, it's been used as a youth center. But plans are afoot to convert it into the office of the Owosso Superintendent of Schools. And I suspect someday it'll be a museum to commemorate the life of James Oliver Curwood."

"What's that building right across the river, Governor Dewey?"

"That's the new high school."

"Wow! Students can see the castle from their classrooms!"

"That's right, Jase. If you were a young English student looking out on Curwood Castle, wouldn't it inspire you to become a novelist?"

"Maybe so, Governor Dewey. Maybe so."

WHEN WE RETURNED TO the Dewey house, Mrs. Dewey was sitting on her front porch reading the afternoon's *Owosso Argus Press*. She waved at us as we got out of the car.

Danny reached the porch first. "We saw the Frieseke painting at the library. Don't worry. It wasn't a nude."

"Oh, all right. I won't," she promised, trying not to giggle at Danny's latest.

Apparently it wasn't working too well because I noticed her tummy was bouncing up and down. She reminded me of Grandma Compton. Danny had her number too. Both women seemed highly susceptible to his odd behavior. I was rather used to it by that time.

"I'll go up and dress. Do you boys want to wash your hands? There's a guest bath at the end of that hallway," the Governor informed us as we entered the house.

While we washed our faces and brushed our teeth with a wet index finger, we discussed the evening ahead. "This should be fun tonight, Danny."

"Which do you think we'll like the most? Getting our new coats and ties at the tailor shop? Or having our picture taken by the nickel guy? Or eating dinner — hmmm — at the City Club? Or meeting the mayor and the foreign sewer officer? Or driving home with Mr. Lund?"

I was studying him, trying to figure out what he meant by *foreign sewer officer*. He decided to help me out. "I was only kidding about driving home with Mr. Lund. I can guarantee that won't be much fun."

Oh, I don't know. Napping's not all that bad.

We met Governor Dewey at the front door. He was dressed in a dark-blue pinstripe wool suit with vest. His white handkerchief extended no more than an eighth of an inch above the top of the pocket over his heart. He wore a stiffly starched white shirt and a blue and white checked silk necktie, tied in a very tight knot. His shoes were highly-polished black wingtips. Since he had no belt, I assumed he was wearing braces. For some reason, I also assumed he was wearing knee-length stockings with suspenders for them as well. I didn't recognize his after-shave lotion. However, because it smelled like the inside of a new wallet, I was fairly sure I knew where he had purchased it.

While Danny and I piled into the backseat, Governor Dewey held the passenger door for his mother. At the church, we hugged Mrs. Dewey goodbye and invited her to come see us in Riverton. She promised she would. Danny gave her a special incentive to make the trip. "Come early on Sunday morning. We'll take you to the Good Mission Church for breakfast with the bums and hobos."

"That sounds perfectly lovely, Danny," she replied, shooting her son a slightly desperate glance. But he wasn't about to help her out. He just smiled and gave the end of his mustache a little twist.

"I'll be home around eight o'clock, Mother. Your bridge partner will drop you back home. Am I right?"

She told him she'd be fine. So off we went.

When we arrived back at Andre's, he seemed fully recovered and enthusiastic. At his suggestion, Danny and I joined him in the back room where we changed into our white dress shirts. Andre helped us knot the identical ties we had selected. Naturally they sported alternate stripes of our favorite colors, blue and gold. Even though Andre carefully demonstrated how to tie them, I was confused. I decided not to worry about it though. For the time being, when I undressed, I would simply loosen the knot and slip the tie over my head. Surely before I arrived at Michigan, someone would show me how to tie it properly.

When he removed our dark-blue blazers from their hangers, I noticed that each was lined with a luxurious light-gold silk. Andre held my blazer for me to try on. When I slipped my arms into the sleeves, I felt an enormous surge of well-being. I looked at myself in his floor-length mirror and could not believe my eyes. Suddenly I had become a man. I turned to Andre and grinned. He clasped his hands together under his chin and cooed proudly. He could barely contain himself.

Mercifully Danny had the same reaction. Andre was even more delighted and, I suspect, greatly relieved. We left the back room to show Governor Dewey our new attire. His reaction was perfect. "My gosh! Fellows, you look like freshmen at the University of Michigan. Well done!"

As we bid Andre adieu, he cooed again. I thought of the pigeons in the top of Grandpa Compton's horse barn. When that image entered my mind, I realized that Andre's shop smelled a bit like horse harnesses too.

Or was it the horses themselves?

BEFORE WE DEPARTED FOR the Schlag Studio, we put our everyday shirts and Danny's medal-laden sweater in the car. I watched him fold the sweater neatly and place it carefully on the backseat. Suddenly I realized that it had been several weeks since I had seen Danny wearing something other than that sweater.

I hadn't realized what a serious problem this was. Weeks later Queenie told me how difficult it was for Mrs. Tucker to convince Danny that he should remove his medal sweater before going to bed. When Queenie related Danny's argument for keeping it on, I recognized his rationale from the summer before.

On his first visit to the farm, because he had forgotten to pack his pajamas, he told Grandma that he had done so intentionally. That way, he rationalized, he could remain fully dressed in his summer uniform, combat boots and leggings included, just in case there was a Nazi air raid on the cow barn. Like his mother, Grandma held her ground, making him remove his uniform and wear one of her nightgowns to bed. He never forgot to pack his pajamas again.

The Schlag Studio was situated on the second floor of the Owosso Savings Bank, just down the block from the City Club. We reached the studio by way of a stairway that led upward from the street below.

When we entered, Mr. Schlag greeted us warmly. When Governor Dewey introduced us, Mr. Schlag bowed slightly and shook our hands. With just the hint of a German accent, he repeated his name. "Felix Schlag. Welcome."

"Mr. Schlag, Danny and I heard how your design for the Jefferson nickel won first place. We think that's just wonderful. And we're very pleased to meet you."

He smiled broadly and shook my hand again. Then he shook Danny's a second time.

With those niceties behind us, we got right down to business.

His camera and lights were arranged in front of a large white sheet hanging from the ceiling. There was a wooden chair centered in front of the sheet. Mr. Schlag suggested that Governor Dewey sit in the chair and that we boys stand behind him with our hands resting on the chair's back. Impressed by his confident manner, we did exactly as he instructed.

He adjusted our clothing and the position of our heads. When we were situated to his liking, he moved to his station behind the camera. Reaching over, he tilted one of his floodlights slightly. When he was completely satisfied, he reached for his remote shutter control that resembled a long hypodermic needle.

He looked at us and ordered, "Smile. That's good. Hold it!"

Snap!

Snap!

Snap!

And that's all there was to it.

As we prepared to leave, Mr. Schlag told Governor Dewey the proofs would be ready for his approval the following afternoon. He offered to drop them by after church. Finally he turned to us. "I have something for you, boys."

He handed us each what looked like a small photograph album. When I felt the cover, I realized it was constructed from extremely thick, stiff cardboard. The cover was laminated with a dark-blue, faux-leather finish and embossed with gold lettering which read:

```
┌─────────────────┐
│                 │
│    Jefferson     │
│    Nickels       │
│    1938 -        │
│                 │
│                 │
│                 │
└─────────────────┘
```

Inside the album were three pages. Like the cover, each was thick laminated cardboard, perforated with nickel-sized holes.

Over each hole, the year and a single letter, representing the mint that had struck the coin, was embossed in gold. Clear plastic strips, inserted under the laminate on both front and back of each page, protected the coins from scratches and kept them clean and dry.

For each year and each minting site of the Jefferson nickel since 1938, Mr. Schlag had inserted a shiny mint-quality coin. To top it off, he had autographed the pale-blue inside front cover, using gold ink.

I opened the folded piece of paper that I had found inside the album. The typewritten document read:

TO WHOM IT MAY CONCERN:
On this day of our Lord, March 23, 1945, I attest to the fact that this book was duly autographed in my presence by Felix Schlag, the designer of the Jefferson nickel.

Signed: *(Signature)*
Date: March 23, 1945
Office: President, Owosso Coin Club

It was signed by the president of the Owosso Coin Club.

Danny and I thanked Mr. Schlag repeatedly as we left his studio. He seemed genuinely pleased by our response to his thoughtful gift.

"Mr. Schlag, I'll keep this album for as long as I live" were my parting words.

And I have kept my promise. In addition, I added newly minted Jefferson nickels for each year the design was used, from 1938 until 2004, a full 30 years after Felix Schlag's death.

ONCE AGAIN WE STOPPED at the car, this time to deposit our albums. When we arrived at the City Club, Governor Dewey's guests were waiting for us just inside the door.

"Sorry we're late, gentlemen. Felix surprised the boys with a gift of an autographed Jefferson nickel album. So we stayed a few minutes longer than planned to inspect the gift and give him our thanks. Didn't we, boys?"

He introduced us to Mayor J. Edwin Ellis and Foreign Service Officer Alvin Bentley. While I was reminded of Danny's *foreign sewer officer* faux pas, I decided not to mention it in such distinguished company.

The headwaiter led us to our table. After we were seated, Governor Dewey summarized all that Danny and I had accomplished and the resultant recognition we'd received during the past year. I was impressed by the elegant terms the Governor used to describe our achievements. Danny was impressed by the enormous pat of butter he managed to bury in a dinner roll before popping the whole thing into his mouth.

When our waiter handed each of us a huge menu, I opened mine and was dismayed. It read like Greek to me. Danny seemed to be experiencing the same trouble. He was evidently annoyed by not being able to order quickly, which was necessary to meet his need for frequent refueling.

"Boys, this menu is a bit confusing. If you like, I'll order for you. Do you both like beefsteak?"

We thankfully accepted Governor Dewey's assistance.

Within minutes, the waiter arrived with our soup course. As he placed it before us, he announced, "Vichyssoise, gentlemen."

Neither Danny nor I knew what that meant. By the sound of the word, I assumed it was some kind of *fishy* soup. To be honest, it looked more like the potato soup Mom made for us at home.

Naturally Danny was the first person to sample the soup. He deposited a giant spoonful into his mouth. Then he made an immediate withdrawal. That is to say, he redeposited the soup back into his spoon.

Frowning at Governor Dewey, he complained, "Hey! Somebody forgot to cook this soup."

Despite a valiant effort, the three men couldn't convince Danny that Vichyssoise was meant to be served cold. Danny turned to me and whispered, "It's just not safe to eat uncooked fish."

By this time, I had eaten about a third of my Vichyssoise and found it to be quite good. But not even my opinion mattered. The waiter came to Danny's rescue by suggesting an alternative, onion soup with a thick cheese-covered crouton floating on its surface. Danny's only condition was that it had to be fully cooked.

Fortunately Governor Dewey had inherited his mother's funny bone. Generally he found Danny's antics to be quite humorous. Frankly I was not always amused.

While Danny concentrated on licking every last molecule of melted cheese from his spoon, I decided to be sociable. Mayor Ellis was a likeable man and an old friend of Governor Dewey. The two of them chatted about the state of the city while I focused my attention on Mr. Bentley. This worked well, because once our dinner arrived, Danny was focused elsewhere.

During our conversation, I discovered that in 1940 at the age of 20, Mr. Bentley had received his bachelor's degree from the University of Michigan. When the war broke out, he enrolled in the Turner Diplomatic School in Washington, D.C., after which he joined the diplomatic service at the State Department.

As a member of the Foreign Service, he had been posted in Mexico for two years prior to his current posting in Colombia. He regaled Danny and me with odd tales about Nazi Germany's forays into South America to stir up trouble for the Allies there.

Later I would learn that Alvin Bentley resigned from the State Department in 1950 and moved back to Owosso to prepare himself to run for Congress on the Republican ticket. In 1952, he was elected to represent Michigan's Eighth Congressional District in the U.S. House of Representatives.

In 1954, while on the House floor, Bentley was among five Congressmen who were shot by four Puerto Rican nationalists. Before being subdued by police, the four sprayed the chamber with 30 rounds from automatic pistols. Having taken a bullet in the chest, Bentley's wounds were by far the most serious, requiring months of recovery before he was able to resume his duties. At their request, the attackers were convicted of capital crimes and sentenced to death by electrocution. However, rather than allow them to become martyrs, President Dwight D. Eisenhower commuted their death sentences and the four were resentenced to a minimum of 70 years in prison.

We made it through the delicious meal without further incident. But, just before we were preparing to leave, Danny requested a doggy bag for the leftover bread. That may have worked if Danny had been content with bagging only the bread remaining in the basket on *our* table.

Danny informed the headwaiter that his motto was *Waste not, why not?*

As he escorted Danny outside to avoid further disturbance to those at other tables, the headwaiter foolishly suggested Danny correct his wording of the old proverb. Danny took his revenge by helping himself to about two hundred *City Club* matchbooks from the huge fish bowl on the front desk.

As he begrudgingly dumped all but a dozen back into the bowl, he explained to the headwaiter, "For gosh sakes, they're just souvenirs for Grandma Compton."

Just after we had said good night to Mayor Ellis and Mr. Bentley and retrieved our items from Governor Dewey's car, Mr. Lund pulled up at the City Club. We shook Governor Dewey's hand and thanked him over and over for all he had done for us. After he gave us a big hug, we got into Mr. Lund's car.

We waved one last time and both of us withdrew into our thoughts to review all that had happened that day. Mr. Lund was busy negotiating Owosso's Saturday evening traffic. He didn't say anything until we had gotten out on the highway. "Tell me, boys. What did you do today?"

"Nothing much," Danny answered him. "How about you?"

When Mr. Lund began his answer, once again I rested my head on the backseat and closed my eyes.

8 DANGER IN RIVERTON

ON THE WAY HOME FROM OUR SCOUT MEETING, Danny and I decided to spend an hour or so working on our Second Class requirements. When we reached the back porch, I noticed the lights were still on in Dad's shed.

Danny noticed too. "Gee! Your dad's still working. Must be behind on his repair jobs."

During the war, shortages and rationing had a profound effect on my father's sewing-machine business. As the size of our armed forces grew, the need for cotton, wool, and synthetic fibers for military purposes grew exponentially. Nearly all raw materials supplied to textile mills were earmarked for uniforms, bandages, bedding, parachutes, camouflage netting, and other war-critical items.

Fabrics for the manufacture of civilian clothing were in very short supply. If garment makers managed to acquire any materials for civilian consumption, they produced only high-end garments, such as women's gowns and men's fine shirts. Underwear for men, slacks for factory-working women, and school clothes for children were seldom available for purchase. But this did not mean these items weren't desperately needed.

Therefore, if you couldn't buy it, you had to make it.

Resourceful American seamstresses launched the hunt for material. No potential source was overlooked, including mothballed clothing in attic trunks, recyclables from the rag bin, seldom used items of clothing hanging in closets, and remnants from church rummage sales. With skillful sewing, any piece of worn or out-of-style clothing could be salvaged for mending, piecing, or altering into usable garments for children and adults alike.

As the war progressed, Americans began to sew with a vengeance. Those who didn't own sewing machines also had to be resourceful. During the war, sewing-machine production lines were converted to the manufacture of weapons and other war materials. As a result, the demand for used sewing machines skyrocketed. People salvaged old ones from attics, garages, and basements. But first, they had to be overhauled and put in working order. With the tremendous increase in sewing, even newer machines required more frequent repairs and adjustments.

Before the war, my father's sewing-machine overhaul-and-repair business had been a modest but profitable pastime to which he devoted a few hours each weekend. Income from this part-time venture merely supplemented the wages generated by his full-time occupation. By the end of the war, he was working seven days a week on sewing machines, logging far more hours than required for his day job.

"Danny, I'm afraid nowadays Dad's always behind on his repair jobs. But he's good at it and enjoys it too. Besides he really helps the war effort by keeping people's sewing machines in good repair."

"Hello! Anybody home?" Danny hollered when we entered the kitchen.

There was no answer.

"I thought your mom would be home by now. Maybe something happened out at the camp," Danny speculated.

Since the previous summer, Mom had spent several evenings each week teaching classes. These were a part of the vocational training program offered to the German POWs at Camp Riverton. Using sewing machines supplied by Dad, she presented hands-on workshops, covering basic and advanced sewing skills.

Taking German pride into consideration, she had wisely named these classes, *Professional Tailoring Workshops*. Because of the practical nature of the curriculum and her skills as a sewing instructor, her classes were among the most popular in the program.

We sat down at the kitchen table and broke out our *Handbook for Boys*. Turning to the Second Class requirements, I told Danny,

"We worked on *Scout Spirit* and *Scout Participation* at the meeting. Let's work on the third part, *Scout Craft.* "

Danny perused his handbook. After a few seconds, he closed it and offered his assessment. "Okay. Here's the deal. We've already completed everything in the *Scout Craft* part. There's nothing more to study."

Having read this part of the requirements earlier, I had arrived at just the opposite conclusion. "Gee, Danny. I don't think it's gonna be that easy."

"What's hard about it?"

"First of all, it's entirely about preparing for a five-mile hike."

"We hike all the time! That's a piece of cake."

"But do you know *six Silent Scout Signals for formations and field work?*" I asked, quoting verbatim.

"Where do you see that? Hmmm. Why are they important for our hike? Since we'll be walking together, we don't need *Silent Scout Signals.* We can just tell each other what to do."

"Okay. Let's get back to that one later. What else is there? Oh, yeah! We don't know how to read a map."

"So what? Gad! We're not going for a hike in the Congo! We'll do it right here in Riverton. We don't need a dumb map!"

"Let's get back to that one later too. Here's another one. Do you know how to *follow the track of a person or an animal in soft ground or snow for a quarter of a mile, reading the meaning of the track?*"

"Of course, I do! As long as the snow doesn't melt, I could follow a man's footprints for a *hundred* miles. As to *reading the meaning,* that's easy! The guy's going someplace! That's all."

I was about to render my opinion of Danny's interpretation when we heard a car door slam.

"I'll bet that's Mrs. A," Danny shouted excitedly. He rushed to the front door and threw it open. "Yes! And Colonel Butler too."

"Hello, boys. It's good you're here," Colonel Butler stated unemotionally.

From his tone of voice, I knew something serious was afoot. His tone brought back memories from months before. As the commanding officer of Camp Riverton, his connections in Washington had provided invaluable information about the whereabouts and welfare of Uncle Van who was listed as missing in action during the Battle of the Bulge. Aunt Maude and my little cousin Johnnie were living with us during that fearful time.

After Uncle Van was reported safe and sound, Colonel Butler was appointed liaison officer to help our entire family travel to Washington for Uncle Van's award ceremony. For gallantry and intrepidity above and beyond the call of duty, he received the *Medal of Honor* from President Roosevelt at the White House. On the same day, Great Britain awarded him the *Victoria Cross* for single-handedly rescuing nearly two hundred British naval officers and sailors. Of course, Danny and I received another pair of *Medals of Courage* at the White House. While we were at the British embassy, we also had the honor of having a secret meeting with Sir Winston Churchill.

"Jase, will you boys run out and ask your Dad to join us?" Mom asked.

Apparently Dad was just wrapping up for the night. When he saw the expressions on our faces, he observed, "You two look pretty serious. What's up?"

We responded by shrugging our shoulders.

After damping down the fire in his potbellied stove and turning off the lights, we headed for the house. We saw flashing headlights and heard the slamming of doors from the street in front of the house.

"Sounds like we've got more company," Danny observed.

He was right. By the time we arrived, Sheriff Connors and Sergeant Tolna had joined the others in the front room.

"What's going on here?"

"John, we have a situation that affects you and your family."

"What kinda situation?" Dad glanced around the room. "And why all the firepower?"

"John, I'll get right to the point — because time is of the essence. I wanted all the interested parties to hear this straight from the horse's mouth," Colonel Butler advised, pointing at himself.

Danny's eyes were as big as saucers.

"We have a deranged guard. Regrettably he's killed two POWs and a fellow guard. But that's not the worst part. He's on the loose and heavily armed. And he's threatened to kill Marie Addison."

"My God! Marie?"
Mom!

COLONEL BUTLER'S BRIEFING WAS delivered with military precision. He didn't mince words.

"All right, gentlemen. The man's name is Sergeant Michael Shane. Six months before he was to graduate from Cal Poly with a degree in mathematics, the Japs bombed Pearl Harbor. He dropped out of school and enlisted. After boot camp, he was assigned to the 101st Airborne Division.

"Shane's very smart but he's no egghead. In college, he won several intercollegiate boxing titles. And he's a top marksman, one of a handful of field-qualified snipers with the 101st.

"Just prior to D-Day, he was one of the paratroopers dropped in behind the lines in Normandy. In the early action, Shane took a bullet through his calf and was assigned to watch over a dozen more seriously wounded men from his company until they could be evacuated.

"During the Waffen SS Normandy counteroffensive, his position was overrun by Germans. He and the wounded were captured, thrown into boxcars, and shipped to a temporary camp near the Belgian-German border. For six months, he watched German guards brutalize the American POWs. Like the rest, he was systematically starved and tortured for no good reason.

"After nearly six months of starvation, beatings, and squalid conditions, he was rescued by the Americans. He was in pretty bad shape, but after a few weeks in an English hospital, he was shipped back to the States for reassignment.

"He reported to Camp Riverton about three weeks ago. After my first conversation with him, I knew he was trouble. I could see it in his eyes. Because his file contained no results of a psych evaluation, I ordered one myself.

"Within days after his arrival, he was into it with the Germans. Constantly complaining they were being coddled by their guards and by the Army's policies. He couldn't see why the POWs deserved — using his terms — their luxury food rations, their warm bunks, or their cushy jobs in the community. He ranted and raved about German POWs who were earning college

credits from Michigan State professors when he had sacrificed his
degree by dropping out to fight the blinking Germans.

"When he learned about Marie's sewing classes, he fumed
about it for days. He told his bunkmates that no foolish female
ought to be allowed inside the camp and that her very presence was
a threat to good order and discipline.

"His language describing Marie became so outrageous POWs
and guards alike complained about it. I warned Marie 10 days ago.
Told her to stay clear of him. I was buying time until the
psychiatrists from Camp Custer could examine him. I was
confident we'd all be rid of him soon.

"By yesterday, I'd had it. I sent him off on temporary duty to
fill in for one of three guards, watching over two dozen POWs
working at a pig farm north of Frankenmuth.

"There was no one living at the farm so the POWs and their
guards were billeted in the big old farmhouse. Since there was no
cook or ready source of groceries, guards and prisoners took their
meals in Frankenmuth. A tavern there served genuine German
food and plenty of beer in the bargain.

"I gave Shane a map, a jeep, and directions. He was *not* happy.
He groused all the way out the door. He demanded that I shut
down that sewing class and throw that — you can guess what —
Marie Addison out of Camp Riverton by the time he returned, or
else I'd be very sorry.

"Anyway, when he got to the pig farm, only one unguarded
POW was there. He was suffering from the flu and had decided to
skip the Sunday night meal at the tavern with the others. Shane
huffed out of the farmhouse and headed for town.

"When he arrived, the tavern was filled with local German-
speaking farm people, the two guards, and all the POWs. Everyone
was swilling down pitchers of beer and dancing to loud polka
music. When the two guards saw him enter, they waved him over.
He walked up to their table and told them to get the — heck —
out of there or he'd clear the place with his tommy gun. They
didn't take him seriously.

"A local woman came up behind him and put her hands over
his eyes. According to witnesses, he spun around and slapped the
woman across the face, he shook his fist at her, and yelled, 'I told

you to get out of my camp! Do you understand that — Miss Marie Addison? If I ever see you again, I'll kill you.'

"To make his point, he turned around and shot a burst from his machine gun at the table, killing two POWs and one of the guards. Then he ran out of the tavern, leaped into the jeep, and sped away."

Colonel Butler paused for a breath of air. I could relate. I hadn't breathed for minutes.

"Questions, gentlemen? Marie?"

WHEN COLONEL BUTLER FINISHED his briefing, no one spoke for a few minutes. Not since the previous fall, when Danny was kidnapped by hateful Nazi POWs had anyone so close to me been threatened with violence. I glanced at Mom and took strength from her calm demeanor. I noticed Dad was holding her hand.

The first question came from Sheriff Connors. "Have the Michigan State Police been informed?"

"Yes. The tavern owner called them immediately. Shortly after that, I received a call from my lead guard in Frankenmuth. Then I called CID — the Criminal Investigation Division — at Fort Custer. It's my understanding that the state police were to have issued an all-points bulletin on Shane. As far as we know, he's still traveling by jeep so he should stick out like a sore thumb."

Turning to Sergeant Tolna, he asked, "You see any APB on this, Jeff?"

"No, Sheriff. But we can radio in and have our dispatcher call the state police directly."

"Let's do that, as soon as we finish up here, Jeff."

"One more thing, with the reduced prisoner population over the winter, we don't have a full complement of guards. CID's sending two squads of reinforcements from Fort Custer that will be here first thing in the morning," Colonel Butler told us.

"Good. Why don't we use my office as a command center?" Sheriff Connors suggested. "When the CID arrives, let's plan to meet there to coordinate our efforts. Jeff, you should be there too. I'll also ask the state police post commander from Lansing to attend. And I guess I should invite my counterpart from Saginaw

County where Frankenmuth's located. I don't want any squabbles — about jurisdiction or authority."

"John, I'll make arrangements to post a Riverton Police patrol car here around the clock until there's no further danger."

"That's great, Jeff. Let's not take any chances."

"Colonel, you mentioned Shane did the killings with a tommy gun. What other firearms was he carrying with him? I'd like the officers manning the patrol car to be properly prepared."

"I was saving this piece of bad news for last."

More bad news?

That got our attention.

"As a practice, on a staggered quarterly basis, our guards turn in their firearms for routine maintenance. At that time, each guard draws a newly refurbished standard set of arms. Our armory sergeant had Shane take three sets of refurbished arms plus a supply of fresh ammunition for the Frankenmuth guards."

"What're you telling us, Colonel?"

"Shane has four tommy guns, four M-1 rifles, and four .45 automatics plus a supply of ammunition in his jeep. And he's an expert marksman."

"Holy smokes! I'd better make that *two* patrol cars," Sergeant Tolna asserted with alarm. "Before we shove off, let me radio in to arrange this security. I'll also check for any late news on Shane."

While we waited for Jeff's return, the sheriff made another suggestion, "Marie — John — I don't like what we've heard here tonight. To put it bluntly, we're dealing with a very dangerous nut. While the Riverton police are top-notch — just to be on the safe side — you may want to consider leaving Riverton for a while. Think about spending a few days with your folks out at their farm."

"That sounds like a good idea, Sheriff. Before we go off half-cocked, let's see what Jeff reports when he comes back," Dad replied.

We didn't have long to wait.

"Everything's arranged, folks," he informed us. "And it's not a second too soon. The state police did put out an APB this morning. And an hour ago, they updated it with new information that affects us."

Everyone in the room leaned forward to hear the news.

"They found Shane's jeep — abandoned — no firearms. They suspect he's stolen a car, but none has been reported missing. So we have no vehicle description to help us."

"Abandoned! Whereabouts, Jeff?"

"On the outskirts of Flint, Sheriff."

"Darn! That can only mean one thing."

"That's right, Sheriff. He's heading this way."

EVERYONE AGREED THAT MOM should leave town for at least a few days. But working out the logistics was another matter. If it had been up to Sheriff Connors, our entire family would have immediately departed for the farm. But each of us, for different reasons, objected to that idea. Dad had an important meeting at work the following morning. Danny was eager for me to be in school so our classmates would believe him when he told them about Shane and revealed his own personal plan for capturing the villain. Naturally I didn't want to miss hearing that.

But Mom's rationale for not going immediately was the clincher. "My folks don't have a telephone at the farm. I can't rouse their neighbors in the middle of the night to deliver a message like this one. It'd scare both households to death. And I can't just show up out there at this time of night, for the same reason."

Sheriff Connors finally conceded that it was safe enough for Mom to stay in the house for one night under the protection of two Riverton patrol cars and four heavily armed police officers. But in exchange for his agreement, the rest of us had to agree to three conditions. First, Mom must allow him to take her to the farm first thing in the morning. Second, my father and I must join Mom at the farm right after work and school. Third, Sergeant Tolna must post two patrol cars and four officers at our house as decoys, as long as Shane was at large.

Even Danny seemed content with this arrangement.

Sometime well past midnight, I fell into bed exhausted. But still, sleep didn't come easily. I tossed and turned all night.

The next morning, I was awakened by a strange repetitive noise coming from our kitchen.

Thwap! Thwap!

Thwap! Thwap!

Thwap! Thwap!

After throwing on my school clothes and brushing my teeth, I staggered sleepily to the kitchen. Mom, Dad, and Danny were sitting in their usual places. But JB was in my chair.

Both Danny and JB wore Tigers' baseball caps on their heads and baseball gloves on their left hands. In their right hands, each held a baseball that they repeatedly snap-tossed into their gloves.

Thwap! Thwap!

Thwap! Thwap!

Thwap! Thwap!

Seemingly oblivious to this annoying sound, Mom and Dad were sipping their coffee and reading sections of the previous afternoon's *Riverton Daily Press*.

Danny was the first to notice me. "Morning, Jase!"

"What're you guys doing?"

"Working on the pockets of our gloves. Go get yours. JB brought some neat's-foot glove oil."

"Hi, Jase," JB greeted me with a quick smile.

I forced myself to smile back.

"Jase, sit here," Mom said as she rose from her chair. "I'll get your breakfast, then I have to pack a bag. Sheriff Connors will be here any minute."

In my haze, I had completely forgotten about the events of the previous evening. Suddenly reality came crashing back into my consciousness.

"Any more news about Shane, Dad?"

"No, Jase. That's what I wanted to know from Sergeant Zeller when I got up. Not a word on his whereabouts."

I was glad to hear Sergeant Zeller was among our police bodyguards. Next to our neighbor, Sergeant Tolna, he was my favorite member of the Riverton Police Department.

On his way out the door, Dad reminded me, "I'll see you after work, Jase. Remember to finish packing your suitcase so we can arrive at Grandma's by suppertime."

"I'll be ready, Dad," I promised.

Mom was sitting in the front room with her packed suitcase when Sheriff Connors arrived. She looked out the window and announced, "The sheriff's here! Jase, I'll see you this evening at the farm."

When she opened the door, Sheriff Connors was standing on the porch.

"Oh, I was just coming out," she explained.

"I got to thinking, Marie. Why don't we drop the boys off at school, just to be on the safe side?"

Danny asked rhetorically, "What's on the other side of *safe?*"

While everyone pondered that one, I returned to my bedroom for my baseball glove and ball. Then I joined my friends in the backseat of the sheriff's patrol car. All the way to school, the three of us worked on the pockets of our gloves.

Thwap! Thwap! Thwap!
Thwap! Thwap! Thwap!
Thwap! Thwap! Thwap!

Before we reached the head of our street, I noticed that the hair on the back of Sheriff Connors' neck was standing on end.

I wonder why?

Disregarding the clamor of our admiring classmates who surrounded us as we exited the sheriff's car, we headed for the schoolyard and a few minutes of three-man catch before the bell rang.

The triangle we formed required Danny to throw to JB who then threw to me. I completed the circuit by throwing to Danny. After a few rounds, I surmised that JB was as talented in baseball as he was in basketball. I also concluded that baseball was not Danny's forte. The demonstration of JB's athleticism was not planned by JB. It came as a consequence of his having to field Danny's wild throws.

On our way into the school after the bell sounded, JB optimistically observed, "Danny, you can throw a ball faster than a bullet, but we really gotta work on your control. Okay?"

"I know that," Danny stated coolly. "I'm just a bit rusty."

I caught JB's subtle wink as we entered our classroom.

Miss Sparks was having difficulty getting the class to settle down for the morning ritual. When she demanded to know what was causing all the ruckus, twenty of our classmates screamed simultaneously that we had arrived at school in the sheriff's car. And they demanded to know why.

She promised that we three could explain ourselves, but only after the completion of our standard ritual for starting the school day. With its silence, the class accepted her offer.

I for one had difficulty concentrating on the Bible reading. Of course, Danny didn't help.

Thwap!

Thwap!

Thwap!

When it was time for our explanation, Danny dropped his baseball glove and grabbed the mike. After waiting for complete silence, he informed Miss Sparks and the class that we were involved in the investigation of a multiple murder and were about to crack the case.

According to Danny, Sheriff Connors was so grateful for our help that he offered to drive us to school in his patrol car. Danny predicted that those who lived in our immediate neighborhood were likely to see other police officers hanging around the Addison house, just waiting for their chance to thank us as the sheriff had.

He capped his brief remarks with the following whopper. "Next week, Jase and I expect a visit from President Roosevelt. But because of strict Secret Service rules, none of you'll be told anything about this visit."

Miss Sparks and our classmates sat in stunned silence.

Obviously that reaction was not what Danny was hoping for. For good measure, he added, "Remember my motto. *Loose lips sink ships!*"

No one in class had a come-back for that one.

DURING MORNING RECESS, DANNY was obsessed with controlling his throws. He claimed he had always dreamt of pitching in the majors. I thought it strange he had never shared that particular ambition with me before. But what did I know?

Exhibiting much more patience than I might have, JB agreed to spend the entire period giving Danny a lesson on proper throwing technique. So JB could spend more time tutoring and less time shagging Danny's errant throws, I volunteered to be his teaching assistant.

We laid out our lesson plan.

First, we would pool our three baseballs, allowing Danny multiple consecutive practice throws without interruption. JB would nab those reasonably within his reach. The others would be my responsibility. Between sets of three, while I rounded up the balls, JB would give Danny feedback to improve his technique.

When I was in position, about twenty yards behind JB, we began. Regrettably Danny's first set of throws belonged to me. All three had missed JB by a country mile. It was incredible. While his pitches appeared to be as hard and fast as those of a major leaguer, they were completely out-of-control. And *I* was completely out of breath from running them down.

"Okay! Okay, Danny," JB advised. "We know you can throw a fastball. But you've got to slow it down if you want to learn how to control it. Let's work on your windup first."

By the end of morning recess, one out of three of Danny's slowed-down throws was arriving within JB's reach. My job was getting easier.

By the end of the lunch hour, Danny was delivering two out of three throws within JB's reach. And by the end of the afternoon recess, often three out of three wound up in JB's glove. At this point, I was lounging in the grass behind JB, studying the emerging dandelions, looking for four-leaf clovers, and wondering when Shane would be run to ground.

"That's it, Danny. You've made good progress. But I don't want you to overdo it and pull a muscle. The bell's about to ring. Let's call it a day!"

"JB! Can we practice after school?" Danny implored hopefully. Suddenly he remembered, "Oh, nuts! You have basketball practice. Shoot! Just let me throw one last pitch. A fastball this time. Okay?"

"All right, Danny. One last pitch. But remember everything you've learned about your delivery."

Before Danny began his windup, JB held up his hand. Turning to me, he suggested, "Jase, I'd stand a little deeper if I were you. About halfway between me and the parking lot would be good."

When I reached my position, JB crouched down in a catcher's stance and shouted, "Let 'er rip, Danny!"

Danny's windup was something to behold. He twisted and bent like a pretzel. And when that spring unwound, the result was amazing. The ball shot straight at JB.

"Wow!" JB yelled.

It was a straight shot all right, but it must have cleared JB's head by at least 10 feet. By the time it reached me, the ball was still climbing. I turned around and watched the ball fly skyward until it reached the apex of its trajectory. There it seemed to stop, right in midair for just a brief instant, before plunging rapidly to earth.

Well, that's not quite accurate. If Danny's fastball had plunged to earth, we wouldn't have heard that horrifying sound.

Sssmashsss! Tinkle! Tinkle! Tinkle!

The three of us stood, looking out over the parking lot. We all knew what had happened but none of us dared to investigate whose car was involved.

When the recess bell sounded, Danny's conditioned reflexes took over. He turned and ran toward the door.

But JB and I stopped him with *shots* from our double-barrel shotgun.

"Danny!"

"Danny!"

"Come back here!" I scolded. "Come with us and find out what happened."

Sheepishly he turned around and slowly walked back to where we stood.

"Let's go," he whimpered.

It didn't take us long to find the victim's car. Danny's reaction was heartbreaking. He moaned, "Oh, no. Don't tell me."

To Danny's everlasting credit, his fastball had landed perfectly. Right in the geometric center of the car's windshield, causing every iota of glass to embed itself deeply in the front-seat upholstery.

We followed Danny into the school to report the *accident.* Right inside the doorway stood the car's owner.

Danny blanched as the owner smiled. "What's new, Danny?"

"Not much. How about you, Mr. Lund?"

DESPITE REASSURANCES FROM MR. Lund that his car was fully insured, Danny spent a miserable afternoon. When the last bell of the day rang, we three walked down the hall amidst the herd of students heading to the gymnasium to watch basketball practice. Because Danny knew I would be leaving for the farm soon after I got home from school, I assumed he would stay for practice. I hoped this entertaining distraction would help him take his mind off his unfortunate last pitch.

When we stopped at the double doors leading into the gymnasium, JB asked, "You coming in, Danny?"

Danny shook his head and stared at his shoes.

"In any case, I gotta go get dressed. But I want you to have this, Danny." JB placed his baseball in Danny's glove. "Go practice that throw of yours. It'll do you good."

Danny looked down at his glove and his mood immediately changed. "Wow! Thanks, JB. Thanks a lot!" He grinned from ear to ear and turned to me. "Can we, Jase?"

What could I say? I simply nodded.

"Yesssss!" Danny hissed gleefully.

"Yeah, thanks a *lot*, JB," I hollered over my shoulder as Danny dragged me down the hall toward the exit doors.

Normally our walk home from school was a leisurely stroll. The slow pace provided Danny a long uninterrupted period of time to share his latest theories and dreams with me. But Danny was bent on hurrying home to get in as much throwing practice as possible before I left for the farm. Instead of walking, we jogged. By the time we reached Forrest Street, I was winded. Looking on the bright side, I figured the more energy Danny expended, the safer the neighbors' windows would be.

I noticed the two police cars parked in front of our house. With the street as the only practical location for Danny's throwing session, those cars needed to be moved out of harm's way.

Sergeant Zeller and another officer I didn't know were sitting on our front porch. When we approached, they arose to greet us. "Hi, boys! What's cookin'?"

"Baseball practice," Danny stated simply.

I told Sergeant Zeller our plans to throw a few balls before Dad arrived home from work. I suggested they move their cars. "Danny's a bit wild at times," I added for emphasis.

"No trouble at all. We'll just park them in your alley."

"Where're the other policemen?"

"Oh, they're sitting on the back porch. We split up. Better for keeping an eye on things around here."

After the police cars were moved, Danny and I took our positions in the middle of the street. Before Danny could throw his first pitch, I heard a car behind me. It was Dad. "Jase, I forgot to mention — I have a repair job in my trunk that needs to be delivered before we leave. Lady lives over by Hamilton School. Should only take 10 or 15 minutes. Why don't you boys stay here and play catch until I get back?"

As soon as Dad had pulled away, Danny ordered, "Hurry, Jase!"

"All right. But take it nice and easy. Like JB advised, you don't want to pull a muscle."

"Okay! Okay! I know."

Impressively Danny threw about a half-dozen balls before his first wild pitch. Fortunately that throw was so wide that it flew through the air and collided with our next-door neighbor's front stoop.

Bam!

"Sure hope Mrs. Mikas is fully insured," I teased.

Danny scowled at me and let go with his next zinger. JB might have snagged it, but I flat-out missed it. It streaked between my feet and headed for New Albany Avenue. While I was running down the ball, I noticed Hans Zeyer, our friend and neighbor, stepping off the bus. He was quite far away, but I recognized his old fedora and tan overcoat.

When I was back in position, Danny threw the ball that he had retrieved from Mrs. Mikas' stoop. I caught that pitch and threw it back to Danny. I looked over his shoulder and saw Dad's car coming up the street.

"Look, Danny! Here comes Dad. We better stop."

Danny pleaded, "One last pitch. A fastball! Okay, Jase?"

As I thought about the disastrous results of his last fastball, I was filled with trepidation. On the other hand, I was encouraged that he had regained enough confidence to risk it. In a split second, I decided to let him throw.

"All right, Danny. One last pitch — your fastball."

For as long as I live, I will never forget the result of that decision.

Danny twisted and wound up like a pretzel again. And then let it fly.

Zzzzzzzzingzzzzzzzzzzz!

His fastball shot over my right shoulder.

Wheeling around, I saw Hans Zeyer in front of Mrs. Mikas' house. He'd covered a lot of ground since getting off the bus. I had honestly forgotten all about him. Instantly I realized the ball was rocketing through the air, straight for his head.

"Duck, Mr. Zeyer! Duck!"

He didn't seem to hear me. I felt helpless.

Thud!

The ball struck him, right in the center of his forehead. He fell to the sidewalk like a sack of potatoes and lay there without moving.

"He's dead! I killed Mr. Zeyer!" Danny screamed. "Jase, I killed Mr. Zeyer!"

Out of the corner of my eye, I saw Sergeant Zeller and the three other officers running toward us from the back of the house. I pointed and ran to Hans.

We all reached him at the very same time.

Sergeant Zeller immediately knelt and grasped his wrist. We all held our breath. The sergeant looked up and pronounced, "He's alive!"

"Thank God!" Danny whispered.

"Run back to the car and radio for an ambulance. His pulse is pretty strong but there's no sense takin' any chances."

"You got it, Sarge," an officer replied as he turned and ran toward the alley.

"Let's get his head up off the sidewalk. Boys, we'll use your ball gloves as a pillow."

We handed him our gloves.

"Okay, fella," the sergeant said, lifting Hans' head from the sidewalk. "Let's get that hat out of your eyes. Here, Jase. Take charge of his hat for me."

When Sergeant Zeller handed me the fedora, I took my eyes off Hans.

"Jase! Look!"

Everyone looked at Danny, who was pointing at Hans. Then everyone looked at Hans, except it wasn't Hans.

"Who's that man, Sergeant Zeller?"

"I thought you fellas knew him," he replied. "He looks kinda familiar to me. Let's see if he's got any identification on him."

Sergeant Zeller unbuttoned the man's overcoat and felt inside his suit coat. "What have we here?"

He held up an Army-issue .45 automatic.

"No wonder you look familiar, you rat! Boys, say hello to Sergeant Michael Shane."

"Shane!" I yelped.

"Cuff him, Don," Sergeant Zeller ordered. He lifted Shane's head and removed our ball gloves. "Here you go, boys. He doesn't need a pillow."

"Shane! I can't believe it!" I exclaimed as we walked back to the house with Dad. "What a lucky break!"

"That was no break — that was my fastball," Danny informed us as he snap-tossed the ball into his glove.

Thwap!

WHEN HE HEARD ON his car radio that the Riverton Police Department had bagged Shane, Sheriff Connors was so relieved he immediately headed for the Comptons to deliver the news. Because Mom was eager to hear the whole story, the sheriff offered to drive her back home so she could attend the debriefing. When the sheriff and Mom walked in, our front room was filled with all the other key players. Colonel Butler. Sergeants Tolna and Zeller. Danny, Dad, and me.

"Didn't anyone make coffee?" Mom asked, looking at Dad and me. "Never mind, I'll put our big pot on. I think I have some cookies too — unless someone I know snitched them," she teased, gently swatting the top of Danny's Tigers' cap as she sidled between feet and chairs to get to the kitchen.

When Dad answered the knock on the door, we heard a familiar voice. "With so many police cars out here, there's bound to be a scoop inside for a humble news reporter."

"Come on in, Chuck. You're always welcome. Anyone here who hasn't met Chuck Nichols from the *Riverton Daily Press* and WRDP?"

"I think I know everyone, John. Thanks." Chuck sat down on the metal folding chair that I had brought him from my bedroom. "I got most of the basics from Sergeant Zeller when we spoke earlier, but I do need a few details to finish my story."

"Join the party, Chuck. Since I've been *vacationing* out at the farm today, I have some questions myself," Mom remarked, placing a huge platter of assorted cookies on the coffee table. "Coffee'll be ready in a jiffy."

"Maybe I should start," Colonel Butler suggested. "You all can chime in or ask me specific questions as I go along. Okay with everyone?"

With the efficiency of a Pentagon briefer, Colonel Butler delivered his update.

"Shane will go back to Fort Custer with the CID folks first thing in the morning. I didn't know this when we met last evening, but they brought an Army doctor — a psychiatrist — up with them. He examined Shane a couple of hours ago. In short, Shane should have never been reinstated. He's definitely Section 8 material. Whether he stands trial for the murders will depend on the results of a detailed psychological evaluation and what the Army lawyers determine is the best course of action at that point in time.

"Those of you who shared my concern for Marie's welfare will feel validated. The psychiatrist claimed Shane was totally obsessed with doing harm to Marie. To Shane's warped way of thinking, Marie just didn't belong in *this man's army* as they say. Of course, those of us out at Camp Riverton share a totally different opinion.

"When Shane's jeep was discovered, we all wondered how he was traveling. We assumed he'd stolen a car. So we'd need to identify that car to track him down. But I guess he outsmarted us. Before he abandoned his jeep, he drove to the Flint bus station and bought a ticket to Riverton. Next he placed all the weapons, except the .45 he was carrying, in a duffel bag and left it in a locker at the bus station. When he was arrested — or should I say *bean-balled* — he had the locker key in his pocket."

"I thought he abandoned the jeep outside of Flint. How'd he get back to the bus station?"

"He'd didn't go back. He left the jeep on the road to Riverton, flagged the bus down, and traveled on over here. When he discovered the New Albany bus would take him to Forrest Street, he hopped aboard and rode out here. Piece a cake!"

"All right, Colonel, I've got a question for you. How'd he know my address?"

"That's easy. He took one of John's sewing-machine business cards from your classroom. Remember that little dish of them you have on your desk? We found one of them in his pocket."

"For goodness sake, I forgot all about them. I meant to bring them home. I don't know why I took them out there in the first place. Not too many POWs bring their sewing machines here for repairs."

"Colonel, I have a question too."

"Shoot, Jase."

"His hat and coat was just like Mr. Zeyer's. How did he know what to wear? And where did he get those clothes so quickly?"

"Jase, that's a very good question. That one really bothered me too. But I had a hunch and called the Saginaw County Sheriff. Sure enough he answered our question."

"Hold that thought, Sheriff. Who wants coffee?" After counting hands, Mom said, "There's cream and sugar on the coffee table for those who use it. Boys, come to the kitchen. I'll pour and you can serve."

In no time, everyone was served.

"Back to you, Sheriff," Mom said when we were all seated again.

"Let's see — now. Oh, yes. I asked if anything was missing from that tavern after Shane made his getaway. The sheriff said he'd just gotten a call from a German fellow. There're lots of them up there. He reported, on the night of the killings, someone snitched his fedora and tan overcoat from the tavern. He'd left them hanging on a hook right next to the door. Apparently Shane grabbed them on his way out to cover his uniform."

"But they looked just like those Hans Zeyer wears," I protested.

"I mentioned the very same thing to the sheriff, Jase. He just laughed and told me that about a thousand other men in the Frankenmuth area wear that very same hat and overcoat. That's why the sheriff didn't think much of the stolen property report. In his words, 'Them Germans are always pickin' up somebody else's hat and coat.' "

"Well, I'll be darned."

"I have a question for Danny," Chuck Nichols said. "I understand you — ah — *lost* your own baseball earlier today. So JB gave you his. When you and Jase were playing catch, you were using only two balls — one ball belonging to Jase — the other to JB. So here's the question. Which ball brought Shane down? Jase's or JB's?"

All eyes were on Danny. His answer surprised everyone.

"Neither. *My* ball hit Shane."

The entire room was silent. My mind was racing. "Wait a minute, Danny! We only had two balls out there. If you had yours, we would have had three."

I felt a little guilty accusing Danny of telling a fib in front of all those people.

"After my meeting with Mr. Lund, I went out to his car and crawled through the window. That's how I got my ball back. I had it in my back pocket when JB gave me his."

"But how come we only played with two?"

"While you were talking to Mr. A, I stuck JB's baseball in the Reilly mailbox. I know JB was trying to cheer me up, but it just wasn't right for me to keep his ball when I'd gotten mine back. I felt guilty."

Felt guilty?

I had never heard Danny utter those words before.

HOMECOMING

WITH ALL THAT HAD HAPPENED, IT WAS HARD TO believe Riverton Y's breathtaking victory over East Lansing had taken place less than a week earlier. While Danny and I were with Governor Dewey visiting Owosso dignitaries, some living and some not, and adding another notch to our slingshots by vanquishing Sergeant Shane, JB was preparing himself and his team for the season finale against the Pontiac YMCA.

Because of the upcoming Easter weekend and the impending start of our relatively short Easter vacation, this final game was to be played in the Hamilton School gymnasium on the Wednesday evening before Easter. JB's reputation as a basketball *phenom* had spread like wildfire throughout Riverton and beyond. At the beginning of the week, Mr. Lund sent a note to all classes suggesting parents, relatives, and friends plan to arrive early. He predicted the availability of standing room only well before tip-off time.

Anticipating JB's competing against them in the '45-'46 season, coaches from Riverton's other junior high schools planned to attend, just to see if JB was for real. Upon hearing this flattering news, both Coach Clark and Coach Temple were elated. They brainstormed ways to highlight JB's talents without diminishing the contribution of the other team members, some of whom would be playing their last game as 14-and-unders.

On the way to school that morning, however, JB was noticeably solemn. This was not the demeanor I expected on a game-day morning.

If you liked to keep secrets, Danny and I were poor friends to have. Long before we arrived at school, we had confronted him. Or rather, I should say, Danny had. "Okay, JB! What's going on? Give, already!" he demanded with the subtlety of a boulder.

But it worked.

"Last night Aunt Mary had a phone call from Mom's doctor. He wondered if she and Uncle Patrick could drive down to Detroit today. He wouldn't say what he wanted to talk to them about."

"Do you think this is about your mother?" the inscrutable one inquired.

"What?" JB gasped incredulously, saving me the trouble of saying the same thing.

"I mean —. It has to be something important about your mother. Maybe she's coming home!"

"If that were it, why would they have to go there to talk first?"

That was a very good question! Because no immediate answer came to my mind, I didn't respond. Apparently, however, Danny felt obligated to provide a credible answer. After thinking about it for several minutes, he rendered his opinion. "The doctor probably thinks your mom's ready to come home. But your mom's not sure. So he wants the Reillys there to tell her it's all right."

JB stopped and stared at Danny. Finally he turned to me and grinned. "I think Danny's got it."

Whether Danny had it or not wasn't as important as the effect on JB. As proof, JB had us save three seats at the game for his family.

Throughout the day, Danny was exceptionally congenial toward his classmates. No favor was refused. Not once did he scoff at an inane comment. Above all, he thanked people for any little thing. This was indeed unusual behavior. Finally my curiosity got the better of me. I decided to use Danny's opener.

"Listen here, Danny! What's going on? Give, already!" I demanded, imitating his *boulder* style.

"Mrs. Libby got a call last night from Barb and Anne's warden. He wondered if she could drive down to Parkersburg Prison today."

"What for?"

"The girls' parole came through. They can come home anytime. But they're afraid of what people will think of them. So they're not sure they're ready to leave prison. The warden wanted Mrs. Libby and Coach Jim to come down and reassure them that it'll be fine."

"Let me get this straight. To answer JB, you *plagiarized* what the warden told Mrs. Libby? I can't believe it!"

Danny locked his lips with his invisible key and stuck it in his pocket.

"When did she tell you this?"

"On my way to your house this morning, I saw Coach Jim and her. They were headed out of town in their new car. They stopped to ask me a favor."

"A favor?"

"They want us to save four seats at the game tonight."

Leapin' lizards, Danny!

ON THE DAY WE received our *New York Medals of Recognition*, the school janitors had placed *Reserved* signs on our chairs. Therefore, Danny insisted we save seats for the Reillys and Libbys the same way. After school we lingered in our classroom long enough for Danny to bat his eyes at Miss Sparks, thereby persuading her to unlock her precious art-supplies cabinet.

During the war, paper of any quality was in very short supply. When Miss Sparks assumed the teaching duties for our class, she was pleasantly surprised to discover her predecessor's stockpile of pre-war paper and art supplies. Danny's success at separating Miss Sparks from seven yellow sheets of coated stock was a tribute to his charm. But his *coup de grâce* was convincing her to mix a special batch of blue poster paint, thus assuring the signs carried the imprimatur of Hamilton School officialdom, to wit, the school colors.

As we sat there with brushes in hand, Danny was unable to decide on the proper wording to inscribe on the seven signs. Being a bit of a minimalist, I suggested *Reserved*. Out-of-hand, Danny dismissed my suggestion, explaining that these signs were too classy for such pedestrian treatment or words to that effect.

So I patiently endured his rambling brainstorm of possible alternatives.

Special Guests! Too elitist.

Keep Out! Not forceful enough.

Wet Paint! Lacked credibility without paint odor.

Warning - Spiders! Might scare small children.

Air-Raid Shelter! Might scare adults.

No Parking! Not enforceable without a badge.

"Come on, Danny! Let's go!"

"How about *Reserved?*"

"Terrific!"

We left our newly-painted signs to dry while we cleaned our brushes in the janitor's deep sink. Then we carefully carried the signs into the gymnasium and up onto the bleachers.

Suddenly we were confronted by a couple of puzzling realities. First, there were no markings on the polished oak bleacher boards to delineate individual *seats*. So we didn't know where to place our signs. Second, we had no way to attach them to the board. Paste or thumbtacks were out of the question.

"Too bad these aren't folding chairs," Danny lamented. "What're we going to do?"

"Hi, fellas! What's up?" Coach Clark hollered to us from the other end of the gymnasium. After we explained our perplexing situation, he thought a minute and then snapped his fingers. "I've got it. Come to my office."

There the coach unlocked his closet door and extracted a huge canvas tarpaulin. "Used to keep home plate dry during baseball season," he explained. Next he opened his desk drawer, removed an old hard-candy tin, and gave it a shake. "Straight pins for pinning notes on the bulletin board. Let's go, boys."

We followed him back to the bleachers.

The coach quickly double-folded the tarpaulin lengthwise and laid it over the bleacher board. It covered about 15 feet. He handed us the tin and directed, "Pin your signs on the tarp. Bring both back to me after the game, if you please."

"Thanks, Coach. Have a good game!" we yelled as he disappeared down the stairway to the locker room.

We followed his instructions exactly. It worked like a charm. While we admired our handiwork, Danny announced, "Someday I wanta be a basketball coach."

I nodded and we left for home.

Because the Reillys were out of town, Mom had invited JB to eat supper with us. When I arrived home with Danny, she invited him too. JB seemed relaxed and in good spirits. Plagiarism or not, Danny deserved credit for the improvement.

"All right, guys. Finish up your desserts. We need to get JB to the gymnasium for warm-ups and find ourselves some good seats," Dad advised.

Pulling into the parking lot, we observed a strange-looking vehicle parked near the gymnasium door. It appeared to be a miniature school bus, painted yellow-green. It was as tall and wide as a regular bus, but only about half as long. Large black letters on its side told us it belonged to the *Church of the Holy Tabernacle.*

As we walked toward the entrance, the bus door opened and a dozen people stepped off. There were eight boys dressed in maroon sweat suits that read *Pontiac YMCA.* They were obviously our opponents. One of the four men wore a maroon ball cap with *P.Y.* embroidered above its bill. I assumed he was the coach and the other three men were fathers.

Danny whispered to me, "Not a very large cheering section. Wait until they see our crowd!"

"They don't have many players either," I whispered back. "And they're not very big."

"Hi, folks. Welcome to Riverton. Follow us. We'll show you the way," Dad offered, with a smile. "How was the drive up?"

JB led the Pontiac coach and team to the locker room while we escorted the three parents into the gymnasium. Warm-ups hadn't yet begun, but still there were at least 50 people sitting in the bleachers. I was relieved to see that our reserved section was still intact with open seats for us on either side.

"Wow! Look at all the people," one of the fathers exclaimed. "Was there an earlier game?"

"No. Everyone comes early to make sure they get a seat," Dad explained. "It'll probably be standing room only tonight."

"You've got to be kidding me. We don't see this many people when we play the Detroit Y!" he told us. "Boy, this is a beautiful gym. Is it new?"

"Built just last year," Dad confirmed.

When the man called our new facility a *gym,* my first instinct was to correct him. No one in our neighborhood called our new facility a *gym.* We had too much pride to use a *nickname. Gym* described our shoes, our bag, and our class. But never our new facility. Hamilton students, parents, and neighbors alike always referred to this magnificent place as our *gymnasium.*

"Gymnasium!" Danny told the man, who responded with a puzzled look.

Mom put her hand on Danny's shoulder and gently pushed him toward our reserved seats. "You did a great job on those signs, boys. Where did you get that big old tarpaulin? Doesn't Grandpa Compton use one that size to cover the haystack in the pasture?"

We were hoping to see the Reilly and Libby contingents before we sat down. But when people started filling the seats around our reserved section, we decided to take our seats. Mom and Dad sat next to one end of the tarpaulin and we boys sat next to the other.

Nearing the end of warm-ups, we waved at JB, who acknowledged us by lifting his chin. Then he turned around and sank a ball that today would be worth three points. After positioning himself to take the tip-off, he glanced up for the last time before turning his full attention to the game.

By halftime, there was some good news and some bad news. Riverton led Pontiac 35 to 6. It was a total rout. And our crowd dominated theirs about 600 to 3. That was the good news. But there was still no sign of JB's mom or the Libby sisters. When the buzzer sounded marking the halftime break, we decided to stretch our legs. Mom came with us while Dad stayed behind to watch our seats.

As we slowly moved with the crowd into the hallway, I confided to Danny and Mom, "I'm really disappointed. I honestly thought they'd be here by now. I know JB'll be very disappointed too."

Mom agreed and then changed the subject. "You boys want some popcorn?"

"None for me, thank you," Danny replied, quite matter-of-factly.

I couldn't believe my ears. Turning to Danny, I demanded, "Why not?"

Smiling broadly, he pointed down the hallway in the direction of Mr. Lund's office. "I'd rather meet JB's mom."

Mr. Lund was in his element. He was regaling our seven reserved-seat holders with a tale that had them in stitches. Some were bent over at the waist. Others had their heads flung back. But each of the seven was snorting, guffawing, or hooting with gusto.

"I had no idea that Mr. Lund was so entertaining," I told Danny as we walked toward the group.

"Oh sure! He was a *real* barrel of laughs the day I told him about his windshield."

WE GREETED BARB AND Anne Libby warmly and told them how glad we were that they were back home on Forrest Street. I had known them all my life, but after my role in their arrest, I wasn't sure how they might feel about me, or Danny for that matter. If the Libby sisters were harboring any residual resentment toward us, they showed no sign of it whatsoever. In fact, they seemed genuinely delighted to see us. I was relieved that we could return to our normal friendly relationship.

The most pleasant surprise of all was meeting JB's mother. Her coloring, eyes, and facial features bore a striking resemblance to Jean Simmons, one of my favorite actresses. If Rose Bradford suffered from melancholia, there was little adverse effect on her physical appearance, charm, or friendliness. When she spoke to you, you felt, as if you were the only person in the world. Clearly JB favored his mother.

"Johnson has told me so much about you two boys. I'm very happy you're his friends. When we moved from Nashville, Johnson left behind friends he'd known since nursery school. Thank you for welcoming him to Riverton and helping him fit in."

Aside from advising him to go easy on the brilliantine, dress more informally, and control his tendency to overuse the sir-ing and ma'am-ing, we'd provided little to help Johnson fit in. As a matter-of-fact, he was fitting in quite nicely all by himself. Thank you, ma'am.

"Are you staying for the rest of the game?"

"Oh, I hope so. We intended to be here well before game time, but we were delayed in traffic — as were the Libbys and Jim. A bridge was washed away in a flash flood on U.S. 23 near Ann Arbor. We just arrived a few minutes ago and would have come right in, but Mr. Lund told us there was standing room only with no seats left in the bleachers. By the way, isn't he a charming man? You're lucky to have him for your principal."

"We're in the *reserved area* Mrs. Bradford so you can sit with us. But there is NO reserved seat for Mr. Lund," Danny told her bluntly, nipping our principal's apparent aspirations in the *rosebud.*

As we filed into the gymnasium, we could see the referee and the three coaches, standing in the center of the court.

"What do you think's going on, Jim?"

"I just noticed the score. It wouldn't surprise me to see Pontiac forfeit the game. By the size and number of the boys on their bench, I'd guess they're pretty worn out and way overmatched. If that's what's happening, I don't know why they kept people here through the halftime break. So I'm just not sure."

"JB!" Danny hollered at the top of his lungs, startling everyone in the reserved section.

When JB looked up, Danny pointed to his mother and clapped. JB smiled and waved. His mother waved back. I'd been looking forward to that exchange for days.

"Ladies and Gentlemen! May I have your attention, please? We have some official business to dispense with and then some good news for you."

You could have heard one of Coach Clark's straight pins drop.

"First of all — for very good reasons — the Pontiac team has forfeited the game. Officially Riverton is the game winner by a final score of 35 to 6."

There were a few *groans* and *moans* in the audience. But strangely, no applause for the Riverton win.

"You may have wondered why Pontiac brought so few players this evening. The fact is the team has been decimated by the flu bug. Ten team members did not make the trip — because they're home in bed.

"Of the eight boys who did make the trip, only one has ever started a game. He's a seventh grader and all the other boys are just sixth graders. I think they were courageous, not only for making the trip but for putting up a good fight against a superb Riverton team.

"How about giving this Pontiac team a round of applause?"

I've never seen anything like what happened next. Every person in the gymnasium rose. The cheering and applause lasted for over five minutes. The Pontiac players and coach were astonished. Forfeiting, even for a very good reason, was embarrassing. But this embarrassment had turned into a rousing celebration for them.

"Thanks, folks. Shucks! That was supposed to be the bad news. But I'll bet it didn't feel that way." The referee turned to the Pontiac coach. "Did it, Coach Barry?"

Spontaneously the Pontiac coach and players began to applaud the audience. The coach removed his hat and waved to the crowd. This was the most inspirational demonstration of sportsmanship I'd ever witnessed.

"Now for that good news! Regardless of the official results, these two teams still want to play some more basketball for you! Would you like that?"

Another round of applause began but it died out quickly. A low hum of conversation moved through the gymnasium as people tried to determine how Pontiac could possibly continue.

"The captain of the Riverton team — who recently moved here from Nashville, Tennessee — has suggested an arrangement they use down there under these circumstances.

"Here's how it works. Each boy gave us his date of birth. The oldest boy was assigned the number one. The second oldest boy, the number two. And so on, right down the line. Now we'll form two teams — *odd* numbers versus *even* numbers.

"Odds, you take the Pontiac bench. Evens, the Riverton bench."

The teams formed around their coaches.

"I'll give the coaches a minute or two to become acquainted with their new talent before we begin the second half. The scoreboard will be set back to zeros. When they're ready, we'll play one full half."

Thanks to JB's creativity, the entire evening resulted in a win-win outcome for all concerned. The crowd witnessed a competitive half of basketball. Both teams shared the recognition and applause. And JB was able to show off for his mother by leading his mixed-city team to a 10-point victory over his opponents. And Danny had reasserted his control over Mr. Lund.

As Danny would say, "All's swell that ends swell."

OUR EASTER VACATION PROVIDED Danny with five uninterrupted days to pursue his two passions, churchgoing and food. On Good Friday alone, we managed to set a daily record by attending five church services, and Danny also posted a record in cookie consumption. I'm not sure of the exact number because I stopped counting when it hit three figures.

When we arrived home, Mom greeted us with a pleasant surprise. To celebrate the homecoming of Mrs. Bradford and the Libby sisters, Mrs. Reilly had offered to host Easter dinner for the Libbys, Addisons, Tuckers, and, of course, the Bradfords and Reillys. Mom volunteered to prepare our traditional Easter entrée, one of Grandpa's smoked hams. The women of the other families agreed to bring the rest of the trimmings.

"Here, Danny! If you want to whet your appetite, take a look at this menu," Mom exclaimed, handing Danny the list of offerings and the family responsible for preparing each item.

Easter Dinner 1945

Baked Ham - Addison
Scalloped Potatoes - Tucker
Baked Sweet Potatoes with Marshmallows - Reilly
Green Peas - Libby
Creamed Corn - Libby
Baked Cheese Grits - Bradford
Molded Waldorf Salad - Libby
Pickled Eggs - Reilly
Hot Cross Buns - Tucker
Daffodil Cake - Reilly
Sugar Cookies - Bradford
Apple Pie - Tucker

After a quick glance, Danny expressed his approval. "Hmmmm, boy! This really makes me hungry! You're going to love my mom's Hot Cross Buns. She only bakes them at Easter time."

"Mom, what in the world are cheese grits?"

"It's a Southern dish. JB's mother firmly believes no meal is complete without grits. I'm eager to try them."

"Then what are pickled eggs?"

"In Mrs. Reilly's family, it's traditional to eat them at Easter. They're simple to prepare. She just places shelled, hard-boiled eggs in a bowl and covers them with undrained pickled beets. The longer the eggs are in the juice, the rosier the color of the eggs. Mrs. Reilly offered to provide these eggs and the cake because of the surplus of eggs from their chicken coop."

She wasn't the only one.

"Hello! It's the egg delivery lady," Grandma Compton announced as she came through the front door. "Anybody home?"

"Grandma! I didn't hear you — pull up," I sputtered. Looking out the window, I saw a blue sedan parked in front of the house. It looked like a Chevy. "Where's your Terraplane?"

"Oh, don't mention that subject. I had to leave it over at Uncle George's to charge the battery. He let me use that awful Chevy out there. It drives like a tank."

"A tank! But, Grandma C, you're an airplane pilot," Danny reminded her. "No wonder we didn't hear you land!"

"Oh, Danny! You're a real corker, all right!"

Danny smiled at her like an admiring fan, which he was.

"Here, Jase. I colored some eggs for you." She handed me a small woven Easter basket. Six shiny, rust-colored eggs were nestled in artificial green grass.

"Grandma C, these are beautiful! Do your chickens lay this color of eggs?"

"No, Danny! These are just regular white eggs. I hard-boiled them with a lot of paper skins from yellow onions. By the time the eggs were done, their shells had absorbed the deep-rust color from the onion skins. This is how my mother colored eggs before there were artificial food colors or dyes. For variety, sometimes she hard-boiled eggs in beet juice. That gave the shells a rosy color."

"But our eggs are never this shiny, Grandma!"

"Oh, that's easy. After your colored eggs are really dry, just rub them with a small amount of Crisco. That'll make them glow."

She handed Mom a green wicker basket filled with egg cartons. "Marie, please put these away so I can take my basket home with me. I gave you an extra dozen. There're three dozen all told."

"Thanks, Ma!"

Mom placed the cartons on the kitchen table and handed the basket back to Grandma. Then she opened one and removed a single egg. Holding it near the window, she remarked, "Oh, these are perfect for coloring — just perfect. Thank you again, Ma. And thank you for the ham. I know everybody will love it. Sorry you're going to be in Mount Pleasant with Raymond's family and can't join us."

"Yes. But they're so proud of their remodeling, I couldn't say no. Oh! Good thing you reminded me. Boys! Do me a favor. Go out to the car and bring in the ham. It's on the backseat. I didn't have enough hands to carry everything."

We ran out to the Chevy and opened the back door. I picked up the ham and cradled it in my arms. "I'll carry it, Danny. You get the doors."

I placed the heavy ham on the counter and waited for the familiar ritual between Mom and Grandma to play out. I'd seen this little show several times before.

"Don't forget to scrape it and wash it off. After that, soak it until early Sunday morning to get the salt out. And change the water —. What am I saying? Marie, you know how to prepare a smoked ham."

"Yes, Ma. I've done it before. But I always appreciate your reminding me how to do it right," Mom replied diplomatically.

"I'll be happy to. I'd bake it at around 325 degrees for 12 minutes a pound. I forget how much this one is — around 15 pounds. It's on the tag. After about an hour-and-a-half, you can remove it for basting with —. What am I saying? You know how to bake a smoked ham."

"Yes, Ma. I've done it before. But —."

"But I don't know how to bake a ham, Grandma C," Danny confessed, winking at Mom. "Tell me more."

"Oh, pish! You're pulling my leg. You're a corker — a real corker," Grandma scolded with a smile. "Oh, my. Look at that time. Heavens! I wanted to be home before dark. I'm off! Happy Easter, everybody!"

With that Grandma was gone, but not in a *flash* without her Terraplane.

A few minutes later, we heard Dad pull into the driveway. "Lord, it's Dad. I'm running behind. I could use your help, Jase. I have to get this ham prepared and put some supper on. Then this evening we have to color eggs. Danny, would you like to help us color eggs?"

"You bet! I just love coloring eggs!"

That was Danny-speak for *I haven't the faintest idea what you're talking about Mrs. A. But I don't want you to know it.*

"Hey! Who was that in the blue Chevy? They need a lesson in shifting gears," Dad remarked as he entered the kitchen. "Wow! What's going on here?"

"It was Ma with a car on loan from Uncle George — probably belongs to one of his other customers. He's charging the Terraplane's battery. She dropped off eggs for coloring and the ham for Sunday. I've got to prepare the ham and set up the egg-coloring production. How would you like to make us a simple scrambled-egg supper tonight?"

"Funny. I was going to suggest just that. Look what I have." He removed a package wrapped in butcher paper from under his arm. When he opened the wrapping, the odor told me exactly what the package contained.

"Smoked whitefish!"

"Good guess. But this is even better. Smoked lake trout."

"Wow! If we had some Pinconning cheese, we'd be all set, Dad."

"Your wish is my command!" He opened his lunch-bucket and brought out another wrapped parcel. "How's a pound-and-a-half of genuine Pinconning cheese, freshly cut from a new wheel at Pete's?"

Whenever Dad and I went fishing anywhere near Saginaw Bay, smoked fish and Pinconning cheese was our special treat. And when we were home, I knew Dad liked to add scrambled eggs to the menu. In fact, scrambled eggs were his specialty.

Since Aunt Maude had left with little Johnnie to be with Uncle Van in Washington, Dad and I fixed our own supper on evenings when Mom taught her classes at Camp Riverton. When it was Dad's turn to cook, most of the time it was scrambled eggs with cheese and hot sauce. Just the way we both liked them. My specialty was cream of tomato soup and grilled cheese sandwiches with mustard.

"Where did you get the fish, John?"

"From Walt Williams — out at the plant. He and his wife have a place up north and they're fond of smoked lake trout. They buy it directly from a fellow who has his own smoker. I asked Walt to buy me a couple of pounds next time he got some for himself."

"I'm not sure I've ever tasted it," Mom said.

"Tell you what. Jase and I'll fix supper while you work on the ham. After supper, we can color eggs. Danny, I assume you can stay for supper. Do you like to color eggs?"

"You bet, Mr. A! I just love coloring eggs!"

Yeah. Right!

Two hours later, we were sitting at the kitchen table totally engrossed in the process. Mom had finished preparing the ham. Dad had fixed scrambled eggs to go with his two delicious surprise packages. Our supper put me in mind of fishing for perch up in Quanicassee. Danny and I had done the dishes while Mom and Dad assembled the needed materials, including eggs, water, vinegar, and various food colors.

Usually Mom only boiled six or eight eggs for Easter coloring, just enough to put a couple in each of our Easter baskets. But, even after the scrambled eggs, we still had more than two dozen left from Grandma's gift. Mom made a command decision, "I'm going to boil them all. That way, whether we color them or not, they'll still keep in the icebox."

Because of the quantity of eggs, Mom used two saucepans for boiling them. Meantime, Mom heated a teakettle to provide boiling water to mix with vinegar and liquid food colors in each of the coffee cups she had assembled on the kitchen table.

"Add just one teaspoon of vinegar to each half-cup of boiling water," Mom advised. "Then mix in about 20 drops of food color. We'll mix the primary colors first — yellow, red, and blue. Later, if we get tired of those, we can blend them to make other colors. Like blue and red to make purple and so on."

I enjoyed using my old crayons to draw a picture or pattern on the eggshells. The wax prevented color from adhering to any spot

I marked. When I finished, my artwork would be etched in near white against the background of the egg's main color. The longer the egg stayed in the cup, the deeper the final color. When we were satisfied with the length of stay, we lifted the egg out of the cup with a spoon and set it on newspaper to dry.

While we sat at the table plying our trade as professional egg colorists, no one uttered a word. Because our concentration was so intense, time passed quickly. When our eggs ran out, everyone was surprised, and I daresay disappointed.

It was quite late when we dropped Danny off with his share of colored eggs and the last smidgen of Pinconning cheese for his midnight snack.

"Thank you, Jase. You too, Mr. A. This was the most fun I've ever had coloring eggs. Next time I'll bring some eggs so we won't run out. Night!"

He was gone.

On the way home, Dad asked me. "Not that it matters a lot, but I got the idea that Danny had never colored eggs before. Do you think that's possible, Jase?"

"Oh, no, Dad. He just *loves* coloring eggs!"

Dad and I both laughed.

DANNY AND I ONLY attended two services on Easter morning. Danny insisted he didn't want to ruin his appetite before that afternoon's feast. He even passed up singing a solo at the First Methodist Church's second service, just to avoid being tempted by the extra-special sweets served between services on holidays.

While the idea of Danny's appetite being *ruined* struck me as implausible, I went along with it anyway. In fact, I was a bit relieved. By Easter that year, my supply of pennies and nickels for collection plates was running extremely low. Income-producing opportunities, including bait gathering, were much more plentiful during the summer months.

Because of Danny's unprecedented abstinence, we found ourselves sitting in our front room with nothing to do. In the kitchen, Mom was busily basting the ham again. This was the eighth or ninth time since dawn. Dad was poring over the Sunday paper for the latest news from the war.

Every so often, he provided us with an abbreviated *newscast*.
"Listen to this. The Allies discovered a massive hoard of artwork and gold stolen by the Nazis. It was hidden in a salt mine in Merkers, Germany. Let's see here — there's Reichsbank wealth, SS loot, and museum paintings among the treasure found. Can you believe that?"

"Interesting, Dad" was my polite response.

"Boys, here's a biggie. A special insert on the front page. The U.S. Marines have launched Operation Iceberg. A massive amphibious landing on the Japanese island of Okinawa. A much larger operation than Iwo Jima. We'll hear a lot more about this battle in the coming days. You can bet your boots on that!"

Now, that one caught my attention.

The Battle of Iwo Jima was the first American attack on the Japanese *Home Islands*. Located some 700 miles south of Tokyo, the island's two airfields were critically important for providing air support for the eventual invasion of Japan. Despite its tiny size of a mere 21 square miles, the island was heavily fortified with vast bunkers and hidden artillery, all connected by an 11-mile network of tunnels.

After days of shelling by American battleships and repeated attacks by a hundred carrier-based bombers, a force of 70 thousand U.S. Marines came ashore, not knowing that the days of bombardment had done little damage to the entrenched positions of the 21 thousand fanatical Japanese soldiers lying in wait.

After hand-to-hand combat, five Marines and a Navy corpsman raised the American flag atop Mount Suribachi, becoming the subject of the most reproduced photograph of all time. More importantly, the American flag flying 546 feet above the beach provided the much-needed inspiration to the Marines who would fight on, for 30 more days, against the tenacious Japanese defenders.

On March 26, 1945, when the fighting ended, the casualties to both sides were staggering. Choosing death over surrender, the Japanese tally was 20,703 dead and only 216 captured. The American count was 6,821 dead, 19,189 wounded, and 494 missing.

During this battle, 23 Marines and four Navy corpsmen were presented the *Medal of Honor*. Of these, 14 were presented posthumously. For the U.S. Marine Corps, this number represented over 30% of the 82 *Medals of Honor* presented during all of War World II.

Analysis of these results gave American military and civilian leaders a dramatic indication for what was in store for our fighting men when the invasion of Japan was launched. As if more evidence was needed, the Battle of Okinawa proved to be even more costly to American fighting men. These sobering results weighed heavily in the decision to avoid the estimated one million American casualties and instead drop the two atomic bombs on Japan to end the war.

"JASE! LET'S GO SEE what JB's up to."

"I'm ready, Danny. Let's go."

The Reilly house was the ideal place to hold our gathering. After all, it was the largest house in our neighborhood. The first floor was about twice the size of our entire house. It consisted of three very large rooms including the kitchen, the dining room, and the living room. Because these rooms were connected and surrounded the central staircase, the traffic pattern was circular. Guests could walk from room to room without impediment or bottleneck. In warm weather, people could even extend their circling to include the broad front and side porches. All the bedrooms were on the second floor.

When Mrs. Bradford invited us to step inside, we were taken aback. Prior to the arrival of their guests, the Reillys had expended an enormous effort to spruce up the place. Because they had drawn back the drapes and cleaned the windows, swept the rugs, and polished the furniture and hardwood floors, everything seemed bright and fresh.

To accommodate the 16 of us, several leaves had been inserted to extend the mahogany dining-room table to its full length. The wide surfaces of sideboards and buffets held silver and china serving pieces including trays, dishes, bowls, pitchers, and tureens. The table itself was set with china, silverware, and crystal. Frankly I had never dreamed such elegance could be found in any home in our humble, blue-collar neighborhood. It reminded me of lunch at Mrs. Dewey's.

The cooking smells, wafting our way from the kitchen, made my mouth water. And dinner was still two hours away. Recalling the menu, I recognized the aroma of sweet potatoes and marshmallow and what, I surmised, was the daffodil cake baking in the oven. Arrangements of forced cuttings of forsythia, quince, and crab-apple blossoms added their luscious scents to the ambience.

"You must be very pleased to be here, Mrs. Bradford. This is such a beautiful home. And now that you've arrived, everyone is very happy."

"I know I am, Jase," JB affirmed.

"Me too," Danny added for good measure.

When Mrs. Bradford smiled, I saw her throat quiver. Unable to speak, she reached out, touched my arm, and nodded quickly.

We heard a light knock on the door. When Mrs. Bradford opened it, we saw Louise Libby. With her was the older lady we'd seen at our awards ceremony in the Hamilton School gymnasium.

"Rose, I wanted you to meet Miss Greta Frantz, who's visiting from Milwaukee." Louise said. "Aunt Greta, this is Rose Bradford. You met Jase, Danny, and JB at the Hamilton School."

Greta Frantz nodded at us and then turned her attention to Mrs. Bradford. The two women shook hands and exchanged greetings. The visitor explained, "I'm Louise's late husband's aunt. Because I wanted to be here when Barb and Anne arrived home, I came by train on Wednesday evening."

"That was the evening I arrived as well. I know Louise was out of town. Did you take a taxi from the train station?"

"No. When I visited Riverton earlier, I became acquainted with Hans and Ada Zeyer who live next door to Louise. I speak German and we hit it off right away. They come from Bavaria as my people did. Anyway they picked me up at the train station. In fact, they insisted I stay at their house since they have an extra bedroom. Now that the girls are home, Louise doesn't have a spare room."

"Will you be joining us for dinner today, Miss Frantz?" Mrs. Bradford inquired.

"I'd love to but the Zeyers have invited me to share their traditional Easter dinner — herbed leg of lamb with carrots and dumplings. I couldn't resist."

"This morning Ada invited the girls and me for a traditional German Easter breakfast. What was that delicious dish called, Aunt Greta?"

"*Eier in gruener Sosse* — eggs with green sauce. With ham, of course."

"We really should return home. I have to check some dishes in the oven. See you in an hour or so," Louise told Mrs. Bradford.

After they left, Mrs. Bradford asked, "Hey, boys. How about giving me a hand in the kitchen?"

She was so charming, who could say no?

LATER THAT EVENING, WE Addisons found ourselves seated at the kitchen table nibbling ham sandwiches. I don't know why, but for some reason, all three of us were wide-awake and famished, of all things.

"Boy, this really hits the spot. After that dinner, I can't believe I still have room for a sandwich," Dad confessed.

"That was some feast, all right," Mom agreed. "Wasn't the dining room absolutely elegant?"

"I've never seen dining-room furniture or silver and china like that. Were those antiques?"

"When we were cleaning up, Mary told us about them. As the older daughter, she inherited all those pieces from her father's sister who married a wealthy Chicago banker. The couple had no children. But they certainly had lovely furnishings. Didn't they?"

"Did you happen to notice what Danny had in his hair, Dad?"

"In his hair?"

"Yep! Two or three strands of green artificial grass from an Easter basket. It must have been there since this morning. I didn't notice it until I walked by him on my way to the sideboard for seconds."

"Perhaps, in a fit of hunger, he dove headfirst into his Easter basket this morning," Dad speculated.

"He told me one of his favorite things about Easter is discovering old jelly beans under the grass. I figure he tipped the basket upside down over his mouth and some of the grass fell on his head."

"Jase, how do you know he didn't put it there intentionally? Maybe he thought it'd go nicely with his doughboy uniform. Camouflage, you know?" Dad suggested.

We all snickered at the thought.

"The whole event was marvelous, but the thing I liked best was seeing Rose and the Libby sisters having such a good time," Mom observed. "To be honest, I thought their return would be more difficult for them."

"You're right, Marie. It's kind of a miracle."

"An Easter miracle, Dad!"

10 GO FISH

MONDAYS WERE USUALLY BUSY DAYS FOR DANNY and me. But on the Monday after Easter, there was no school and no scout meeting. We could just relax. However, after breakfast as we sat in the warm sun on our back porch, we decided to make productive use of our time by counting the tiny white and purple crocuses that had miraculously appeared overnight in the bed next to the porch. We were so preoccupied with this important task that we failed to notice JB walking across the lawn toward us.

"Hi, guys! Got a minute?"

His voice startled me but I recovered quickly. "Sure! What's up?"

"Do you remember the conversation we had — when we first met — about Homer Lyle's bait business?"

I certainly did remember. But it wasn't much of a conversation. It was more of a surprise announcement by Danny that *we* had decided to stop being Homer's sole suppliers of night crawlers and other baits. Danny had also announced, if JB were interested in taking over for us, *we* would put in a good word to Homer on his behalf. Finally he assured JB there was good money to be made, if he were interested.

In an apparent desire to please and impress JB, Danny had overlooked the needs and desires of his partner, Jase Addison, and our bait-business boss, Homer Lyle. There was another person who had a say in the feasibility of Danny's suggestion. He was former Marine Private Homer Jensen, who had served only briefly in the Pacific before Japanese bullets ended his military career.

When he joined the Marine Corps, Danny and I became Homer Jensen's temporary replacements. Now that he was back home, I wasn't certain whether we still had a job, let alone the ability to pass it on to JB. After all, Homer Jensen was Homer Lyle's heir apparent to his bait business.

While all of these thoughts flitted around my head like butterflies, my partner looked dreamily at the crocuses and sighed. I assumed the sigh was my cue to answer JB.

"JB, I'm not sure Danny should have said —."

Before I could finish, JB held up his hand and assured me, "Believe me, I understand. But I didn't want to overlook the possibility. I can see that Danny shouldn't have encouraged me. And that's not a problem."

JB looked knowingly at me. I nodded back at him. Danny's face had been saved one more time.

Much to my surprise, Danny drifted in from left field and lazily announced, "Jase, I forgot to tell you. I talked to Homer Lyle on Saturday."

What?

"A friend of his is retiring from a bait business over near the Chippewa Town Dam. He asked Homer One to find somebody to take it over. So Homer Two will run it. They'll need the three of us to provide bait for both shops. Homer One knows it's a bit too early to gather bait. But he wants to start JB's training this afternoon — if that's all right with you two."

Once again, I felt like a mouse under Danny's paw.

As a refresher course for us and to keep JB company, Danny and I decided to sit through JB's training. Besides we agreed that Homer One, as Danny now insisted on calling him, was always entertaining. Even Homer Two promised to stop by if he could.

After we had introduced JB, Homer One insisted on getting right down to business. So we headed for his backyard bait shack. Leading the way, our instructor hobbled along on his crutches. From behind, we could see the devastating effect of arthritis on his twisted spinal column.

Just inside the door, Homer One had arranged four wooden boxes in a tiny circle. When we were seated, our instructor dramatically cleared his throat and began. Holding up two arthritic fingers, Homer One told us that he would talk about two subjects. The first subject would be night crawlers and the second would include all other baits.

Because they were his best-selling fish bait, Homer One focused on night crawlers first. Crawlers were also the easiest bait for boys to collect without much special knowledge or training. JB assured Homer One he was available to start right away. He admitted being excited by the prospect of having every coffee can of crawlers net him 50 cents or more. Homer One quickly reminded JB that our share was exactly 50 percent of the price he charged to his customers at the time. If Homer One was charging his customers 12 cents a dozen for crawlers, we were paid six cents a dozen for those we supplied. In the dry late summer, when crawlers were hard to come by, his price could easily double or, in extreme droughts, even triple.

Our instructor explained that night crawlers were just large fat earthworms. They populated everybody's lawns and gardens throughout the region. They improved the condition of the soil by breaking down plant materials like leaves, stems, twigs, and blades of grass. But, he advised, night crawlers were particularly partial to maple leaves. Crawlers stored in a wooden worm box could be kept alive and healthy forever simply by adding more maple leaves. Of course, you also had to ensure the contents were kept moist.

"But crawlers kin't stand oak leaves. No siree, Bob! Use oak leaves — and ya'll poison every crawler in your worm box. They's jest too sour."

Homer One showed a typical worm box to JB. This simple, wooden worm box had a hinged cover for depositing and removing crawlers, replenishing maple leaves, and wetting them down every few days. The best worm box was relatively small for easy handling. In addition, if you happened to lose all the crawlers stored in one box, you still had the rest of your inventory safely ensconced in your other boxes.

You stored these boxes on a foundation of bricks, up off the ground, to allow excess moisture from the dampened maple leaves to escape. This prevented undesirable fungus buildup. If you kept your boxes outside, you placed cement blocks on the box covers to discourage furry thieves, like raccoons and possums, from dipping into your crawler supply for a midnight snack.

Homer One fully expected us boys to stockpile some of our crawlers and sell them to him during dry spells, when prices escalated. That was okay with him because he didn't have enough worm boxes or room in his bait shack to store all he needed anyway. The important thing was for us to know how to store, feed, and care for our crawlers. There was nothing worse than working for several nights to build up your supply only to suffer the death of your stock because you forgot to moisten your maple leaves.

He suggested we harvest crawlers from lawns other than just our own. "Crawlers needs lawns. An' lawns needs crawlers. So ya never wanta remove the whole worm population from any one lawn," he warned.

We told JB about our bargain with the Forrest Street neighbors. In exchange for watering their lawns every afternoon, we had their permission to stop by, for an hour or so every evening, to gather night crawlers. They all looked forward to our visits.

After dark, freshly-watered lawns yielded dozens of long, fat healthy specimens. Using a flashlight, you crept quietly through the wet grass in search of your pink-orange prey. They would be stretched out nearly to their full length, with only the tip of their tails tucked inside their holes for a quick escape if you were not fast enough.

"Good crawler hunters use a light touch when snatchin' up crawlers. That's the only way not ta hurt 'em. Your grab's got ta be quick and firm enough ta git 'em. But light enough ta not squash 'em," Homer One advised.

At certain times of the year, experienced crawler pickers collected two crawlers with one grab because the amorous pair seemed more interested in hugging each other than avoiding a change-of-address to your worm box.

Supplying Homer One and Homer Two with night crawlers would prove to be a lucrative activity for the three of us, but it was not all fun and profit. Spending the entire evening stooped over was a true backbreaker. Also, it often was cold, damp, and lonely work. And the hours, from dark to midnight, were hardly ideal for growing boys. But, for years, we did it anyway. Money saved from my *worm business*, as my family called it, contributed significantly to my financial independence, especially at college.

Homer One's second lesson provided an overview of various baits, including how they were stored and generally where and how they were obtained.

Hellgrammites, the Dobson fly larvae, are shiny and black with dozens of prickly feet and one big pincher on their noses. They are carnivorous, aggressive, and very ugly. Full-grown hellgrammites are about two inches long.

Of all the baits Homer One sold, hellgrammites were by far the most difficult to catch. To achieve the best results, two people were needed. You and your partner placed a six-foot wide net, spread between two four-foot vertical poles, downstream from the rocks under which hellgrammites were likely to lurk. While holding the net pole with one hand, you used the other to turn over rocks and wipe the hellgrammites off their undersides. If you selected the right rocks, swift current would carry the dislodged hellgrammites downstream into your net.

Crabs or crawfish inhabited the same rocky shoals as hellgrammites. When you picked up rocks, crabs would dart in all directions. But some inevitably found their way into your net. If you were lucky, you could add a dozen or more three- or four-inch crabs to your take, along with your hellgrammites. Fishermen used either the whole crab or just the tail section for bait. I always had success using crab tails for bluegills and rock bass.

After carefully plucking hellgrammites and crabs out of the net, you placed them in the perforated inner pail of your minnow bucket. This pail was tethered to your wrist and floated along behind, partially submerged in water. Keeping hellgrammites and crabs in cool fresh water was the key to delivering them to Homer One in the best shape.

Although fishermen differed on which of these two baits worked best, Homer One was adamant. "Hellgrammites is ideal bait fer bass and panfish. Fer one thing, fish loves hellgrammites. Fer another, they's got such hard shells that once they's on the hook, they don't come off easy. Unless a fish munches mosta your hellgrammite, you kin use him over and over agin."

Suckers and chubs were used as baitfish to catch the *Real* Big Ones, northern pike and muskies. A redhorse sucker could easily measure a foot or more in length. Often, large chubs and suckers were used as *decoys* when spearfishing for *Real* Big Ones through the ice. These baits were caught from the bridges over the Chippewa with hook and line using fishing worms as bait.

Because they were the most expensive item in Homer One's inventory, it was important not to lose them. To prevent our catch from expiring in the hot sun on an unshaded bridge, when we had accumulated a half-dozen or so in our minnow bucket, we would make a fast run on our bicycles to deposit them in Homer One's aerated tank.

The smaller shiners were an equally fragile baitfish, but we netted them in great quantities in the small creeks and ponds around Riverton. A good net full of shiners easily required two or three minnow buckets. Our brimming buckets sloshed wildly as we pumped our bicycles at top speeds back to Homer One's with our live shiner supply. Small shiners were always a winner with walleyes, bass, perch, and panfish.

Crickets were late summer baits. They thrived beneath lumber and brush piles. But their favorite habitat was under sections of cardboard laid over fields of grass. Because these black hoppers loved to eat paper, we created cardboard homes, not only providing them protection but also their dinners.

Grabbing crickets required practice. If you applied too much pressure to the fat adult crickets, two bad things could happen. First, you could squeeze your prize to death, which is frowned on in the *live* bait business. Second, your catch sometimes *squeezed* back with a sharp bite to the inside of your hand. The best technique for avoiding bites and crushed crickets was to cup the cricket with both hands and lower him into your dry minnow bucket for transport back to Homer One's wood frame and fine wire-mesh cricket cages.

"Since y'er Riverton boys, I ain't gonna tell ya nothin' about fishing worms ya don't already know. When ya dig a new garbage pit — or spade yer garden, ya kin gather small worms that I'll add ta my fishing-worm box — fer sale ta those in town who's too lazy ta pick up a shovel."

Homer One was right. We didn't deliberately hunt fishing worms. They seemed to be a by-product of our other bait-hunting or normal digging activities. Nonetheless, we helped Homer One maintain a supply of small worms that he sold by the hundred to lazy Rivertonians.

We boys were familiar with corn borers. Who hadn't seen them in sweet corn, acquired at the weekly produce sales at the stockyard parking lot? We just didn't know that these plump little worms were ideal fishing bait, especially when fishing with tip-ups for yellow perch through the ice on Saginaw Bay. Even in the winter months from snow-covered fields at the Compton farm, we could gather corn borers lying dormant inside cornstalks left standing after the corn had been picked.

Finally Homer One wondered if we had ever used live mice for bass fishing. I had to admit that Dad had a mouse harness, but we had never taken the trouble to catch live mice to fill it. But I'd heard that bass really went for them in a big way. Homer One confessed that he didn't have much call for this particular bait, although he personally had had terrific luck with it back in his fishing days.

On our way home from Homer One's house, Danny predicted, "This is going to be a very profitable summer, guys!"

JB and I concurred.

FOR ALL MY BOYHOOD preoccupation with bait, both live and artificial, one of my very favorite fish was caught without using any bait at all. Of course, I'm referring to the Great Lakes smelt, dipped from Michigan's spawning streams in the middle of a chilly spring night using homemade nets. My rationale for holding the smelt in such high esteem can be summed up in one word, *Taste*.

During my youth, I'm sure I taste-tested every freshwater fish found in Michigan's lakes, ponds, and rivers. Moreover, I was fortunate to have been able to conduct my tests under the very best conditions. Because both my father and I loved the taste of properly prepared good-to-eat fish, we often indulged ourselves by taking our fresh catch to shore, cleaning it promptly, and immediately cooking it over our campfire.

To ensure cooking did not in any way diminish the natural flavor of the fish, we always relied on the same simple recipe. In a small, brown paper bag, we blended a half-cup of flour, a tiny dash of pepper, and a single pinch of salt. Next we dropped the freshly cleaned fish into the bag and shook the bag once to coat the fish. After dusting the excess flour from the fish, we fried it lightly in butter over a low fire.

Over the years, we used this process to identify those species that we agreed were tops in taste. Our selections included the yellow perch. The bluegill. The walleye. The native brook, brown, and speckled trout. And our very favorite, the lowly smelt.

Technically smelt are not a Michigan freshwater fish at all. This saltwater fish is native to the Atlantic Ocean off the northeastern coast of North America. In 1912, smelt were planted in Crystal Lake, Michigan, which lies close to Lake Michigan in the northwestern part of the Lower Peninsula. From there, the wily smelt made their way into all five Great Lakes where they found a most hospitable environment in which to thrive.

Shunning light and warm water temperatures, the newly hatched fry seek out the deepest and coldest parts of the lakes, usually some miles from shore. There they feed on an abundance of aquatic life including insects, insect larvae, crustaceans and other aquatic invertebrates, and smaller fish. In turn, smelt are preyed upon by lake trout, whitefish, walleyes, yellow perch, and in recent decades various species of salmon, which have been introduced into the Great Lakes.

Lowly may be a fitting label for the smelt. First, it's not a flashy dresser. Resembling a sardine, smelt have long, thin silver-white bodies painted with thin coats of subtle iridescent purple, pink, and blue hues. Three years after hatching, the fully grown Great Lakes smelt achieve an average length of only seven to eight inches.

Every April, mature smelt leave their deep-water homes in waves and ascend rivers and streams to gravel beds where they spawn. When I was a boy, Riverton smelt fishermen eagerly awaited news of early catches near the points where a number of rivers enter Lake Huron along the western shore of Saginaw Bay. These entrance points offered the largest concentration of spawning smelt and were closest to Riverton.

Our fishermen friends disagreed about which river offered the best smelt dipping. The choices of rivers were numerous, including the Tawas, the Au Gres, the Rifle, or the Kawkawlin. Truth be known, each of these rivers produced an abundance of smelt each spring. But, like every other smelt fisherman, Dad and I had a special spot that we returned to year after year.

After rising from several creeks to the north, the East Branch of the Au Gres River travels south for 15 miles or so. Abruptly, the river is diverted by the Whitney Drain, a man-made canal, and heads straight east for Saginaw Bay. Looking back on it, I assume the river was diverted for flood-control purposes.

Nonetheless, just before reaching the shoreline of the lake, the river runs under the *Singing Bridge*, built to allow U.S. Highway 23, a coastal road in that part of the state, to cross over the river. The bridge is named for the sound it makes as winds off the lake *hum* through its superstructure. Apparently the *Singing Bridge* was as appealing to smelt as it was to us because Dad and I never failed to fill our lard pails every time we dipped there.

When the word came that the run was on, Rivertonians by the hundreds loaded lard pails, smelt nets, hunting jackets, waders or hip boots, and raingear into the trunks of their cars or the beds of their trucks and headed north. Because the fishing sites were within a two-hour drive, there was no rush to get there. Depending on the amount of moonlight, the light-sensitive smelt waited in the depths until 10 o'clock at night at the earliest. Then they ran furiously until perhaps two o'clock in the morning when the fish gods blew the time-out whistle until the next night. This nightly pattern repeated itself for two or three weeks and then stopped as abruptly as it started.

When the smelt were running heavily, a strong man could easily fill a lard pail with a dozen dips. Strength was required to lift smelt-heavy nets out of the rushing water, generally characterizing the best smelt-dipping sites. Dad and I always limited our take to two lard pails. This provided more than enough for our family, a sizeable portion for Grandma and Grandpa Compton, and the same for the Tuckers. However, some smelt fishermen took pride in filling the beds of their pickup trucks with smelt. Apparently they loved the attention they received the next morning when they delivered large portions of fresh smelt to every family in their neighborhoods.

Because Dad's Chevy had limited storage and passenger room, Dad and I often went smelt dipping alone. On two occasions, I remember inviting Grandpa Compton to join us. And once, Sergeant Jeff Tolna. Because smelt dipping was a dangerous business, I never requested permission to bring Danny or any other young friend along. Taking a chance on an inexperienced fisherman could, and often did, result in death by drowning.

While waiting for the nightly run to commence, some people ran into trouble by choosing to kill time at a local tavern. Not infrequently, Dad and I observed a fisherman, clearly under the influence, stumbling by us in the dark. Feeling your way along treacherous, steep banks above the rushing river was dangerous enough, even with your faculties fully intact. Playing it safe, Dad and I always waited for the run while feasting on the smoked fish, hot French bread, and Pinconning cheese, which we always bought on our way north at the trading post in Kawkawlin. Hot coffee was our drink of choice.

Like all fish on our tops-in-taste list, smelt were best enjoyed soon after being caught. Because the harvest was so abundant and concentrated over just a couple of weeks, Riverton families attempted to devise methods to preserve smelt, too numerous to be consumed before they spoiled. These methods included freezing them in water-filled, waxed cardboard containers. Canning them like bully beef. Drying them in the sun Eskimo-style. Cooking them into vats of fish soup for later consumption. Pickling them like herring. Packing them in salt like cod. And smoking them like hams and bacon. In the end, much of the surplus was not processed because people simply ran out of time and resources.

On the verge of spoiling, excess smelt were fed to chickens, ducks, and pigs or carted off to nearby fox farms. As a last resort, smelt were plowed under in Victory Gardens, following Squanto's advice to the Pilgrims about planting a fish in each corn hill.

But Dad and I were purists. We only consumed smelt by using our standard method for optimizing the flavor of fish. With a two-hour drive home, the smelt were not exactly freshly caught. To make up for this, we devised a method for greatly decreasing the time spent on cleaning smelt. Because their scales were miniscule, they could be removed quickly with a swipe of a coarse rag. Unlike walleyes, they didn't have to be filleted. Smelt bones disappeared during cooking on the grill or in the frying pan. Finally smelt were so small they could be cleaned by a mere two snips of the scissors. I won't describe this method in detail, but anyone who has cleaned a fish before will follow my meaning.

Using our recipe for cooking fresh fish, each spring we produced platter after platter of golden-brown and sweet-tasting ecstasy! And the cost? Only a few hours of lost sleep!

11 SCOUTING AHEAD

BOTH DANNY AND I KNEW FREDDIE HOLLAND WAS delighted to have JB as a member of his Wolverine Patrol. As its leader, Freddie could have vetoed the idea by telling Scoutmaster Mel there were already too many Wolverines. We did have the largest patrol in the troop, but Freddie was a good leader and his patrol always outperformed the others. One additional scout wouldn't detract from his ability to give us novices the benefit of his valuable tutoring on scouting skills.

As odd as it seemed, Danny was beside himself when our meeting on the Monday following Easter was canceled. Because he and I had tentatively set that next Saturday as our day to take the required five-mile hike, Danny arranged for Freddie to meet with us to ensure we were doing everything necessary to complete our Second Class requirements.

Right after school on Friday, we met at the Methodist church. Freddie was certainly prepared for our questions. While Danny and I depended heavily on referring to our *Handbook for Boys* to lead us through the discussion, Freddie had committed the requirements to memory. It was most impressive.

"Since you've completed the first two parts of the requirements for Second Class, today we'll focus on the third part, *Scout Craft*. Of course, this is the toughest part because it covers five areas of expertise."

Freddie inventoried those areas without batting an eye: Preparing for the Hike. Finding the Way. Cooking a Meal on the Trail. Being Observant. Taking the Hike.

"Because you're planning to take your five-mile hike tomorrow, we don't have much time to work on the other four areas. But, if we knuckle down, I think we can nail them," Freddie declared optimistically. "Instead of me reciting what's right there in your book, why don't you ask me specific questions about the requirements?"

Danny didn't hesitate. "I don't understand why we have to demonstrate six *Silent Scout Signals* when Jase and I'll be hiking right there together. We can just talk to each other if we need anything."

Fearing another round of Danny challenging the requirements, I intervened. "Danny, Freddie doesn't want to discuss *why* the requirements are there. He's here to help us understand them and show us how to demonstrate them to him."

But Freddie didn't seem to mind the question.

"Danny, assume you're in the jungle, stalking a killer lion with your patrol. You sure better be able to communicate silently — or someone's going to be eaten. Or let's say you're on Iwo Jima. And you're ordered to lead your men on a patrol behind Japanese lines to spy on their positions. Can you talk out loud to each other in those conditions?"

Danny shook his head. Then, to my amazement, he stood up and demonstrated the *Silent Scout Signals*.

"This one's *Assemble,*" he informed us, circling his hand above his head. "And this one is *Down* or *Take Cover.*"

Frankly I wasn't sure Danny knew any of the silent signals. But he surprised me even further.

"This is *Halt.* This is *Parallel File Formation.* Here's *Circle Troop Formation.*"

Instead of the required six signals, Danny demonstrated all 13 shown in the handbook.

"Very good, Danny. I —." Freddie stopped when he realized Danny hadn't finished.

"This means *You're Out.* This is *You're Safe.* Here's *Basket Counts.* This is *Unnecessary Roughness.* Here's *Time-Out.* And —."

"**Whoa, boy!**" I yelled, attempting to shut off the signal machine. It worked.

Danny stopped and looked smugly at Freddie and me.

"Why did you go on like that?" I finally demanded.

"Just being practical, Jase. In the next year, what're our chances of stalking a killer lion in the jungle or taking a patrol behind enemy lines?"

"Pretty slim," I had to admit.

"Right! But what're our chances of taking in a game of baseball, basketball, or football?"

I told him I understood by nodding my head.

Turning to Freddie, Danny asked, "Want me to show you how to dig a one-man latrine now?"

BEFORE ENDING OUR SESSION with Freddie, we agreed that Danny and I had met all Second Class requirements except two. Our planned hike the next day would satisfy one of them. But we still needed to cook a meal outdoors. Weather permitting, Freddie would meet us at Trumble Park on the following Wednesday evening to fulfill that last requirement.

"You'll need to sharpen your hunting knives and hatchets. Before you gather and prepare your firewood, I'll check their edge. You'll have to lay your fire properly and then light it. Remember you're only allowed two kitchen matches. Before next Wednesday, I suggest you practice lighting a small pile of kindling a few times."

Danny and I looked at each other. Neither of us had acquired our official hunting knife or hatchet yet. We'd counted on making a bit of bait money to finance those purchases, hopefully before the spring Camporee.

"Freddie, Jase and I don't have knives or hatchets. Would it be all right if we bring Mr. Addison's axe? We use it to chop old sewing-machine cabinets into firewood. And can we use the Japanese sword my uncle got for me at Gottacanal?"

Danny was referring to the menacing four-foot samurai sword his Uncle Jack had collected as a souvenir while serving with the Marines during the Battle of Guadalcanal. For some reason, his uncle thought the sword would be a suitable gift for Danny. Fortunately Mrs. Tucker had confiscated the weapon after seeing Danny show off in front of Chub and a bunch of his buddies.

During Danny's swordsmanship demonstration, with one samurai swing, he managed to lop off the entire upper half of Mrs. Tucker's favorite spirea bush. When he protested her seizure of his weapon, she promised to return it after he graduated from college. Although I never told Danny, I had joined the rest of the neighborhood in a collective sigh of relief.

"But, Danny — your mother," I reminded him.

He smiled and cast his patented not-to-worry look in my direction.

"Hmm, I see," Freddie mused, holding his chin between his fingers. "Maybe I can help you out."

As senior patrol leader, Freddie was entrusted with a key to the Troop 46 storage closet. He opened the door and went inside. Danny and I watched as he reached up to the top shelf and wrestled a large cardboard box to the closet floor. He lugged the cumbersome box out of the closet and opened its lid. Inside we saw a vast collection of scouting paraphernalia. Handbooks and Merit Badge booklets. Neckerchiefs and slides. Pins and badges. Web belts and shiny brass buckles. Jackknives and waterproof metal match containers. Canteens and first-aid kits. And cooking-utensil and silverware kits. And, most importantly, handsomely sheathed hunting knives and hatchets.

"Where'd all this stuff come from? It looks brand new."

"Jase, three or four years ago, Weinstein's — you know the department store — decided to discontinue carrying scouting equipment and uniforms. So Mrs. Weinstein generously divvied up their leftover inventory and donated a big boxful to each Riverton troop."

"Do you just give it out to new scouts — or what?"

"No, Danny. Only to those boys who come from indigent families." Sensing we didn't know the meaning of the word, he added, "Needy, you know?"

That label certainly didn't apply to the Addisons or the Tuckers. We may not have been the richest families in Riverton, but our hardworking parents certainly saw to our basic needs and then some. The one thing both families had in abundance was pride.

"Gee, Freddie. I'm not sure that we —."

Before I finished, Danny looked at me. "Jase, it looks like we won't complete our Second Class requirements until the end of summer."

"Wait a second, guys! Don't get me wrong. We also *loan* out this equipment. I'm not talking about charity in your cases. We'll loan you each a hatchet and a hunting knife. You sign for them on that form pasted on the cover of the box.

"When you get enough money together, you buy replacement hatchets and knives down at Madison's. You put those new ones in the box, and we scratch your names off the list. Then the loaners become yours to keep. We've done this dozens of times. Why do you think all this stuff is new? It's been bought new and returned to the box by guys just like you."

"Will you explain to our dads how we got our new hatchets and knives?"

"That's a good idea. The committee's meeting here in the morning to discuss raising funds to buy new camping equipment for the Camporee. Since I'll be there, I'll remind everybody about our loaner program then. Is that agreeable to you guys?"

We smiled at Freddie and nodded. Freddie handed each of us a brand new hatchet and a hunting knife, sheathed in sturdy heavy-duty leather, sporting an embossed Boy Scouts of America symbol.

"If one of you has a wood-burning set, I suggest you burn your initials into the leather inside your sheaths. That way, you won't get them mixed up with somebody else's."

When Freddie handed us our loaners, sheer joy surged through my body. The weight, the feel, and the smell of Freddie's gifts were almost too much to bear. Apparently Danny felt exactly as I did because he joined me in thanking Freddie over and over.

"Help me lift this box back up onto that shelf — then we'll continue with your requirements."

The three of us awkwardly hefted the heavy box back into place. Freddie locked the closet, and we sat back down to finish our session.

"Where were we? That's right. After your fire's burned down to a nice bed of red-hot coals, using your cook kits —. You do have cook kits. Right? Oh, sure you do. I remember them at Camp Moon Lake. Anyway, using your cook kits — or another method I'll mention in a minute — you cook a full meal starting with raw meat, fish, or poultry. And at least one raw vegetable.

"You don't have to bake any bread, but I suggest you do. Bread's good with meat and vegetables. There's an easy way to bake it. Just mix a large ball of biscuit dough and bring it with you in a can. When you get to the park, find a thick stick, clean off its bark, roll the dough into a long cigar, wrap it around your stick, and then poke it into the ground next to the fire. It's best to angle the stick so the dough's over the coals. You have to rotate it, every so often, to expose all sides of the bread to the fire as it bakes. It's called stick bread. And it tastes like a smoky biscuit.

"You're allowed to cook your meal without your frying pan or the lidded cooking pot in your kits. You can grill kabobs on a skewer over the fire. Or bury a mud-covered potato in the coals. Because this is your first cookout, my advice is to keep it simple. Use your frying pan and pot.

"That's about it. Any questions?"

Danny and I shook our heads. We thanked Freddie one more time and headed for home.

On our way, I noticed that Danny was very quiet. Seeming to read my mind, he explained, "I'm really happy about our new hatchets and hunting knives, but I sure was looking forward to cooking with my samurai sword."

I sure was looking forward to cooking without the danger of becoming a boy kabob!

IT WAS BEGINNING TO look like Danny and I would fulfill our Second Class requirements well before the Court of Honor. With plans in place with Freddie for us to cook a meal outdoors, the only thing we needed was to complete our five-mile hike. There was just one hitch. We were going on this important hike first thing Saturday morning. But on Friday evening, we had yet to decide on our destination and the route to get there.

Knowing Danny's tendency to procrastinate and obstruct, I'd enlisted Dad's help to nail this down after we finished our session with Freddie. I also cautioned Dad not to make his participation too obvious. He understood completely. To be sure Danny was at our house, I proposed we discuss this topic after supper. To save time, I suggested he eat with us. Anticipating Danny's question, I had checked with Mom to see what she was planning for supper. She suggested one of Danny's favorite Friday-night meals.

As usual, Danny's reaction was a bit inscrutable. "That's a great idea, Jase. We need to decide tonight about our hike route so we can dream about it after we go to sleep."

"I hadn't thought about that," I told him honestly.

"Don't mention it," he responded.

"If you say so," I replied, not having the faintest idea why.

While I kept waiting for him to ask me what we were having for supper, he never did. When we entered our back door, Mom greeted us and informed Danny, "We're having your favorite Friday-night supper — macaroni and cheese with catsup!"

Danny smiled at her. "I know. Jase told me. Yummy!"

Thinking I must have dozed off and talked in my sleep on the way home, I pinched myself. No such luck. It was just another Dannyism. For the sake of my sanity, I decided just to let it go.

After supper, Danny and I kept our seats while Mom and Dad cleared the table and started washing dishes. Gingerly I broached the agenda. "Where do you want to hike tomorrow, Danny?" I inquired innocently.

"My good man, there's but one destination I desire. I insist we trek to the Compton estate," he informed me, using the voice of James Mason.

Ignoring the accent, I reminded him bluntly, "It's over 10 miles to the farm. Not only will it wear us out, but it's twice as long as required."

"Ah, but you forget the great benefit of making the expedition. When we arrive, Madam Compton will prepare a feast like none other. Yes, my good man, it'd be more than worth the effort even if it were a 20-mile journey. But you know all these things. Forgive me for patronizing you, dear sir."

By this time, Mom and Dad had dropped their dishtowels and turned around to gawk at Danny.

"Besides we know the way. We couldn't get lost."

Without noticing his accent had disappeared, I reiterated, "But it's 10 miles, Danny! We've never walked that far before."

With the show apparently over, Mom and Dad returned to drying the dishes.

"What do you mean? How far is it to Hamilton School?"

I decided it was time to involve Dad.

"Do you know, Dad?"

"Oh, it's about a mile there and a mile back here, I'd say."

"So that's two miles a day, Jase," Danny calculated. "How many times do we walk it each week?"

"Five times. So what?"

"So this — that's 10 miles a week. Why's walking 10 miles to Grandma Compton's so hard?"

I was beginning to lose patience, but I bit my tongue long enough to deliver one last point.

"Because, Danny, we would be walking *this* 10 miles all at once. That's a lot different than walking 10 miles back and forth to school spread over a week."

I was certain my point would close the argument. *Silly me!*

"But you're forgetting one important fact. We'd be keeping each other company so it'd go faster."

"Danny, it's too far. And that's all there is to it," I stated resolutely.

Danny nodded his head and smiled. "Okay, I agree. It's 10 miles out to the farm. Right?"

At last, I'd won my case.

Then he added, "What if you walk five miles of it — and I walk the other five?"

This was making me very tired. "What're we gonna do, Danny? Carry each other?"

"No, Jase. Don't be silly. It's simple. We take one bicycle with us."

Mom and Dad turned around and stared at Danny, trying to figure out what he was trying to say. I was just as baffled as they were.

"You walk the first five miles and I ride the bike. I keep you company while you're hiking. I walk the last five miles while you ride the bike. We both end up walking five miles and we both get supper at Grandma's house. Get it?"

There had to be something wrong with Danny's plan but I just couldn't see it. *There must be a flaw somewhere.*

Mom didn't seem to think so. "That sounds like a marvelous plan, Danny," she told him.

Finally Dad and I both agreed. *But why did we have to hike so many miles to reach it?*

"Even though we know how to get there, the requirement says we need a map to follow using Dad's compass. And this will prove to Freddie that we walked five miles."

"But like you said it's 10 miles. Does that require a map and compass too?"

I was nearly ready to turn my friend into a catsup-covered Dannyburger when Dad came to his rescue. "Hey! I've got just the map you need — right in this drawer. Jase, please get your crayons so we can plot your course."

When I returned to the kitchen, Dad had spread the Chippewa County map out on the table. Danny and he were following the roads to the farm with their fingers.

"What color do you want, Dad?"

"Orange, naturally," Danny insisted.

I didn't ask why.

Dad took the crayon and began to trace our route by marking a large orange swath next to the road we'd be following.

"Watch this now! Start here on Forrest Street. Head southeast on New Albany Avenue until you come to a dead end in downtown New Albany. Turn left and keep on walking — or biking — north on Saginaw Road all the way up to Riverton Road. Turn east and take that all the way over here to Barrington Road. Turn north and the farm is — right there!" He made a circle on the map.

"Dad, can you figure out where the halfway point is? We'll eat our lunch there. That's where Danny'll start hiking and I'll start riding the bike."

Dad reached behind him and pulled the ruler out of the kitchen drawer. He began examining the map very closely. "Oh! There it is! One inch equals — um ah. So that's about four inches. Two more there. Okay, we got the total! So half is about — here!"

His finger pointed right at the spot where the orange swath bent at a right angle.

"The halfway point is right at the corner of Saginaw and Riverton Roads. What a perfect spot to stop for lunch! There's a well there. And a picnic table and even an outhouse."

"Where's that, Dad?"

"Oh! Sorry. You know the little school on the corner where we turn onto Riverton Road — right across from the little grocery store and gas station where Grandma always goes."

"Oh, sure, Dad. Danny and I've been there lots of times with Grandma."

Danny gave me a puzzled look. "You know, Danny. They have those gigantic ice-cream cones for only three cents a scoop."

Danny's eyes opened wide and he leaped out of his chair, "You mean the *station?* That's what Grandma calls it — the *station!* Huge ice-cream cones! Friendly man! Yes!"

For a minute, I thought maybe Danny should walk the first five miles. Having the station as his goal might prevent him from tiring. But suddenly I came to my senses.

What's the station compared to the bounty of Grandma's kitchen?

ON HIKE DAY, DANNY arrived for breakfast as usual. Before entering the kitchen, he parked his bicycle next to the porch. We'd decided to take his bike because his father had given it a clean bill of health after its mechanical checkup the day before. Danny was wearing his usual doughboy outfit, including untied heavy combat boots. Not the best shoes for hiking five miles.

His new hatchet and hunting knife were hanging from his belt, adding unnecessary weight as well. To top it off he was wearing a canteen that sloshed as he walked, and his war-surplus backpack contained something that looked fairly bulky. Presumably this was his lunch and perhaps some raingear. With all he carried, I was sure that he'd moved up at least one weight class. Joe Louis, beware!

Eager to get under way, we didn't tarry at breakfast. When we finished, I pocketed the map and Dad's compass, scooped up my lunch, and waved goodbye to Mom and Dad. From the back porch, Danny wished them a *fond farewell* and we were off. Rather than make a big deal about Danny's extra load, I decided to hold off until we reached the halfway point. I figured he wouldn't be bothered much until he entered his hiking phase. Meanwhile he would benefit from the mechanical advantage provided by his bicycle.

As we traveled southeast along New Albany Avenue, the bright early morning sun was blinding. We pulled our Tigers' caps down over our eyes and looked at the ground. When traffic permitted, Danny's boundless energy manifested itself in his circling round and round me in dizzying loops. Though I considered suggesting he conserve his energy, I knew better. He just pumped his pedals and whistled like life was a bowl of cherries.

When we reached New Albany about two miles into our trip, Danny suggested we stop for lunch. At this point, it was only nine o'clock in the morning. We had a full three miles to go before we reached the schoolhouse at the halfway point. Naturally I thought he was joking, and I said so. Evidently he was quite serious. When I scoffed at the idea, I think I hurt his feelings because he immediately cranked up his speed. From a distance, I watched him spin around the corner onto Saginaw Road. He was out of sight for several minutes until I reached the corner. When I turned to head north, I spotted him. He had stopped at the old mill dam where he appeared to be feeding a flock of mallard ducks, swarming around his feet.

He looked up and waved. Jumping on his bike, he raced toward me. When we were within shouting range, he informed me that his accidental encounter with the flock of ducks was a sign of good luck. I didn't have the heart to tell him that those mallards were permanent residents of the Chippewa near the dam. So far, the only luck of the day had definitely benefited the ducks. They seldom wheedled a free meal from a passing human this early in the morning.

After we cleared New Albany, my pace settled into a rhythm that caused all my thoughts to vanish. During this time, Danny rode just ahead of me at a very slow pace. For the next two miles, we hardly spoke a word. My mind did come alive as we approached the farm on our right.

Each spring, one or two sap-collecting buckets hung on each of the dozen sugar-maple trees lining the road in front of the farmhouse. My parents and I always made a point of taking this route to Grandma's house in the early spring. Because not much maple syrup or sugar was produced in our part of the country, I felt fortunate to witness that rare operation each year.

After seeing the buckets, I knew the schoolhouse would be visible just over the next hill so I picked up my pace. Danny sensed

my excitement and rode on to the hilltop. He stopped his bicycle
and cupped his hand over his eyes.

"There it is, Jase. It's the school and the station. We're almost
there. Hang on!"

While I didn't feel like running the rest of the way, I was
nowhere near collapse. I wasn't sure why Danny told me to hang
on. Because I needed all my breath to finish my five miles, I kept
that thought to myself.

By the time I entered the schoolyard, I looked up to see Danny
emerging from the outhouse. He walked to the pump and jerked
the handle up and down until a gush of water shot out. He washed
his hands and face.

Shivering, he announced, "Boy! That water's cold!"

I allowed myself to collapse on the bench of the picnic table.
Danny joined me. "Can we eat lunch now, Jase?"

I nodded yes.

"Want some water first?" Without waiting for my answer, he
raised his canteen and took a large gulp. "Boy! That's good. Fresh
and cold."

"Did you get that water from the well?"

"Sure! Why not?" He looked at me incredulously, as if I didn't
know where water came from.

"Did you put any water purification tablets in your canteen
before filling it?"

He answered with a question of his own, "Do you think there's
anything wrong with the water here? It's a school. The teachers and
kids drink it. Don't they?"

I took from his response that he hadn't treated the water. I told
him, "I was planning to ask the man who owns the station — just
to make sure."

"That's a good idea — for you, Jase," he advised.

"Just for me?"

"Yep! I'm safe. Before I came to your house this morning, I
swallowed two water-purification tablets — just to make sure, like
you said."

"But, Danny, that's not how they're supposed to be used.
Besides —." I stopped abruptly. Over his shoulder, I saw a freakish
gust of wind blow open the outhouse door. I decided this was a sign

for me to forget what I was about to tell Danny concerning the side effects of the tablets. I guessed he already knew about them.

"Can we eat lunch now?" he repeated, extending his backpack across the picnic table.

"Sure, Danny. I'm hungry. How about you?"

Mom had really outdone herself. She had packed three big bologna-on-pumpernickel sandwiches, a snow apple, and a wedge of pound cake. Before I finished half my lunch, Danny, as usual, had wolfed down all of his. He seemed restless. I doubted that it had anything to do with getting back on the road right away.

"While I finish, why don't you go over to the station and check out their dessert offerings?"

"That's a great idea!" he said, loping off toward the station. "Want me to get you something?"

"I don't have any money. Besides I'm nearly stuffed. Don't forget to ask the man about the pump water!" I hollered.

He gave me a thumbs-up, opened the door, and popped inside the store.

After finishing my cake, I packed our gear into the bicycle basket and waited for Danny's return. Before long, I heard the door bang open and saw Danny, carrying two bottles of strawberry pop, heading my way. He had a wide grin on his face.

"Hey! I told you I didn't have any money, Danny!"

"That's all right. I've got plenty," he assured me.

This was an unexpected announcement. On Easter Sunday, we had discussed our dangerously low levels of financial solvency and how good it would be to restart our bait business to replenish our funds.

He handed me my pop. "The pump water's fine, but I thought you might like a treat. Wanta candy bar? I gotta few of them too."

"Listen — see! You came into some dough. Tell me where you got it — see!" I did my best imitation of Edward G. Robinson.

"It's rental income."

"What does that mean?"

"Remember how Chub kept asking if he could wear my *New York Medal of Recognition* to school?"

"Sure. You didn't let him — did you?"

"He met my price. I told him I'd rent it to him for one week

— starting today — if he could come up with 25 cents. He said
he'd get it out of his piggy bank. Because he was an FSG member,
I told him I'd trust him. I gave him the medal, and he was
supposed to put the 25 cents in my backpack. When I stopped to
feed the ducks, I found the money."

"But that was only 25 cents. Looks like you spent it all on pop
and candy bars."

"Oh, no. I have a lot left — for emergencies."

"How come?"

"Chub still doesn't get denominations. He thinks a coin's
worth depends on its size. To him dimes are worth less than
pennies. So he gave me 25 dimes instead of pennies."

"You're going to pay him back, aren't you?"

"Sure! Right after I sell my samurai sword."

"What do you mean?"

"Right after I graduate from college."

"Danny!"

"Jase, can't you take a joke?"

"How many *dimes* will it cost me?"

BEFORE WE STARTED ON the last leg of our hike, I suggested
that Danny lessen his load by placing his canteen, hatchet, and
hunting knife in the bicycle basket. Not unexpectedly, he refused,
citing some convoluted logic having to do with Lewis and Clark.
Down the road a mile or two, I figured he was likely to change his
mind. I decided not to push it. But Danny's pure stubbornness was
something I often underestimated.

We soon fell back into our rhythm and its accompanying
silence. I pedaled slowly behind my friend, watching him plod
along with the strings of his combat boots whipping the tarmac
road surface. The sun was shining brightly. By early afternoon, the
temperature had risen to a comfortable level. It was a perfect day for
our hike. As we passed various farms, men and women going about
their business paused to wave at us and shout encouraging words.

After reaching what I reckoned was the seven-mile marker, I
told Danny I could use a drink from his canteen. We paused in the
shade of a giant elm tree for a huge slug of water and, this time, I

accepted one of his candy bars. His spirits and energy level were high. I didn't detect the slightest sign of fatigue in his bearing.

Nonetheless, I asked, "Do you want to rest awhile, Danny?"

"Why? Are you tired?"

In answer, I climbed back on the bicycle and rang the bell in mock impatience. He gave me a smirk, hitched up his belt, and headed off toward our destination.

We were making very good time.

When I realized the next crossroad we would encounter was Barrington Road, I felt exhilarated. I stopped the bike, pulled out the map, and estimated our distance to the Compton farm.

"Danny, I'm pleased to announce that according to the map, we only have about a mile-and-a-half to go!"

His reaction was understated. Without turning around or speaking, he waved his left hand at me and continued plodding along. I fell back into my silent trance and the time passed quickly.

When we were within 50 feet of Barrington Road, I let out a whoop. Startled, Danny turned around to look at me. Suddenly his left foot slipped off the tarmac and twisted unnaturally, throwing Danny to the ground. He sat up quickly. Terror filled his eyes.

"Danny! Are you all right?"

"My ankle — it really hurts," he cried, rubbing the outside of his floppy combat boot.

"I told you to lace up your shoestrings!" I snapped. Immediately I regretted my words. "Sorry, Danny. I shouldn't have —."

"That's fine, Jase. You're right about that. What should we do?"

"Let's take off your boot and have a look."

He loosened his shoestrings further and attempted to pull off the boot. But no luck. A combination of pain and swelling prevented us from assessing the damage. He looked at me again. This time his forlorn expression nearly made me cry.

"We need to get you off the road. Let me help you over to that tree. You can wait there and I'll ride ahead to the farm. Grandma can come and get you in the Terraplane."

He nodded and held up his arms. I helped him to stand upright on his one good leg. With his arm around my shoulder, he shuffled down into the ditch and back up to the base of a huge oak tree. After flopping to the ground, he leaned back against its trunk. He closed his eyes and rested for a second.

"Really hurts. Huh?"

"Jase, it really does. I'm sorry. I wanted to finish the hike."

"Ah, don't worry about that. I'm sure you made at least five miles. Remember Dad told us it was farther than 10 miles to the farm."

"Oh, yeah," he moaned. He tried to smile but the pain prevented it. He wiped his eyes and gritted his teeth. I had never seen him in this condition before. His bravado had all but disappeared and he looked beaten.

"Hey! Chin up! I'll be back in a jiffy. Have a drink of water — or another candy bar while I'm gone. And — and — relax!" I told him, running short of encouraging words.

"Jase, hurry back. Will you?"

"Sure, Danny," I promised as I mounted the bicycle and shoved off.

When I passed the Donaldson farm, I noticed their car parked in front of the house. That was a good sign. I hadn't mentioned to Danny the possibility that Grandma might not be home. And the idea of Danny being hauled to the house behind a team of horses on Grandpa's bouncing stone boat was not an appealing option.

When I crested the slight hill approaching the lane to the woods, I peered ahead to the farm. I was certain I saw Grandma's Terraplane at rest in the garage. A great sense of relief motivated me to pedal even faster.

When I pulled into the driveway, I noticed Grandpa as he opened the cow-barn door and stepped inside. Normally I would have shouted a greeting, but I didn't want to waste time. I skidded to a halt, let the bicycle flop over on the grass, and burst into the house.

"Grandma! Where are you? Danny's hurt! Grandma!"

"Oh, laws! What's happened? Quick! Tell me."

"It's his ankle! Terrible sprain — I think. We couldn't get his boot off to see. He's really in pain."

"Where?"

"Down under the big oak tree by the intersection of Barrington and Riverton Roads."

Without another word, Grandma grabbed her purse and ran to the garage. Come to think of it, I'd never seen her run before.

We hopped into the Terraplane and within seconds were streaking south toward the patient. As we approached the intersection, I saw the big oak. But I couldn't see Danny because, when I'd left him, he was sitting on the far side of the tree.

"That's the tree, Grandma!" I exclaimed, pointing ahead.

"Okay! Hold on tight," she warned as she stomped down on the gas pedal.

She skidded around the corner and slammed on her brakes. The car stalled with a *chug*. A mammoth cloud of dust that had followed us from Barrington Road engulfed the Terraplane. I looked out through the haze for Danny but I couldn't see him.

When the dust finally settled, I looked again. And again. "Grandma! He's gone!"

Grandma leaped out of the car and began to shout. "Danny! Where are you? Danny!"

I joined her chorus of shouts with a chorus of my own. After a minute or two, futility overtook us and we stopped. For an instant, I thought maybe Grandma wouldn't believe me. I left the road, crossed down into the ditch, and up to the oak tree. There I saw the proof I needed.

"Look, Grandma!" Picking up the evidence, I showed it to her. "A candy bar wrapper! This was definitely the tree."

Grandma put her hands on her hips and scowled. She shook her head. She was stumped and so was I.

Suddenly she announced, "I know where he is. One of the neighbors must have picked him up and taken him home! Quick, Jase. Get in the car."

Before my door was closed, Grandma had started the car with a roar. She popped the clutch and turned the steering wheel hard to port. We spun out onto Riverton Road and laid rubber for 50 yards as she tore toward the neighbor closest to the oak tree. After we skidded to a stop in front of Mr. Hagan's lumberyard office, I saw the two friendly German POWs who worked there. When we got out, Mr. Hagan stuck his head out of his door.

"What's up, folks?"

Grandma quickly explained the situation. Mr. Hagan shrugged his shoulders and confessed he had not seen hide nor hair of Danny. He suggested we check at the Donaldson farm. Grandma thanked him brusquely and returned to the car.

We launched the Terraplane into the air, and we flew at the speed of sound back up Barrington Road. We landed just as Mr. and Mrs. Donaldson stepped off the porch. They stopped in their tracks and waited for the dust to settle.

"Hello, Jane! Where's the fire?"

"It's Danny! He's lost. Have you seen him?"

"No. Afraid not. We were just heading to town. We'll keep an eye out for him."

"Thanks, I'll check the other neighbors. Bye now."

Over the course of the next half-hour, Grandma and I paid calls on the Henrys, the Blakes, the Raus, and several others whose names I didn't know. She even hailed Audrey Kirby, the RFD mailman, to see if he had any information about the "missing lad" as he called Danny. Mr. Kirby said no, but he'd pass along the word to all the households on his route.

After a dozen more stops, Grandma ran out of ideas, at least any good ones. Judging from the fear in her eyes, she was entertaining the same terrible thoughts that had entered my head. In short, I was beginning to suspect foul play.

Grandma pulled the car to the side of the road and looked at me frantically. She didn't say anything but I could tell she was getting desperate. Finally she admitted, "This is not a good situation, Jase. We need help."

"What're we going to do, Grandma?"

She answered by tromping on the gas and streaking back to the Henrys. She slammed on the brakes and hopped out of the car. Within seconds, she had placed a call to Sheriff Connors. She thanked Mrs. Henry for the use of her telephone.

When she returned to the car, she reported, "Sheriff Connors will meet us at the house. He wants you to tell him everything that happened before he takes action."

While we drove back to the Compton farm, I wondered how many times the sheriff had come to our rescue since I'd known Danny. I also wondered how long we could expect the sheriff's winning streak to last.

When we pulled into the driveway, I had one thought and one thought only. "I hope he's all right, Grandma."

"Me too, Jase. Me too."

WHEN SHERIFF CONNORS ARRIVED, we assembled on the screened-in porch. First, I told him about our hike and why I'd left Danny at the oak tree. Next Grandma inventoried all the steps she and I had taken before calling him. He knew us sufficiently well to know that this was not a frivolous case. During the preceding year, he had been involved with dangerous situations involving Danny and me on at least a half-dozen occasions.

Grandpa also sat in on the briefings. Up to that point in time, he was unaware of Danny's disappearance or our attempts to locate him. When the sheriff left to use his car radio to launch a formal search, Grandpa confessed, "I must say, I don't know how you two boys have managed to cause so much commotion in such a short period of time."

When he returned, the sheriff informed us, "I've assigned three cars — plus my own — to canvas every farm in this part of the county. We've laid out the search pattern in ever-expanding circles from that oak tree. If we don't find Danny or a clue of his whereabouts within an hour or so, I'll have to involve the Michigan State Police. Oh! One more thing. I had the dispatcher call the Tuckers — and they'll notify the Addisons. I thought they'd feel more comfortable here. So I took the liberty of inviting them out — if that's all right with you folks."

"You read my mind, Sheriff. I'll put some things together for an impromptu supper. You and your men are welcome to join us," Grandma told him. "I'll start by putting on a big pot of coffee."

An hour later, Danny's parents and mine arrived at the farm. Grandma and I repeated everything we had told the sheriff. Of course, Danny's folks were very concerned, but by no means panicky, since they had been through similar Danny-occurrences before.

While Mom and Mrs. Tucker busied themselves in the kitchen with Grandma, we menfolk sat on the porch and talked about fishing, just to take our minds off the troublesome situation. As time wore on, we grew weary of even that topic. As darkness fell, we fell silent.

I sensed an increase in the level of tension in the house. Grandma must have sensed it too. She came to the porch door and announced, "Soup's on, boys. Come on in and fix yourselves a plate while we wait for news from the sheriff. Dad, come on now!"

Everyone went through the motions of having supper, but I noticed no one had a very big appetite. I picked at my food and finally put my plate back in the warming oven. "Sorry, Grandma. I'm just not hungry. Maybe later. Would that be all right?"

"That's fine, Jase. We'll hear something soon. I know we will."

Another hour went by and still no news. We were all becoming antsy.

"John, do you think we should go over to the Henrys and call the sheriff?"

"No. I think he'll let us know the minute he hears something, Marie. Let's just wait here and try to be patient."

I knew Dad was right, but I wished *somebody* would do *something*.

"Look! Here comes a car!" Grandpa pointed to the headlights, coming our way from the south. "I'll bet it's the sheriff."

Grandpa was right. The sheriff pulled into the driveway. By this time, Grandma had turned on the yard light. All of us were out on the porch to see if the sheriff had found Danny. But the sheriff emerged from his car alone and walked toward the house. I could tell by his body language that his news was not good.

When he reached the porch, trying to be cheerful, he smiled and greeted everyone. We all followed him into the kitchen where he finally broke the news. "Folks, we've canvassed every house within 10 miles of that oak tree. No one knows a cussed thing about Danny or his whereabouts. I just stopped by to see if — by chance — you'd heard anything before I call the state police in on this."

"Not a thing, Sheriff. We're as mystified as you are."

"All right then. I'll call Lansing and have them put out a state-wide bulletin. I sure am sorry I don't have better news for you."

Like everyone else in the kitchen, I was completely focused on the sheriff's every word. However, something in the back of my mind caused me to look away and listen. I heard a faint, but familiar, sound coming from the driveway. It was the *clop-clop-clop* of a single horse and the *squeak-squeak-squeak* of wagon wheels.

I ran to the porch and looked out. There it was!

Under the glow of the yard light, a colorfully painted Gypsy wagon, pulled by a magnificent black and white horse, came to a stop. Perched atop the wagon was a beautiful young Gypsy woman and, sitting next to her on the driver's seat, was the missing Boy Scout.

"Danny! Grandma, it's Danny — and Gisella!" I yelled at the top of my lungs.

Within seconds, we all rushed out to the driveway to welcome our lost sheep. Naturally we were relieved to see him safe and sound, but I bet I wasn't the only one who felt a bit irritated because of the worry and concern he'd caused us. Not to mention the cost and bother of the sheriff's four-car search of the countryside.

Danny seemed oblivious to our concerns. Knowing him, the rapt attention of an attractive young Gypsy lady did nothing but improve his disposition. Gisella helped Danny down from his perch and held his hand as he limped to the house. She came in with him, I suppose, to explain the circumstances under which she was delivering my friend to Grandma's house well after dark.

"Gisella, where's Jenci? Is he all right?"

"Jenci iss just fine, but he iss asleep so Lorant stay with hem. They're back at our new campsite — in your woods. I hope that iss all right."

"Of course it is! Where on earth did you meet up with our Danny?" Grandma asked, wrapping her arms around him.

"We come up Barrington Road when we see Dahny sitting under oak tree. He look very sad. We stop to ask if we help hem. He tell us he iss hiking to your house and sprain hes ankle. Lorant look at it and tell Dahny to lace up hes boots — very tight. Then he walk with not so much pains. He try to walk and iss very happy that no hurt so much."

"But that was hours ago. Where have you been since?"

"We offer to bring hem here, but he iss in no hurry. He say Jase go ahead to keep you company until he arrive. But he iss really hungry and give me sad look again. I feel so sorry for hem that I ask hem to have a leettle something to eat before we bring hem here. He seem very excited."

Grandma and I looked at each other. "I'm beginning to understand, Gisella."

"When we get there, he tell us that hes hike iss for Boy Scouts and he must cook meal. We tell hem we going to have chicken. He offer cook for us. But before that, he say he build our campfire —

for Boy Scouts. He iss most insistent. So — I suppose — we give in."

"Don't worry about a thing, Gisella. I'm happy you're camped nearby. I'll come over and see you tomorrow. Now why don't you go on home to your son and husband? And thank you for taking such good care of little Danny here," Grandma told her, squeezing Danny again. A good bit harder than the first time, I thought.

We all thanked Gisella and gave our best to Lorant and Jenci.

The sheriff announced he was heading back to his office to fill out paperwork associated with a certain *missing-person* case. I could tell he wasn't any too happy. Uncharacteristically he even left without saying goodbye.

After their departures, we returned to the kitchen where Danny was surveying Grandma's table for his next snack. His mother walked over to him, took him by the arm, and sat him down on a kitchen chair. Hard! She was not happy.

Before she could say something she would regret, I thought I would give it a shot. "Danny, have you any idea how worried we were about you? And how much time and effort the sheriff spent to find you? Sometimes I just don't understand you!"

When I finished, I realized that everyone in the kitchen was staring at Danny, waiting for his response.

When it came, it wasn't something any of us expected.

"Hey, Jase. I'm a Second Class now. I used my new hatchet to prepare firewood and started Gisella's campfire with just *one* match. I cooked a meal with poultry and one raw vegetable. Now I've completed all my requirements. As soon as you cook your meal, you'll be finished too."

There wasn't a closed mouth in the room.

I don't know what possessed me, but I just had to ask, "What raw vegetable did you cook, Danny?"

"It's a Gypsy vegetable — called a *dumpling*."

12 CANS FOR TENTS

ALL DAY SUNDAY, DANNY WAS MYSTERIOUSLY ABSENT from our midst. After his *Gypsy Holiday*, as Dad called it, he had been sentenced to a 24-hour lockup in Mrs. Tucker's cellblock. Not being a signatory to the Geneva Convention, she did not comply with rules barring cruel and unusual punishment. For her errant son, her brand of torture took the form of a total immersion course on etiquette.

Shortly after his parole on Monday morning, we were the beneficiaries of her student's learning. We were seated around the breakfast table, when Danny tapped lightly at the kitchen door. Mom got up and let him in. He refused to make eye contact, but she pretended not to notice.

"Good morning, Mr. and Mrs. Addison. Hello, Jase. I've come to give you this." He handed Mom and me each a sealed envelope. "Inside, you'll find my written apology for acting irresponsibly on Saturday. I'm truly sorry if I caused you to be concerned about me. I had no good reason for acting the way I did. And I promise it'll never happen again."

"Thank you, Danny," Mom replied. "We were all *very* concerned because we care *very* much about you. I think I speak for all us when I say your apology is accepted and you're totally forgiven. It takes a lot of courage to own up to your responsibility."

Immediately Dad and I echoed Mom's sentiments.

"Won't you sit down and have some breakfast with us, Danny?"

"That would be very nice, Mrs. Addison, but I'm not quite finished with what I have to say."

"Oh, I'm sorry. Please continue."

"Yesterday I mailed a letter of apology to Grandpa and Grandma Compton. And when you go out there next or when they come here, I'd like to make a personal apology to them too."

"That would be very nice, Danny. It's too bad they don't have a telephone or you could call them on the phone in your father's garage."

"I'm not allowed to use that telephone anymore."

I didn't think he ever used his father's phone. I guessed his mother made it a condition of his parole, just in case he was tempted to use it in the future.

"We'll certainly let you know about any opportunity for you to see them."

"Jase, I've something more to say to you. After school today, I'm taking the bus to deliver a letter to Sheriff Connors too. I hope he's there. But, if not, I'm supposed to wait until he comes in, even if it takes all night. I may be late for scouts."

Boy, this was serious! Mrs. Tucker wasn't fooling around.

"And one last thing, Jase. I'd like to go with you to Trumble Park on Wednesday night to complete my cooking requirement for Second Class with Freddie. I didn't really do it right with — on Saturday. Dumplings aren't raw vegetables. They're — ah — my mother told me, but I forget."

He looked at Mom. "Mrs. Addison, are *dumplings* mushrooms? Or what?"

Without waiting for her answer, he looked at me. "Is Wednesday all right with you, Jase?"

"Sure, that'll be fine. You should do pretty well. Look at all the practice you got with Gisella!"

"Jase!" I suddenly remembered that Mom wasn't a signatory either.

"Sorry, just kidding," I claimed, hoping that would let me off the hook.

Mercifully Dad changed the subject. "I should tell you boys about the committee meeting on Saturday morning. We discussed the type of tents the troop would need for the Camporee. Then we appointed two of our members to work with Scoutmaster Mel and Freddie Holland to make the final decision. For your information, it boils down to a pair of choices — either pup tents or explorer tents."

"What's an explorer tent, John?" Mom asked as she set a heaping plate of scrambled eggs and bacon at Danny's place. After giving her a wide grin, he slipped quietly into his chair and picked up his fork.

"They're larger than a pup tent. Room enough for four people. To give them that extra room, they have sidewalls. In fact, in the scout handbook, they're called *wall* tents."

"Do we have to buy all one kind, Dad?"

"Boy, Jase. That's a very good question. Exactly the same one Freddie had. According to him, sometimes scouts want to carry their tents on their backs when they go trail camping. You can't easily carry an explorer tent, but you can carry a pup tent. That's why Freddie's involved — to help the committee make the best decision."

"But that's not the big news!" Dad reported, almost smugly. "The committee accepted my idea for raising funds to purchase the tents. I suggested we sell those handy four-ounce cans of household oil. You know, Jase. Like those I give to my sewing-machine customers. We just provide you boys with maps, and you go door-to-door through every neighborhood in town. Whoever sells the most gets a prize. What do you think?"

"Will people want to buy oil, Dad?"

"What home can't use a can of household oil? Besides they'll only cost the customer 20 cents. Who could say no to a boy in a scout uniform, trying to sell them something they can use — and for only 20 cents?"

The more Dad talked, the more I liked the idea.

"That's not the best part. I think I can buy these at about nine cents a can from Harry Roberts, the Standard Oil distributor. That's where I buy those I give to my customers. The question is will he have enough in stock or be able to order enough to supply as much as we'll need?"

"How much is that, Dad?"

"If we hit every house in town, we'll need — hundreds of cans! Do you know how many houses there are in Riverton?"

I'd never given it a thought.

"Just over four thousand, Mr. A," Danny answered, licking the last bit of egg from his fork. "But don't forget — if we do a good job of selling — some households will buy more than one. Maybe we sell one for the garage. One for the basement. One for the kitchen. One for the sewing room. Need I say more?"

"I'm sold, Danny. I'll take four cans," Mom quipped, passing him an imaginary dollar. "Keep the change!"

"I plan to stop by and talk to Harry after work this afternoon. Want to go with me, Jase? Danny, you'll be busy. Right?"

"Yes, I'll be at the county jail."

"Probably better than the Tucker jail. Right, Danny?" I teased.

Danny shot me a dirty look. At that, everybody laughed.

DANNY WAS DEFINITELY NOT himself at school on Monday. He hardly spoke a word. And, when he did, his voice was soft and polite. During recess, he chose to stay at his desk instead of joining JB, Butch Matlock, and me outside for a game of catch. His unusual behavior was disquieting to everyone, especially Miss Sparks, who seemed unsure of herself in dealing with this new Danny.

Exposure to this remorseful version of my friend at breakfast had given me an advantage. Before arriving at school, I'd decided to allow him to do his penance without my input for however long and in whatever form it took. In the end, I knew we would all be better off. That way, the Danny we all knew and loved would return even sooner.

At recess, JB wondered, "What's up with Danny? Is he sick or something?"

"Yeah, why's he acting so strange?" Butch added.

They caught me off guard. I hesitated to tell them the whole story because some of it wasn't particularly complimentary to Danny. On the other hand, they were his friends and they cared about him too.

Finally I settled for a truncated version of the truth. "This past Saturday, on our scout hike to my grandparents' farm, Danny went off with some Gypsies without telling us where he was. When we couldn't find him, we were very worried so we called the sheriff to help. Even though Danny came back on his own, he got in trouble with his folks. He's apologized to everyone, but he still feels terrible about it."

I hadn't realized that Butch's younger sister, Judie Matlock, was standing right behind me, listening to my explanation. Before JB and Butch could react, Judie sighed, "Oh, I hope Danny's all right."

Turning around, I suggested, "I'm sure he will be, Judie. But I bet you could help. Why don't you go inside and say *Hi* to him?"

"Do you think that would be all right, Jase?"

Knowing how fond Danny was of Judie, I assured her, "Coming from you, it'd be more than all right. He'd love it."

That's all the encouragement Judie needed. She ran for the door and disappeared inside. Like a true FSG member, Butch shook his head and summed up the situation in one word, "Girls!"

We all laughed and continued our game.

When school ended, we walked out together. According to plan, Dad was waiting for me in the parking lot. When we approached his car, he rolled down the window and asked, "Danny, would you like a ride to the bus stop?"

"No thanks, Mr. Addison. That would take you out of your way. I'll just walk there with Butch and JB. Thank you for offering."

Once we were under way, Dad observed, "I see Danny's still contrite and polite. I kinda miss the old Danny. How about you?"

"Don't worry, Dad. He'll be back." While I didn't know it until later, I should have said, "— back with a vengeance."

The office of Harry Roberts, the general manager of Standard Oil's Riverton distribution facility, was located in a combined warehouse, garage, and office building in the southwestern part of town. Dad and Harry had been friends since grade school. Because of the fascinating array of huge oil and gas tanks, complicated pumps and gauges, drums and cases of oil, and mammoth oil-delivery trucks in the fenced-in main yard, I always liked going there with Dad to observe the operation. In addition, Mr. Roberts was a friendly fellow, who obviously enjoyed our visits.

"Hello, John. Nice seeing you too, Jase. I've been following your escapades with Danny in the *Daily Press*. I must say — I'm very proud of you. Now, what can I do for you fellows?"

Dad explained his idea for selling cans of household oil door-to-door to raise funds for Troop 46's new tents. Mr. Roberts immediately expressed his approval of Dad's idea and pledged to help us anyway he could.

"How many cases of four-ounce cans are we talking about, John?"

"It's really hard to be sure, but I'd say somewhere between 50 and 100."

Mr. Roberts' response was a long, low whistle. Then he informed us, "Before the war, that would have been an easy order to fill, but with oil and gas rationing — and the shortages —. Boy, I'd have to do some hunting. Right now I don't have anywhere near that much on hand. But one thing's for sure. Whatever I can find, the price won't change because of OPA's price controls — you know — the Office of Price Administration. The company is a real stickler on that point. Shortages or not, what I find for you will still be priced at nine cents a unit."

"How much can you sell me now, Harry?"

Reaching for his bulging black three-ring binder, he replied, "I can tell you in a minute. Let's see. According to this, I have 19 cases in the warehouse. And after a day or so of calling around, I might be able to find 19 more. But that's not close to what you need. I'd hate for you to get the scouts all excited about this idea and then run out of product for them to sell."

This was perplexing. Dad made a quick calculation in his head. He was always good at that. "If we only ended up with 38 cases — and I understand that's not even a sure thing — we'd come up way short of what's needed to put 30 boys in tents by the Camporee. I'm afraid to commit to that course of action. I hope you understand, Harry. Looks like we'll just have to find another way to raise funds."

"Mebbe so, John. But before you pull the plug on your dandy idea, let me put a call into our area manager to see if there's any way of finding you enough to make it worth your while. Meantime, you might consider —. No. Better not."

"Did you have another idea, Harry?"

"Not another idea, but possibly another source. But I'm torn. They're a competitor — but that's not it. How do I say this? John, you're a friend. From some things I've heard through the grapevine

— rumor mostly — I don't know if I should recommend this place to you or not."

My curiosity was really peaking at this point.

"Come on, Harry. What're you trying to tell me?"

"John, you remember down in Detroit last year — when they found that wrongdoing on the part of distributors — like me — and gas station owners too?"

"Oh, sure! I read all about it in the paper. Was that the case where distributors and stations were caught selling black-market gas — some of it stolen?"

"Exactly! And counterfeiting and stealing windshield stickers. Keeping fraudulent books. Selling gasoline over the OPA price ceilings — by extortion in some cases. Members of organized crime — and all those businessmen were arrested."

"Now, what's that got to do with oil for Troop 46?"

"You remember old Hank Jefferson? Used to own Riverton Auto Center — and the Ajax Oil and Gas distributorship. Out New Albany Avenue, just past the lumberyard."

"Sure, I go by it every day on my way to work. But I've never done business there. Except for the times we used to ride our bikes out that way and stop for a drink of pop from their cooler. But did you say Hank *used to own* that business? Who owns it now?"

"A fellow named Joe Rajak bought Hank out last year."

"Don't think I know him. Is he from around here, Harry?"

"Nope. Came up from Detroit," Mr. Roberts informed us, raising an eyebrow.

"Harry, you're not implying —."

"John, that's why I hesitated to get into this. One thing you have to understand. Those of us in the oil and gas distribution business all know each other. Yes, we're competitors, but we're also friends who've known and trusted each other for years. It's a close-knit fraternity that doesn't instantly welcome outsiders. Rajak is an outsider who came to town with a bucket of cash and bought his way into our club. And he came here from Detroit just about the time things heated up down there. As you can imagine, rumors started flying about Rajak and the source of his money. Normally I stay clear of gossip, but people I trust have told me some things."

"I understand completely, Harry. But, again, what's this got to do with oil for Troop 46?"

"From what I hear, Joe Rajak can likely provide you with as many cases of oil as you need. And it's possible that we can't."

"But is he on the up-and-up?"

"I honestly don't know. But I felt an obligation to suggest you at least go talk to the man and see for yourself."

"You're right. It never hurts to talk. Maybe we'll run out there and see what he has to say. But I'd hate to do business with him instead of you — even if he's as pure as the newly driven snow."

"I'm not going down without a fight, John. I'll get on the wire and see what I can find. On your way back, I suggest you swing by here. Hopefully I'll have some good news for the scouts by then."

What Mr. Roberts had told us was spinning in my head. Black-market gas. Counterfeit stickers. Organized crime. Extortion.

"Dad, do you think Mr. Rajak is a black marketeer?"

"That's a pretty serious charge to make with no evidence. I'd prefer to think he's an outsider — like Harry said — who's most probably an innocent victim of some nasty rumors. Let's give the man the benefit of the doubt. If he's fair and reasonable and can supply our oil, it'll benefit the troop. And that's what this is all about."

WE PULLED INTO THE parking lot of Riverton Auto Center, a fancy name for an Ajax Gas Station. Off to one side of the station, we saw a small office building behind which stood the usual assortment of tanks, pumps, and gages associated with the oil and gas distribution business.

After parking the car, we entered the office where we found a husky, bald man smoking a cigar. He wore a white dress shirt and a loud floral tie, black trousers with black suspenders, but no suit coat. The other person was a bleached-blond lady in a very tight blue dress. She chewed her gum as rapidly as she typed. I assumed he was Mr. Rajak and she was his secretary.

"Hello, my name's John Addison. Are you Mr. Rajak?"

"Pleased ta meetcha. What can I do for yah?" the man demanded, without confirming his name or offering to shake hands.

"I understand you bought out Hank Jefferson. When I was a boy —."

"Listen, bub. Don't mean to be impolite, but I gotta company to run here. See?"

"Right! I'll get down to business. I'm a member of the men's committee for Boy Scout Troop 46. We're raising funds to purchase new tents for —."

"Didn't yah see the sign at the door? It says *No Solicitors!* Beat it."

"Joey! Mind your manners," the blond lady scolded.

"You tend to your typing. Or I'll —!"

"Ooooo! I'm quivering in my boots," she whimpered insincerely. Ripping the sheet of paper out of her typewriter, under her voice she added, "Jerk!"

Turning his attentions back to Dad, Mr. *Jerk* snarled, "Are you still here?"

"Mr. Rajak, I'm here to talk to you about buying cases of household oil," Dad explained, seeking to be understood by a man whom I had already begun to despise.

"Why didn't yah say so in the first place? Whatya need?"

"Fifty to 100 cases of four-ounce cans of household oil," Dad blurted out.

"I can get that for yah. When do yah need 'em?"

"First of all, how much are we talking about per unit? Please keep in mind this is for a Boy Scout troop."

"Yeah, yeah! Heard yah the first time," Rajak grumbled. "Let me check." He perused a ledger book that lay wide-open on his desk. "That would be 15 cents a unit. $3.60 a case. Getcha all yah want of household oil at that price."

"I was under the impression that the OPA ceiling on four-ounce cans of household oil was nine cents a unit."

"We have a special *exemption*. See? Yah want the oil or not?"

"What brand is it?"

"Ajax, naturally."

"I was looking for a brand like Standard Oil. A name house-wives might recognize."

"I can get Standard for yah. Little higher price though. When do yah need 'em?"

"Let me get back to you on that, Mr. Rajak," Dad told him, pushing me out the door.

As we drove back to Harry Roberts' office, it was easy to see that Dad was furious. I was too but I thought it best not to say anything. We pulled in and Dad turned off the engine. He just sat there thinking. Finally he put his hand on my arm and instructed, "Jase. You can forget what I said about *innocent victims.*"

That's all he had to say.

"Let's see if Harry did any good."

When we opened the door, Mr. Roberts was all grins. "John, you're not going to believe this, but I got you 100 cases of four-ounce cans of Finol, our best grade of household oil. When I called my area manager and told him about your fund-raiser for the scouts, he waved a wand and came up with all you need — and maybe more. And here's the best news. Standard Oil would like to donate this oil to your troop — at no charge. I'll have it here in two days."

We were ecstatic. The swing of emotion, between the Rajak visit and Mr. Roberts' fantastic news, had been dramatic indeed. Dad could hardly talk.

"Why was your area manager so eager to help — and so generous?"

"First of all, he loved the idea of selling household oil door-to-door for a troop fund-raiser. Apparently he's on the committee of his son's troop. They're about to replace their camping equipment too. He felt your idea would be extremely helpful to them. But more importantly, he's committed to scouting. He himself was an Eagle Scout and his son is about to pass the last requirement to become a Second Class. Tonight the boy is cooking supper for the family on a campfire in their backyard."

"Hope they like dumplings," I said.

Mr. Roberts gave us a funny look. But neither of us could stop laughing.

SUSPECTING WE MIGHT BE running late, Mom had prepared a platter of cold cuts and some potato salad for us before setting off to teach her class at the POW camp. Dad and I just had time for a quick sandwich before hopping back into the car.

When we arrived at the First Methodist Church, the parking lot was nearly full. I thought perhaps there was a meeting of the church board or some other related group. But when we reached the basement where our meeting was held, I realized the cars belonged to the troop committee members who were all present that evening.

After the opening ceremony, Scoutmaster Mel had Freddie report the decision regarding the purchase of tents. Freddie explained the troop would purchase enough explorer tents to sleep roughly half of the troop and enough pup tents to sleep the other half. The *troop* included 30 scouts and up to six adults camping with them. Thus we would purchase five explorer tents and eight pup tents plus some additional cooking gear and lanterns to light our campsite. The entire budget amounted to exactly $250.

Next Dad announced Standard Oil's donation of up to 2,400 cans of oil. After the applause, he pointed out that we now could afford to lower our price from 20 cents a can to 15 cents a can. This price would be a full dime under the retail price downtown. And it would still generate revenues of up to $360.

He suggested we use the extra dollars to give cash prizes to the top sellers. A $12 prize for first place, $8 for second, and $4 for third. With the money leftover, he recommended the creation of a Camp Moon Lake *scholarship fund* to subsidize the camp fees for deserving scouts.

Scoutmaster Mel addressed the committee members. "Are there any objections to accepting Mr. Addison's plan as presented?"

There were no objections.

Then Dad suggested we divide Riverton into four quadrants defined by Main Street running east and west and Addison Street running north and south.

"I suggest each of the four patrols be assigned to a quadrant. Because a couple of quadrants might be considered more desirable than the others, let's make these assignments by drawing lots.

"Finally I suggest we assign each committeeman to a quadrant. They would be provided a certain number of cases of oil for which they would maintain an accounting. Each boy would acquire his oil from someone assigned to his quadrant. If this plan is acceptable, the oil is due to arrive at the Standard Oil office in two days. I suggest we all meet down here after work on Wednesday to divvy up the supply."

Addressing the committee members again, Scoutmaster Mel asked, "Are there any objections to accepting Mr. Addison's plan for assigning sales territories and distributing oil as presented?"

Again there were no objections.

I was very proud of Dad. He had secured our oil, calculated the finances to set the price, and created a sales and distribution plan to achieve our goals. Yep, I was very proud of him indeed.

After the meeting adjourned, we were walking from the church to the car when we heard a siren coming down New Albany Avenue toward the church. We were curious to see where the patrol car was headed. When it pulled into the church parking lot, we were amazed. I recognized it as Sheriff Connors' car.

"Thank you, Sheriff. And please thank Mrs. Connors again for supper. It was delicious. I really appreciate the ride too. Good night!" Danny effused as he got out of the car. Turning toward us, he shouted, "Am I too late for the meeting? I have some ideas on how to assign the sales territories."

He's back!

13 BLACK MARKET REVENGE

DANNY'S DRAMATIC LAST-MINUTE ARRIVAL AT OUR scout meeting the night before once again demonstrated the power of his charming personality. With the addition of politeness and humility to his already formidable weapon of persuasion, Danny even managed to win back the affections of Sheriff Connors.

For the record, Danny had also charmed Dad back into his fan club by endorsing every aspect of his fund-raising plans for Troop 46. Danny was so effusive about the plans' probability of success that he personally guaranteed he'd sell more cans than any other boy in the troop, thereby ensuring the sale of all 2,400 cans. Despite his puffery, I believed he'd achieve exactly what he promised.

When I entered the kitchen the next morning, Danny was practicing his Standard Finol sales pitch on Mom. Despite herself, she seemed totally captivated by his message.

When he saw me, he abruptly cut short his sales presentation and went straight to the closer, "So how many cans will it be, Mrs. A? Three or four?"

"Well, Danny. I'm sold. Make it four, please," Mom responded, also succumbing to his charms.

"Now, just a minute here! You can't come into my kitchen and sell my mother before I have a chance. This isn't even your territory," I asserted, grasping at straws.

"Jase, don't forget. *First to reach the border always gets the order.*
"The quickest fellers are the finest sellers.
"Sales diminish for those who don't finish.
"Opportunity knocks so pull up your socks.
"Be there in advance or you don't stand a chance.
"A man with a fish is —."
"Danny! Knock it off!"
"Those who eat liver, always deliver," he solemnly pronounced in conclusion.

During this exchange, Dad sipped his coffee and read his paper apparently unaware of Danny's performance. It wasn't until Danny began listing the *Features* and *Benefits* of Standard Finol that Dad decided to leave early for work.

A few minutes after he said goodbye, we heard him again on the back porch. When he entered the kitchen, he was holding a small square of paper in each hand. I couldn't imagine what they were.

"John! You're back. What is it?"

"That's what I'd like to know. Someone stuck these under my windshield wipers. They look like the real thing too."

He placed the two pieces of paper on the table. Each displayed a red square containing a white block letter "C." Since the beginning of gasoline rationing more than two years earlier, every American was familiar with these stickers. One or another of their kind was affixed to the windshield of every car in the country. The vast majority of cars displayed either "A" or "B" stickers, far less desirable than the coveted red "C" stickers.

"Who on earth would put these on your windshield? Is this a practical joke? Or is someone trying to get you in trouble with the authorities?" Mom hypothesized.

"I have no idea, Marie. But I can't be late for my morning production meeting. If you wouldn't mind, I'll turn this over to you to track down. I'd start with Jeff Tolna," Dad suggested. Looking at the kitchen clock, he added, "He may still be home. Boys, why don't you run down and see if he can stop by on his way to work?"

Following Dad's instructions, we raced down the street toward the Tolna house. We noted immediately that his patrol car was not in the driveway, but we knocked on the door anyway, just to be sure. No one answered.

"Sometimes he drops Mrs. Tolna off at her job at Madison's, but Sherm should be home. Where do you suppose he is?"

"Gosh, Jase. I'm sure he's with Chub."

"How'd you know that?"

"Lately Chub's been leaving the house real early. When we ask where he's going, he says to meet *a friend.*"

"Who could that be?"

"He only has *one* friend, Jase."

Danny was right. Chub and Sherm had been inseparable lately, claiming their FSG membership made them *blood buddies* or words to that effect.

"We better go back and tell Mom that Sergeant Tolna isn't home."

When we crossed Forrest Street, I noticed Louise Libby's car parked in her driveway as usual. Suddenly I stopped and looked again. There were red squares stuck under her windshield wipers. We walked to her car and, sure enough, another pair of "C" stickers.

"Danny, let's check Mr. Reilly's car."

We found another pair of red stickers. A check of the Shurtleif car revealed the same.

Something very strange was happening here.

We walked to the Tucker garage. In the lot, there were five cars waiting for repairs. All five had red "C" stickers under their wipers. After crossing New Albany Avenue, we passed by two more cars, both sporting a pair of "C" stickers.

Stopping in front of Pete's store, we waited for traffic to clear. A bus stopped across the street at the Mission Church. Another pair of red "C" stickers was stuck under the bus' giant windshield wipers.

As we crossed the street, Mr. Smalley, our favorite bus driver, stepped out of the bus and removed them. "Well, I'll be. Who on earth would tuck these under my wipers?" He looked up and saw us. "What do you make of these, Jase?"

"We just walked around our neighborhood. Every car we saw had them. Did all the buses at the bus garage have them this morning?"

"I don't remember seeing any but these, and I only noticed them in the last block or so. I stopped a distance back to check the pressure in my left rear tire. Right in front of your house, Danny. I had to wait there for the maintenance truck to come and give me a shot of air. It's possible someone put them under my wipers while I was standing behind the bus."

"Probably at the same time they put the stickers on the cars in the Tucker parking area," I speculated.

We told Mr. Smalley we were planning to report Dad's red stickers to Sergeant Tolna. Mr. Smalley looked at his watch. "Could you boys take these pieces of evidence as well? I don't want any trouble with the police or OPA. Right now, I'm really running late."

While we were walking toward home, Mr. Reilly pulled up beside us. "Morning, boys! What you got there?"

After we quickly told him our story, he handed us his pair of "C" stickers and also requested that we take custody of them. He thanked us and drove off to work.

"Maybe we should have collected them all, Jase."

"Why don't we? You go back to your dad's garage, by way of New Albany Avenue and then down Chester Street. I'll cover Forrest down to the end. Meet you back at my house in a few minutes."

We ran our routes and returned to the house out of breath. We spread out our collection on the kitchen table. Mom gasped, "My gosh! How many are there?"

We quickly counted them. Forty-four red "C" stickers covered the table.

"This is serious business. I'm going across the street to the Shurtleifs to call the police. I know you boys might be late for school, but I'm sure Jeff will want to talk to you. So please wait here."

We followed Mom as far as the front steps and sat down to wait. As we silently stared at the Shurtleif house, something caught my eye. I walked over to the Shurtleif car and pulled another two red stickers from under the windshield wipers.

When I returned, Danny had a question. "Didn't you tell me you got all the cars on Forrest Street?"

"I did. Somebody must have planted another pair when I was at the other end of the street."

We looked at each other and shook our heads. Suddenly Mom emerged from the Shurtleif front door and walked back across the street.

"Sergeant Tolna is on his way. He's stopping to pick up Harry Chambers. Wants you boys to wait until they get here."

"Why's Mr. Chambers coming, Mom?"

"In addition to his regular law practice, he's been appointed as the head of enforcement for OPA in this area of the state. He prosecutes black-market and rationing-abuse cases. Jeff told me he's very interested in what you've found. Apparently these stickers are worth hundreds of dollars apiece on the black market. We have a fortune on our kitchen table."

Hundreds of dollars apiece!

I handed Mom the new additions. I told her these had to have been placed on the Shurtleif car within the past 30 minutes.

"This is getting more and more interesting!" Mom declared.

In the deep voice of a radio mystery-show announcer, Danny boomed, "And now for the thrilling conclusion of *The Case of the Red-Sticker Robin Hood.*"

SERGEANT TOLNA AND MR. Chambers were astounded when they saw our collection of "C" stickers. After close examination, Mr. Chambers picked up one of them. "This is what I was looking for."

"What's that, Harry?"

"Jeff, see the plate number printed on the edge of this one? Like currency and postage stamps, these stickers are printed at the Bureau of Engraving and Printing in Washington. On each sheet of 25 stickers, BEP imprints a unique plate number — same as on postage stamps. After the sheets are printed, they're cut into individual stickers and packed in cartons containing 300 stickers. Every 25th sticker has a plate number. From the plate number, we can determine whether these are real or counterfeit."

"Where would somebody get their hands on quantities of the real thing, Harry? I should think security would be pretty tight around these. They're very important in the effort to conserve gasoline for use in the war."

"Unfortunately we've had several incidents where cartons of gasoline stickers and ration stamps have been stolen off the BEP loading docks or hijacked from delivery trucks. The FBI, working with the enforcement folks at OPA and the War Production Board, has formed a task force to track down the perpetrators of crimes like this."

"Could these be part of the same batch of stolen stickers discovered in the Detroit cases, Harry?"

"Sounds possible. Although, as far as I know, the FBI confiscated that gang's entire supply. But when organized crime is involved, you never know," Mr. Chambers declared.

"It's hard to believe we could have elements of the mob working here in Riverton."

"They'll go wherever the money is, Jeff. And these stickers are valuable to people who want to cheat the system. You'd be amazed how many car owners have been charged with using unauthorized stickers and how many gas stations have been closed for selling stolen or counterfeit stickers or black-market gasoline. It numbers in the tens of thousands."

"That's incredible! I simply cannot understand how American citizens could commit crimes like this — especially people right here in Riverton. Without adequate gasoline, our men on the front lines will suffer more casualties. Don't they know that?"

"Marie, I've been around law enforcement long enough to conclude there're some people who just don't believe rules apply to them. Don't you agree, Harry?"

"Absolutely! Furthermore, they convince themselves they won't be caught."

Until that moment, I had believed all Americans, especially Rivertonians, stood shoulder-to-shoulder, sacrificing whatever it took to win the war. Suddenly my idealism came crashing down on my head. At first, I felt sick to my stomach. Then betrayed. And finally angry. Very angry.

I left the kitchen and went back into my bedroom. I was sitting on my bed when Danny walked in and sat down beside me.

He didn't speak but his presence comforted me. I was certain he felt exactly as I did.

Finally he spoke. "Let's find out who's behind this, Jase. That way we'll both feel much better."

"You mean like President Roosevelt told us after Pearl Harbor."

"That's exactly it! Let's turn our anger into a powerful force for good."

We stood, shook hands, and marched back to the kitchen. We were ready to take on the bad guys. All we needed was our assignment.

"Boys, Sergeant Tolna and I need you to tell us exactly what happened. Give us the details from the minute Jase's dad told you to run down to the Tolna house until you arrived back here with the stickers. Take your time and don't leave anything out."

We did exactly as Mr. Chambers directed. It probably took us a full 10 minutes to explain all that we had seen and done before presenting the 44 stickers to Mom and discovering another two on the Shurtleif car while Mom telephoned Sergeant Tolna.

When we finished, Mr. Chambers sat back in his chair and scratched his head. "Jeff, can you use your car radio to patch me through to the long-distance operator? I'd like to call Washington about this plate number. While we're waiting for the operator to complete the call, I have an idea to discuss with you. Okay?"

Mr. Chambers had us wait inside while the two of them made the call. They were gone for quite awhile. When they returned, Mr. Chambers revealed his plan and our roles in it.

"First of all, I checked with OPA headquarters in Washington. Based on that plate number, these stickers were stolen from a truck dispatched from headquarters to the Detroit OPA office. They were part of a carton that wasn't recovered in the raids on the Detroit distributors. Evidently this carton was being held — perhaps here in Riverton — until things cooled off a bit. I really doubt whoever had these valuable stickers intended to distribute them at no charge to your neighbors. That has us baffled.

"From what you boys tell us, the person or persons distributing the stickers did so in broad daylight without regard to your presence. Even though the reason for distributing them remains a mystery, Sergeant Tolna and I would like to know who's doing it. That way, we can trace them back to the original thieves.

"We're afraid if we add extra police patrols to the neighborhood, we might spook the —. What was it Danny called him? *The Red-Sticker Robin Hood.* We'd like you fellows to organize a surveillance of the neighborhood using the Forrest Street Guards.

"Just a lookout, mind you! The minute you spot anyone placing a sticker under a wiper, you immediately make a beeline for the Tolna garage. We'll have officers waiting there in a patrol car ready to speed to the scene of the crime. No risk-taking. Just watching and reporting. Understood?"

We proudly accepted our assignment, agreed to the rules, and assured Mr. Chambers we would be on patrol right after school. During lunch hour, we would round up the FSG members and organize them to implement the plan. He wished us luck and departed for his office.

Sergeant Tolna drove us to school. By the time we arrived, everyone was outside for the morning recess. The sergeant offered to explain to Miss Sparks and Mr. Lund, if necessary, why we were late.

Before we could make our exit, however, a hundred members of our Hamilton Fan Club surrounded the car. With some effort, we pushed our way through the crowd and into the school. After Miss Sparks told Sergeant Tolna she'd explain our late arrival to the principal, Sergeant Tolna wished us luck and departed.

During what was left of recess, we told all FSG members to meet us right after the start of lunch hour. Our meeting would take place at the old tennis court, tucked in a remote area of the schoolyard. To emphasize the meeting's importance, we told everyone it was a matter of *national security* and what we would discuss was *top secret.*

Predictably within 60 seconds after the lunch bell sounded, the complete roster of FSG members circled around Danny and me in the far corner of the tennis court. We enjoyed complete privacy. No one was within 50 yards of us.

Before assigning patrol territories, we had to know how many surveillance specialists we had at our disposal. Accordingly the first order of business was to ensure all those present were available right after school. Danny took charge. "How many people absolutely cannot — I repeat *cannot* — work on a top secret assignment in our neighborhood starting right after school this afternoon? Raise your right hand."

Chub and Sherm glanced at each other. They both shrugged and simultaneously raised their left hands. At least they were consistent.

Danny looked at me and muttered, "Thank goodness!" Turning to the two youngest FSG members, he ordered, "You're excused. Shove off!"

"But we want to hear the *top secret* stuff, Danny!" Sherm protested. "Can't we stay?"

"Listen. See! If you stay, I'll rub your two heads against that chain-link fence until you're bald. Sure, stick around. It'll be fun," Danny assured them.

Never knowing whether Danny was serious or not, the two lesser members departed, muttering how unfair it was.

"Good riddance," Danny proclaimed before turning his attention to the issue at hand.

We spent the next few minutes describing the strange happenings of that morning, summarizing our meeting with Mr. Chambers and Sergeant Tolna, instructing them on the reporting procedure, and answering their questions the best we could.

Next we handed out the patrol assignments. Queenie and JB were to cover both sides of New Albany Avenue between the Mission Church and the Tucker garage, including Pete's store, the Graham Market, and all the houses in between. Danny and Butch would take both sides of Chester Street from the Tucker garage to the river. And Dilbert and I would be responsible for Forrest Street from the Mission Church down to the river.

"Don't forget, everybody, if you see anyone putting a red sticker on any car, one of you run like crazy for the Tolna garage while the other person stays put to observe the perpetrator. We'll continue our patrols until dark. That should give us about an hour this time of year. In the morning, we'll start again at sunrise unless we nab the rat tonight."

AFTER SCHOOL, WE HURRIED home. We stopped briefly for last-minute instructions at the Mission Church before setting off on our patrols. Dilbert and I decided to walk directly to the river end of Forrest Street. By the time we got there, all cars should have arrived home from work. On our return, we would carefully inspect both sides of the street. If we were thorough, it would be nearly dark when we reached my house. The other members of the FSG surveillance team would meet us there right after dark.

A careful search of the windshield wipers along Forrest Street failed to produce a single red sticker. We sat down on the porch steps and waited for the other patrols to join us.

The streetlight in front of our house came on, officially signaling nightfall. The light cast long shadows from the Shurtleif maple tree onto their driveway where their car was parked. I told Dilbert about collecting two pairs of red stickers from that car earlier in the morning.

"So that's why you checked it before and after we made our patrol," he observed.

I'd been fooled once before and didn't want to be fooled again. When it came to the Shurtleif car, I suspected *Robin Hood* was playing games with me. I was in that frame of mind when I noticed a new shadow, moving quickly across the driveway next to the car in question.

Poking Dilbert with my elbow, I whispered, "Quick! Run to the Tolna garage and tell the police I think there's someone prowling around the Shurtleifs' car. Follow the bushes so he doesn't see you. Tell the police to call Sergeant Tolna and then approach the Shurtleif's with their headlights off."

After Dilbert ran off, I stared into the shadows and squinted my eyes to discern any sign of life across the street. But the streetlight cast a barrier of dusty illumination, making it difficult to distinguish anything but large shadows there. I cupped both ears to hear a telltale noise. Nothing.

Glancing down the street, I saw the dark form of the patrol car from the Tolna garage slowly moving up the street toward me. A block or two down New Albany Avenue, I heard a siren *scream* and *whine*. It too was headed my way.

When the noisy and brightly-lighted police car skidded onto Forrest Street, the entire Shurtleif driveway was caught in its headlights. The car, moving up the street from the Tolnas, suddenly roared its engine and leaped forward with siren blasting and headlights shining brightly.

Both cars steered straight for the Shurtleif car before slamming on their brakes just short of the vehicle.

"Darn," I exclaimed to myself. In the glow of police headlights, I saw yet a third pair of red stickers tucked under the Shurtleif wiper blades.

"This is the police. Come out with your hands in the air. On the double!"

The sound had blasted from Sergeant Tolna's patrol-car loudspeaker.

"This is your last warning! Come out with your hands up!"

Over the noise of the powerful idling engines of the twin patrol cars, I heard a tiny, almost indiscernible sound. Although it was familiar, I couldn't quite place it.

Into the light, a pair of perpetrators slowly walked forward. One had his hands raised far above his head. The other only raised one hand. His other hand was pulling the source of the familiar sound. Sherm's squeaky red wagon.

"Don't shoot, Dad!" cried *Robin Hood One.*

"It's us, Sergeant Tolna," confessed *Robin Hood Two.*

Just at that very instant, another car skidded to a halt under the streetlight. Out sprang Mr. Chambers carrying his special-issue .45 automatic at the ready. When he saw who stood in the limelight, he promptly holstered his weapon.

Everyone just stood there, staring at poor Chub and Sherm, who stood quivering with three of their hands in the air.

"All right, everybody. Relax!" Sergeant Tolna announced, loud enough for all to hear.

By this time, all FSG patrols had assembled on our front walk. I didn't have to explain what happened. To get a better look, we walked across the street. After slipping on a pair of leather driving gloves, Mr. Chambers reached into Sherm's wagon and extracted a hefty carton. It had been torn open at one end. He turned the parcel around and read the label.

"This is it. The carton's addressed to the Detroit OPA office," he confirmed. "Have you two boys been putting these stickers on cars in the neighborhood for the past couple of days?"

After looking at each other, they both nodded.

"Where did you get this carton of stickers, boys?"

They looked at each other again. Then Sherm admitted, "We found them."

"Where?"

"At the dump," declared Sherm. "At the foundry," declared Chub simultaneously.

Sherm's dirty look caused Chub to change his story. "I forgot. At the dump, just like Sherm said."

"Are you sure?" Mr. Chambers snapped.

They both nodded their heads vigorously.

Danny whispered, not all that softly, "The little rats are lying."

I knew them well enough to agree.

"Have you been placing these on cars again tonight?"

They both nodded their heads.

"You can put your hands down, boys. I think you'd better show us all the cars you put them on. Okay?" They immediately dropped their hands to their sides. The wagon handle banged to the driveway in the process.

"Now, let's start with the closest car you put them on tonight. Then the next closest car. We'll just follow your path backwards right around the neighborhood. Do you understand?"

They both nodded and struck off for the first car. Sure enough, it was the Shurtleif's car.

But the second car surprised everybody. The pair walked over to the patrol car from the Tolna garage and plucked a pair of "C" stickers from under the wipers.

Sergeant Tolna glared at the two patrol officers who were stuttering, trying to explain their embarrassing situation.

Sherm helped them out. "I keep my wagon — and the carton of add-vermints — in our garage. When Chub and I came home from school, we went there to get them. We opened the garage door and saw the police car. We were very quiet because we didn't want to wake up the policemen. They were taking naps. So we got the wagon, left them two add-vermints, and closed the garage door. We were real quiet — weren't we, Chub?"

"That's right! They didn't wake up once. Honest Injun!"

"Did we do something wrong, Dad?"

"You're both safe, Sherm. You weren't in uniform and on duty this afternoon."

THE PRELIMINARY INTERROGATION OF the two young *Robin Hoods* failed to induce them to reveal the source of the carton. They did, however, agree to retrace their steps, enabling the two police officers to collect all the stickers distributed earlier that evening.

Even though they knew that ultimately Chub and Sherm were likely to spill the beans, Mr. Chambers and Sergeant Tolna decided it was important to check the carton for fingerprints, as soon as possible. Naturally Chub and Sherm would be fingerprinted to rule them out. Assuming additional prints were found, these would be wired to the Michigan State Police and FBI for identification. These procedures were best accomplished at police headquarters.

To facilitate communication, Mr. Chambers suggested all interested parties assemble in the Chambers & Chambers conference room one hour hence. He had Mom and Dad inform Danny's parents of the circumstances and then bring them to the meeting. Danny and I would ride with him while he accompanied Sergeant Tolna to headquarters in case his help was required to expedite any aspect of the investigation.

"How about your wife, Jeff?"

"She's out of town on a buying trip for Madison's. So I'm it tonight."

After carefully placing the carton into the trunk of his patrol car, Sergeant Tolna loaded Sherm and Chub into the backseat. Before he closed the door, I heard Sherm ask, "Dad, if we're under arrest, don't you have to turn on your siren?"

Once the door was closed, I couldn't hear Sergeant Tolna's response. But, from the look on his face, I could tell he wasn't amused by Sherm's suggestion. This didn't seem to bother either of the *prisoners*, who appeared to be having the time of their lives. Since they heard they were to be fingerprinted, they hadn't stopped chattering and giggling.

In contrast, Danny was very quiet. While we waited for Mr. Chambers, I asked him what he had on his mind. In no uncertain terms, he revealed, "This is very embarrassing! I know if I had two minutes alone with those twerps, they'd talk their heads off."

I believed him.

As we drove to the Chambers and Chambers law offices, I thought about Danny's idea. Because aspects of it had merit, I suggested a modified version to Mr. Chambers. "Before the meeting, Danny and I would like to spend a few minutes alone with Sherm and Chub. Because of our influence with them, we believe we could convince them to tell the truth."

"That sounds like a good idea. Let me tell you why. We found at least four sets of prints on the carton. Two of them are smaller — probably belonging to the boys. And the others are from two adults. Going through channels to ascertain their identity could take days. If you could influence Sherm and Chub to tell us what they know, it could save us a lot of time. When Sergeant Tolna arrives at my office with the boys, I'll recommend giving you fellows a shot at getting them to talk before our meeting starts."

Sergeant Tolna and Mr. Chambers huddled briefly. Sherm and Chub were shown into a vacant office. Sergeant Tolna closed the door behind them. Then he motioned for Danny and me to come over. "Listen, guys. Give it a try. But go easy on the torture. All right?" he cautioned with a wink.

"Okay if I go first?" Danny nodded and followed me into the small office.

When the pair saw it was us, their chattering immediately stopped. Their eyes widened and both of them started fidgeting in their chairs. We stood above them looking down. They glanced at each other and grinned nervously.

A thought flashed into my mind. *Maybe they'll crack without our saying a word.*

The longer we stood there without speaking, the more agitated the two became. Finally Sherm cried, "Why are you guys here? When are we going to the meeting — with my dad and the other adults?"

Ignoring his question, I posed one of my own. "Do you fellows like being FSG members?"

They both nodded their heads enthusiastically. More fear crept into their eyes. I glanced at Danny and he shook his head very slowly, which generated even more anxiety.

"Why are you asking us about FSG, Jase?" Chub wheezed, as if he were nearly out of breath.

"Why do *you* think I'm asking, Chub?"

"Because you're mad at us for not telling where we got the add-vermints. Right?" Chub squeaked.

Danny shot me a quick puzzled look. Evidently he didn't know what *add-vermints* were either. Instead of asking, I decided to slow things down. I just stared at Chub. He couldn't stand it and broke the silence. "Aren't FSG members supposed to keep their promises, Jase?"

"Did you promise somebody not to tell who gave you the red stickers?"

They both nodded their heads.

"The person who gave you those stickers was breaking the law. Do you know what that makes you?"

Their look told me they didn't quite understand.

"You two are *outlaws!*"

For the first time since entering the room, I had raised my voice. It really worked. The tempo of their squirming and fidgeting hit the boogie-woogie level. Taking advantage of their soaring anxiety, I turned to Danny. "Can *outlaws* belong to FSG?"

He shook his head very slowly.

That did it. The tears began to gush. Both boys wailed. Very loudly! I feared Sergeant Tolna would think we'd inflicted physical abuse on the twerps. After a full two minutes, the uncontrollable outburst finally died down to mere chest-heaving sobs.

To ensure they could both hear and understand my question, I waited a few moments more before asking, "Danny, suppose Sherm and Chub told the *whole* truth — and nothing but the truth — to Mr. Chambers and Sergeant Tolna. Do you think we could *possibly* convince the other members to let them stay in FSG?"

Danny leaned back against the wall, folded his arms, and stared at the ceiling. This went on for what seemed like five or ten minutes. By then, the sobbing had all but disappeared. Both

Sherm and Chub seemed spellbound by Danny's pose. Breathlessly they waited for his ruling.

Even I was getting impatient to hear his opinion.

Danny brought his eyes down off the ceiling and looked at me before speaking. Finally he announced, "I don't know, Jase. The other members are not going to like what Sherm and Chub have done. But if they tell the whole truth — right here and now — tonight! I *think* we can convince them to keep Sherm and Chub in FSG."

Both Sherm and Chub leaped from their chairs and ran to hug Danny, shouting, "We'll tell! We'll tell! We'll tell!"

So much for promises!

WHEN WE ENTERED THE conference room, Mr. Chambers pointed to the four chairs reserved for us across the long conference table from all the adults. This arrangement reminded me of a Congressional hearing I had once seen in a newsreel at the Chippewa Theater. In this case, we were on the side of the testifying witnesses. Sherm and Chub were unusually relaxed and calm. With Danny and me agreeing to vouch for them and save their FSG memberships, their earlier anxiety seemed to have vanished.

Mr. Chambers began his inquiry. "By the looks on your faces, the four of you appear to have had a productive session. Is that so?"

Having chaired the session, I answered for the four of us. "Yes, Mr. Cham —."

"We'll tell everything!" squealed Sherm.

"Yep, everything," confirmed Chub.

Leaning back in my chair, I decided to relax and enjoy the show. Danny joined me.

"All right, boys, you may start at the beginning and tell us the whole story," Mr. Chambers advised.

Chub began. "We learned in school that birds build nests in the spring. So that's why we went there."

What a terrific start!

"Ah, went where, Chub? And please tell us when this was."

"On Saturday, when Jase and Danny took their scout hikes, we took Sherm's wagon to the lumberyard to look through their trash pile for wood. We found a whole bunch of good wood. We took a wagon load back to Dad's garage. He's showing us how to build bird houses. Aren't you, Dad?"

Mr. Tucker nodded his head slowly, not knowing exactly where Chub was heading.

"Then we went back for more wood. It was hard pulling the wagon because wood kept falling off. We went back for — how many times, Sherm? Three?"

"Four! We got four loads. When we got back there for more, we were thirsty. I had a nickel in my pocket — some of my Christmas money. But when I put it in the pop machine at the gas station, it got swallowed," Sherm told us.

"What gas station, Sherm?"

"You know — the one next to the Hopkins Lumberyard. What's it called, Chub?"

"The Ajazz gas station. After we lost Sherm's nickel, we met — ."

Sherm interrupted. "This is the part we promised not to tell about."

Sergeant Tolna looked knowingly at Mr. Chambers who nodded his head and smiled. That was most curious, but I put it out of my mind to concentrate on what the boys were saying.

"It's all right, you guys," I told them. "Tell everything like you promised you would."

"Okay. We lost my nickel and told the gas-station man about it. He told us we would have to go to the office and talk to the lady there. She's really pretty, with blond hair and a nice blue dress. Right, Chub?"

"Really pretty! Uh, huh."

I thought about the gum-chewing secretary of Joe Rajak, the nasty owner of the Ajax gas station and distributorship. From my perspective, she wasn't particularly attractive. Evidently, to the thirsty younger set, she was *really pretty*.

"When we knocked on the door of the office, nobody answered. We heard loud voices and a lady crying. Then this big, bald man banged the door open and walked to his car. He seemed really mad. He took off down New Albany Avenue and that was the last we saw of him."

"Yeah! His tires were really spinning."

"That's how we got the job!" Sherm concluded, folding his arms as though he had finished his testimony.

At that point, I intervened. "Remember! You're to tell everything, Sherm. So what job are you talking about?"

Chub took over for Sherm. "After the man left in a hurry, we could still hear the lady crying inside. But we waited because we wanted to get a nickel from her to buy some strawberry pop — 'cause we were really thirsty. When she stopped crying, we knocked again. This time she let us in."

"I told her I lost my nickel. She took three nickels out of a big metal box in her desk and told us to buy three pops. She wanted strawberry. Didn't she, Chub?"

"Yep! That pretty lady was really nice to buy us each our own bottle of strawberry pop. We were going to split one before that. Yep! That really pretty lady was really nice. When we gave her the strawberry pop —. That's when she told us we could make two dollars apiece. Two dollars for each of us! *Natch-really,* we said yes!"

"She went back to the desk and took out another key. She opened the closet and brought out that carton full of add-vermints."

"That's when she told us what they were for. It was a secret. Should we tell that too, Jase?"

"Tell everything, Chub."

"Okay, then. There's a new pop coming to Riverton. That's what the add-vermints are for."

"A new pop?" Mr. Chambers asked. "I don't quite understand."

"Red Cherry! A brand new flavor."

"What did the stickers have to do with cherry pop, Chub?"

"Red sticker. Big *C* for *cherry.* Cherry Red pop! It's a brand new flavor, Mr. Chambers."

"She told us, if we put the add-vermints under people's *windshell* wipers in our neighborhood, she'd pay us two dollars apiece. That's when she wanted to know if we could keep a secret. We told her yes!" Sherm explained. "She swore us to *secret-cy.* Not to tell anybody about where we got the *add-vermints*. But we had to. Right, Jase?"

After I nodded, Chub took over.

"Then she took four dollars out of that box and gave me two and Sherm two. And it's a good thing we were there right then too. Wasn't it, Sherm?"

"Yep! After she paid us our money and gave us the add-vermints carton, know what she did?"

"Tell us, Sherm."

"Okay. She dumped all the rest of the money from the box right into her purse. Then she took her purse and — ."

"Right! She left her office without even closing the door. Before driving away, she thanked us again. I think she went downtown to put all that money in the bank."

Danny politely offered some information about banker's hours to his younger brother. "Banks are closed on Saturday, dummy!"

"Oh! I didn't know that," Chub admitted, shrugging his shoulders and looking to Sherm for support.

The boys stopped talking, as if they had finished again.

"What did you do next, boys?" Mr. Chambers continued.

Sherm concluded their testimony. "We finished our pop, closed the office door for the pretty lady, and took the add-vermints home. We put the wagon with the carton in our garage. Then we put the four dollars in my piggy bank. The next day — Sunday — we started putting the add-vermints on cars. If we hadn't got arrested, we would have finished and not told anybody. Right, Chub?"

"Right, Sherm! A promise is a promise." He paused, apparently realizing by his testimony he had broken his promise to the *pretty* lady. He deftly blamed his lack of fidelity on us. "But Jase and Danny made us tell you. Didn't they, Sherm?"

Sherm nodded his head and so did Chub. They both sat back in their chairs and waited for something to happen.

No one in the room spoke.

At that very second, a man I didn't know opened the conference-room door and requested to speak with Mr. Chambers in private. He excused himself and left the room. A second later, he asked Sergeant Tolna to join them in the hall.

We all looked at each other, wondering what on earth was happening. We soon found out. On their return, they appeared to be very excited.

"Please excuse us. We just received two pieces of very good news. Now we can share some information about this case, which I believe will be of great interest to you all," Mr. Chambers told us, smiling proudly.

"But first things first! Sergeant Tolna and I want to thank Sherm and Chub for sharing the whole truth and nothing but. Their story was exactly what we needed to tie up some loose ends. I'm referring to the case we've been building for some weeks against Joe Rajak and his — ah —*pretty* secretary, Olive Tyndale. Before I forget, we want to thank Jase and Danny for persuading the young boys to give us the full story.

"You should know that very early this morning, we arrested Joe Rajak on a number of charges, including selling stolen gasoline, kerosene, and fuel oil. He's also charged with diluting the Ajax gasoline with kerosene, which is considerably cheaper than gasoline. Using extortion, he's forced many of his customers to pay prices that exceed OPA ceilings for numerous gas and oil products, including common household oil. His leverage with these customers comes from his having sold them counterfeit gas stickers. Obviously they couldn't very well complain to the authorities. Finally, in order to deceive OPA auditors, he kept two sets of books — with considerable help from his secretary. So he's also being charged with fraudulent bookkeeping."

Dad winked at me when Mr. Chambers mentioned overcharging people for household oil.

"But I still haven't given you the first piece of good news. After his arrest, Rajak was sent to the Michigan State Police lockup down in Lansing. When he was booked, he was fingerprinted. And guess what? Surprise! Surprise! His fingerprints match those found on Sherm and Chub's add-vermints carton. Now we can add the charge of being in possession of stolen government property with probable intent to sell it. This last charge rounds out an airtight case, which'll put Rajak away for many, many years."

Upon hearing this news, I only had one thought. *It couldn't have happened to a more deserving rat!*

"Don't forget the second piece of good news, Harry," Sergeant Tolna reminded him.

"I didn't forget, Jeff. I've been trying to think of how to break it to Sherm and Chub."

Danny poked me and whispered, "So much for the *pretty lady!*"

"Well, here goes. At this moment, I'm not sure what's more upsetting to Joe Rajak. His arrest and the possibility of being in prison for the rest of his life or — how did he put it — his secretary's *betrayal, embezzlement,* and *thievery.* In any case, he gladly provided the address of Olive Tyndale's mother in Chicago. As he correctly predicted, when she left Riverton with the stash of cash and the company car, she headed straight for mom. Miss Tyndale was picked up about two hours ago and is singing like a canary to OPA enforcement people from the Chicago office.

"Only Sherm and Chub can decide whether she's *pretty* or not. But I know for sure she's got a very good singing voice. And right now she's using it to provide damaging information about Rajak to lessen her own jail time. I love to prosecute two crooks when they're having a falling-out."

Dad declared. "I don't know when or where, but soon we've got to honor Jeff and Harry with a special occasion, at which we can properly express our appreciation."

"Here! Here!" added Mr. Tucker.

Danny provided the clincher. "And FSG will furnish all the Cherry Red pop you can drink!"

14 AMERICA MOURNS

FREDDIE HAD RECOMMENDED WE BUILD A SIMPLE
hunter's fire for our first attempt at cooking a meal over a campfire.
First, we'd need two relatively green logs about six inches in
diameter and two feet long. These would be laid side by side on
the ground. Depending on the direction and strength of the wind,
they could be either quartered into or placed at right angles to the
wind. The two logs must be separated by a distance slightly smaller
than the diameter of our cooking pots and frying pans.

We would strike our first match to a loosely packed ball of
fluffy tinder, blowing gently until it ignited. Next we would add
thin wood shavings and tiny dry twigs until the fire was well-
established. Finally we'd feed it increasingly larger pieces of dry
kindling until we achieved enough of a blaze to create a bed of hot
coals over which we would cook our meal.

Knowing the type of fire we'd use made it easy to select the
correct tools (hatchet and hunting knife) and primary cooking
utensils (lidded pot and frying pan). We'd also need a spatula and
canteens of water for cooking and drinking. Seasonings and Crisco
were required as well. Of course, we'd need our nested silverware
kit and aluminum dinner dish that was part of our cook-kit. And
we couldn't forget matches!

Planning these *mechanical* aspects of our cookout was relatively
simple. We'd have to do this for any meal we cooked. The real
difficulty was selecting our menu. Not that the actual

requirements were that stringent. Choosing which raw meat, fish, or poultry and which raw vegetable shouldn't have been all that challenging. But it was for us. We were stumped.

"Isn't a hot dog considered raw meat?" Danny was trying to keep it simple and still follow the rules. "And catsup comes from a vegetable. But I guess it's already cooked. How about diced onions on our hot dogs? They're vegetables. No, we're supposed to cook them. How would cooked diced onions taste on hot dogs? Is pickle relish a vegetable?"

Mom came to our rescue. "Boys, I know this is your meal to plan, but may I offer a suggestion?"

We eagerly welcomed her help.

"Grandma brought us some nice pork chops. They're thawing in the icebox and should be ready to cook by this evening. How does that sound?"

"Great!" Danny exclaimed.

"When it comes to raw vegetables, it seems to me your choice is limited to what we have in the fruit cellar. This time of year, the pickings are pretty slim. Carrots, onions, and potatoes. But they're all vegetables that can be cooked separately — or even together with a little careful timing."

"We'll do it. Let's go down and get what we need. We can clean them before we go to school. Is that all right, Mom?"

"Certainly. Help yourself."

"Oh, one last thing, Mrs. A. We need to make a ball of dough for our stick bread. Shouldn't we do that now so it has time to *raise* — or something?"

"That's right, Danny. So it can *rise*. I'll assemble the ingredients while you bring up the vegetables."

All during school that day, in my head I rehearsed Mom's recommended cooking times and sequences of the various items on our menu. First, she suggested we boil the peeled and sliced potatoes and carrots. After a few minutes, we could begin to fry the pork chops and sliced onions. When they were done, we should remove them from the frying pan and cover them to keep them warm. Finally we should add the slightly under-cooked boiled vegetables to the frying pan to brown them.

Of course, we'd have to keep our eye on the stick bread, remembering to rotate it often for even baking throughout and to avoid burning one side through neglect. And we mustn't forget the seasonings. While all this was going on, we'd have to ensure our fire wasn't burning too hot or dying out.

During my years in scouting, I achieved the rank of Eagle Scout of which I'm still very proud. I also learned some scouting truisms. For example, most food cooked over a campfire is either seriously under-cooked, i.e., raw. This usually occurs as a result of hunger-driven haste. Or it's burned beyond the point of being edible. This typically results from inattention.

Every scout knows campfires always generate more than enough smoke to blind an elephant.

Moreover, whenever you go camping, you may count on an infestation of blackflies and mosquitoes to invite themselves for dinner, featuring *you* as the main course. But looking on the positive side, food cooked over a campfire always tastes best when seasoned with wood smoke, ashes, and citronella.

But there's more. If you happen to be both *camping* and *cooking*, you will probably enjoy the added pleasures of near-drownings. Second-degree sunburn. Lawsuit-generating snipe hunts. Bouts of homesickness. Chiggers and full-body poison-ivy outbreaks. Tent fires. Knife cuts. Wandering rabid beasts. Asthma and allergy attacks. Fishhooks in fingers and ears. Food poisoning. And rain-soaked sleeping bags. Now that is what I used to call pure ecstasy! I would not have missed it for the world. Scouting is the best training for manhood ever devised!

But I digress.

After school, we loaded our food supplies and cooking gear into our bicycle baskets and backpacks. We hung our full canteens, waterproof match containers, first-aid kits, hatchets, and hunting knives on our web belts, slung our cook-kits with attached silverware kits over our shoulders, bandolier-style, and set off for Trumble Park. Freddie was waiting for us on the clearing overlooking the stream that ran through the park and past the public swimming pool. I noticed a neat pile of firewood that had been stacked by the park rangers near an outdoor brick fireplace. I wondered if Freddie would let us use wood from that handy supply or force us to forage from the nearby woods.

Freddie was traveling light. His canteen and silverware kit were hanging from his belt and his backpack revealed only a small bulge, presumably his supper. For a minute, I wondered if he had brought a sack lunch from home. He sat down at a nearby picnic table to perform his job of observer. Evidently he was impressed by our preparation and our complete inventory of supplies and equipment, as well as the teamwork we exhibited while going about the business of building our campfire and laying out the makings of our supper.

Apparently satisfied that we knew what we were doing, he rose from his seat and came over to offer advice, not in the way of helping us but in the vein of improving our techniques. For example, he showed us how to wet a finger and hold it up to check wind direction. Using two fine logs from the park's supply, we oriented our Hunter's Fire properly, prepared our tinder from puffs of dried milkweed silk and dry-rotted bark, created a pile of wood shavings using our super sharp new hunting knives, and laid out our kindling in piles by size. After striking our first and only match, we achieved our objective. Our campfire was lit.

Following the recommended progression, it took about a half-hour for our bed of coals to begin to form. At this rate, producing enough hot coals to cook our supper would take even more time than we had predicted. I made a mental note to start my next campfire well before I planned to start cooking.

Seeing our progress was nicely under way, Freddie returned to the picnic table and opened his backpack. "Come here a second, fellas. I want to show you my supper." By the time we reached him, he had set a large Graham Market coffee can onto the table. "This is my coffee-can dinner."

"What's inside?"

Freddie removed the lid. The can was packed with food. Using a fork from his silverware kit, he gently removed some of the items from the top of the can. "The bottom layer has large chucks of raw potato. Then there's a layer of carrots. I added some canned sweet corn, not much, because I was running out of room. On top, I laid these three strips of bacon, mainly for flavoring. And I added a little salt and pepper too."

"How'll you cook it?"

"First, I fill it to the top with water." After showing us how, he replaced the top and thumped it a couple of times with the heel of his hand.

"Okay, that's firmly in place. Now I need to punch a few holes in the top to allow the steam to vent." He pulled his official Boy Scout jackknife from his pocket and opened the awl. Touching its tip to the top of the can, he hit the jackknife with the heel of his hand. After punching three good-sized holes, he announced, "That's it! Let's bury it in your coals."

Freddie didn't actually *bury* the coffee-can dinner. He banked coals all around it as high as the lid, explaining, "I don't want ashes to get into those vent holes."

"When will it be cooked?"

"After the water starts boiling, steam will start escaping from the vents. I'll leave it in the fire until the steam dies down. That means the water's almost boiled away. Then I'll remove it and let it set for a while. It'll cook some more before cooling down enough so I can eat it. It should be ready about the time you fellows are through cooking your meal."

"Boy, that's an easy way to bring a dinner to a cookout. Isn't it, Freddie!"

"Yep. And I bet it'll taste a lot like your meal."

"We should have brought coffee-can dinners. Could we have passed our cooking requirement if we had, Freddie?"

"Technically you would have. But look how much more fun you'll have actually cooking every part of your supper."

Despite the labor involved, it was definitely worth it. Perhaps it was beginners' luck, but our meal was cooked perfectly. And for some reason, it tasted better outdoors than it ever would have in our kitchen at home.

We traded sample bites with Freddie, who was delighted with our success. He proudly announced that we had passed each and every one of our Second Class requirements.

Danny was quick to take advantage of Freddie's good mood. "Freddie, when are you available to work with us on our First Class requirements?"

"How about the day you graduate from college, Danny?"

Now how did Freddie hear about that?

ON OUR WAY HOME from Trumble Park, Danny and I were bursting with pride from having completed our Second Class requirements. Freddie assured us he would complete all he paperwork necessary for us to receive our awards at the Court of Honor in Lansing.

He also reminded us that we were free to work on any Merit Badge that struck our fancy. We were no longer restricted to the original four for which our fathers were counselors. Having said that, Freddie became pensive and hesitant.

"Do you want to say something else, Freddie?"

"Yes, I do, Jase. I earned my Eagle Scout rank, as fast as I did, because I focused on the requirements for promotion rather than on those things that interested me most. When scouts reach Second Class, they can work on any Merit Badges they want. I know some scouts who have a dozen or more Merit Badges but have never gone beyond Second Class. Don't get me wrong. There's nothing wrong with that. Doing the work needed to become an Eagle is hard — and it isn't for everyone. And that's my trouble."

"What do you mean, Freddie?"

"I don't know which kind of guys you are. I'll put it simply. Which would you prefer, staying Second Class and working on fun and easy Merit Badges? Or working long and hard on the requirements for Eagle and having the satisfaction of earning scouting's top rank?"

"You took the second choice, Freddie. And you'll soon be too old for Boy Scouts. Have you ever had any regrets?"

"None whatsoever! But that's just me. And I don't judge people who don't share my attitude. If they enjoy having fun and not working too hard, who am I to say they're wrong?"

I looked at Danny. I knew how much he wanted to complete the four Merit Badges for which our fathers were counselors. But they were not core requirements for making Eagle Scout. Therefore, I thought Danny might choose to spend his remaining years as a scout pursuing enjoyable Merit Badges. However, I also knew he was proud, smart, and clever. If he set his mind to it, he could achieve any rank scouting had to offer.

"Which choice would you make, Jase? Be honest now."

"You first."

"All right, I'll tell you. I'd like to pursue fun Merit Badges —."

"I kind of thought you'd say that," I admitted.

"Wait! Let me finish. I was saying — I'd like to pursue fun Merit Badges *after* I earn my Eagle. So Freddie, how can I make Eagle as fast as you did? Tell Jase too. He wants to be an Eagle Scout. Right, Jase?"

I smiled and replied, "You bet!"

"Boy, that's a relief!" Freddie confessed. "Okay, here it is in a nutshell. I followed a simple two-part plan to advance rapidly to the top with the minimum investment of time.

"First, I didn't spend one minute working on any Merit Badges until after I completed my First Class requirements. Why? Because you need to be a First Class before you can be a Star, Life, or Eagle.

"Second, when I became a First Class, I only focused on Merit Badges that would give me my Eagle because most of them can also be used toward your Star and Life ranks. So essentially I earned the last three ranks at the same time."

"But, Freddie, we have a little problem."

"A problem? What's that, Danny?"

"I won't graduate from college until I'm too old to be a Boy Scout. Are you sure you can't help us with our First Class requirements a little sooner than that?"

"Now that I know what you guys really want, I'm ready to start right now. Go home and read the First Class requirements and write down all your questions. I'll see you tomorrow at school, and we'll agree on a regular time to meet each day until you've passed all your requirements. Deal?"

"Deal!" we both exclaimed, beaming.

THE NEXT MORNING AT breakfast, all Danny talked about was how Freddie was going to help us make Eagle Scout in record-setting time. Danny even announced he was planning to invite President Roosevelt to present our Eagle Scout medals at a Court of Honor. FDR had presented our second *Medals of Courage* at the White House. The least we could do was offer him another opportunity to pin a medal on our chests. After all, he really seemed to enjoy doing it.

I reminded Danny that President Roosevelt was extremely busy nowadays. Danny thought about it for a minute and then offered a fallback position. "I'm sure President Roosevelt will make room in his schedule for us. Especially when we tell him if he can't make it, we intend to ask our friend, Governor Dewey."

"Governor Dewey?"

"Sure! I know he's not President yet. But next time he runs, I bet he wins. We'll help him again with his campaign. Maybe this time he'll buy us black suits like those he wears. Won't our white shirts and Michigan ties look good with black suits, Jase?"

"But Governor Dewey's pretty busy too."

"Jase, he already came here to award us our *New York Medals of Recognition*. The Eagle Scout medal is a lot more important than that one."

"Do you really think so?"

"Sure! Hmmm! I wonder how much Chub will pay to wear my Eagle Scout medal to school."

"You want that answer in pennies or dimes?"

Danny ignored that one. On the other hand, I could see he was still trying to identify a worthy person on whom to bestow the honor of awarding his Eagle Scout medal.

"I've got it! We'll ask Winston Churchill, Jase. Remember when we saw him in Washington, D.C.? Oops! Is it all right to talk about that now?"

"Sure, President Roosevelt and Prime Minister Churchill were having secret talks about the Yalta Conference with Mr. Stalin. But that happened in February. Don't you remember? About a month or so ago, President Roosevelt briefed Congress on the conference. Can't be very secret now."

"In any case, we're lucky to have three good candidates. Winnie, FDR, and Governor Dewey. What do you think, Jase?"

"I think we should consider a fourth person. One who's not so famous or busy as those three. We'd be more likely not to be disappointed. Don't you think?"

"A fourth choice? Hmmm! Oh, sure. It's obvious."

"Who would that be, Danny?"

"Joseph Stalin! He can't be too busy in Russia now that spring is here. No snow to keep him from coming."

"Let's go to school, Danny. We have to see Freddie and show him our list of questions about the First Class requirements."

"Right. He'll know which of these four guys should present our Eagles. Let's ask him."

"I'd rather hold off on that one, Danny."

All through the morning, Danny babbled about earning his Eagle Scout. A few of our classmates became convinced that he already had it. They wanted to know why he wasn't wearing it on his sweater with his other three medals.

His standard reply was "It's at the cleaners."

At our meeting with Freddie during lunch hour, several of Danny's admirers inquired about his new Eagle Scout medal. Despite Danny's attempts to dismiss these questions as misunderstandings, Freddie was no fool. He tactfully reminded Danny that to earn his Eagle Scout he must satisfy his scout leaders that, on a daily basis, he lived up to the *Scout Spirit* as defined by the *Scout Oath, Scout Law, Scout Motto,* and *Scout Slogan.*

Yes. Freddie threw the book at Danny. Of course, I'm referring to the scout handbook. After his dressing-down, Danny became rather subdued. We handed Freddie our list of questions and agreed to meet at my house right after school. Freddie's commitment to our advancement was a great compliment to us. I reminded Danny we needed to honor it and be grateful.

"I know, Jase. I got a little carried away. I'll apologize to Freddie when we meet this afternoon."

Occasionally Danny surprised me with his humility and his courtesy. Those occasions usually occurred between the Dutch rubs and Chinese handcuffs that he was fond of inflicting on Chub, Sherm, and their ilk.

Danny and I hurried home right after school and immediately retreated into my bedroom to wait for Freddie. We were studying our scout handbook when he opened my bedroom door. True to his word, Danny apologized for bragging about being a shoo-in for Eagle Scout and thanked Freddie profusely for offering to help us.

Suddenly I heard Mom scream, "Oh, my God! No! It can't be true! Oh, my God!"

When I reached the front room, I saw Mom sitting on the couch with her hands covering her face. She was sobbing uncontrollably. I put my arms around her and held her close.

After years of girding myself for bad news, my conditioned response kicked in. "Is it Uncle Van?"

She shook her head and pointed to the radio. I had been so alarmed I failed to notice that it was tuned to WRDP. I heard the familiar voice of Chuck Nichols, sounding unusually subdued. Danny and Freddie were staring at the radio. Freddie reached down and turned up the volume. That's when all of us learned why Mom was so distraught.

"Ladies and gentlemen, for those of you who may have just tuned in, we have received a special announcement from the White House that President Franklin D. Roosevelt has died. Despite desperate attempts to save his life, the President was pronounced dead at approximately 3:35 p.m. Eastern War Time by his personal physician at the Little White House in Warm Springs, Georgia. No details have been released as to the immediate cause of death.

"Vice President Truman arrived at the White House at approximately 5:30 p.m. at which time, Mrs. Eleanor Roosevelt informed him of the President's death. Within minutes, the Cabinet was assembled and Harry S. Truman took the oath of office to become the 33rd President of the United States. President Truman is 60 years of age.

"We'll continue to monitor this tragic story and update you immediately as details become available. Please tune in to our regular seven o'clock evening news for complete coverage. This is Chuck Nichols coming to you from the WRDP newsroom. We now return you to our regular programming."

When Dad walked through the door, all four of us were standing in the front room with tears streaming down our cheeks.

"My God! What's happened? Tell me. Is it Van?"

"No, Dad. It's not Uncle Van. It's even worse — for everyone!"

ON MARCH 1, 1945, President Franklin Roosevelt addressed a joint session of Congress to report the results of his meeting at Yalta with Churchill and Stalin. Those in attendance were shocked when the President chose to remain seated as he delivered his remarks. His statement began with these words. "I hope that you will pardon me for the unusual posture of sitting down. It makes it a lot easier for me not having to carry about 10 pounds of steel around the bottom of my legs."

His grayish skin tone, loss of weight, glassy eyes, and halting speech were telltale signs of his deteriorating state of health. Yet, when Franklin Delano Roosevelt died of a massive cerebral hemorrhage seven weeks later, his death was met with shock and grief across America and around the world. When he delivered the news to Parliament, Winston Churchill broke down, saying, "I feel as though I have been struck a physical blow." In a rare public expression of sentiment, Joseph Stalin ordered all Russian newspapers to print pictures of President Roosevelt on their front pages.

Roosevelt had served as President of the United States for more than 12 years, longer than anyone before or since. During his term of office, though physically crippled by polio, he led the country through two of its most challenging crises, the Great Depression and World War II. Across the political spectrum, President Roosevelt was admired for his ability to provide hope and courage to the oppressed throughout the world and here at home.

On the morning of April 13, 1945, a train carrying the President's casket departed for Washington, D.C. Grieving Americans of all colors and creeds silently mourned as the passing train, moving at no more than 35 miles an hour, traveled north through the Carolinas and Virginia. On April 14th, President Truman, with members of the immediate family, cabinet members, and other high-ranking government officials, met the train at Union Station.

As the casket made its solemn journey along Pennsylvania Avenue to the White House, the procession was afforded full military honors. Units of the armed forces and mourning citizens lined the street. Behind the casket, flag bearers carried the American and the Presidential flags.

After the casket was placed in the East Room, a 23-minute funeral service was conducted. The next morning, the casket was transported by train to the Rose Garden at the Roosevelt estate in Hyde Park, New York. A 21-gun salute was fired and taps played as the casket was lowered into Roosevelt's final resting place.

When news of the President's death reached the country, out of respect, public buildings and schools were closed, sporting events and theater performances canceled, and special church services conducted to comfort a bereaved citizenry. Flags were flown at half-mast for a 30-day period in tribute to Franklin Roosevelt.

During that month's time, Italian partisans captured and hanged Benito Mussolini, Adolph Hitler committed suicide, and all Nazi armed forces surrendered unconditionally to the Allies. May 8, 1945 was declared V-E (Victory in Europe) Day. Massive celebrations took place in New York's Times Square, Chicago, and Los Angeles. President Harry S. Truman, who celebrated his 61st birthday on that day, dedicated the victory to the memory of his predecessor, Franklin D. Roosevelt.

SPRING HAS SPRUNG

DURING THE WEEK FOLLOWING PRESIDENT Roosevelt's death, like most Americans, I went about my daily activities in a trance. Danny called it his week of sleepwalking. While we were still committed to Freddie's strategy for achieving early Eagles, our hearts were not fully engaged. School was even worse. I felt sorry for Miss Sparks, who was trying her best, to force-feed knowledge into sixth-grade brains that were, for all practical purposes, AWOL.

News reports of the Allied Army's liberation of two Nazi concentration camps, called Buchenwald and Bergen-Belson, added to our depression. By all accounts, the sheer scale of atrocities committed by the Germans at these camps was staggering. Newsreels depicting scenes of these horrible crimes against humanity were downright sickening. I would learn later that the death toll from these two camps alone was more than 106 thousand. Among those who perished were Jews, Gypsies, anti-Nazi Christians, communists, homosexuals, Jehovah's Witnesses, and even some Soviet POWs, who were supposedly protected by the Geneva Convention.

After several days of FDR-induced doldrums, Danny and I were sitting on my back-porch steps. He broke the silence by asking, "Have you noticed how warm it's been lately?"

"Yes. But why do you ask?"

"I think spring is finally here."

"Really? I haven't noticed."

"Sure, it is. Just look around. For one thing, the trees all have buds and a lot of them have leaves already. The birds are picking up pieces of string and twigs for making nests. And they're singing — a lot — early each morning. The tulips and daffodils are sprouting up. The forsythia and quince have blossoms. And look! There're even dandelions in your yard. Do you know what else? Tiny shoots of asparagus are coming up in the ditch along Mrs. Mikas' alley.

"People in the neighborhood are starting to spade their Victory Gardens. I love the smell of newly dug soil, especially after a spring shower. Don't you? Have you seen the baby rabbits munching the new clover next to the Reilly's garage? And what about all the puffy white clouds and deep blue skies? Even the level of the spring floodwater covering the swamp is a lot lower lately. And the days are really getting longer. Right?"

I realized I was staring at Danny but I couldn't seem to help myself. Had I just heard my first zoology lecture? Or was it botany? Maybe it was meteorology? In any case, my sluggish mind wasn't absorbing his message.

He gave it one last try.

"Do you know what day tomorrow is?"

I had to think a minute before answering. "It's April 17, 1945."

He gave me a look of exasperation.

"It's the Detroit Tigers' Opening Day!"

My heart immediately filled with excitement.

It's spring!

IN 1944, THE DETROIT TIGERS made a run for the American League pennant but came up just short. Despite a commendable record of 88 wins and 66 losses, the final standings had the Tigers losing the pennant race to the St. Louis Browns by a single game. Pitching was Detroit's strength that year. Left-hander Hal Newhouser won 29 games and teammate, Dizzy Trout, won 27. For his efforts, Newhouser was selected as the American League's Most Valuable Player.

Prior to opening day of the 1945 season, like all Tigers' fans, I was convinced this was our year. But on that day, St. Louis once again asserted itself by handing Detroit its first loss of the season, a 7 to 1 shellacking. In that game, even the Browns' one-armed outfielder, Pete Gray, hit a single off Detroit's starter, Les Mueller.

By the 1945 season's end, however, the Browns were six games behind the pennant-winning Tigers, who edged out the Washington Senators by a slim game-and-a-half margin. The Senators surprised us by ascending from the American League cellar in '44 to give the Tigers a run for their money in '45.

But surprising performances were not uncommon that year. Many teams were bolstered by returning stars who had put their baseball careers on hold to serve in the armed services. Baseball standings were in a constant state of flux that season.

In July, the Tigers benefitted greatly by the return of future Hall of Famer, Hank Greenberg, who had missed four seasons while serving in the military. Despite the layoff, Greenberg at age 34 hit a home run in his first game back and went on to be voted to the American League All-Star team. More importantly, on the last day of the regular season, his grand-slam homer against the Browns clinched the pennant for the Tigers.

Also on that day, the Tigers' pitching staff got a boost by Virgil Trucks' return from naval service. Trucks shook off the rust and pitched for the Tigers' first win over the Chicago Cubs in Game 2 of the World Series.

Under the able leadership of Detroit's manager, Steve O'Neill, the Tigers beat the Cubs in the 1945 World Series, 4 games to 3. After their Series' victory, *Detroit News* sports writer, H.G. Salsinger, attributed the Tigers' win to the "superb pitching of TNT, meaning Trucks, Newhouser, and Trout."

Newhouser won Game 5 and Game 7 of the 1945 World Series for the Tigers. He also won the pitching Triple Crown in wins (25), ERA (1.81), and strikeouts (212). For the second straight year, he was voted the American League's MVP. After retiring from baseball along with teammate, Greenberg, he was voted into the Baseball Hall of Fame.

In the minds of Tigers' fans, the decade between Detroit's 1935 World Series victory and this 1945 win was much too long to wait. But little did we know, the next Tigers' World Series win wouldn't come until 1968 when Detroit defeated the St. Louis Cardinals, 4 games to 3.

Again that same year, pitching was the Tigers' strength. For the first time since 1934, a major-league pitcher won more than 30 games. In 1968, Detroit's Denny McLain won 31 games and Mickey Lolich chalked up 17 wins. McLain was voted the American League MVP and Lolich was the World Series MVP.

The second-place vote-getter for the league MVP that year was their man behind the plate, Bill Freehan. During most of his 15-year career with Detroit, he was considered the premier catcher in the American League. At the University of Michigan, before signing with the Tigers in 1961, Freehand set the all-time Big Ten Conference season record by batting .585. He also played football for the Wolverines and was a fraternity brother of mine.

As a boy, there were many avid Tigers' fans in my life, including Danny, Uncle Van, and Dad. But my most respected fan of all was Grandpa Compton. He knew the Tigers and their history inside and out. His enthusiasm for the Detroit team and his passion for the game of baseball were incomparable.

Each and every time I possibly could, I would join Grandpa in front of his old console radio where the three of us would lose ourselves in the pure joy of Tigers' baseball. Of course, I'm referring to Grandpa and me plus Harry Heilmann, former Tiger hitting ace and Hall of Famer, who for decades skillfully broadcast Tigers' games straight from Briggs Stadium right into the Compton front room for the personal enjoyment of Grandpa and me.

AFTER THE TIGERS' OPENING-DAY defeat by the St. Louis Browns, Danny and I sought the solace of our back porch once again. While we sat there, my mind revisited Danny's spring-awareness lecture from the afternoon before. I focused on the remark he had made concerning the appealing odor of freshly overturned soil. I had never heard that idea expressed before, but I completely agreed with it.

In fact, after thinking about it for a day or so, I realized that my attraction to this unique *perfume* was the primary reason behind my desire to spend so much time at my grandparents' farm during the spring and early summer. This was the period during which Grandpa Compton prepared or *fitted* his fields for sowing crops. And the sweet smell of the Compton farm's rich earth was nearly addictive to me.

I told Danny how I felt. "Do you remember when you talked about the smell of freshly overturned earth — like in the Victory Garden? I wanted you to know I agree with you about that. It's why I like being at the farm this time of year."

"Funny you should mention that, Jase. I really like the smell too, but those weren't really my own words."

I didn't understand his meaning.

"I read them in a book at the library. It was about farm life on the prairies of — South Dakota — I think. The book was called *A Son of the Middle Border*. The author was a man named Hamlin Garland. When we go to Grandpa Compton's farm, I think of that book."

"What made you pick up that particular book?" I was incredulous.

"I thought it was about sheepdogs. But anyway, I have a question, Jase."

I didn't understand his *sheepdogs'* explanation, but I decided it would be best to ignore it. "Ask away!"

"I've been to the farm a lot of times. But I really don't know what Grandpa Compton grows there. When we went hunting, we walked through corn fields. And I saw Grandpa and you cutting and loading hay. But to be honest, all those other plants growing there — I mean — they all look alike to me. Can you tell me what they are? I mean —. What all does he grow?"

Again I was incredulous. I knew Danny had never spent any time on a farm before I met him. But my knowledge of farming was extensive because Grandpa was a willing teacher. For years at the farm, I had watched, questioned, and learned. Until this conversation, I hadn't realized how much I knew about farming compared to Danny.

"I'm sorry you never mentioned this before. I'll try to answer your question as best I can. And I promise, when we go to the farm from now on, I'll show you the different plants and the crops they produce."

"Great!"

"Danny, the simple answer to your question is this. Farms around Riverton are blessed with a perfect combination of soil conditions and climate to produce abundant yields of soybeans, peas, and white beans. Those crops are all legumes. The other crops are non-legumes like corn, wheat, and oats. Of course, Grandpa grows hay to feed the horses and cows in the wintertime. It happens that hay is a mixture of legumes and non-legumes."

"Are the white beans the same as the navy beans you can buy in boxes at the grocery store?"

"They're pretty much the same. In the Midwest, the beans Grandpa grows are sometimes packaged and labeled as *Michigan Beans* too."

"What're *leg rooms?*"

"Generally legumes are plants with pods, like beans and peas. But alfalfa and clover are also legumes. They are among the plants that make up the hay we cut and store in the barns."

I explained to him that legumes are ideal rotation crops. To rotate crops, one year Riverton-area farmers plant legumes in a field. In the next year or two, they sow non-legumes like wheat, corn, and oats in that same field. Then they repeat the cycle. By practicing this crop rotation religiously, they can prevent depletion of certain plant nutrients in the soil, especially nitrogen.

Once the South's leading cash crop, cotton is a good example of a non-legume plant. After the Civil War and before crop rotation was used, in a desperate attempt to recover economically from the war, Southern cotton farmers replanted their fields year after year with cotton. As a result of this practice, these fields nearly became barren from the failure to replenish the depleted soil.

Strangely enough, George Washington Carver, who introduced the practice of crop rotation with legumes, is credited with saving the very Southern cotton plantations on which he and his ancestors labored as slaves. Of course, Carver's favorite legume was the peanut. His studies yielded hundreds of uses for this lowly legume, not the least of which was Danny's and my beloved peanut butter.

Like all good Michigan farmers, Grandpa Compton had taught himself the chemistry and the biology of farming. He knew legumes replenish the form of nitrogen in the soil needed by all plants to live and flourish. Legumes achieve this through a symbiotic relationship with certain *nitrogen-fixing* bacteria, which collect in nodules on the legume's roots. Living on nutrients provided to them by their host plants, these bacteria work feverously to extract nitrogen gas from the air and to convert it into a solid plant-edible form.

"Do you understand, Danny?"

"I think I better wait to meet these plants in person. When will Grandpa be planting seeds?"

That was a good question. In the late winter and early spring, as the ice and snow began to melt, Grandpa spent an enormous amount of time and energy on removing excess water from his fields. For the most part, this amounted to old-fashioned, back-breaking manual labor. Over the years, he laid tile and cut in additional ditches to improve drainage and reduce the spadework required.

Because of the vicissitudes of weather, you couldn't predict the exact date on which Grandpa's plow would first slice into the awakening soil. Each field dried according to its own unique timetable. Its drying rate depended on its location (high or low ground), soil composition (proportions of humus, clay, and gravel), and efficiency of its natural or man-made (field tiles or ditches) drainage system. When the fields were finally dry enough to plow, Grandpa stopped his winter work of repairing and refurbishing farm vehicles, implements, and buildings to focus his energy fully on the tasks of the planting season.

Early each morning, he hitched the appropriate team of horses (heavy or light) to the appropriate implement (plow, disk, or drag) and engaged in the long process of fitting each of his fields according to the crop to be planted. Back and forth, back and forth, day after day, week after week, he and the horses marched across the fields until their soil's condition met his precise standards.

The first step in fitting a field was plowing. The plow sliced through the wiry grasses covering the field's surface and turned them under. Hopefully, plowing would succeed in killing the stubborn vegetation to prevent it from competing for nutrients with the new crop. Plowing also exposed the wet humus to the warm sun and wind and hastened the drying process.

Grandpa used a McCormick moldboard plow employing three huge steel plow blades, polished by the soil to a lustrous silver finish. Each plow blade had a removable plowshare or *tip* that Grandpa sharpened regularly to lessen the burden for his pulling team. These plow tips could be replaced in the field if they were badly chipped or broken by *round heads* as we called the annoying stones and boulders that popped up each spring.

After plowing, came disking. The *disk* was a farm implement housing a long row of razor-sharp, 18-inch disks that rotated as the equipment passed over the field. Disks sliced lumps of roots, vegetation, and humus into workable bits.

The last step in the fitting process was dragging. The *drag* always reminded me of the bed of nails used by Hindu yogis for napping. In this case, the heavy bed was fitted with nails that pointed downward. During dragging, these spikes exposed undetected stones and boulders, leveled the field, and also removed unwanted scraps of vegetation and leftovers from last year's crop.

"When all the draining and fitting is complete, it's time to drill. Do you understand?"

No answer.

"Danny?"

Zzzzzzzzzzzzzz!

IN HIS ROLE AS troop fund-raising coordinator, Dad kept a weekly tally of household-oil cans sold by each scout and by each patrol. When Freddie drew lots with the other patrol leaders, the Wolverines ended up with Riverton's least affluent territory, the southeastern quadrant of the city. That was the bad news.

The good news was every member of our patrol lived in that quadrant. We all knew our territory and its people very well. The other piece of good news was that nearly every factory in Riverton was located in our territory. Finally our quadrant was home to 90 percent of Riverton's bars and taverns. That was the best news of all.

Most patrols would have avoided our quadrant like the plague. Not us. We knew the generous people and we knew the pikers. As a result, we didn't waste time trying to sell to cheapskates. Instead, we focused on the easy sells among our bighearted neighbors and friends.

The factories represented the human equivalent of smelt runs. Through the gates, just before and after shift changes, hundreds of workers streamed into and out of these factories. Each of the three daily, double runs of potential household-oil buyers was made up of people who lived all over Riverton and in the many small communities in the far corners of Chippewa County. We knew these workers had money and often demonstrated ostentatious behavior to impress their coworkers. They also bought in frenzies like a school of ravenous perch at Quanicassee. We were happy to help them spend their excess pocket change for a good cause, namely purchasing our new tents.

If we missed a sale at the gate, we always had a second crack at a prospect at one of the two-dozen drinking spots, where a substantial proportion of the workers headed after their shifts ended. There was no softer touch than a man, trying to impress his buddies at a bar. This was especially true if the salesperson was a boy, wearing a scout uniform. The longer prospects spent at the bar, the more their beverages washed away their anti-spending inhibitions.

For all these reasons, we convinced ourselves that the affluent residential quadrants north of Main Street offered far less potential than our own territory. Dad's first weekly tally proved our theory. Of the total sales of over 800 cans, our patrol accounted for more than half. As he predicted, Danny was the troop's leading salesman with 88 cans to his credit. In his own *humble* way, Danny let the other patrols know how he felt about their relatively poor sales performance. His fellow Wolverines attempted to stifle his comments. After all, how wise was it to create three patrols of irate competitors?

In the end, Danny paid dearly for his disrespectful behavior. His comeuppance occurred when several unrelated factors collided to create a perfect storm whose fury nearly drowned Danny under waves of retributive justice.

Factor #1 resulted from an unfortunate traffic accident involving a Riverton motorist and a boy on a bicycle. A month before we launched our oil sale, a 10-year-old boy rode his bicycle at top speed through a red light and into the passenger-side door of a car passing legally through the intersection. Chief of Police Leonard Remke's mother was the driver of the car. She was unhurt, but the boy suffered a broken left leg and various cuts and bruises.

After the accident, although completely exonerated from any wrongdoing, Mrs. Remke made it very clear to her son how she felt about the competence of children operating bicycles on Riverton's city streets. She insisted he immediately implement a plan to teach children the rules of the road and grant authority to school safety patrols to enforce these rules throughout the city.

Factor #2 occurred the following Saturday. Chief Remke and Donald Foreman, the superintendent of Riverton's public schools, were having lunch after their weekly golf game at the Riverton Country Club. After soundly trouncing his opponent, the chief thought it an opportune time to propose his mother's plan to the superintendent.

To compensate for his trouncing, Foreman agreed to implement the plan, providing Remke agreed to have his police officers train all Riverton safety patrols in the proper enforcement of traffic laws as they pertain to bicycle operators. To put some teeth in the enforcement process, safety patrols would be provided pads of traffic citations, which they could issue when they spotted a violation. Each Riverton junior high school and the senior high school would appoint a student judge to preside over the school's bicycle traffic court. The court would have the authority to sentence offenders to various forms of punishment commensurate with the seriousness of the offense.

Both men agreed that a pilot program should be run at one of Riverton's four junior high schools. Knowing the heavy workload currently burdening their principals, Foreman told the chief that none of them was likely to volunteer. After flipping a mental coin, he would arbitrarily select one of the four as the pilot school.

Factor #3 occurred when Mr. Lund, the new principal of Hamilton School, walked into the dining room with Miss Sparks on his arm. The couple was seated only a few tables away from the chief and the superintendent. When Lund spotted Foreman, his face immediately turned red. Both men knew that social fraternization between principal and teacher was strictly forbidden.

"Chief, the pilot program will be conducted at Hamilton School. After we finish our lunch, I'll introduce you to Jack Lund, Hamilton's principal."

"After lunch? Boy! That was fast!"

"So is Jack Lund!" Foreman snapped, scowling in the direction of the red-faced principal.

Factor #4 occurred the following Monday morning when Mr. Lund selected Sammy Perioche as judge of the Hamilton bicycle traffic court. Sammy was already the student coordinator of the Hamilton safety patrol. When he assumed the added responsibility of judge, he removed himself from the safety-patrol watch list. He selected his friend, John Bosco, to take his place at the busiest intersection under his command, the corner of New Albany Avenue and Hamilton Street.

In addition to their safety-patrol jobs, Sammy and John were leaders of the two Troop 46 patrols assigned to sell cans of oil in the quadrants north of Main Street. They were the principal recipients of Danny's derisive remarks. Thus, of all the members of the troop, they were the two most likely to take the greatest pleasure in causing Danny's downfall.

AFTER TWO WEEKS OF oil sales, Dad's weekly tally confirmed that the Wolverines continued to dominate the other patrols. With over 1,700 cans sold, our patrol again accounted for more than half. Specifically we had sold 891 cans. We also had the best three sellers in the troop, with Danny sitting on top with 231 cans to his credit.

After the results were announced, despite pleas from Scoutmaster Mel, Freddie, Dad, and me, Danny was insufferable. He focused his semi-malicious comments on the patrols led by Sammy and John. Justifiably so, the two leaders were livid.

Even though his comments were way out-of-bounds, technically Danny was correct. The two patrols did have the most affluent territories in town. Logically they should have had more sales to show for their efforts. I reminded myself that sometimes what a person says can be *correct* and at the same time not be *right.* That's how I felt about Danny's remarks on that occasion.

When Danny entered our kitchen the next morning, I immediately knew something was different. He was wearing ankle clips around both his ankles. As you pedaled your bicycle, this device was designed to keep your flopping pants' leg or cuff from becoming entangled in your bicycle chain.

Our bikes were equipped with chain guards. Some weeks before I had politely informed Danny it really wasn't necessary to wear a clip on his right leg. His reaction was *exaggerated.* He told me wearing clips on both ankles provided him with better balance, resulting in more even wear on his rubber bike tires. He insisted he did this to conserve rubber, thereby helping the war effort. Finally he invited me to join him in this noble practice.

Now why hadn't I thought of that on my own?

"Good morning, everyone! Happy May Day!"

"Morning, Danny. You're pretty chipper. What's up?" Mom observed.

"May's here so we're riding our bikes to school, starting today. Right, Jase?"

I was distracted, pondering whether Danny would still wear two ankle clips in the summer after we cut over to shorts. I concluded there was a better than even chance he would.

"What?"

"May Day! We ride our bikes to school. Right?"

This was the first I'd heard of it. But I didn't let on. "Right, Danny. It's May Day!"

After we shoved off for school, Danny seemed *highly agitated.* He continually rode his bicycle in circles around and around me. It was dizzying. When we reached New Albany Avenue, he shot through the stop sign and crossed the street without checking for oncoming traffic. He zoomed into one of the double driveways at Pete's Store and out the other. Cars coming from Riverton had to brake to avoid hitting him. Drivers honked their horns and shook their fists.

But Danny was undeterred. He continued behaving like a madman. Pedaling along New Albany, I hugged the right curb to give passing cars as much room as possible. Danny did the opposite. He rode down the centerline between the rows of cars traveling in opposite directions on either side of him.

"Danny! Please don't do that! You're going to be hit by a car," I warned. But he paid me no heed.

Down the centerline he streaked, heading toward Hamilton Street, the turnoff for our school. Still hugging the curb, I followed cautiously behind. As Danny approached the intersection, I saw John Bosco step off the curb and hold up his hand-carried *Stop* sign. Beside him was an older lady who was pulling her heavily-laden, two-wheeled grocery cart behind her.

Honoring John's sign, cars in both lanes came to a stop. Apparently Danny saw this as just the opportunity he needed. He picked up speed and raced toward John and the lady. When John saw him coming, he frantically waved his sign in Danny's direction. Instead of stopping, Danny steered directly for John, I assumed, to scare him. When Danny roared by, only missing John by inches, his back tire rolled over the wheel of the grocery cart, flipping it into the air. The contents of three full grocery bags flew in all directions. Danny zoomed around the corner onto Hamilton Street and never looked back.

"Danny! Come back here," yelled John. "Danny! Stop in the name of the law!"

I skidded to a stop and quickly parked my bike. Running out into the intersection, I hurriedly began collecting the lady's groceries. As John helped her to the curb, he tried his best to calm the poor lady. When he saw what I was doing, he nodded his approval. While I repacked the bags as quickly as possible, cars headed in both directions stayed put, allowing me to complete the job. When I finished, I hastily pulled the cart to the curb. The traumatized woman snatched the cart handle out of my hand and marched away, mumbling to herself.

"Danny has gone too far this time, Jase. This is a serious offense. I'm issuing a citation and he's going to be in deep trouble."

How could I disagree? I didn't attempt to defend Danny's outrageous behavior.

After reassuming his post at the curb, John continued to appear rattled.

"Arc you sure you're going to be all right, John?"

"Thanks, Jase. I think so. Just give me a minute. We'll let the traffic clear while I hold these kids back," he told me, pointing at his three new customers from the third grade.

After he recovered, John held up his *Stop* sign and led the three younger children across the street. I wheeled my bicycle along with them. When we reached the other side, he thanked me again and asked me to do him a favor. "Jase, will you please talk some sense into Danny? His attitude stinks right now. I really do like him, but he's making it harder and harder."

I promised John to try my best and headed to school to track down Danny. I found him sitting in his seat in Miss Sparks' classroom.

"Where have you been, Jase? I've been waiting for you. I've got an idea —."

"I've been cleaning up your mess, Danny!"

"What mess?"

"Don't you know you nearly scared that old lady half to death? You spilled her groceries all over the street! I've been with John, picking up groceries and talking to him about your behavior. That's the *mess*, Danny! And that's not the only mess you're in. John's giving you a ticket!"

"Honest, Jase. I didn't know I caused her groceries to spill. I'm really awfully sorry. Think we could go by her house after school — and apologize?"

"You better start with John," I advised. "He's really angry with you." Danny looked forlorn. But I didn't feel sorry for him.

"Danny, please come with me."

Turning toward the door, I saw Mr. Lund, Sammy Perioche, and John Bosco. Danny slowly rose from his seat, looked at me sadly, and walked to the door. Mr. Lund took Danny's elbow and led him out of the room.

I didn't see Danny until the next day after his father dropped him off at school. He seemed morose and ashamed. I couldn't blame him.

AT RECESS, I FOUND Danny. "How are you?"

He simply responded, "Terrible."

"What happened yesterday — after you left the classroom?"

"John gave me the ticket — just like you said. Sammy held my trial in Mr. Lund's office. He found me guilty of violating four traffic laws. It's all written down in my arrest record."

"Arrest record?"

"Yep. I may not be able to go to Michigan now, Jase. You'll have to find another roommate."

"Oh, it can't be that serious."

"You can say that. But you're not the one serving my sentence."

"Sentence?"

"First of all, I'm forbidden to ride a bicycle for the next six months. Dad chained my bicycle up in his garage. He and Mom are really upset with me."

After Danny's beaten-down condition, resulting from his recent one-day stay in Mrs. Tucker's prison, I couldn't imagine what he might endure over the next six months.

He continued, "For the next month, I have to stand duty as an assistant safety patrol — every morning and afternoon with John Bosco. And I have to serve a week's community service with the police. Sergeant Zeller will pick me up right after supper every night. And we'll go out on traffic patrol until 10 o'clock. I'm supposed to *observe and learn.*"

"How will you work on your First Class requirements with Freddie and me? And how'll you sell oil?"

"I haven't figured that out yet. But I do know one thing. I'm never going to get arrested again. This is too hard."

All that next week, I only saw Danny in Miss Sparks' classroom. He even stopped coming to breakfast at our house. It seemed strange not to have him in my life. But, each day after school, Freddie and I continued work on my First Class requirements. Frankly, without Danny present, we had accomplished a great deal. Strangely Freddie and I never talked about Danny. In fact, nobody talked much about Danny. Not even Mom and Dad.

The next Monday evening, Dad and I drove together to the scout meeting. He was eager to share the results of that week's sales with everyone. I wasn't quite sure why he was so excited. After all, his best salesman was under house arrest. When we arrived, the lot was filled with familiar cars.

"Dad, are the committee members here again tonight?"

"Yes. Scoutmaster Mel got the word to everybody."

"Boy, Dad. This is going to be a special sales report. Huh?"

He just smiled at me.

When we entered the church basement, Danny was there. His presence was a surprise. "I thought you'd be out on traffic patrol tonight with Sergeant Zeller."

"I've been paroled. Let off for good behavior. I'm finished with my community service. I observed and learned a lot."

"Are you glad to be here tonight? Dad's report must be really good. He seems very excited about telling everyone."

"I'd be excited too," Danny confirmed slyly.

I didn't understand. But that was not a new condition for me when Danny was involved.

After the opening ceremonies, Scoutmaster Mel quickly turned the meeting over to Dad for his report.

"Thanks, Mel. Gentlemen, I'm proud to announce that as of this afternoon we've sold every last one of the 2,400 cans of oil. We've met our goal. Our tents and equipment will be purchased within a few days. Congratulations, everyone!"

After the applause died down, Sammy inquired, "Who're the big winners, Mr. Addison?"

His question was echoed by everyone in the basement.

"All right! Quiet, please. Here're the details. First of all, the Wolverines did it again. Of the 2,400 cans, they sold a total of 1,501. That's more than any other patrol."

Our patrol led the cheer for the Wolverines.

"Now, listen up. Here're the prize-winning salesmen, starting with third place. From the Wolverine patrol — with 221 cans sold — the third-place prize of $4 goes to Jase Addison."

I was very surprised to hear that news. I thought surely someone from another patrol would have beaten me out for third place. But the troop's applause felt extremely good anyhow.

"The second-place prize of $8 goes to another Wolverine. With 278 cans sold, the winner is Freddie Holland."

The entire troop gave Freddie a loud round of applause.

Finally it struck me. I had no idea who could possibly be the first-place winner. Last week, Danny was in first with 231 cans. But he hadn't sold oil all week. To take first place, someone had to best Freddie's mark.

"It must be someone from another patrol," I whispered to JB.

"With a grand total of 504 cans sold, the $12 first-place prize goes to — Danny Tucker!"

The room was completely silent. We were all in shock. Undoubtedly everyone in the room was asking himself the same question. How could Danny possibly have sold 273 additional cans since the last meeting? Hadn't he been under lock and key all week?

"Danny! Come up here and tell your friends how you managed to pull it off," Dad suggested.

Danny walked to the stage. Looking directly at me, he hesitated. "Before I tell you that, I think Freddie's got an announcement. Freddie?"

Freddie stood up. "Danny's right. During this past week, two scouts in the Wolverine patrol completed all their requirements for First Class. They are Jase Addison and — Danny Tucker."

More silence.

"But how did Danny — ?"

Before I finished my question, Danny spoke.

"Jase and I owe Freddie our gratitude. He worked very hard to ensure we met our First Class requirements before the upcoming Court of Honor. Every afternoon after school — for weeks now — Freddie's met with Jase and me to help us. This past week he met with Jase after school, and he was good enough to ride along with me in Sergeant Zeller's patrol car — for two hours every night — to help me finish my requirements."

I stared at Danny in awe. *How did he do it?*

"Now I suppose you're wondering how I sold so many cans of oil while I was completing my public-service sentence. Let me put it this way. Sergeant Zeller was a great help. When a very large police officer walks into a bar with a scout in uniform, for some reason, everybody there needs a can of oil."

Oh, Danny!

16 SHROOMS

USING HIS POWER OF PERSUASION, DANNY OFTEN convinced people to do what their common sense told them not to do. Not that Danny's intentions were ever malicious. He was no Svengali. However, occasionally, his ability to persuade backfired, especially when he boasted about his success in influencing people to carry out his wishes.

On some level, I'm sure he was aware that he might incur Sergeant Zeller and Freddie's wrath. But when he bragged about completing less than a full week's worth of lessons from his public-service sentence, he forgot to check his audience.

Who but the most masochistic among us would have ever confessed, as he did, with his father present? Danny seemed to overlook the fact that Mr. Tucker was married to Mrs. Tucker, the dreaded warden of Danny's private slammer. In the words of Shakespeare, Danny had been hoisted by his own petard.

While we were leaving the church basement, we heard the clamor of honking horns, sirens, church bells, factory whistles, exploding firecrackers, and shotgun blasts. It sounded like New Year's Eve. When we opened the outside door, the din intensified.

"What's going on here?" Dad wondered.

All of us scouts and fathers stood in front of the church, perplexed. But at that very moment, we were rescued by one of the unsuspecting *interested parties.*

"Speak of the Devil!" Dad announced. "It's Sergeant Zeller."

"Fantastic news, folks! Germany has surrendered unconditionally. The war in Europe's over! President Truman has declared tomorrow V-E Day — Victory in Europe Day. Schools will be closed. There'll be a big parade downtown at noon. People are flooding into the center of town tonight. All the stores are still open. It's like New Year's Eve down there. Thought you'd want to know!"

After we thanked him, like a town crier of old, Sergeant Zeller sped off to deliver his news flash to people in other parts of the city.

"Wow! That *is* terrific news! It's sure been a long time coming. Maybe our boys can come home now."

"I sure hope so, Dad."

For some odd reason, I remembered an exchange I had with JB just after we had met. He wondered if my father had been in the military. Of course, JB's father had volunteered to become a navy doctor and was killed in action. I explained that Dad was a tool and die maker in a defense factory. His skills were considered war-critical, meaning he was exempt from the draft. Seeming to understand, JB accepted my explanation. But I'm not sure I did. Not fully anyway. I was a little like Dad in that regard.

Although many men in the army would have changed places with Dad in a second, he felt somewhat ambivalent about his status. On one hand, he was certainly grateful to be out of harm's way and home with Mom and me. But, because so many of his friends and family were in the service, he sometimes wondered whether he was acting patriotically responsible.

Of course, without the talents of skilled men like my father, tools-of-war such as the Norden bombsight or the atomic bomb could not have met their critical delivery dates. Without their availability, the war would have lasted months or even years longer than it did. This delay would have proven very costly in terms of human life and coin.

"Yep! I sure hope so, Dad," I repeated.

Wanting to share this exciting time with my best friend, I looked around for Danny. He wasn't in the group. And neither was Mr. Tucker.

"Dad, have you seen the Tuckers?"

At that moment, they both came out of the church. Danny's body language told me he had just gotten an earful from his father. Everyone shouted the news of the surrender at them. When they walked by, I asked, "Want to go downtown tomorrow to watch the parade with me?"

"No, Jase. I'm afraid I'll be staying at home for — for the duration. I'll see you when I get out — I mean — later."

His father steered Danny toward the parking lot. That would be the last I would see of him for several days. This time his mother made arrangements with Miss Sparks for Danny to keep up with his schoolwork from home. Furthermore, Danny was not allowed to leave the Tucker house. Mrs. Tucker was committed to doing all she could to prevent a recurrence of Danny's recidivism.

"Looks serious, Jase."

I didn't say what I was really thinking. I was angry and very disappointed that Danny allowed his selfishness and ego to get himself and others in trouble again. He'd really pay the price this time. Without his companionship, so would I. All I could do was hope that this time he would learn his lesson.

Needing to forget Danny for a while, I changed the subject. "Dad, let's go home and tell Mom the good news."

"All right, Jase. Let's do exactly that. Hey! I nearly forgot — congratulations on being one of the top three sellers."

"Thanks, Dad. Think of how much better I'd have done — if you'd been a policeman!"

ON MAY 7, 1945, Germany's unconditional surrender formally brought an end to the war in Europe. After five years, eight months, and six days of bloodshed and destruction, what was left of the encircled German army had no choice but to capitulate. In the French city of Reims, the surrender took place in a small red schoolhouse, which served as the headquarters for General Dwight D. Eisenhower, Commander of Allied Forces in northwestern Europe.

The surrender instrument was signed for the Germans by Colonel General Gustav Jodl, the new Army Chief of Staff. Lieutenant General Walter Bedell Smith, Chief of Staff for General

Eisenhower, signed for the Allies. The next day, a second surrender document was signed near Soviet-occupied Berlin by Russian Field Marshall Georgy Zhukov and German General Field Marshall Wilhelm Keitel.

As soon as news of the surrender was leaked by the press, massive celebrations erupted all over the free world. In London, an estimated one million celebrants flooded the streets from Trafalgar Square to Buckingham Palace. King George VI and Queen Elizabeth appeared on the palace balcony with Prime Minister Winston Churchill to greet the cheering crowds. Eyewitness reports described American sailors and rejoicing young English women, forming endless conga lines in Piccadilly Circus.

New York emulated London. Masses of humanity flooded Times Square, as well as the financial and garment districts. Tons of paper floated downward from office-building windows. New Yorkers danced, kissed each other, and held up newspapers, whose headlines proclaimed the victory. The celebration went on and on into the wee hours of the next morning.

The western Allies declared May 8, 1945, as the official day for celebrating Victory in Europe. Because fighting continued on the German Eastern Front, the Soviets postponed the official victory celebration until May 9th. After cessation of hostilities, the Soviets referred to this struggle as their Great Patriotic War. In the decades immediately following the war, most Germans considered May 8th as their day of defeat. But in 1985, West German Prime Minister Richard von Weizsacker redefined V-E Day for Germans by calling it "The day of liberation from the Nazi government."

Well before noon on V-E Day, the Addisons, Reillys, and Bradfords were standing in front of Woolworth's awaiting the impromptu parade that was forming a half-mile away at the north end of Addison Street. While Riverton's V-E Day turnout was considerably smaller than that of London or New York, we were equal in our enthusiasm and excitement.

The atmosphere on the sidewalks lining the parade route reminded me of the Chippewa County Fair. Neighbors and friends chatted and laughed, genuinely happy to see each other on this momentous occasion. The Reillys and Bradfords decided to see if

Woolworth's carried sunvisors. Not wanting to miss anything, they promised to return promptly.

"I'm glad they've gone. Now I can tell you two a secret," Mom whispered conspiratorially. "Rose has been offered a position at Riverton Memorial — as a surgical nurse. That's her specialty. Mary Reilly was so excited she told me and then swore me to secrecy. I've been bursting to tell you about it. But, Jase, she hasn't told JB yet. Mum's the word."

So much for secret-keeping among the women in our neighborhood.

"Marie, is she going to accept the position?"

"I don't know — but it's extremely flattering. When the director of the hospital learned of her superb qualifications, he called Mr. Reilly to ask if he could stop by and speak with Rose. That was just yesterday."

"Boy! It didn't take him long to make up his mind."

"So many medical professionals are needed for the armed forces that nurses with her skills are very hard to find, especially here in Riverton. Rose told him she needed a few days to think about it. She'll decide by Friday. So mum's the word."

We'd been so engrossed in Mom's secret that we failed to notice the approaching couple.

"Hello, John. Happy V-E Day!"

Dad looked up and smiled. "Hi, there, Walt. Vickie. Come over and meet my family."

The tall man with rugged good looks approached us with a broad grin on his face. By his side was an equally friendly and very attractive lady.

Dad made the introductions. "Folks, this is my friend Walt Williams and his wife Vickie. Walt and I work together at Burke's. And Vickie works there too — in the accounting department."

"The Williamses are the source of the delicious smoked lake trout, Jase!" Mom reminded me.

"If you liked that, you'll love what we're featuring at the cottage this weekend. Right, Vickie?"

"We got a call last night from a friend up in Mesick. They've gathered a few shrooms already. With the warm weather they're calling for over the next few days, this weekend should be great shrooming," Vickie predicted with a smile. "We're going up after work on Thursday night for a couple of days. We want to get there ahead of the weekend crowd. We're both taking vacation days on Friday. You probably have a lot of days on the books too, John. Why don't the three of you join us? We have plenty of room at our cottage. And it'll be a great time. We'll show you all how to shroom. Then we'll prepare a gourmet feast!"

I didn't know where Mesick was, and I had no idea what *shroom* meant. But both Williamses were so enthusiastic and welcoming, I blurted out, "Can we go, Dad? I'll clear it with Miss Sparks."

"What do you think, Marie?"

Mom liked the idea too. That week, she had no tailoring classes at the POW camp after Wednesday evening.

We had a plan.

"We'll iron out the logistics at work tomorrow, John. Right now, we have to find Vickie's sister and her husband. Nice meeting all of you. Look forward to some fun and great eating this weekend."

Great eating! Probably a shroom is a fish.

Before I could clarify this with Dad or Mom, we had more visitors.

"Hello, Addisons!"

We turned to find Coach Jim and Louise Libby walking toward us. I hadn't seen them since our Easter dinner at the Reilly's.

"Jim — Louise! What's new with you two?"

When Louise looked at Jim, they both started grinning. "Should we tell them all our good news?"

"What good news? Tell us right now, Louise," Mom insisted excitedly.

"Okay! Let's see. Where should I start?"

"Tell them about the girls, first," Jim advised.

"Gladly! Thanks to Jim's glowing recommendation and some great help from Donald Foreman — the Superintendent of Schools — both Barb and Anne have been accepted by *Michigan State Normal College* in Ypsilanti. They enroll in June — for a summer session. After that, they'll stay on for the fall and spring semesters. It'll take four years for them to graduate. They're going to room together in the dormitory. We're absolutely elated — and so is Aunt Greta."

"That's *wonderful* news, Louise!" Mom exclaimed, giving her friend a hug.

"Excuse me, Mrs. Libby! What's a *normal* college?"

"That's a good question, Jase. When I first heard the term, I wondered exactly the same thing. *Normal* means using a *standardized* curriculum to train high school graduates to be teachers. The goal of normal colleges is to establish teaching standards — or *norms*. That's how state teachers colleges came to be called *normal* schools."

"I didn't know that," Dad admitted.

"Do you have any more pleasant surprises?"

"Why don't you give them *your* news, Jim?"

"Okay, I will. In a nutshell, you're looking at the new principal of Riverton High School."

"What? That's terrific, Jim! How did that happen? Wait a minute. What happened to —what's his name — the current principal?"

"That's Oliver Terhune. Ollie's going to be the new principal at Flint Central. Much larger high school than Riverton High. A lot of very qualified candidates applied, but Ollie was selected. I'm very happy for him."

"What's going to happen to your coaching?" Dad broached the subject that had just entered my mind.

"Essentially I'll be the Director of Athletics. While we'll hire a new football coach, I'll stay closely involved."

"You just had an undefeated and state-championship season. I certainly should *hope* you'll stay involved. But I sure don't want to take anything away from your being selected as principal. That's quite an honor — after only having been back on the job for a few months since your — absence."

Dad was referring to the years Jim spent as our neighborhood bum. Fortunately his Gentleman Jim years were far behind him.

"One good thing about Jim's new job is that he'll hire all of the new teachers. In a few years, Barb and Anne will be job-hunting. I'd like them to teach close to home — which brings me to my next piece of good news. Aunt Greta is selling the family home in Milwaukee and moving to Riverton. She wants to be close to us because the girls and I are her only family."

"Good thing they'll be living in the dorm in Ypsilanti. You'd be crowded with five of you in the house," Mom observed.

"No, the girls can keep their own rooms for vacations because Greta won't be living with us."

"Oh, for gosh sakes! Where will she live?"

"Next door — with the Zeyers," Louise told us with a smile. "It's the best of all worlds. She and the Zeyers are absolutely overjoyed with how it's all worked out."

"Well, I'll be. Do you have anything else to share with us?"

"Yes. We've set our wedding date. Mark your calendar for Saturday, the 2nd of June. We'll be married by Reverend Noble at the First Methodist Church, and we'll also have our reception there."

"That's where you announced your engagement on Thanksgiving. Or was it Danny who announced it?"

"Any more good news?"

"Who's got good news? Tell us all — quick — before the parade starts," Mrs. Reilly demanded.

So we heard Jim and Louise's newscast twice. Once they had finished, we heard the *boom-boom-boom* of the Riverton High School marching band's big bass drum.

After we arrived home from the V-E Day celebration, we sat in our front room reviewing the day. "Today we celebrated the end of the war in Europe. That was very important, but we sure had a lot more than that to celebrate. Didn't we?"

"It was a great day, Dad. It really was. But there were two things wrong with it."

"I know one of them. Danny wasn't with us. Right?" Mom guessed.

"That's one. I really missed him."

"I can't imagine what the other one is."

"I never found out what *shroom* means."

WALT AND VICKIE WILLIAMS were members of the passionate group of Michiganders who were addicted to the practice of hunting, gathering, cooking, and consuming delicious wild mushrooms. Of these *shrooms*, as they are known to aficionados, the most highly prized are the illusive and delectable *morels.*

At work the next day, Mr. Williams and Dad worked out the details of our shrooming trip. After supper, Dad shared the plans with Mom and me. Pointing at a spot on the Michigan road map he'd spread out on the kitchen table, Dad told us, "The Williams' cottage is located right about here. It's just north of Mesick on the south bank of the Manistee River. That's a great river for canoeing and fishing — especially for brown trout."

"How far is it from here, John?"

"About 140 miles. There're pretty decent roads though. Probably take us a little over three hours driving time. Weather's supposed to be good for the next few days. It'll be a nice drive in the evening."

"Do the Williamses go up there often?"

"Because there's just the two of them, they're pretty flexible. I gather they go up about every other weekend. They enjoy all kinds of fishing — and gathering morels this time of year. Walt tells me the woods in that area produce more morels than anywhere else in the world. Mesick calls itself the *Mushroom Capital of the United States.*"

"That's odd," Mom remarked. "In the Sunday paper a couple of weeks ago, I read about a Pennsylvania town that calls itself the *Mushroom Capital of the World.*"

"Anyway, getting back to the trip. They'll pack their station wagon in the morning and come here right after work to load our bags. Then we're off."

"What about meals up there? Should I be taking something?"

"Vickie mentioned we'd be stopping at a little market in Mesick near their cottage."

"Ma brought us something today that will be perfect for a supper. Yep, I'll make it my surprise."

"Dad, have you ever gone *shrooming?*"

"Not for a long time. Your mom and I went a couple of times with a friend of mine from high school — Paul Smithy. His dad took us up to an area not far from Roscommon. When Paul joined the navy a couple of years before Pearl Harbor, that was the end of that."

"Is he still in the Navy, Dad?"

"No. After the attack on Pearl Harbor, under cover of smoke from the burning ships, his destroyer was able to escape without being seen by the Japs. Unfortunately a few days later, his ship was torpedoed by a Jap submarine. None of the crew survived. From what his dad told me, evidence showed they'd drifted along with the debris for many days. But ultimately they lost the battle with sharks. It wasn't a pleasant story."

"John, you never told me how Paul died."

"I didn't see any reason for you to have to know all that. Not quite sure why I told you tonight. I guess it's because we're talking about going for morels. The last time either of us went, Paul was there. Anyway, Jase, he was a good guy and one of my oldest friends. And boy! Did he ever love his morels — especially the Blacks."

Dad reached for the book that Walt Williams had loaned him. Its pages were dog-eared and its cover so worn you could hardly discern the title. Dad had to read it for us. *Guide to Edible Mushrooms.* Walt swears by this book. He thought we'd like to study a bit before leaving for Mesick."

"Walt says the only morels we'll find up there will be the Blacks. They're the first ones that pop up in the spring. The Whites sprout a little later. Some people call them Yellows. I always had a hard time knowing the difference. Since Walt says we might see one or two, we should know what they look like too. Walt marked the pages where both are described."

Dad opened the page and showed us the color plate of a small black mushroom. It looked like a miniature, partially-folded dark-brown umbrella. The morel's appearance reminded me a bit of the picture of the human brain depicted in our health-class textbook, but its wrinkles and creases were more symmetrical. Dad thought the surface resembled the brown rippled ridges of a sea horse.

After hearing our comparisons, Mom shook her head. "Ugh! You two need help."

Under the picture, the description read as follows:

Black Morel (*Morchella elata*)

The Black Morel is the first to fruit in the morel season. It usually appears just after or during the False Morel fruiting season. The Black Morel ranges in size from .5 inches to 12 inches. Its colors range from charcoal-black to dark-brown. Lighter colors are found in other species of the Black Morel including *Morchella conica* and *Morchella angusticeps*.

Like all true morels, the Black Morel has a hollow stem to which the cap is attached. Because of its meaty texture, most people say the Black Morel is the best eating of all morels.

To be honest, I was a bit disappointed by what I saw. Because of its superlative reputation, I was expecting the Black Morel to have a more grandiose appearance. Instead, here was a puny-looking mushroom. I shared this impression with Dad.

"Jase, just wait until you taste one after it's been fried in butter. Almost as good as smelt."

That got my attention. No more doubts for me.

The color plates of the Yellow Morel (Morchella esculenta) and White Morel (Morchella deliciosa) were so similar that we couldn't tell them apart. In its description, the Yellow Morel was called a Gray Morel. The author speculated the White could be an immature Yellow. We were confused.

But one thing was certain. The Yellow and/or White Morels looked far more substantial than the Black. They were thought to be almost as delicious. Besides Mr. Williams didn't think we'd see any Yellow/White Morels when we went shrooming in Mesick that weekend.

"We forgot to check out the False Morel. We're likely to see some of them," Dad reminded us, referring back to the Black Morel's description. He flipped through the pages of the guide. "Here it is. The False Morel isn't a morel at all. Hmmm. It looks bigger, fatter, and uglier than a Black Morel. They say it's called a

Red Mushroom. Or a Lorchel. Or a Beefsteak Mushroom. Oh, Lord!"

"What is it, John?"

"It says that some people can prepare and eat the False Morel without any problems. But others have very serious side effects including —. Holy Smokes! There're a half-dozen symptoms. I wouldn't wish any of them on my worst enemy. Oh, I love that last one."

"What is it, Dad?"

"Even possible death!"

"I wish you hadn't read that, John."

"You and me both. Boy, I'm glad we're going with the Williamses."

"And I'm glad their guide book is so beat up. It tells me they do their homework."

That was an understatement!

ON THURSDAY MORNING BEFORE leaving the house, we were all packed and ready to go shrooming. The Williamses had warned us that during this time of year Mesick temperatures could range from the 70s to the teens. For our comfort, they advised we pack layers of clothing that could be added or removed easily.

For a day or so before our departure, they also suggested we avoid the use of perfumes, colognes, and scented soaps that might attract nasty blackflies. When picking blueberries in the bogs north of Riverton, we sometimes experienced swarms of these little monsters. In our book, there was only one remedy for blackflies. Dad called it the chicken-liver cure. We simply grabbed our berries, ran to the car, and drove straight home. We Addisons hated blackfly bites a whole lot more than we loved blueberries.

At recess, JB suggested we find Chub and inquire about Danny. I agreed but not without reservations. Chub's tendency to exaggerate, when in the spotlight, sometimes caused him to deliver less than truthful testimony. But when we found him, he gave us the straight story. "Mom lets Danny help Dad out in the garage. He does that all day until Miss Sparks stops by with his schoolwork. After he finishes that, he and Queenie listen to big band music. Then he goes to bed."

"Big band music! He's lost his mind."

Chub agreed. "I really hate big band music. I just go outside where I can't hear it."

At last, I had found something to like about Chub.

"How long do you think Danny'll have to stay home?"

Chub thought about JB's question for a long time. Finally he answered, "Until he goes to college — I bet."

I assumed we'd just witnessed a sampling of Chub's exaggeration. But I couldn't be certain with Mrs. Tucker overseeing Danny's punishment.

"Danny also wanted me to tell you to have fun in Mesick."

"How did he — ?"

"Yesterday after work, Mr. Williams had Dad tune up his station wagon for the trip. Danny heard them talking. Oh! There's one more thing. Danny said to tell you he's sorry."

"About what?"

"About all the blackfly bites you'll get in Mesick."

BY FIVE O'CLOCK, WE had finished loading our luggage into the back compartment of the Williams' station wagon. As planned, Mom and Mrs. Williams had made a dozen sandwiches and jugs of coffee and hot cocoa. No one would suffer hunger pangs on this trip.

Mr. Williams and Dad sat up front while I sat in the backseat, sandwiched between the two ladies. When we pulled out onto New Albany Avenue, Mr. Williams glanced at his watch. "Sunset's at 8:49 p.m. this evening. Allowing for a gas and rest stop in Clare, we should be at the grocery store in Mesick well before dark."

"Marie, I understand you and John have gone shrooming before," Mrs. Williams remarked.

"Several years ago, we went a few times with a high school friend of John's. We did gather a good number of morels but — from what I know now — we were awfully lucky not to have found any false ones. Compared to Walt and you, we were rank amateurs. And Jase has never gone. Perhaps you could give us some tips."

"We love talking about morels. Since we bought our cottage 12 years ago, shrooming's become our passion. If you live in Mesick and don't shroom, people around there think there's something wrong with you. We played dumb — which we were — so people took us under their wings and taught us what we needed to know. We're happy to share all we've learned with you. Why don't we start by answering your questions?"

"I'll be happy to go first," Dad volunteered. "Do morels only grow in Michigan?"

"Each year, morel sightings are reported as far west as California, east to Long Island, and south to Texas. But the vast majority of sightings occur in the upper Midwest. Within that area, the upper half of Michigan's Lower Peninsula has *the* very best shrooming — at least for morels. By the way, a friend of mine says the largest morel he ever saw was gathered by Mr. Frank, the Michigan Conservation Officer assigned to Chippewa County. It was growing on a farm about six miles south of Riverton."

"That's hard to believe, Walt."

"I have a question too. Exactly where in the woods are you most likely to find morels?"

"Marie, if you ask a dozen experienced shroomers, you'll hear a dozen different answers. But from our experience, you'll find them most often near dead or dying trees — elm, fruit trees like apple, and even pine. They seem to like well-drained moist soil. After a mild humid night, they'll pop up from under leaves. So places where leaves naturally accumulate are good."

"I had difficulty spotting them — even when they were right in front of me," Mom confessed.

"You're not the only one. The morel's coloring and texture help them blend in with the leaves, rotting stumps, and logs on the ground. Seeing the big ones is fairly easy, but spotting the smaller ones takes a trained eye. When you do find one, you've located the right soil and other conditions. You'll probably find more near that spot."

"Do you always gather them in the same spots?"

"We sure do. We have certain places we've found by trial and error over the years. We do our shrooming very early in the morning. Incidentally that's when we gather the best tasting morels. They're the ones that have freshly sprouted the night before. During the height of the season, we don't want any locals to stumble on our hot spots by accident. Those shrooms are in our onion bags real early in the day. Isn't that right, Vickie?"

"All shroomers have hot spots, but they never tell anybody where they're located. Secrecy is common among shroomers. A friend of mine says morels are like gold. Around Mesick, you never reveal the location of your *gold mine*, even to your closest friends."

"During shroom season, we always come up during the week or on the Thursday before the weekend. That way we can gather ours before those down-state weekenders arrive. Even the clumsiest tourist can get lucky. Like the old saying — even a blind pig finds an occasional acorn."

"Too bad you can't train pigs to hunt morels like the French do for truffles."

"Funny you should say that, Marie. When we first came up here, there was a sign on the edge of town that read *The French have their truffles. Michiganders have their morels.* Remember that, Vickie?"

"Whatever happened to that sign?"

"Somebody burned it down. Maybe a disgruntled Frenchman."

"Or maybe a blind pig," I suggested. Everyone laughed. "Seriously though. The *Guide* states that Black Morels come first and the Whites follow them. When do the Blacks first appear?"

"That depends on two factors — temperature and moisture. Mushroom experts say the ideal weather for stimulating Blacks to sprout are day-time temperatures in the 70s with temperatures at night no lower than the 40s. Our experience squares with that.

"But even with ideal temperatures, Blacks won't sprout until the moisture's just right — when it's not too moist and not too dry. Around Mesick, most years, these factors come together during the first two weeks of May. That's usually when you'll see your first Blacks."

"Sounds like there's a lot more luck than science involved here, Walt."

"Experts will readily agree with you on that. When it comes to estimating when and where they'll first sprout, there's a lot of just plain luck involved. But when you finally do spot a Black Morel, there's a right way and a wrong way to harvest it."

Being on solid ground was a relief to me. I wasn't sure I could become passionate about hunting such an illusive quarry. Of course, that was before I'd enjoyed my first taste of a properly prepared Black Morel.

"To pick a morel, you simply break it off at the base of the stem. I personally use a pinch and twist move. They're fairly easy to break so it's not difficult. You don't want to pull up the root because that's a sure way to get dirt on the edible part of the mushroom. Dirt's very hard to remove from a morel because of its texture.

"Next you shake the morel lightly so the spores — the mushroom seeds — fall onto the ground. Because of their loose knit, onion sacks are the preferred collection bag. While you tromp through the woods, the spores can escape through the bag. We don't want to take those precious seeds home with us. We need them right there in the woods to grow next year's crop."

When we entered the town of Clare, Mr. Williams announced, "Up ahead is the gas station where we like to stop. It's a little more than halfway to Mesick. They have clean restrooms and a nice table where we can have a cup of coffee and one of the ladies' sandwiches."

When we stopped beside the pump, Mom and Mrs. Williams took the sandwiches and jugs to the log picnic table in front of the combined general store and gas station. Dad and Mr. Williams watched as the attendant checked the oil and the tires. Finally he washed every car window, using his squeegee and clean rag.

When I joined the ladies at the table, Mom was saying, "The next thing I want to learn is the best way to prepare and cook the morel."

"Honestly, Marie, I'm glad we've stopped to eat something. I can't talk about cooking morels without my mouth watering and my stomach growling. If I have a sandwich and cocoa, maybe I can avoid suffering from a morel craving."

"Vickie, you and Walt talk about morels the same way Jase and his father talk about smelt."

"That's true, Mom. On V-E Day, when I heard Mr. and Mrs. Williams talking about *shrooms*, I assumed they were fish."

"Well, Jase. Maybe they're not fish. But it's sure easy to get hooked on them."

ONCE WE WERE BACK on the road, Mrs. Williams instructed, "You men just keep your eyes on the road. I'm conducting a cooking class back here."

"Can't we listen in? Maybe add a comment or two?" Mr. Williams inquired.

"Maybe so! But only if you behave yourselves," she replied, winking at us. "Marie, this won't take long because morels are so easy to prepare."

"Years ago, the morels we gathered with Paul Smithy were always turned over to his mother," Mom told us. "She was very fussy about sharing recipes and so on. When she cooked the morels, I wasn't allowed in her kitchen. She told me that I was a guest and should act like one. So I did. The point is — I don't know the first thing about preparing them."

"Believe me, Marie. You'll be an expert in five minutes. The first thing we do when we get home is rinse them in clear water. I usually just fill the sink and immerse them. This removes the dirt, particles of wood, and bugs."

"Bugs?"

"Unfortunately they seem to attract a certain number of critters. The best way to make sure you've cleaned them thoroughly is to slice them lengthwise into two halves. After cleaning them, I place them on a damp kitchen towel. That keeps them moist while I refill the sink with cold water. Then I add a bit of salt — less than half a teaspoon — and let them soak overnight. Bugs don't like that treatment at all.

"Some people won't soak them in saltwater for more than an hour. They believe longer soakings allow morels to absorb too much salt — and spoil their natural flavor. We've done it both ways and haven't noticed any difference. Of course, we're not using a lot of salt. You can experiment and decide for yourself.

"When they've finished soaking, I rinse them in clear water again and lay them between towels to soak up the excess water. If you're not going to cook them right away, you can store them between moist layers of towels for a while in the icebox until you're ready.

"Most of the time, we serve morels over steaks, chicken breasts, or veal cutlets. Before frying, I slice them lengthwise again. We like the strips about two to two-and-a-half inches long. If the morels are the larger ones, you can cut them in two to produce that size. In any case, they'll shrink a bit when you cook them. Next we fry them — on a low heat — in butter with just a touch of salt and pepper. To be sure they're not overcooked, I stir them quite often. If cooked properly, they'll be hot and soft when you serve them."

"Can you store them for a time?"

"Sure. The best way is to freeze them right after you cook them. Just put them in a canning jar with a tight cover — butter and all. Leave a little room for expansion. Store the jar in your freezer. Later just heat them. They'll taste like you just fried them."

"Is that all there is to it? I wonder why Mrs. Smithy was so secretive."

"There's another way they can be stored," Mr. Williams added from the front seat. "Some people thread them and hang them to dry. Just like you would chili peppers. After they dry, they can be stored. Later, when they're soaked in mild saltwater overnight, they'll return to their original size. And after they're cooked, they still taste great."

"That's right. I'd nearly forgotten about that technique. Because we generally fry and eat what we gather right away, we seldom have enough left to save for later."

"Vickie, shall I tell them about our run-in with the hawk?"

"Only if you leave out the part about me screaming and running away!" Mrs. Williams snickered.

"About two seasons ago, we were out hunting morels when Vickie was attacked by a huge hawk. Must have had a wingspan of three feet. Without warning — screeching like a banshee — that hawk came swooping down to within inches of Vickie's head. This happened over and over. As you can imagine, it nearly scared her to death. So she took off running back to the main trail.

"Like a dope, I just stood there watching her go. Suddenly that crazy hawk came after me. Frankly it made me mad. So I picked up this stick — or club — about four feet long and two-and-a-half inches in diameter. Each time that hawk swooped, I'd swing my bat. I missed every time. Neither the hawk nor I got hurt. Finally I gave up and followed Vickie back to the trail.

"Later, after I thought about it some, it finally dawned on me. That hawk probably had a nest in the area. She was just protecting her young from us humans. After this episode, we settled down and decided to resume our hunt for morels. Would you believe it? About 300 yards from our initial attack that same hawk — or its twin sister — attacked us again. Two hawk attacks in the same day. How about that?"

"Maybe I should have brought my shotgun, Mr. Williams."

"Sure, Jase. I could use it like a club. That way nobody'd get hurt."

WE STOPPED AT THE Williams' favorite market to stock up on groceries for our two-day stay. Mom announced that our main course for Saturday night was a gift from Grandma Compton. "She wanted us to have something special to enjoy with our morels. That roll wrapped in butcher paper that I brought from home is a hefty beef tenderloin. It'll make several huge filets. How's that sound?"

Thank you, Grandma Compton!

The Williams cottage was just down the road from the market. But before unpacking the car, our hosts insisted we take a look at the cottage and see the view before the sun disappeared below the horizon.

The instant we stepped inside, I could see why they were so adamant. The interior was caringly finished in wood paneling the color of golden honey. In the light of the setting sun, the sparkling Manistee River was visible through the expansive windows that covered one wall of the main room. Beyond the windows, a stained wooden deck was furnished with black wrought-iron furniture. Its deep-green cushions were stacked neatly just inside the sliding glass doors.

"Your cottage is absolutely gorgeous. The finish work is exquisite, and the view is breathtaking. You must be very proud of it."

"Marie, we've worked here on this cottage two weekends a month for eight years. You're our first guests since we called the project complete. And, yes. We're extremely pleased with how everything has turned out."

"My goodness, it certainly has paid off. Frankly I've never seen a place as warm and welcoming. Have you, John?"

"I'm flabbergasted. I was prepared to camp out. That's what most people's cottages amount to. This is a real gem. Thank you for inviting us to stay here."

When we came down from the clouds, Mrs. Williams asked what we wanted for our late supper. I didn't know about the others, but I craved a pillow and a long night's sleep. Quickly we settled on chicken-noodle soup and grilled-cheese sandwiches.

While Mom and Mrs. Williams put the meal together, we men sat in the comfortable main room facing the immense fieldstone fireplace. Mr. Williams had just struck a match to start a fire that had been laid before our arrival. Wavering streaks of yellow light, emanating from the briskly-burning fire, painted every honey-colored wall in the room. Mesmerized by this setting, I leaned back in my brown-leather easy chair and closed my eyes.

When I awoke, I heard voices coming from outside the room where I lay. At first, I was confused, not knowing where I was. My suitcase was on a white wicker chair next to a light-colored maple chest of drawers. I slipped on my jeans and sweatshirt, pushed into my shoes, and walked toward the voices.

"Good morning, sleepyhead. Do you realize how long you slept? Just short of nine hours. How do you feel?"

"Very rested, Mom. And, to be honest, a little hungry too."

"That's because you missed your supper last night. We tried to wake you, but you weren't having any part of it. There're some scrambled eggs on the stove. Make some toast and then we'll be off for your first day of shrooming."

"My tongue still gets tangled on that word," I admitted. Both the Williamses chuckled at that.

"We had the very same problem. Maybe it's our Riverton accent — but when we first bought the cottage, that word simply refused to roll gracefully off our tongues. We were branded *tourists* until we could pronounce it like the natives. Jase, by the end of two days, I'll bet you'll be able to say it right every time. Or at least every other time."

Not wanting to hold up the shroom parade, I quickly devoured my breakfast. In response to the temperature reading on the thermometer outside the kitchen window, we dressed warmly in layers as suggested. Before departing, we assembled on the deck for Mr. Williams' short briefing.

"Here's an onion bag for each of you. I suggest you hang it on your belt. That'll free up both hands. It's early so it'll be difficult hunting deep in the woods. Shrooms are hard enough to find in the bright daylight, let alone in the dark. First, we'll check out two or three of our favorite hot spots that're lighted by the morning sun. That should take us an hour or so, and then we'll make our way into the *deep, dark forest primeval!*"

Our first potential hot spot was just inside the woods next to a fern-covered meadow. The area under the sparsely-growing trees was also covered with ferns. Given all I'd learned about the ideal habitat for morels, this did not appear to be a likely hot spot. It looked more like an extension of the fern field we had just crossed. But there were large decaying stumps of formerly gigantic elm trees hidden among the ferns. The stumps had been cut so low that ferns had grown up around them, hiding them from view.

"Bingo! Here's our first nugget of gold. Circle around, my friends, and take a gander. You'll want to see how it grows naturally before I pick it."

We circled around the mammoth stump and I looked down. I didn't see a thing. Mr. Williams pointed his toe at what looked like an irregularity in the bark still remaining on the sides of the stump. I bent over for a closer look. Sure enough, there it was. But the day's first morel didn't come close to meeting my high hopes and expectations. It wasn't much larger than my thumb.

"This shroom has just sprouted overnight. You can tell because there's hardly any stem showing yet. Watch carefully. This is how I suggest you pick a morel."

He leaned over and demonstrated his pinch-and-twist method. Next he shook what must have been invisible spores over the ground near the margin of the stump and the bed of ferns. Finally he gently deposited the baby morel into the sack hanging from his belt.

"Remember! Where there's one shroom, there'll likely be more. This area of stumps extends from here all the way to that large blue spruce. I suggest we spread out and cover it thoroughly as we head that way."

Because I had taken up position on the left end of our line of shroomers, I was nearer to the dense woods than the others. I inspected two stumps very closely but didn't spot a thing. When I bent over to peek under a large fern, what I saw caused me to shout, "Mr. Williams! Dad! Look what I've found."

Everybody came running, assuming I'd spotted a prize morel. But my prize was of another nature. When everyone reached me, I suggested that they bend over and look under the large fern.

Mom took a close look. "What is it, Jase? Oh! Now I see. Isn't it darling? How did you ever see it? Its spots blend in so perfectly with the sun-mottled patterns under the ferns."

"What is it, Marie?"

"It's a pretty little fawn. Probably just born recently. It's so tiny."

"You're right, Marie. We see newly-born fawns in the area every shrooming season. Because fawns don't have much of a scent, the does safely leave them and go off to feed. We make a practice of leaving them alone. No sense in upsetting their mothers."

I backed away and circled around to the right to avoid leaving my scent too near the fawn when I walked past.

After the excitement subsided, I got down to work and searched diligently for my first shroom. By this time, I was determined to be the next person to spot a winner. Just as that thought entered my head, I saw it. A huge morel standing nearly a foot high.

"Mr. Williams! Come quickly. Wait until you see this morel! Dad! Mom! Look at it. It's huge!"

I was ecstatic. My temples were pounding. I felt like yelling but I managed to maintain my composure.

Mr. Williams arrived first. He took one look at my prize. "Jase, I'm very happy you found this mushroom. But I'm afraid it's not a gold nugget. It's more like fool's gold. It's a False Morel — or as some people call them — a Beefsteak Mushroom."

"It sure looks like a morel — to me at least." Out of the blue, it came to me. "Nuts! This is the poisonous one."

"That's why I'm happy you found it. I want everyone to see what it looks like. Sometimes when these False Morels are a bit smaller they're extremely difficult to tell from the real thing. But here's the test."

Mr. Williams removed his hunting knife and cut the mushroom off at the base. He laid it on a nearby log and sliced it lengthwise as you would when cleaning a morel. "See here. This mushroom is solid. Just filled with that cream-colored meat. Some call it *cotton*. True morels are hollow inside. That's the test. If they're not hollow, leave them alone. These are man-killers."

"Thank goodness for that!" I declared with relief.

"What do you mean, Jase?"

"I'm still a boy, Mr. Williams!"

BY THE END OF my first day of shrooming, each of us had gathered a number of true Black Morels. Back at the cottage, we assembled in the kitchen to admire our take. My bag alone contained over 60 shrooms of which I was very proud.

Each of us poured the contents of our onion bags into the bushel basket on the kitchen table. Our catch was varied, ranging in size from about two inches to several morels that would have stood at least six inches tall. In the end, the basket contained about two-thirds of a bushel.

Before we started the day, I had no idea what a good day's shrooming would produce. However, having strained my eyes and back for nearly seven hours, I was very satisfied with what we had to show for our effort.

"Quite honestly, this is much more than I expected from the first day of shrooming season. I think our hot spots are really beginning to pay off, Vickie."

"Don't forget, it's Friday. We got up here before the *amateurs*. And our team had five very talented shroomers."

Mrs. Williams and Mom began to organize the ingredients and utensils for preparing supper. The main course was to be chicken and dumplings, one of my favorites. We men began the morel cleaning and preparation process. Friday's morels, properly prepared and cooked, combined with Grandma Compton's filet mignons would be our Saturday evening gourmet feast.

Once again, the slumber gods beckoned early. I don't know what it is about being *Up North*, but when I'm there, everything smells, tastes, sounds, and feels better, including a good night's sleep.

The Williams' practice of arriving before the weekend crowds proved to be a wise one. Even though we launched our Saturday shrooming an hour earlier, we encountered more competing shroomers in the first hour than during the entire previous day. Even with only a day's shrooming expertise under my belt, I found myself resenting these newcomers who were violating the sanctity of *my* woods with their loud voices, laughter, and smelly pipes and cigars. The Saturday crowd was much too rowdy! How quickly I had become a purist!

When we entered the woods where we had the day before, I was immediately confronted with further evidence of the callous nature of amateurs in our midst. Sadly my first morel of the day had been crushed by the careless boot of a non-observant neophyte.

Nonetheless, my second day passed as quickly as my first. But my onion bag held nowhere near the quantity of morels that it had when Friday ended. More than disappointed, I was embarrassed and somewhat ashamed. But I wasn't the only one. When we combined the contents of our onion bags in the basket, we Addisons were dismayed to behold far less than a half-bushel of morels.

"Boy! This wasn't our day. Was it, folks?" Dad said sadly. "I honestly thought with our early start and our improved eye for our quarry —."

"Whoa! Before anyone gets too disappointed, this is exactly the target I set for today. We've seen it over and over. The Saturday take is always about half of Friday's. Think about it! Yesterday many of the shrooms we picked were two or three days old. You won't see many large ones like those until two or three days from now. And for any we missed yesterday, there were twice as many shroomers out there to find them. Don't be discouraged. This is par for the course."

Reluctantly I accepted the logic and truth of Mr. Williams' words.

"Is anyone hungry for some melt-in-your-mouth grilled filet mignon covered with buttery Mesick morels?"

I sure was! And an hour later, I was blessed with my first taste of these exquisite mushrooms.

For centuries, the morel has been exalted by kings and rulers, sought by master gourmet chefs, and traded by exporters of rare commodities, including truffles and caviar. Cookbook authors hail the morel as the perfect accompaniment to beef, veal, lamb, pork, and seafood. Morels are sold fresh, dried, powdered, and as an essence to flavor virgin olive oils. Large morels are cherished when stuffed with lamb or sausages. Small morels are revered when added to sauces, soups, and stews.

Editors of food magazines and cookbooks cannot agree on the correct words to describe the morel's flavor to readers. Is it meaty, nutty, exquisite, addictive, rich, subtle, delicate, or hearty? Why is the morel's flavor enhanced when butter, cream, or Madeira is added to a sauce or stew? Why is the distinctive flavor of the morel not lost or diminished even by drying the mushroom?

These are questions for the ages. I doubt they'll ever be answered.

But after tasting the Black Morel for the first time, I knew that I would always answer Mom's question just as I did on the evening of May 11, 1945, in Mesick, Michigan.

"Jase, have you ever tasted anything more delicious?"

"Never, Mom! Never!"

17 DANNY'S PLEA BARGAIN

The Eddie Conroy Story
Toledo, Ohio

AS CONROY DROVE NORTH, HE ASKED HIMSELF over and over what possessed him to trust her. His setup was perfect. Even though he wasn't paid a lot of money, the couple provided his room and board. Since they hadn't questioned his cover story, he felt safe. After his second week of working on the farm, they invited him to stay until the war ended and their son returned from his stint in the army.

Beginning with his orphanage days, he always had difficulty lying to older women. One day after spending six months at the farm, perhaps to gain her approval, he revealed his secret to the farmer's wife. Without conferring with her husband, she immediately picked up the telephone, called the FBI, and informed them Conroy was a *deserter*. Coming from her, that word hurt him deeply. After trusting her with his secret, she'd betrayed him.

Without thinking, he grabbed her car keys from the kitchen table and ran out of the house, leaving his meager possessions behind. Every dollar he had earned still remained unspent in his wallet. He drove north at a speed that wouldn't attract attention. After the car ran out of gas outside Toledo, he stuck up his thumb and landed a ride immediately.

When the friendly driver wanted to know where he was heading, Conroy answered honestly. "Anywhere I can find a good job."

"You look fit enough. If you're not afraid of work, I might be able to use a man like you. What's your name?"

"Smith."

"I'm Rankin. Pleased to meet you."

WE AWOKE EARLY ON Sunday morning. I could hear the others in the kitchen chatting and putting breakfast together. Suddenly I remembered. Today is Mother's Day. I reminded myself not to forget to give Mom the card I brought for her.

Instead of getting out of bed right away, I just lay there, reviewing all that had happened since we'd arrived on Thursday night. Staying in the well-appointed cottage surrounded by lush forests. Watching the mesmerizing sun setting over the clear, bubbling waters of the Manistee. Finding my first Black Morel and being fooled by the huge False Morel. Discovering the hidden fawn. Getting to know and enjoy the Williamses. Becoming addicted to the flavor of the morel.

What a great weekend this had been!

After breakfast, we packed our things, including the remaining morels, and got into the station wagon. The never-ending flow of interesting stories, hilarious jokes, and harmless teasing helped make the time fly. We were home before we knew it. We said our goodbyes and carried our bags to the house.

Thumbtacked to the front door was an envelope addressed simply to *The Addison Family*. I recognized the handwriting. "It's from Mrs. Tucker."

We hurried inside, dropped everything on the floor, and waited eagerly for Dad to open the envelope. Quickly he perused the note and then shared it with us.

Dear Addison Family,

Welcome home! Happy Mother's Day, Marie!
So you won't have to bother cooking, we Tuckers would
like to invite you to have supper with us tonight. We're
having roast venison so, if you were lucky enough to find
some morels, you might want to bring a few along to
enhance the flavor of the roast.
The roast will be done about 6 o'clock but come over,
as soon as you can. We have news to share with you that I'm
sure you'll be happy to hear.

See you soon,
Sam & Christine Tucker

"I wonder if Mrs. Tucker's forgotten your aversion to venison, Jase."

"That's all right, Mom. I'll eat a whole deer if it involves something positive about Danny."

Because of the number of morels we'd prepared and cooked for Saturday's supper, our half of the leftovers would provide an adequate accompaniment for the Tucker's venison roast. We changed our clothes, packed our buttery morels, and departed for the Tucker house.

On the way over, I wasn't sure what they had in store for us. With Danny involved, predicting the future was impossible. I decided to go with the flow.

WE PULLED INTO THEIR driveway at about 4:45 p.m. When Mr. Tucker opened the door, we saw the entire Tucker family, waiting for us in their front room. Mr. Tucker seated Mom and Mrs. Tucker on the couch. He and Dad took the pair of easy chairs. We four kids occupied the kitchen chairs that were wedged between the pieces of upholstered furniture. Obviously this meeting had been carefully planned in advance.

Mrs. Tucker spoke first. "We're very happy you're home because we're eager to tell you what's happened since last Monday's scout meeting. Both Sam and I have spoken to everyone involved. As a result, we've made some decisions and our children completely agree with them. However, two decisions are yours to make. I'll tell you about them in a minute.

"First, Danny exercised very poor judgment during the time he was performing community service with Sergeant Zeller. Thus, Danny will repeat his sentence by riding with Sergeant Tolna for another week. Jeff has assured us that Danny will *observe* and *learn* — or else."

That made good sense to me. I looked at Danny who nodded his head in agreement.

Then Mr. Tucker took his turn. "We've talked to Scoutmaster Mel and Freddie Holland about Danny's completing his requirements for First Class when he was supposed to be performing community service. We told Freddie to withdraw his First Class paperwork. At the upcoming Court of Honor, Danny will only be awarded the Second Class rank. He'll have to demonstrate his mastery of his First Class requirements all over again — this time under the supervision of Scoutmaster Mel."

Again Danny nodded in agreement.

"When he persuaded Sergeant Zeller to help him sell household oil at bars and taverns, Danny again violated the spirit of his sentence. He also used the help of another person. Therefore, his final sales figure will revert back to his previous week's total, making him ineligible for any of the sales' prizes. Freddie now becomes the first-place winner. Jase comes in second. And — ironically — John Bosco is the third-place winner."

Danny nodded again.

"Because Danny's underlying offense was operating his bicycle recklessly, it will be sold to the highest bidder. The proceeds will be contributed to the Troop 46 camp-scholarship fund."

Danny looked at me, presumably to gauge my reaction to this news. I nodded, and he responded with a sad smile.

Of all people, Queenie delivered the next decision. "Danny will give Jase his half of the radio they won in the furniture-store contest. Jase, the radio is completely yours. You can take it home with you tonight."

"But he —."

Queenie raised her hand. "It's fine, Jase. Believe me. Because JB and you depend on Danny to help provide bait to Homer One and Homer Two, Danny will be allowed to work with you. However, the first $15 he earns will go to me for the purchase of my own radio. It'll be kept in our bedroom upstairs, and I will control the station we listen to."

I looked at Chub whose eyes told me he had lost this argument. However, Danny nodded his agreement in a perfunctory way.

Looking directly at me, Mr. Tucker declared, "The last decision is up to your parents — but it greatly affects you, Jase. Since your Aunt Maude and little Johnnie no longer share your bedroom, Danny suggested it might be more convenient to share your room during the bait-gathering season. Because of the odd hours you'll be working, he feels the two of you living together can better coordinate the bait business with JB who lives next door. He's assured us that your profits could increase substantially by such a move. As I mentioned, this decision rests solely with your parents."

Dad and Mom looked at each other and immediately nodded their agreement. Danny and I grinned at each other.

"There's another decision that affects you, Jase," Mr. Tucker stated. "Last fall, out of gratitude, E.F. Graham offered to send you to church camp for four weeks this coming summer. But Danny tells us the demands of your bait business will keep you in Riverton all summer. Mr. Graham has agreed that Chub can take your places. If you agree, starting in a couple of weeks, Chub will go to Camp Harmony for the entire eight-week summer session. How do you feel about this, Jase?"

I looked at Chub whose hands were clasped together in prayer. His eyes were begging me to agree.

"That would be perfectly fine with me."

Chub ran to me and threw his arms around my neck. He jumped up and down and screamed, "Yes!" about 40 times.

"I guess that about settles everything. Do you boys have any questions?"

Danny looked at Mom. "All right if I come home with you tonight, Mrs. A?"

AFTER THE MEETING, EVERYONE seemed pleased with the outcome. Even Mom and Dad went out of their way to tell Danny how thrilled they were to have him as my roommate. The only person I wondered about was Mr. Tucker. With Danny moving to our house for the bait season and *encouraged* to work long and hard to pay off his $15 obligation to Queenie, he could no longer assist Mr. Tucker in his car-repair business.

Ever the opportunist, Chub seized the moment. "Dad, if Danny's running away to work in the worm business, can I take his place and help you in the garage?"

I wondered why Chub had chosen that particular language to characterize Danny's temporary move to our house. Facing the prospect of life filled with big band music, perhaps Chub had contemplated that very option for himself. Regardless of his reason, no one seemed to notice his choice of words except me.

"Chub! You read my mind. You'll make a fine assistant mechanic. Danny didn't seem to have much interest in that line of work, but I've noticed that you do. Tomorrow morning before you go to school, we'll go over your duties. You can work for me until you go to camp. All right?"

While Chub nodded his head furiously, Mr. Tucker smiled and messed Chub's already messy hair.

That made it unanimous. Every Tucker seemed satisfied.

Mrs. Tucker and Mom went to the kitchen to put supper on the table. When Mrs. Tucker opened the oven to check on the roast, the scent of venison made me slightly queasy. But with everyone enjoying themselves, I decided not to spoil the occasion by mentioning my aversion to the main course.

"Jase, you want to see what I've fixed you for supper?" Mrs. Tucker held the oven door open. "Come take a look."

I couldn't believe my ears. *Was she teasing me?* I looked at Mom who nodded her head and pointed to the oven with her chin. I peeked inside. There was a quart-sized glass dish filled with something covered with a thick bubbling layer of golden-brown cheese.

"It's macaroni and cheese — just for you. Danny told me it's one of your favorite dishes."

"Oh, Mrs. Tucker, you didn't have to prepare something especially for me."

"Are you kidding? Nothing's too good for my son's roommate," she said with a smile.

"Thank you, Mrs. Tucker. I really love macaroni and cheese."

"We even opened a gallon can of catsup just for you, Jase," Danny informed me.

After supper, we loaded Danny's meager inventory of clothing and other personal belongings into the backseat of the Tucker station wagon. Queenie handed me the portable radio. "Here, Jase. It's tuned to the big band station for your listening enjoyment." She smiled and jabbed Danny with her elbow.

"See you at your house, John," Mr. Tucker hollered as he made a right turn out of his driveway.

When we arrived home, Mr. Tucker was standing next to the station wagon. After parking, we walked over to help carry Danny's things into the house. When Danny and I finished loading our arms, there was hardly anything left for Mom and Dad to carry.

But Mr. Tucker soon remedied that situation. Opening the tail door of the station wagon, he instructed, "John and Marie, come help me carry these inside." The entire rear compartment was filled with shiny, wrapper-free cans of mystery food. "Thanks to Chub, I can't tell you what these contain. But each week while Danny's staying with you, I'll come by with another load."

"But, Sam! That's not necessary."

"Have you forgotten my son's appetite? Of course, it's necessary. Shoot! Once a week may not be often enough. Danny'll let me know when you're running low. And don't worry about it. Our basement's full of cans, just like these. Now you can enjoy some surprise meals just like the Tuckers."

There was no arguing with Mr. Tucker. I was very happy about that. And I could tell my new roommate was too.

"Let's open a can or two — right now! Okay, Mrs. A?"

"We'll discuss that after your clothing's put away and Aunt Maude's cot is made up."

"Anything you say, Mrs. A. You're the boss! From now on, you won't get any arguments from me. I promise."

This time, Danny said what he meant and meant what he said.

18 ON MY HONOR

EVERYONE, INCLUDING DANNY, WAS CERTAIN WE would adjust quickly to living together. Each morning, with three of us preparing to depart for work or school, competition for our only bathroom could present a problem until we worked out a system. By tradition, Saturday was bath night at the Addison house. With only one bathtub and no hot-water heater, this was not a simple exercise. Because the Tucker house also had a single bathtub and no hot-water heater, Danny was used to this situation.

Meal arrangements were no issue. Since meeting Danny the summer before, he had become a regular part of the Addison mealtime routine. In fact, occasions when he was missing from our table seemed somewhat strange to us.

On the first morning of Danny's stay, the four of us were sitting at the breakfast table as usual. When I saw JB about to knock at the kitchen door, I waved him in.

"Morning, JB," Mom said. "What's new?"

"Mom has accepted a nursing position at Riverton Memorial Hospital. She started this morning."

"That's terrific news! I'm so happy she's going back to work. How do you feel about it?"

"Mrs. Addison, I've been waiting for this day since Pearl Harbor."

"Speaking of work." Dad looked at his watch. "I keep forgetting I'm not going today. I've taken another vacation day to help Scoutmaster Mel and Mr. Tucker purchase the new tents and camping equipment."

"When are you leaving, Dad?"

"Madison's doesn't open until half-past eight, but I've been looking at my watch every 10 seconds. Danny's dad isn't even picking me up until an hour from now."

"Lucky you! You have an hour to work in the Victory Garden, John."

"That's a great idea. I need to finish spading and raking. I'll go change into my old shoes. Again, JB, tell your mother how happy we are about her new position. So long, fellas."

"Let's go to school early. And see what's happening," Danny suggested.

"You think Miss Sparks knows you're out of jail, Danny?"

"Danny! That's right. You shouldn't be here," JB told him. "When did you get out?"

In the minds of people familiar with Danny's case, Mrs. Tucker's lockup was as real as Sing Sing. These two prisons did have a lot in common. Both were notoriously tough places to serve a sentence.

Quickly Danny gave JB an overview of his plea bargain.

"You lost your bicycle! How will we transport our minnows, crabs, and hellgrammites back to Homer One's with only one bicycle?"

JB had a very good question. I was *im*pressed by how much he had absorbed from Homer's lecture and *de*pressed by having my consciousness raised to this very serious issue.

"We'll need to think long and hard about this. But somehow we'll solve it."

Mom looked up from her movie magazine. "Isn't Danny's bicycle going to be auctioned off by Troop 46 to support the camp-scholarship fund?"

Danny and I nodded.

"You boys need to find a way to submit the highest bid."

Danny spoke for all of us. "Easier said than done, Mrs. A."

The Eddie Conroy Story
The Singleton Residence
Riverton, Michigan

CONROY IMMEDIATELY TOOK TO his new job. While it did involve some manual labor, the work offered a wide variety of tasks and an opportunity to breathe fresh air. He quickly made friends with Rankin and his coworkers, a close-knit group of honest, hardworking men. Despite his own spotty record in this regard, he felt like one of them. To top it off, his new employment paid more than he had ever made in his life. He used some of his earnings to purchase a used car for exploring the Riverton area on weekends.

Once again, Conroy began to think his troubles were over. His future looked bright. All he had to do was maintain a low profile, work hard and squirrel away his earnings, and avoid doing anything to attract the attention of the law. After a year or two, he'd have the wherewithal to leave the country and live worry-free in some pleasant foreign setting. That thought comforted him every night as he drifted off to sleep.

During his ninth week on the job, everything changed. On a morning delivery, he found himself in a room all alone. Quite by accident, his eyes came to rest on a particularly valuable article, laying on a dressing table for anyone to see. In one area of expertise, Conroy was not just anyone.

His mind raced back to his teens when his foster father, a well-respected Cincinnati jewelry appraiser, had taught Conroy how to assess the value of gemstones. His lifelong fascination with diamonds, sapphires, and rubies was born. Unfortunately this was not the first time this obsession had landed him in trouble.

After the disappearance of a valuable piece of jewelry entrusted to his foster father for appraisal, his relationship with those foster parents ended abruptly. Conroy was sentenced to a two-year term in a juvenile correctional institution or, as it was called in those days, a reform school. When he reached the age of 18, the remaining portion of his sentence was forgiven, in exchange for his agreement to join the navy.

When a marine drill sergeant at boot camp had the audacity to refer to him as a *yellow puke*, Conroy's budding naval career was placed in jeopardy. By this time, he had grown into a strapping lad who thought himself capable of inflicting serious physical harm on drill sergeants and other similar figures of authority. Unfortunately, on this occasion, he failed to take into account the martial arts expertise of combat-hardened marines. That particular life's lesson cost him three weeks of recuperation at the Great Lakes Naval Hospital. Nearing the end of his stay, with the help of a young navy nurse, Conroy unilaterally terminated his relationship with the U.S. Navy by, as an old salt would say, *going over the hill.*

He shook these unpleasant memories of the past and pocketed the diamond bracelet from the dressing table. By midafternoon, he recognized the danger posed by that decision. If the police were called in by the owner, Rankin could easily direct them to Conroy. He had to hide the bracelet in case he was searched. His choice of hiding place was rather unusual, but he assured himself that no one was likely to find it.

DANNY WAS WELCOMED BACK to school by everyone, especially Miss Sparks. When he walked in, her genuine surprise and delight was clearly evident.

Butch Matlock immediately posed the $64 question. "How'd you get out of jail so fast, Danny?"

"Good behavior, Butch. Good behavior."

Danny didn't share the details with his classmates as he had with JB. This was a good sign. Evidently he trusted JB as much as I did. A high level of trust would be the key to the success of our bait-business partnership.

Butch added, "You have a certain admirer who'll be very happy you're free again."

Danny gave Butch a puzzled look.

"My sister Judie! She's been beside herself with worry since you stopped coming to school."

Butch *really* understood the nuances of the female mind! Wouldn't Judie be *dee*-lighted to know Butch had told everybody, including Danny, how his incarceration had affected her?

When we arrived home after school, Dad was sitting in the kitchen talking to Mom as she prepared supper. Eager to hear about the tent purchase, we three scouts joined them.

Dad was excited to give us every detail of the transaction. "Mr. Tucker and I met Scoutmaster Mel at the store at 8:30 sharp. Before we got there, Mel had called Mr. Markel to make sure he would be there. He's the manager of Madison's sporting-goods department — including the official scouting equipment and supplies.

"Mr. Markel really knows his stuff. Because he was so willing to share his knowledge, we understood everything about what we bought. Before we arrived, he'd unboxed a pup tent and an explorer tent — just to show us how to erect them properly. And he inventoried all the tent components and functions. Finally he did the same with the cooking and camping equipment we ordered. He was very generous with his time. We were there over two hours.

"We told him about our setup practice —. Oh, shoot! You boys haven't been told about that yet. This coming Saturday — a week before the Camporee — we're going to practice setting up tents and equipment at Courthouse Park. All the committeemen and scouts will be there. Mr. Markel's volunteered to come too — just to make sure we do everything properly. How about that for service?"

"Where's the equipment now, Dad?"

"You boys won't believe what Mr. Tucker came up with. Danny, you're familiar with your father's large flatbed trailer. Right?"

While Danny nodded his head, I didn't think he really knew what Dad was talking about.

"After we made our purchase, we went to your house and installed the sideboards. Then we called Madison's and had the tents and equipment delivered to your Dad's garage. The delivery guys just off-loaded our order from their truck onto the trailer.

"Next Saturday we'll use your station wagon to pull the entire load out to Courthouse Park. When we finish the practice setup, we'll repack everything, load it back onto the trailer, and store it in your garage until the Camporee. What do you think of that?"

Danny provided an appropriate one-word answer. "Ingenious!"

AFTER THE OPENING FORMALITIES, Scoutmaster Mel announced, "Scouts and committeemen, we have a number of items to cover tonight. So grab a chair and form a big circle in this area. When everybody's comfortable, we'll start our powwow."

After the obligatory jostling, poking, and shoving, we were finally seated in our powwow circle in front of the stage. "Listen up, scouts. The Court of Honor is in Lansing this coming Thursday evening. I've received the Council's official inventory of awards for our troop. For the first time in the troop's history, every scout will receive an award. Congratulations, scouts!

"Remember! We meet here in the parking lot at 6:30 p.m. Everyone should be in full scout uniform with brightly shined shoes and brass. No exceptions. The Court of Honor begins at 7:30 and will last for a good two hours. So tell your folks you won't be back before 10 o'clock."

"Mr. Tucker will tell you about this next item. Sam?"

"You boys are familiar with the bicycle Danny received for Christmas. He's decided to donate it to the camp-scholarship fund. We thought we'd have some fun by conducting a different kind of auction for the bicycle." Mr. Tucker held up what appeared to be a sign-up sheet. "On this sheet, bidders can raise the last bid by entering an amount and signing their names. The bidding starts tomorrow and lasts until five o'clock on the afternoon of May 25th. That's the day we leave for the Camporee. The winner will be announced at our campfire meeting that evening."

Scoutmaster Mel whispered something in Mr. Tucker's ear.

"Thanks, Mel. Folks, I forgot a couple of important details. This bidding sheet will be maintained in the church office by Miss Bundy. She'll accept new bids from 8:30 a.m. to 5:30 p.m., Monday through Friday — and on Sunday after church. If you're interested, talk to your parents and enter your bid. Be sure to tell them it's for a good cause."

"Mr. Tucker, I have a question." We all looked at Striker Loomis, the troop's champion hockey player. "Why's Danny donating his bicycle? I'm just curious because I know he loves that bike."

Caught off guard by Striker's question, Mr. Tucker was at a loss for words.

"Dad, I'll answer this one. Striker, I operated my bicycle recklessly while riding to school last week. I endangered a pedestrian — an elderly lady — and could have caused a traffic accident. John Bosco, the safety patrol on duty, gave me a traffic ticket, which I deserved. And Sammy Perioche, the judge of the Hamilton School traffic court, sentenced me to a week's community service, among other things. I deserved that too. I decided to donate my bike because I abused the privilege of having one. And that's the long and short of it, Striker."

"Sorry to hear that, Danny. But it sounds like you're doing the right thing. Thanks for telling me."

"I need to say a couple more things," Danny continued. "Last week, Mr. Addison announced I'd won first prize in the sales contest. That was wrong. I used Sergeant Zeller to help me sell oil. I really don't deserve any prize.

"Finally I'm sorry for the way I've been behaving lately. You're all my friends. In the future, I'll try very hard to treat you that way."

This had to have been difficult for Danny. An ego the size of his doesn't shrink without considerable pain. But I was proud of him for clearing the air.

Wanting to move right along, Scoutmaster Mel called on Dad.

"Thanks, Mel. And thank you, Danny. That had to be tough for you to do."

I saw a faint smile on Danny's lips. His family and the Addisons were the people that meant the most to him. And all of us had forgiven him.

"I need to correct the record regarding winners of the sales contest. The new first place winner is Freddie Holland. Second place goes to Jase Addison. And in third place — our new winner is John Bosco. Congratulations, boys. Well done!"

Spontaneous cheering and applause filled the basement.

"The dollars generated by your excellent salesmanship were put to good use just today. Scoutmaster Mel, Mr. Tucker, and I spent the morning at Madison's where we purchased our new tents and camp equipment. This coming Saturday morning, we will all — scouts and committeemen alike — meet at Courthouse Park to practice setting up this new equipment.

"Mr. Markel, the manager of Madison's sports and scouting equipment department, will be there to coach us. Because Troop 46 is a host for this year's Camporee, our campsite should be the model of perfection for all participating troops. This practice session will help us meet that goal.

"The place and time? The campground next to the fairgrounds. Mr. Tucker and I'll be there with the equipment trailer at nine o'clock sharp!!!"

On the way home, Danny seemed unusually quiet. I assumed it had to do with the emotional energy he had expended at the meeting. "What's on your mind, Danny?"

"I still haven't figured out how to submit the highest bid to get that bike back for our bait business. But I will. On my honor!"

IN THE DAYS LEADING up to the Court of Honor, most members of Troop 46 were preoccupied with the awards they were about to receive. But we three bait moguls were preoccupied with the reopening of our business. Our first task was to establish the financial rules of our partnership. Although JB initially protested, we insisted on sharing profits equally, regardless of an individual's contribution.

Experience had shown that frequently Danny and I would work exactly the same number of hours and produce a significantly different number of crawlers in our coffee cans. One night I would have more and the next night Danny would. In the end, we felt everything balanced out pretty evenly.

We cleaned our four existing night-crawler boxes and filled them with fresh maple leaves for the dining pleasure of the soon-to-be plump pink occupants. We assembled the used coffee cans we needed to transport our catch to Homer One's. For simplicity's sake, Homer Two would pick up his shop's bait supply at Homer One's.

We checked our supplies of fresh batteries and tested our flashlights. We paid a call on all our neighbors to reaffirm our arrangement with them to water their lawns on a regular basis. In exchange, we were allowed to catch the night crawlers that would invariably emerge after nightfall in response to our sprinkling. We targeted Wednesday as our first crawler-gathering night.

Realizing we needed more crawler storage, JB scrounged some decent lumber from the attic of the Reilly garage and skillfully constructed two fine boxes, using the tools in Dad's shed. We proudly added his boxes to the existing stack beside our basement door. Because of the size and value of our anticipated inventory of night crawlers in our half-dozen boxes, we placed a full-sized cement block on the cover of the top box. This weight would prevent skunks, raccoons, or possums from overturning the stack to feast on our high-protein crawlers.

As an added precaution, Danny suggested we install a *burglar alarm*. His idea was to tie a string of old tin cans around the cement block. If a black bear happened to visit, the alarm would alert us. Mom was not thrilled with the prospect of having a can-cluttered area around the back porch. Besides, she explained, Riverton hadn't had a bear incident in years.

THE STORY SURROUNDING THAT bear incident had become a town legend. It all began on a warm June evening following a Riverton High School graduation ceremony at Waters Field. Emboldened, after sipping a quantity of celebratory hard cider, four freshly graduated RHS boys decided to put a scare into the community by releasing the mangy pair of old black bears from their residence, a barred cage in the center of Courthouse Park.

Laboring for nearly an hour, they finally hacksawed through the heavy padlocked chain that secured the cage door. Apparently the boys were oblivious to the two old bears that, out of curiosity, were leaning against the door, watching the boys finish their work. When the door flew open, one of the bears tumbled out of the cage. The terrified boys screamed and scattered to the four winds. All this activity so frightened the other bear that he scurried back into his den, the brick structure provided for the bears to hibernate, nap, or sleep overnight. Traumatized by the incident, he didn't emerge for several days.

The bear that had fallen out of the cage immediately liked the game the boys were playing. To have some more fun, he decided to run after one of them. In search of a safe haven, this young fellow ran directly from the park to the sheriff's office with the bear rumbling along behind him. When the boy burst through the door, the desk sergeant and dispatcher leaped up in amazed surprise. The three of them were standing there openmouthed when the old bear, eager to come in and join the party, began to scratch at the door.

The three dove over the counter and crouched behind the dispatcher's desk. The fun-loving bear, thinking this was part of the game, smashed the door glass, reached inside, and managed to open the door. Following the rules of the game, he too leaped over the counter.

That's when the sheriff stormed out of his office and yelled, **"What the Sam Hill is going on out here!"**

When the bear reared up to greet him, the sheriff drew his pistol and drew a bead on the animal. Fortunately the bear avoided being targeted by quickly ducking down behind the counter. There he soon lost interest in the game-playing and began investigating the contents of the dispatcher's lunch-pail. While the bear enjoyed his snack, the three men and the boy made their escape. Out of harm's way, they barricaded the three doors leading into the dispatch area.

Immediately they agreed that this was a matter for Mr. Frank, the Michigan Conservation Officer assigned to Chippewa County, popularly known as the *county game warden*. The sheriff marched to his patrol car to radio him. On his return, he informed the others, "The warden's going to check the condition of the bear cage and then come directly here."

On arriving at the sheriff's office, the warden promptly sized up the situation. "Sheriff, I need someone to drive my car slowly back to the bears' cage. I'll be sitting in the trunk."

"Not sure what you're planning here, Mr. Frank. But if you think that'll work, I'll do the driving."

"Fine with me. Get in and roll down the windows. I want you to be able to hear my instructions."

Mr. Frank's first order was for the sheriff to back the warden's car to within about 10 feet of the barricaded door. The warden opened his trunk revealing his magic weapon, a bushel of snow apples. He removed a handful of apples from the basket and walked toward the barricade.

By this time, a reporter from the *Riverton Daily Press* and his photographer had heard the commotion and wandered over from the county courthouse. "What's going on here, Sheriff?"

"Nothing! Just go about your business."

Knowing the old sheriff pretty well, the reporter ignored his orders. He quickly sized up the situation and told his photographer to ready his camera. Meantime, the babbling new graduate confessed all the details of the story to the reporter who dutifully recorded every last word in his notebook.

Not particularly sensitive to the public-relation issues at stake, the warden impatiently ordered, "You other fellows clear away that barricade and pull the door wide-open. Then get out of the way — pronto!"

That was the photographer's cue to start snapping pictures.

When the door swung open, the bear stood up on his back legs and peered over the counter. In the warden's hands, the bear spotted his next snack. Tossing the empty lunch-bucket aside, the bear nimbly leaped over the counter. With his arms extended toward the apple-toting warden, the mangy black bear shuffle-stepped forward toward his snack.

"Here you go, Oscar," the warden called as he tossed the first apple at the bear.

Looking like a furry Hank Greenberg, the bear deftly snatched the apple from midair with his left paw and popped it into his mouth.

The warden lowered himself into the trunk of the car and gave his orders. "All right, Sheriff. I've got him hooked. Let's head for the park — real slow-like — nothing over 10 miles an hour."

And so the comic parade left the sheriff's office and slowly made its way back to the cage. There they went. The embarrassed sheriff, driving the warden's car at a snail's pace. The warden, seated in his trunk, dispensing snow apple after snow apple to big Oscar. The old bear, loving this latest game, shuffle-stepping on his back legs toward home. And this whole show recorded for posterity by a madly scribbling reporter and a shutter-snapping photographer.

When the procession reached the cage, following the warden's instructions, the sheriff pulled up close to the cage door. The warden jumped out of the trunk and grabbed the partially filled basket. After flipping one to Oscar, the warden opened the cage door and stepped inside.

"Mr. Frank, what on earth are you doing?" the sheriff screamed in alarm.

"I'll be all right, Sheriff. I know these animals," he explained. To prove his point, he called out to the bear, "Come on, Oscar."

With that, he dumped the remaining apples on the floor of the cage and stood off to one side. The bear dropped down off his back legs and shot into the cage through its open door. When Oscar was fully occupied, popping the last of the snow apples into his mouth, the warden calmly walked out of the cage and closed the door. He wrapped the chain around the door bars, pulled a new padlock from his pocket, and snapped it shut over the chain.

"There you go, Sheriff. Case closed. Let's go home."

"Wait a minute! Where's that other bear?"

"Oh, he's huddled inside the brick building there — scared as a kitten. We won't see him for a while."

"Thanks, Sheriff. You gave us our headline for tomorrow's paper. Much obliged!"

In response to the reporter's taunt, the sheriff just growled. But that was nothing compared to his response when he saw the headline and photos displayed on the front page of the next day's *Riverton Daily Press.*

DANGEROUS ESCAPEE *BEAR*-RICADED IN SHERIFF'S OFFICE
Heroic Apple Vendor Comes to Lawmen's Rescue

The entire front page was covered with highly amusing photographs with comic captions. My personal favorite showed Oscar standing behind the counter, peering into the empty lunch-bucket. The fried-chicken sandwich, caringly prepared by the dispatcher's wife, protruded from the bear's mouth. The caption read:

New Sheriff's Deputy on Well-Deserved Lunch Break

ONE OF THE ADVANTAGES of having Courts of Honor in Lansing was the frequent participation of Governor Harry F. Kelly. He dearly loved bestowing badges on young Michiganders who had distinguished themselves by earning the ranks of Star, Life, and Eagle Scout. During his time in office, Governor Kelly was known for his support of scouting. When demands on his time prevented him from personally participating in a scout event, he always ensured that a high-ranking member of his cabinet represented him.

While we had personal friendships with political leaders, including Franklin Roosevelt, Winston Churchill, and Thomas E. Dewey, Danny and I had never had occasion to meet Governor Kelly. We were hopeful that the upcoming Court of Honor would offer us that opportunity. We felt we already knew him because of all the positive things Governor Dewey, his close friend, had told us about him.

After graduating from law school at Notre Dame, Governor Kelly volunteered to serve in World War I. At the Battle of Château-Thierry, he was wounded and lost his right leg. For multiple acts of heroism on the battlefield, he was awarded the *Croix de Guerre* with palm leaves.

His public service career was similar to Thomas E. Dewey's. From 1929 to 1934, Kelly served as assistant prosecuting attorney for Wayne County, in which the city of Detroit is located. From 1939 to 1942, he served two terms as Michigan's Secretary of State.

Running as the Republican candidate, he was elected to two terms as governor, serving from 1943 to 1947. While in office, he was nicknamed "The War Governor." In 1944, he was an influential delegate to the Republican National Convention where fellow governor and Michigander, Thomas E. Dewey, was nominated for the office of President of the United States.

During his public-service career, like Dewey, Governor Kelly earned high marks for his campaigns to rid government of corruption. Putting a cap on his commendable career, he served with distinction on the Michigan Supreme Court from 1954 to 1971.

Prior to the Court of Honor, Danny and I ignored rumors concerning whether or not Governor Kelly would make an appearance. While seeing the governor in person would be a satisfying experience, we were not receiving Star, Life, or Eagle badges. Our awards would be presented by some lesser dignitary. Having recently received awards from the President of the United States, we were understandably a bit blasé about awards from a mere state attorney general or the like.

Attending the Court of Honor would be my first visit to the auditorium on the Michigan State College campus in East Lansing. In my imagination, that auditorium was a very special place. All through my grade-school years, we had heard special radio programming that originated there, including musical and dramatic productions broadcast to public-school students throughout the state. As a boy, I placed the MSC Auditorium in the same league as Carnegie Hall. When attending the University of Michigan, I enjoyed my first live performances of this caliber at Hill Auditorium on the Michigan campus. But my first love will forever be those early radio broadcasts from MSC.

On Thursday afternoon, we were innocently sitting in class when the call from Lansing came into Mr. Lund's office. Instead of sending his secretary to summon Danny and me, Mr. Lund did the job personally. When he walked into the classroom, he appeared to be in a state of extreme agitation. I had only seen him this way once before. That was the day Governor Dewey visited Hamilton School. I looked at Danny who mouthed the words, *Governor Dewey*. I nodded and looked back at Miss Sparks' desk where Mr. Lund was whispering loudly and waving his arms to make his point.

Finally Miss Sparks nodded her agreement. Mr. Lund scurried from the classroom and Miss Sparks put her head in her hands for a minute, before saying, "Danny and Jase. Would you please come here?"

We scurried to her desk.

"Boys, Governor Kelly is coming by this afternoon to see you. He wants to pick you up and take you home from school. Apparently you have a Boy Scout affair in Lansing tonight — where the governor was hoping to meet you. But he's been called away to a meeting in — in Grand Rapids — I think. On his way, he thought he'd drop by here and spend some time with you."

"That's great, Miss Sparks. But is Mr. Lund okay?"

Miss Sparks rolled her eyes back and shook her head. Finally she pleaded, "Will you boys do me a *really big* personal favor?"

We both nodded. *How could we ever deny Miss Sparks anything?*
"Would you do your best to meet your famous friends
somewhere other than Hamilton School?"
"Pretty bad. Huh?" Danny asked.
"The worst!"
Nuf sed!

DURING AFTERNOON RECESS, WORD of Governor Kelly's
visit spread rapidly among Hamilton's students. Many of our
friends wished us good luck. Others wondered why the governor
was coming in the first place. There was much less of the pre-
arrival hysteria that had surrounded Governor Dewey's visit or
some of our police-escorted arrivals in recent months. This was
beginning to be old hat to all of us. Well, almost all of us.

Mr. Lund was the only person who exhibited any hysteria
whatsoever. By an hour before the governor's estimated time of
arrival of four o'clock, our principal was beside himself. Because the
ETA coincided precisely with the normal end of the school day, Mr.
Lund ordered teachers to disregard the bell and hold students in
their classrooms until the governor arrived, received his proper
greeting from Mr. Lund, and departed with Danny and me.

Upon hearing this news, a highly perturbed Coach Clark paid
a call on our principal who immediately softened his stance. He
decided that students would be allowed to depart at four o'clock,
but only by way of the building's south door. Safety patrols would
be stationed along the sidewalk to ensure the student body moved
quickly out the door, through the schoolyard, and onto the
Hamilton Street sidewalk. From there, they could walk either
north or south toward home. This would keep the north entrance
and parking lot clear of student clutter while Mr. Lund delivered
his welcoming address to the governor and his entourage.

Fifteen minutes before the ETA, at Mr. Lund's insistence,
Danny, Miss Sparks, and I were standing at parade rest on the
sidewalk next to the north parking lot. Mr. Lund was flitting here
and there, inside and outside of the building, to ensure the
planned student evacuation was properly organized.

Suddenly I heard the north doors bang open. Mr. Lund screamed, "Miss Sparks! I don't know why I didn't think of this earlier. I'm sounding the last bell now. That way the students will be clear of the school before the governor arrives. What do you think of —?"

Before he could finish, the last bell rang.

Bong-Bong-Bong!

Unfortunately Mr. Lund's early-release strategy had one fatal flaw. He failed to warn the teachers about the change of plans. Instead of spending the last minutes of the day preparing their classes for an orderly departure from the south doors, the teachers were caught completely off guard. En masse, the Hamilton student body bolted from their classrooms and raced for the north exit.

Mr. Lund turned to see the onrushing mob heading straight for him. Instinctively he turned around, spread his arms, and pressed his back against the double doors, attempting to block their escape. Without regard for their principal, the students stormed the exit. Both doors banged open and the horde swarmed out on the sidewalk and swirled around us. Poor Mr. Lund was hopelessly pinned between the door and the school's brick wall.

So much for my reduced-hysteria theory!

At that precise moment, Governor Kelly's limousine pulled into the parking lot. It moved slowly toward us, taking care not to collide with or run over any of the three hundred kids who engulfed the vehicle. The huge limo came to a halt in front of us and the back door opened wide. Governor Kelly stepped out and shook Miss Sparks' hand.

To be heard above the din, Miss Sparks shouted, "Governor Kelly, welcome to Hamilton School. I'm Miss Sparks. I'd like to introduce two of my favorite sixth-grade students, Jase Addison and Danny Tucker. I apologize for the confusion — the final bell of the day rang just as you arrived. As you can see, the students are very thrilled to see you here."

"No apologies required. We timed our arrival to enable me to say hello to the entire student body," Governor Kelly hollered. He turned to the student mass and waved both arms above his head. The resulting cheer was deafening. The governor took Miss Sparks' hand again and shouted, "That was perfect. Thank you for greeting me so nicely. Goodbye."

While waving at the frenzied mass of students, he swept Danny and me into the backseat of the limousine and slipped in beside us. While we were inching our way out of the driveway, I heard the faint voice of Mr. Lund proclaim, "On behalf of the administration, faculty, and students, we wish to welcome you to our —." I peeked back to see Mr. Lund staring at our taillights as we pulled out onto the street and accelerated toward home.

The governor's first words to us were "I just realized I didn't have a chance to meet Mr. Lund, your principal. Tom Dewey wanted me to say hello to him. Was he there today, boys?"

"Oh, he was there, Governor Kelly. But he's quite shy," Danny advised.

GOVERNOR KELLY SEEMED A bit surprised to learn that Danny was living at my house. But when he realized the reason had to do with our thriving bait business, he was impressed. Because I thought it was important for the governor to meet Danny's parents, I suggested we stop at the Tuckers. When we pulled into the driveway, Mrs. Tucker was in the backyard, hanging out the wash. From the open garage door, I could see Mr. Tucker's feet sticking out from under an old Pontiac he was working on.

When Danny and I emerged from Governor Kelly's black limousine, Mrs. Tucker's mouth popped open. The two wooden clothespins she was clutching between her lips tumbled end-over-end to the ground. She adjusted her hair, put on a smile, and walked toward us.

"Mrs. Tucker? How nice to see you. I apologize for the surprise visit, but I'm just on my way to Grand Rapids. My friend, Governor Dewey, insisted I stop to meet these two young heroes and their families. How'd you do?"

After wiping her palms on her apron, Mrs. Tucker shook the governor's hand. "Welcome, Governor Kelly. I'm very pleased to meet you. If you're a friend of Governor Dewey, you're a friend of ours. And you're exactly right. We're all very proud of these two boys."

"I'll go get Mr. Tucker," I offered. Without waiting for a response, I trotted over to the garage. Because he was loudly singing *Don't Sit Under the Apple Tree*, he didn't hear me coming. Not wanting to frighten him, I decided just to tap his toe with mine. When I did so, he jerked, and his head hit the underside of the car with a resounding *thump*. It was certain to have been a painful thump as well.

"Sorry, Mr. Tucker!"

"Who the —?" he sputtered, rolling out from under the car. "Jase, what're you doing here?"

"I — ah —. You have a visitor, Mr. Tucker."

Rubbing his forehead, he stood up and wiped his hands on an oily rag. He walked over and stuck his head out the door. "Well, I'll be. That's Governor Kelly. Isn't it, Jase?"

Ignoring the oil and grime, Governor Kelly shook hands with Mr. Tucker like they were old friends. "Just came by to congratulate you folks on raising such a fine young man. I'd hoped to meet you at the Court of Honor tonight, but I was called away for an important meeting in Grand Rapids. Anyway how does it feel to be the father of a hero like Danny, sir?"

"To be honest, Governor, it's painful at times. Sometimes I wish Danny and Jase were just ordinary boys. I really wonder how limousine rides with governors will affect them in the long run."

"Sam, you —." Danny's mother was about to scold her husband, but she stopped herself.

The governor held up his hand. "Sir, before becoming governor — like my father before me — I was a pretty fair lawyer. And I know an honest answer when I hear one. If you weren't a caring father, you would have never told me that. And I commend you for feeling that way. No wonder your son's a hero."

After shaking hands once more, Governor Kelly waved us back into the car, and we headed for my house. When we arrived, Mom and Dad were standing on the front porch. They quickly walked to the car and opened our back door before the driver could.

"Welcome, Governor!"

When Governor Kelly stepped out, Dad's mouth fell open. "Oh, my gosh! I've got the wrong governor. I thought you were Governor Dewey."

"Think nothing of it. Sorry for the surprise. I'd hoped to meet you at the Court of Honor tonight, but I had to change my plans. On matters of some urgency, I'm attending a meeting in Grand Rapids. Our friend, Tom Dewey, will also be there. When he found out I'd be driving by way of Riverton, he insisted I drop by and say hello to these young men and their families."

After shaking hands with my folks, the governor stood in the front lawn and chatted for a long time. He told us how his sons had been very active in scouting when they were our age. He glanced at his watch. "Boys, if you wouldn't mind dressing in your uniforms, I'd like to take a picture before I leave."

Within 10 minutes, the governor and we were standing on the porch steps. Following his driver's instructions, we all responded, "Cheeeeeese!" After promising to send prints of the picture, the governor was off.

We stood there, looking up Forrest Street as the dust settled. "You boys certainly make life interesting. Don't they, John?"

"Yes, they do. But I wouldn't have it any other way."

We had a quick bite of supper and piled into the car. When we arrived, the MSU Auditorium far exceeded my expectations. At last, I had seen the place in person.

Danny and I were given directions to join the other members of Troop 46 who were seated in the section of the auditorium near the stairway to the stage. Also seated there were over two hundred scouts eager to receive their honors.

The Court of Honor opened with ceremonies closely resembling those we used back in Troop 46. Acting as master of ceremonies, the senior scouting executive for our council announced that, owing to pressing official business, Governor Kelly would not be available to participate in the ceremony that evening. In his place, the state attorney general would present the awards. When I heard that news, I chuckled to myself.

"I'll bet you fall asleep before you get your First Class badge," Danny predicted confidently. "But don't worry. I'll wake you when it's time."

After making his promise, he folded his hands, slumped down in his seat, and fell fast asleep. But that was all right. Danny knew I always looked out for both of us.

So I did.

ON THE MORNING OF the practice setup, Dad, Danny, and I walked from our house to the Tuckers. Since we were early, we went to the back door and tapped on the glass. Mrs. Tucker let us in. "Come on in, fellas. Sam's running a little late. He had his sleep interrupted last night."

Danny became very concerned. "What happened, Mom?"

"I'll let your father tell the story. He was there and I was asleep."

When Mr. Tucker entered the kitchen, he seemed a bit groggy. "Morning, everybody. Sorry I'm late, but I ordered a scrambled egg and toast sandwich to go. We can leave in a jiffy."

After saying our goodbyes, we headed for the garage. We walked around to the large sliding doors behind which I knew the trailer of camping equipment was parked. Mr. Tucker stuck his sandwich in his mouth and reached into his pants' pocket. He found a key and unlocked the padlock hanging on the garage-door hasp.

"When did you start locking the garage, Dad?"

After removing his sandwich, Mr. Tucker replied, "Since last night after the police left."

"What happened, Sam?"

"About one o'clock in the morning, something woke me up. That's unusual because normally I'm a pretty sound sleeper. I thought the sound came from outside somewhere. I got out of bed, put on my slippers and robe, and went out to the back porch. I stood there for a few seconds, just listening. Everything was calm and quiet — for a while anyway.

"I was about to go back to bed when I heard a rustling noise coming from out here in the garage. I figured that a raccoon had gotten in through the roof or an open window. So I got my 12-gauge and loaded her up. I tiptoed to the garage side door and opened it very quietly. When I looked inside, I was amazed to see the sliding doors here were partially open — oh, about four feet or so. In the glow from the streetlight, I saw the silhouette of a man."

"Trying to steal something, I assume. What was it?"

"He was standing on top of the flatbed trailer, pawing over those pup-tent boxes."

"Stealing a pup tent? That makes no sense, Sam."

"You're right about that. In any case, there he was, trying to pull one of those tent boxes away from the rest. So I looked him over carefully — best I could in the dark — and decided to take a chance. I crouched over behind the end of the workbench back there, leveled my shotgun at him, and flicked on all the lights. I yelled as loud as I could, '**Stop! Thief!**'

"He took one look at me and tumbled backwards off the front of the trailer. I heard him hit one of the sliding doors on his way out. By the time I got back here, he was halfway down the block. I wasn't about to chase him in the dark wearing only slippers. So I let him go. A few seconds later, I heard a car start and tear out of the neighborhood. He was probably parked at the bottom of the hill."

"My gosh, Sam! That's unbelievable. What do you think he was after?"

"I have no idea and neither do the police. I called them immediately. Jeff had just gotten off duty so he came right over. His fingerprint guy and a couple of his officers showed up as well. They lifted prints off the top ends of all those boxes. But I couldn't provide them a description, either of the man or the car. As far as I could see, nothing was stolen. Jeff suggested I lock the garage from now on. And he arranged for the patrol cars in this area to check the garage a number of times each shift for signs of another break-in or for anyone hanging around. So there it is. Now you fellas know as much as I do about it."

"Why on earth would anyone want to steal a pup tent?"

Danny offered his opinion. "Maybe he's a deranged camper."

WE HITCHED THE TUCKER station wagon to the trailer and, after relocking the garage, set off for Courthouse Park. When we arrived at the campgrounds, we were a few minutes late, but we figured that Mr. Tucker had good reason for sleeping in a bit that morning.

Before we got out, Mr. Tucker cautioned, "I almost forgot. Until he completes his investigation, Jeff requested we not mention what happened in the garage to anyone outside our two families."

We agreed and piled out.

"Have any trouble, Sam?"

"None at all, Mel. Sorry we're late. Everybody here?"

"All the scouts and committeemen are present and accounted for. Mr. Markel will be along shortly."

After Dad removed the end board from the trailer, several scouts formed a line to pass the equipment cartons from the trailer to the shady area under the big oak tree. Scoutmaster Mel had selected that spot to practice setting up camp because it would be out of the hot morning sun during the time we'd be there.

When all of the cartons were off the trailer and lined up neatly on the ground, Scoutmaster Mel raised his three-fingered salute and circled his hand above his head. We all assembled around him.

"Good job, scouts. Today we're going to proceed as follows. First, we'll assign a specific tent carton to those individuals who'll be sleeping in that tent. We'll mark each carton with your names. From now on, you're responsible for the care and maintenance of the carton, the tent, and the related equipment inside.

"Second, we're going to pitch all pup tents there — north of the oak tree — and all explorer tents in that area — south of the tree. Those of you who've never pitched a tent can learn from those who have."

Scoutmaster Mel looked at his watch. "Mr. Markel will be along in a few minutes. When someone has a pup-tent question for him, all those pitching pup tents can hear his answer. And the same thing is true for those pitching explorer tents. Any questions?"

There were none.

"All patrol leaders, please step forward. You'll mark each carton with the responsible persons' names." He handed a thick black marking crayon to each of them. "When your tent, poles, stakes, ropes, and so on are out of your cartons, stack the cartons neatly back onto the trailer so they're out of the way. You can retrieve them for repacking your tents after the practice setup. When your own tent is pitched, please open the cooking and camping equipment boxes and have a go at setting that up. Mr. Markel will give you a hand if you need it.

"All right, scouts. Let's get to work."

With Mr. Markel's able assistance every tent was pitched, every cooking pot assembled, and every camp lantern tested successfully. The entire process took just under two hours. We all thanked Mr. Markel for his assistance and invited him to return the following weekend to see the real thing, the Camporee. He promised to be there.

We broke down our tents and equipment and repacked them in their cartons. Dad and Mr. Tucker supervised the careful loading of the trailer.

Before we departed for home, Scoutmaster Mel again circled his three-fingered sign above his head. "Scouts, I have a few reminders. First, don't forget our regular meeting on Monday evening. At that time, we'll take care of last-minute details in preparing for the Camporee.

"Second, the silent auction for Danny's bicycle is still in progress. The latest bid received was a very low one. Tell your friends and families, if they need a fine bicycle, to go to the church office and enter their bid.

"Third, you all received new badges at the Court of Honor. Please ask your mothers to remove the old badges from your uniforms and replace them with the new ones. If you have more than three or four Merit Badges, you'll want to purchase a Merit Badge sash at Madison's and sew your new badges onto it.

"Well done, scouts. See you all on Monday!"

WE BACKED THE TRAILER into the garage and chocked the wheels. While we were locking the sliding doors, Sergeant Tolna's car pulled into the driveway.

"Hello, men. How's the tent business?"

We told him how impressive the campsite looked when the new tents were erected. We invited him to the full Camporee that next weekend, and he promised to come.

"Any news on the break-in, Jeff?"

"That's why I'm here, John. It's about the fingerprints we lifted last night. We found prints from at least six or eight different individuals on those cartons. We need Sam's and yours to help us eliminate non-suspects. Sam, you were in the navy. John, you have a security clearance. I could send off to Washington for your prints, but it'd be quicker if you could just come down and be printed."

"I suppose we did touch the cartons when we were at Madison's and probably when the two guys delivered them here. You want to do that now, Jeff?"

"If you don't mind, John. You boys want to come along? We can all squeeze into my car."

"Can we, Dad? I've never seen anybody fingerprinted before."

"Sure. Let's all go together."

Because Danny insisted on sitting in the front seat, I was the *squeezee* between Dad and Mr. Tucker in the back. As we approached the intersection of Hamilton and New Albany, that same elderly lady was pulling her two-wheeled grocery cart slowly across the street. Sergeant Tolna stopped to allow her to pass in front of us.

When she reached us, she peered into the police car and saw Danny. She wrinkled her nose, shook her fist, and squeaked, "It's about time you were arrested! You reckless pedestrian killer, you!"

"Who's she talking about?" Danny inquired innocently.

Ignoring Danny's comment, Sergeant Tolna responded, "That's a sign telling us to get moving on your community-service sentence. Right, Danny?"

"I'm available any evening after night crawling."

"I was just thinking. With all the cases involving you two boys in the past year, we ought to have your prints on file too. Gentlemen, is it okay to fingerprint your sons?"

It was agreed. Danny and I would also be fingerprinted.

"We need to be sure we have the prints of all the Madison's employees who may have touched those cartons. I've already gotten Mr. Markel's and his assistant. And their stock boy. Now you've mentioned delivery men. How many were there?"

"Two of them. Their first names were embroidered over their left shirt pockets. I can remember them both. Can you, Sam?"

"That's not hard. They were both named John."

"That must cause confusion on the loading dock."

"I'll get their prints on Monday. Anybody else?"

After racking their brains, Dad and Mr. Tucker couldn't remember another person.

"We have an additional piece of business to take care of, Sergeant Tolna," Danny declared. "I was arrested, charged, and tried for reckless bicycling. But I never had my mug shot taken."

"Actually, Danny. I'm not sure we —."

"Remember, Sergeant Tolna. *Sloppy law enforcement is the precursor to lawlessness.*"

"Where on earth did you hear that, Danny?"

"It's printed on the back of every Riverton Police traffic-citation pad. I read it when I was doing my first community service with Sergeant Zeller."

"To be honest, Danny, I never noticed it before. Thanks for pointing it out to me."

"*Observe* and *learn,* Sergeant Tolna. *Observe* and *learn.*"

WHEN MISS BUNDY WAS given responsibility for administering the silent auction, she immediately took charge. Much to our surprise, she had a good head for merchandising. Her first decision was to issue an order. "Danny, why would anyone want to bid on a pig in a poke? Go home and get your bicycle. Then park it there next to the bulletin board. Chop! Chop!"

By the time we returned, Miss Bundy had prepared a sign, which she promptly taped to the handlebars.

BICYCLE FOR SALE
SILENT AUCTION

PROCEEDS BENEFIT
BOY SCOUT TROOP 46 CAMP SCHOLARSHIP FUND.
SEE MISS BUNDY IN CHURCH OFFICE.

Her second decision involved another facet of her sales strategy. "Unless people see how the auction is progressing, they won't be motivated to bid. We need to post an abbreviated bid sheet on the bulletin board. We'll show the amount bid, the date and time, and the bidder's initials. That'll inform people where the bidding stands, while adding a bit of mystery and intrigue. Mark my word! Bidders will come a-running.

"I'll keep the official sheet, including the bidder's full name and address, locked in my desk drawer. That'll be for my eyes only," she pronounced.

During the 11 days of bidding, JB, Danny, and I must have checked the bulletin board at least two dozen times. Why we thought that would help us get another bicycle for our bait business escapes me. But every time we were near the church, we stopped in to stare at the latest bids and try to decipher the bidder's initials.

The bidding had started very low. The first bid was $3.00. After a week, the latest bid was only $7.50. When Miss Bundy saw us shaking our heads outside her office, she came out to give us the benefit of her experience. "You just wait. In a couple of days, the bidding will get serious. Don't worry about the amount this early in the game. Focus on the number of bidders, especially those who've submitted more than one bid."

We took her advice and reviewed the bidding. There were a total of 18 bids. Most were just increases of 25 cents. But we noticed that four of the bidders had bid twice and one had placed three bids.

"*AGF.* Who do you think that is, Jase?"

"JB, I don't know anybody with those initials. But he must really want that bicycle."

Miss Bundy's prediction proved to be absolutely correct. On Wednesday and Thursday, the two days before the auction closed, the bid amount rose from $17 to $47. And only three active bidders remained. *AGF, BBB,* and *MS.* Continuing to top the bid of the other two, *AGF* seemed determined to win the auction.

After school on Friday, we had to hurry home to finish packing our gear and leave for the Camporee. But we allowed ourselves one last visit to the bulletin board a half-hour before the five o'clock close of bidding.

"Gee! *BBB* has bid $63. I wish we could stay around to see if that's the final bid. Before coming to the park, Scoutmaster Mel will stop to get the winning name and amount from Miss Bundy. We'll know at the campfire meeting tonight."

"Or maybe before," Danny added mysteriously.

19 A CAMPING WE SHALL GO

AS ONE OF THE HOST TROOPS, OUR CAMPSITE WAS adjacent to the check-in booth near the entrance to the campground. Ours was also the farthest from the center of Camporee activity, located at the rustic amphitheater overlooking the wooden stage on the bank of the Chippewa River. All other campsites lay between ours and that spot. However, our location enabled Mr. Tucker to park the equipment trailer within a few feet of our site. All the other troops had to off-load their gear at check-in and lug it for distances up to a half-mile to their weekend homes.

Another benefit of our campsite was its proximity to one of two large restroom facilities. The one near us even offered hot-water showers if we were so inclined. The other was located near the amphitheater. Many troops simply dug nearby latrines instead of subjecting their scouts to a half-mile hike just to use the facilities. Fortunately pumps to provide drinking and cooking water were conveniently located throughout the campground.

To display our brand new tents and equipment prominently, Scoutmaster Mel and the four patrol leaders had agreed on a U-shaped layout for our camp. The five explorer tents formed a tight row along the back boundary of our site, with two rows of pup tents extended from both ends of the explorer row to the front boundary. Our troop campfire, cooking equipment, and food-storage containers were located in the center of the U. Because we were a host troop, we had two large picnic tables at our disposal.

These were placed end-to-end near the campfire to form a long dining or meeting table. The open end of the U faced the campground entrance road to provide a panoramic view of our model campsite for newly arriving troops from every corner of the Chippewa Council area.

Having practiced our setup the Saturday before, we pitched our tents and set up our *kitchen* in just under an hour. Because light rain was predicted for the weekend, we *ditched* each tent. This was accomplished by digging a trench directly under the tent walls to collect and distribute rainwater running off the tent. Because our site gradually sloped from front to back, rainwater was directed to the back of the site. To prevent erosion, we saved the clumps of sod and would restore the trenches upon our departure.

Because JB was one of his tentmates, Freddie assigned the pup-tent position right next to his explorer tent to Danny and me. While this first slot meant we wouldn't have far to walk to converse with each other, there was another advantage. We didn't have to wait for others to erect their pup tents to ensure we had positioned ours correctly, relative to their location. Because we were first in our row, we were the benchmark.

In 1945, every American knew what a pup tent was. Once a household word, meaning a two-man shelter made of treated canvas, the pup tent has gone the way of crystal radios. To be honest, I hadn't noticed its demise. Advances in tent design and tenting materials hastened the end of pup tents as we knew them. When I was a boy, soldiers slept in them on the war's front lines and Boy Scouts used them to earn Camping Merit Badges. Today, to many Americans, a *pup tent* is a shelter for their dogs.

Whatever happened to dog houses?

As far back as I can remember, young boys in my neighborhood camped out. Admittedly it was only in the backyard and probably only lasted a couple of hours beyond sunset. But there was a very good reason for that. Who could predict the precise moment when the Green Monster of Forrest Street would emerge from behind Mrs. Mikas' plum trees? You just never knew.

By now, you are probably wondering what this has to do with pup tents. Here is the answer. When we camped out in the backyard, we constructed our *tents* by tossing an old blanket over a low-slung length of clothesline. Once both blanket ends had been anchored with rocks, bricks, or other heavy objects, our shelter came very close to looking like a pup tent.

Naturally the official Boy Scout pup tents we used in Courthouse Park were not held up by clothesline. Instead there was a four-foot pole, made from sturdy pre-war aluminum piping, propping up the front end of the tent and another propping up the back. These poles were held erect by tightly strung cords, extending from canvas loops at each end of the tent's roof to stakes in the ground. The sides of the tent were anchored, not by rocks or bricks, but rather by pre-cut and properly shaped wooden tent stakes driven into the ground through several canvas loops, located at intervals along the lower edge of the tent's sides. The tension of the cords and the side stakes could be adjusted to make the pup tent as taut as a snare drum.

The pup tent covered an area approximately the size of a double bed, with a bit of extra space beyond the pillow area. Unlike the blanket over the clothesline, both ends of the pup tent were closed. At the foot of the bed, two flaps could be tied or untied to keep out the wind and rain or to allow you to enter or exit. The *flap* at the head of the bed couldn't be opened, and it extended outward to make a tiny space for storing backpacks and other gear.

When Danny and I finished pitching and ditching our tent, we inspected the ground under the tent to ensure there were no rocks or roots to poke up through our bedrolls. We decided not to dig the shoulder or hip holes, recommended for maximum sleeping comfort by our *Handbook for Boys*. Satisfied that this area was relatively free of sharp objects, we laid out a large sheet of oil cloth, slick-side-down, for a ground cloth. This waterproof cloth would be a barrier to any moisture trying to wend its way up the capillary express to our bedroll.

"Do you think we should unroll our bedding yet, Jase?"

"I think it might stay drier if we keep it rolled up until we go to bed."

Back in those days, none of us had a genuine sleeping bag. We assembled our homemade version using a mattress cover from a single bed. Into this, we carefully inserted a *bed,* consisting of two specially folded army blankets and a flannel inner sheet. After tightly rolling our bed from its bottom to its top, we encircled and tied it with strong lengths of binder twine or leather thongs. When rolling up our bed, we did so in a manner to ensure the folds of the blanket were on the bottom when it was unrolled. That way, the weight of our body would hold them in place and keep our bedroll from developing gaps and openings through which the night air could whistle. When we slipped into bedrolls, we were careful not to disturb our blanket folds. Once inside, we were snug and warm.

Before going to bed, we removed our clothing, except for underwear and socks. After folding it, we stacked it on top of our shoes. During the night, this accomplished two purposes. It provided us with a pillow and it kept our clothing and shoes warm and dry. On frigid mornings, we could easily access this pile and dress before exiting our toasty bedrolls.

On a few camping trips, I remember the nights being so warm that we wiggled out of our bedrolls and slept on top of them. On those occasions, we encountered another problem, pesky mosquitoes. I don't remember returning from a summer camping trip without smelling, as if I had showered in citronella.

Ah! The joys of camping.

AFTER STORING OUR GEAR in our tent, Danny and I picked up JB and walked the campsite perimeter to assess the troop's progress. Dad and Mr. Tucker were sharing an explorer tent with Scoutmaster Mel and Mr. Reilly. But Scoutmaster Mel had yet to arrive.

In passing, we overheard Mr. Tucker telling Mr. Reilly about the garage break-in. "The police fingerprinted anyone who might have touched those cartons. Altogether, seven of us were printed. They compared our fingerprints to those they found on the cartons to eliminate the prints of us non-suspects. Oddly all the prints on the cartons were eliminated."

"How could that be, Sam? Didn't you say the thief was pawing through the cartons?"

"Jeff thinks he might have been wearing gloves."

"Sure, that makes sense. Did you discover anything missing from your garage?"

"No. And that *doesn't* make sense. Neither does the fact that he was searching through the cartons. We may never know what he was after."

"Who wants to ditch the tent?" Dad asked, holding up a trenching shovel.

They seemed fairly well-organized so we continued our tour. The four patrol leaders were helping their scouts with the finer points of tent-pitching. All in all, our campsite was settling in nicely.

Having completed our sidewalk-superintendent duties, we volunteered to help the two committeemen who were preparing supper. Since we had arrived late in the afternoon and had to set up the camp before sunset, the meal planners decided to keep supper simple. Hot dogs with all the trimmings. Pork and beans. Pete's finest potato chips. And all flavors of Riverton pop.

Our first task was to peel and slice onions. While the three of us stood slicing and sobbing, I thought about the bicycle auction. Because I was eager to hear the results, I had been keeping an eye out for Scoutmaster Mel. At half past six, he still hadn't arrived.

"Think anything went wrong with the auction, guys?"

"Gee, I don't know," JB admitted.

"Nope! Not a thing," Danny declared confidently.

"Why are you acting so smug? Do you know something we don't know?"

"What? You mean like who's going to win the auction?"

"Of course!"

"AGF or *BBB."*

"Geez, Danny! I could have told you that!"

"If you knew the answer, why'd you ask the question?"

I *really* loved these exchanges with Danny.

Because troop check-in and setup were the only scheduled Camporee events on the first evening, Scoutmaster Mel had planned a Troop 46 *campfire meeting.* As far as I knew, the only agenda item was the announcement of the auction winner and the amount to be added to the camp-scholarship fund.

After finishing their setup, the other scouts and committeemen wandered over, plopped down at the picnic tables, and watched us prepare supper. When Scoutmaster Mel finally arrived, he recognized the inequity of the situation and took action, "You cooks need a hand? You've got me and these 20 loafers sitting at the picnic tables to draw on."

With so little remaining to be done, we suggested they start serving themselves. Then we did the same and sat down at the table with Dad and Scoutmaster Mel. "Mel, do you have the results of the auction?" Dad asked matter-of-factly. My ears perked up.

Having just bitten off a third of his latest hot dog, Scoutmaster Mel nodded and pointed at his mouth. After a series of *chomps* and *gulps,* he replied, "Yes, I have, John. But this thing had more twists than a pretzel. It's a long story. I'd like to wait and tell everyone at the campfire meeting. Okay?"

"You bet, Mel. Relax! Have another hot dog. Why does everything taste so much better when you're eating outside?"

After supper, we all pitched in and cleaned up the cooking area. When the sun had sunk below the western horizon, the wind picked up and the temperature took a nosedive. Scoutmaster Mel advised, "Let's start the meeting at eight o'clock sharp. It's getting cooler. I'll stoke up the fire. Everybody best put on a jacket or sweatshirt before the meeting."

Danny and I opted for sweatshirts. JB slipped on his letter sweater from Stony River Academy. When we reassembled around the campfire, we were a motley-looking troop of boys, but we were warm and contented.

SCOUTMASTER MEL OPENED THE campfire meeting like any normal scout meeting. We recited the *Scout Oath, Laws, Motto,* and *Slogan.* While we were at the Camporee, Scoutmaster Mel advised it was important to keep the virtues and values of scouting in mind. He called them the *Fundamentals.* We were among 30 or more troops in attendance that weekend. Since these Fundamentals had brought us together, they would be the basis for the learning, fellowship, and fun we would share. As he uttered these inspiring words, the brightly flickering campfire painted the entire scene with splashes of gold. We basked in the glow of fellowship.

"Before we enjoy the lighter festivities, I want to recap our agenda for the next two days." After inventorying the events and competitions scheduled for Saturday and Sunday, he informed us, "Tomorrow evening, the *Order of the Arrow* has a wonderful show for everyone at the amphitheater starting at eight o'clock. You can invite friends or family to join us for supper before the show. Given our afternoon schedule, we should be eating somewhere around half-past six.

"For your information, Mr. Markel and Sergeant Tolna will be here. Let me know if you have guests coming so we can water down the soup or —. What are we having tomorrow night?"

In unison, everyone shouted, "Spaghetti and meat balls!"

"You really didn't think I'd forgotten *that*. Did you?" Scoutmaster Mel guffawed.

"Speaking of the menu, you might want to try your hand at snipe hunting. Snipe are quite plentiful here, especially this time of year. A dozen snipe would make a delicious addition to tomorrow night's supper. See Freddie if you're interested."

Danny turned to me and whispered, "What's a snipe?"

Normally I would have told him the truth. But I was still smarting from my latest nonsensical exchange with him. "It's a small night bird — looks like a quail or a woodcock. You catch it with a flashlight and a paper bag."

"That's right. Now I remember."

Wait until Freddie hears this!

Scoutmaster Mel continued, "After my *tale* about the bike auction, Freddie has a spook story for us called *The Hook*. To top off the evening, Striker Loomis will lead us in a round or two of rousing camp songs. How does that sound?"

When the buzz of approval died down, Scoutmaster Mel began. "Now let me tell you about the auction. You're not going to believe what's transpired. As you'll recall, I'd planned to stop by the church to learn from Miss Bundy who was the highest bidder and how much they'd bid.

"The bidding closed at five o'clock. But a few minutes before five, I received an urgent telephone call from Miss Bundy. She told me there was a mighty brouhaha going on between the last two bidders, and my presence was required in her office. *Chop! Chop!* Because she only uses those words in dire circumstances, I dropped everything and headed for the church."

Scoutmaster Mel turned and looked directly at me. "I'll stop here and ask Jase a question. Miss Bundy told me you boys were there this afternoon around half-past four. Is that right?"

I nodded, not sure why he was asking.

"When you left the church, who was the high bidder and how much was the bid?"

"It was *BBB's* bid for $63."

I looked at JB and Danny for confirmation. Both nodded.

"And who was the other bidder, Jase?"

"*AGF.*"

"Exactly! And they were the two bidders who were having the row in Miss Bundy's office. When I arrived at the church, I discovered I knew them both — and so do some of you. Miss Bundy had approved their requests to use misleading initials to mask their true identities. Anybody want to guess who one or both of these bidders are?"

No one responded. That is, until Danny raised his hand. "I know who *AGF* is."

"I had a hunch you would, Danny. Anybody know the other bidder?"

No response. Danny raised his hand again. "I know who *BBB* is too."

I was flabbergasted. "Danny, how is that possible?"

Without answering, he locked his lips with the invisible key and tossed it over his shoulder.

"All right, Danny. Looks like you know all the answers. Let me ask you this one," Scoutmaster Mel stated calmly.

"What was the highest bid of the day?"

Danny thought for a minute. "Probably $100."

"You're absolutely right."

"Who was the winning bidder?"

"Probably *AGF,*" Danny guessed again.

"Danny, you're close. There was no bid higher than *AGF's*. But *AGF* wasn't the winning bidder. Know why?"

At first, Danny looked puzzled, then a broad grin appeared on his face. "It was a tie. Wasn't it?"

"You're absolutely correct!"

My head was spinning. A tie! "What're they going to do? Saw the bike in two?" I sputtered.

"No! Just the opposite. Each of them has agreed to donate $100 to the camp-scholarship fund. Then together they'll present the bicycle to the party on whose behalf they were bidding."

"Why would they do that, Mel?"

"It's simple, John. After calming down, they discovered they were bidding against each other to purchase the bicycle for the *same* party. Let me clarify by asking Danny another question or two."

"Who's *BBB,* Danny?"

"E. F. Graham. The initials stand for 'Boys' Bait Business.' He wanted to buy back the bicycle for us to use in our business. I told him not to pay more than $100."

"And who's *AGF,* Danny?"

"Aunt Greta Frantz. She's the Libby sisters' aunt. She wanted to buy the bicycle for us too. I also told her not to bid more than $100."

"Danny, I can't believe you *arranged* all this?" Dad told him.

"Actually it wasn't my idea."

"Whose idea was it?"

"Mrs. Addison told us we needed to think of a way to submit the highest bid. So I thought of two ways, just in case one didn't work out." Danny winked at JB and me, saying, "So, guys, it looks like our bait business has two bicycles."

We were stunned.

With his mission accomplished, Danny turned to Scoutmaster Mel. "Can we hear Freddie's spook story now?"

The Eddie Conroy Story
New Albany, Michigan

CONROY HAD NOT VISITED the park since the previous week when he'd followed the trailer from the Tucker garage. His clumsy attempt at burglary had only intensified his obsession with recovering the bracelet. But his careful observations from afar revealed that Tucker had locked him out and the Riverton police had increased patrols in the vicinity of the garage.

He decided to be patient. On his way home from work the next Friday, he noticed Tucker, accompanied by the same man and two boys, hitch the trailer to his station wagon and drive off in the direction of New Albany again. After turning into the park, he saw the increased population of Boy Scouts and adults. He concluded this was a big campout of some sort.

He observed the Tucker station wagon and trailer pull up near the campground entrance. After stopping on the road opposite the trailer, Conroy watched as that same group of scouts and adults began to unload the trailer and empty the cartons of their contents. He spotted the mark he had placed to enable him to recover the bracelet. While the boys who came with Tucker carried Conroy's loot to the rear of the campsite, he watched carefully, fixing the location of his quest by noting trees and other physical objects to help him find it after dark.

Exiting his car, Conroy casually walked to the Camporee check-in booth. Quickly he determined there would be upwards of 600 Boy Scouts spending the weekend in the Courthouse Park campgrounds. Politely he requested a copy of the *Camporee Activities and Events* list stacked on the counter. During a cursory review, he spotted his opportunity.

As he drove away from the park, he exclaimed aloud, "While you're having your *Order of the Arrow* ceremony, I'll have my *Order of the Diamond Bracelet* ceremony. See you Saturday night at eight o'clock sharp, scouts."

ON SATURDAY MORNING, DANNY was very grumpy, and I really couldn't blame him. Very late the night before, I'd awakened when he stumbled into our tent. This was long after Freddie and I had left him in the woods, holding his brown paper bag and flashlight. When I asked what luck he'd had, he mumbled something about the two big ones that got away. I replied, "Funny thing! That was the same luck I had on my first snipe hunt with my cousins." What I didn't say was no one ever goes on a *second* snipe hunt. While I felt a bit sorry for him, it didn't prevent me from immediately falling back to sleep.

Danny wasn't the only grumpy one. Three other novice snipe hunters, including JB, were also members of the bitter bunch. On the morning after my initiation into the Snipe Hunters of America, my feelings were an acerbic blend of anger, resentment, and embarrassment. Like every other American kid, driven by a desire to fit in, I'd fallen for the snipe hunt ruse. However, having gone on a snipe hunt was a terrific motivator. I could hardly wait to bag my first snipe patsy. And Danny was it.

Danny, JB, and I stood in line with our cook kits, waiting to be served hefty portions of scrambled eggs, Canadian bacon, and campfire-burnt toast. When we joined Scoutmaster Mel at the picnic table, he cheerfully greeted us. "Just the trio I was looking for. How would you three like to volunteer for a special assignment tonight?"

Being the only non-grouch in the threesome, I responded positively, "You bet! What do you want us to do?"

"I'd like you fellows to take charge of the marshmallow roast after the *Order of the Arrow* event. You'll have to leave the show about 20 minutes early. First, you'll need to put some wood on the fire. The marshmallows, roasting forks, and paper napkins are in the blue food case there. You can set them up here on the picnic table.

"After going through the troop closet at the church, I could only find three roasting forks. I thought you three could just roast marshmallows for everybody. Since each fork can hold six marshmallows, you can produce them about as fast as people can eat them."

After breakfast, we still had time for a few games of *split* before the day's activities began. This dangerous game requires throwing your hunting knife so it sticks in the ground very close to your opponent's foot, but I'm sure this game has been outlawed by parents today. When we were boys, we played split with our adult leaders looking on. Frankly I'm amazed we didn't have more casualties. I believe we only played it at scouting functions because I don't remember ever playing split at school or between church services. On the other hand, unlike a camping trip, I seldom strapped on my hunting knife before school or church. Maybe that had something to do with it.

Each of the three host troops was required to plan and conduct its share of the wide variety of Camporee events and competitions over the weekend. Many of these addressed the requirements for advancing in rank or earning Merit Badges. One of Troop 46's assignments was *Axe Safety*. Patrol Leader John Bosco and Committeeman Patrick Reilly demonstrated how to carry and pass an axe safely to another person, how to fell a tree, how to prepare firewood, and how to sharpen an axe. Our troop was also assigned *First Aid, Bird Identification, Capture the Flag, Compass Reading,* and *Competitive Knot Tying.*

Danny was adamant about our choice of morning events. I staunchly protested by reminding him we were members of the *Boy Scouts* not the *4-H.* But in the end, perhaps out of snipe-hunting guilt, I agreed to attend *Animal Husbandry.* The session was held in the Courthouse Casino, the brick meeting hall located in the center of Courthouse Park. Each July, my family attended the Compton reunion that was held in that building.

When we walked in, the hall was filled with farm kids. Being a part-time farmer myself, I could tell by the coating on their work shoes and by the familiar scent of their cologne, *Eau de Barnyard.*

The handout confirmed the inadvisability of our attendance.

Program Title
ANIMAL HUSBANDRY

Program Leader
Mr. Harvey Hickenlooper
Teacher, RHS Agriculture Department
Faculty Advisor, Future Farmers of America

Merit Badges Covered

Poultry Care	Sheep Farming
Pigeon Raising	Dairying
Beekeeping	Rabbit Raising
Beef Production	Dog Care
Hog & Pork Production	First Aid to Animals

"Danny, I'm not sure we're —."
"I'm very interested in one of these Merit Badges."
"You are? Which one?"
First Aid to Animals. So we'll have to stay for the entire program."
Farmer Tucker had spoken.

BECAUSE HE BECAME REALLY bogged down in *Beekeeping* during his three-hour program, Mr. Hickenlooper only managed to cover four of the 10 promised Merit Badge topics. Danny's targeted subject hadn't come close to being discussed. When he suggested we attend the repeat offering of *Animal Husbandry* that afternoon to catch the First Aid topic, I put my foot down.

Since there were so many more interesting programs, we couldn't decide on what to attend. When we saw JB at lunch, we inquired about his choice for the afternoon. *"International Morse Code,"* he declared without hesitation.

Frankly we had not even considered that option. But you would have never known it by Danny's response. "We were torn between that one and *Animal Husbandry."* Addressing me, he suggested, "Let's join JB for some *mars coating.* Okay, Jase?"

Another one of Danny's studied decisions!

To accommodate the expected large turnout, the Morse code program was held in the campground amphitheater. The leader was Jesse Norman, a retired navy chief signalman and counselor for the *Signaling* Merit Badge. The badge required scouts to demonstrate their mastery of Morse code using a number of methods for sending and receiving. On the stage, Chief Norman had assembled the most common instruments used to do so. A flashing light, buzzer, radio code key, and wigwag flag.

A scout in the front row raised his hand. "I understand how dots and dashes can be created in the form of a *flash, buzz,* or a *click.* But how do you do it with a wigwag flag?"

"Good question! I was about to show you how it's done," our leader replied as he picked up the flag. "These are official-sized wigwag flags. Each is a two-foot square attached to a six-foot wooden shaft. Notice that one flag is white with an eight-inch red square in the center. The other is red with an eight-inch white square in the center.

"The red flag can easily be seen against a light background like the sky, sand, or snow. And the white flag is used against a dark background like dark trees or a dark building. Understand?

"Wigwag signals all start with the flag staff held in an upright position. Like this," he told us, holding it with both hands. "To make a *dot,* you swing the flag left — down to the horizontal position — and back up again. And to make a *dash,* you swing the flag right — down to the horizontal — and back up again." He demonstrated both movements. "With a little practice, most people are able to read dots and dashes pretty quickly."

As he moved the flag to and from both positions, he spoke the code. "Di-Di-Dah" and "Dah-Di-Dit."

Within a few minutes, I was able to read the positions with little or no concentration.

"I want to show you the common devices used to send Morse code. But our primary objective for our short time together is to teach you a method for quickly learning the *International Morse Code.* Over the years, I've taught this method and, believe it or not, there're some individuals who can master the entire code in less than two hours — and never forget it."

We all looked at each other, wondering if we were one of those people.

"Just so you know — I personally was not one of those fast learners. It took me several days before I was able to *hear* or receive the code — and thereby *understand* it. Or to *speak* or send the code — and thereby *think* in the code.

"Practically speaking there's no *easy* way to learn the code, but like my old Navy instructor used to say, 'There is a *less hard* way.' First, we're going to throw away those alphabets with the dots and dashes beside each letter. You never want to think in terms of *dot-dash.* Instead we'll talk in terms of *didah* not *dit dah.* "

He lost me there.

"I probably lost some of you when I made that statement. But my able assistant will pass out a sheet of paper entitled *Morse Code Lesson Groups.* On that sheet, you'll see 12 groups of code representing progressively more complex letters and numbers. As soon as everyone has a copy, we'll go over it and you'll see what I mean."

When everyone had a sheet, he began. "For now, I just want you to focus on the first group of code. When you see how this group is constructed, you'll understand the progressive — *less hard* — way to learn Morse code."

I focused on the first group.

MORSE CODE LESSON GROUPS (1 - 12)

GROUP 1

E	Dit
T	Dah
A	DiDah
O	DahDahDah
I	DiDit
N	DahDit
S	DiDiDit

"Earlier I said you need to think in terms of *didah* — not *dit dah*. Listen carefully. When I say *didah,* there's no pause between the *syllables*. When I say *dit dah,* there's a distinct pause between these two *words*.

"Look at the first three letters in Group 1. If you mean to send the letter *A,* you can't pause between the syllables. If you do pause, you won't be sending the letter *A*. You'll be sending the letter *E* followed by the letter *T*. Are you beginning to see now?"

Immediately the entire sheet, organized in the 12 groups, became crystal clear to me. After a few minutes of concentrated study, I had memorized the Morse code for all 26 letters of the alphabet, all 10 numbers, and the essential punctuation marks. To this day, I have no idea how it happened. But I have always been grateful that it did.

Several years later, while serving as a naval officer, my being able to *see* or *hear* and simultaneously *understand* Morse code certainly impressed the radiomen and signalmen in my division. When we were at sea during the Cuban Missile crisis, I memorized the Cyrillic transliteration tables which enabled me to communicate with Russian ships by flashing light.

When I looked at Danny, he nodded and smiled broadly. I assumed he'd memorized the code as well. Blinking my eyes rapidly, I sent my first message in Morse code. He immediately blinked back, *"YES. I KNOW. YOU'RE MY BEST FRIEND TOO."*

AFTER OUR BEING THOROUGHLY *coated with mars,* Danny and I blinked at each other all the way back to our campsite. Because JB had not benefitted from the same astonishing learning experience we had, I felt a bit guilty about excluding him while we played with our new toy. I blinked my concern to Danny, who agreed by suggesting a blinking moratorium until we were alone. After blinking my acceptance of his idea, I shut down my blinker.

However, I continued unconsciously transmitting my inner thoughts in Morse code by slapping my leg as I walked along. When Danny's leg responded to my thoughts, I was jarred awake. "That's quite enough," I vowed aloud.

"What is?" JB wanted to know.

"Danny and I can't seem to stop sending code to each other."

"No kidding? I hadn't noticed."

"Sorry, JB. I know it's rude. But we've agreed to stop it. Right, Danny?"

"RIGHT," Danny's leg replied.

The form of his answer escaped me until JB wondered, "What did Danny say, Jase?"

"What? Oh, he agreed to stop."

JB didn't answer. He just shook his head. When we arrived at our tents, JB announced he was going to stretch out on his bedroll for a little rest before supper. Following JB's lead, Danny and I did a little stretching ourselves. The minute I closed my eyes, I was gone.

"Danny! Jase! Wake up. They're almost finished serving supper. Grab your cook kits and let's get over there together. When we finish, I suggest we go to the *Order of the Arrow* show together and get seats together so we can leave together for our marshmallow duty."

"That's a lot of togetherness," Danny quipped.

"Just the way I like it," JB quipped right back.

After being served, we carried our supper to the picnic table where Sergeant Tolna, Mr. Tucker, Mr. Markel, and Dad were engaged in, what appeared to be, a serious conversation. I figured they were talking about the Tucker garage break-in. When we approached, they suddenly became silent.

As a bit of a tease, I probed innocently, "What were you talking about? You seemed so serious."

By looking at Sergeant Tolna, the other men gave him the option of answering my question or not. He communicated his decision by changing subjects. "Spaghetti's really good, you guys."

Without JB noticing, I looked at Danny and quickly blinked, *"SECRET STUFF."*

Danny nodded and blinked back, *"LET IT GO."*

I nodded and then focused on my supper. Until I took my first bite of spaghetti and meatballs, I hadn't realized how hungry I was. Second servings were mandatory for all three of us.

Ritualistically we washed our cook kits and silverware in the warm soapy water and dipped them into the scalding rinse water. By the time we walked back to our tents, the sun had begun to set. We slipped on our sweatshirts and jackets, grabbed our flashlights, and joined the river of campers streaming toward the amphitheater. Before we arrived, the sun sank below the horizon turning our river into an endless, narrow moving band of bobbing flashlights.

The *Order of the Arrow* was an organization of scouts who had been recognized as honor campers. The members were chosen because they had demonstrated exceptional camping expertise and maintained a cheerful disposition as they exemplified all the scouting Fundamentals as Scoutmaster Mel had called them. Before the end of our scouting careers, all three of us would be tapped for *Order of the Arrow* membership.

The show turned out to be an entertaining blend of Indian lore, scouting Fundamentals, choreography, and pyrotechnics. After everyone was comfortably seated, the Chippewa Council senior scouting executive took the stage and welcomed us to the Camporee and to the evening's entertainment. Mercifully he was a man of few words, the last of which he used to request we extinguish all flashlights in preparation for the show.

On that moonless night, we sat quietly in total darkness, listening to the tree toads. Suddenly we heard the haunting call of a screech owl, no doubt rendered by an experienced birdcaller. The eerie sound had come from our right, upriver from where we sat. Straining our eyes in that direction, we searched the darkness for a hint of what would happen next. Above the trees along the riverbank, we saw the shimmering golden glow of firelight, radiating upward into the coal-black sky. The source of the light had yet to come into view. Faintly at first, the rhythmic beat of a tom-tom floated toward us from the direction of the brightening firelight.

Suddenly a long and sleek canoe appeared. A trim wooden structure, resembling an inverted, six-foot spatula, jutted from its bow. On its flat, forward-most area was a large cast-iron pot filled with blazing pitch-filled pine cones. Illuminated by the bright fire, a tall Indian chief stood stoically in the bow with his arms crossed. He wore a splendid full headdress of white, fluffy red-tufted eagle feathers, which formed a full circle around his head and trailed down his back to the deck of the canoe. In the stern, a kneeling Indian brave deftly dipped his canoe paddle, stroke after stroke, to propel the vessel slowly toward the stage before us. It was indeed a magnificent sight to behold.

When the canoe came alongside, the chief stepped out onto the stage. He took exactly three moccasin-clad footsteps toward us. Stopping abruptly, he spread his arms above his head and appealed to the Chippewa fire god by shouting the time-tested entreaty, "Wau—wa—to—sa."

Suddenly, out of the trees, a great ball of fire shot straight from the heavens into the center of the huge stack of tinder, kindling, and firewood piled high in front of the stage. The campfire exploded and suffused us all with yellow-white light.

Actually the great ball was a bucket filled with rags drenched in kerosene. A strong wire ran from the center of the kerosene-soaked firewood pile through the bucket's bail to a sturdy eyebolt screwed into the crotch of an oak tree some 20 feet above. When the chief's entreaty startled us all, the courageous Boy Scout who had shinnied up the tree, struck a match to the bucket, and sent it earthward.

Standing behind the roaring fire, the chief regaled us with a 30-minute soliloquy, comprising Indian lore, nature stories, and scouting Fundamentals. The chief was obviously an experienced speaker, whose script had been carefully drafted by the scouting front office. The more I listened, the more I suspected the chief was the high-school student who read the daily school announcements and cafeteria menu over the school speaker system, a member of a winning debate team, or the star of his school play. Or perhaps all of the above.

When the chief concluded his fine act, he beckoned to the audience. All the newly tapped *Order of the Arrow* members stood up and formed a line to come onto the stage for their initiation. That was our cue to steal away and launch our marshmallow mission.

While we walked toward our campsite, Danny declared, "I'm glad the guy who played the chief remembered all his lines."

"Why's that, Danny?"

"Instead of yelling, *Wau—wa—to—sa*. What if he'd yelled, *Mil—wau—kee?*"

AS THE FESTIVE SOUNDS faded behind us, the surreal jet-black night engulfed us. The once-sufficient light from our flashlights seemed to dim, retreating in the face of overpowering darkness. We ourselves sought the silent solace of our own thoughts. Without the perspective of clearly defined landmarks on the way back, our walk seemed interminable. Moreover, the interrupted sleep of the night before and the long active day were beginning to take their toll. Fatigue gnawed at my bones like a mangy old dog.

Finally, in the distance ahead, we saw the faint glow of streetlights that dotted the park. When the path changed from dirt to paving, I knew the darkness on our left obscured the many buildings that housed county fair events each August. But, try as I might, I couldn't distinguish a single one of them. I even extinguished my flashlight and strained my eyes, but it was no use. Darkness ruled that night.

When we hit the entrance road, I saw the dark shape of a car that someone had backed off the road and into our campsite. I assumed it was a late-arriving attendee of the *Order of the Arrow* show who hadn't taken time to park properly. To reach our campsite, we walked single file between the parked car and a giant forsythia bush. JB led the way.

Suddenly he stopped, causing Danny and me to pile up behind him.

"Hey, why'd you stop?"

"Shhhhhhh!" JB warned, pointing ahead. Whispering he added, "Someone's in your tent."

Even though the campfire had died down considerably, it cast enough light for us to see the silhouettes of our tents. At the far end of the left-hand row, stood the tent belonging to Danny and me. JB was right. The beam of a flashlight danced on its inside wall.

For the life of me, I couldn't understand why anyone would be there. We hadn't brought anything of particular value. Desperate attempts to explain this situation flitted back and forth inside my head like sparrows in the top of a barn. It still made no sense to me.

"What'll we do?" JB whispered.

I pointed behind us toward the entrance road. Understanding my signal, the other two followed me. We huddled behind the oddly parked car.

"So what'll we do?" JB whispered again.

Up to this point, Danny had remained unusually silent. But abruptly he announced, "We gotta get him!"

"How do you propose to do that?"

Danny motioned for us to huddle up. The three of us joined arms and leaned in. To explain his plan, Danny told us to visualize the face of a clock. We were located at the entrance of our campsite. That was the six o'clock position. Our tent was located at the 11 o'clock position. If we wanted to move quickly to the tent without being seen, we had to avoid using a frontal approach because a straight line from six to 11 would take us right by the campfire. Instead, Danny proposed we circle counterclockwise and approach our tent from the rear. And what he suggested next was ingenious. When our huddle broke, each of us knew his assignment.

After turning off our flashlights and clipping them to our belts, we executed Danny's plan. Our path took us outside the right-hand row of pup tents up to the one o'clock position. From there we turned left and crept behind the row of explorer tents until we reached the 11 o'clock position where we situated ourselves directly behind our pup tent.

At that instant, the intruder jerked the rear pole out of its upright position. This caused the back end of the tent to sag. But Danny ignored this unexpected occurrence. As planned, he pointed to the front of the tent. That was my cue. I ran to the front and immediately yanked on the pole cord, pulling its stake out of the ground. Danny yanked out the rear stake. The pup tent completely collapsed. We dove onto the collapsed tent, pinning the intruder to the ground. At first the man struggled, but within a minute or so, he gave up. He couldn't move a muscle with three good-sized boys lying spread-eagle on top of his canvas covering.

"Help!"

"Stop! Thief!"

"Police!"

For the next 10 minutes, we yelled incessantly at the top of our lungs.

"**All right, boys. We're coming!**" I heard Scoutmaster Mel shout from the entrance road. Before we knew it, our entire troop, the committeemen, Sergeant Tolna, and Mr. Markel stood around us, staring down on our collapsed tent and our subdued lump of quarry.

"When we got back to fix the marshmallows, we saw someone with a flashlight inside our tent. He seemed to be looking for something. So we pulled out the front and rear stakes and jumped on top of him."

"You fellows stay right there on top of this rascal," Sergeant Tolna directed as he drew his police revolver. "The rest of you boys stand back."

He lifted the front tent flap, revealing the intruder's left foot. He tapped the shoe with his pistol barrel and explained the reality of the man's situation to him. "Mister, I'm Sergeant Tolna with the Riverton Police Department. That was my loaded revolver that just tapped your toe. I want you to come out — very slowly — with your hands up high. Do you understand me?"

"Yes, sir," the man croaked weakly. "Don't shoot! I'm not armed. Can you get these guys off my back so I can get out of here?"

"All right, boys. Slowly roll back off him so he can get out."

The man wiggled out from under the tent and stood up with his hands on top of his head.

"Turn around," the sergeant ordered. Holding his pistol in his left hand, he clicked his handcuffs on the man's wrists and walked him toward the campfire. "Come over here so we can get a look at you."

Dad and Mr. Tucker threw some wood on the fire. A burst of light flooded the scene. They turned around and stared at the man.

"My gosh! It's one of the Johns!" Dad exclaimed.

"John Smith! To be precise," Mr. Markel added. "He works for Joe Rankin down in shipping and delivery. It looks like your theory on the two crimes being connected was correct, Sergeant."

"I remember Mr. Smith from the day we fingerprinted him. Real friendly that day, weren't you, Smith? By the way, what's your real name? And while you're at it, where's the loot?"

"Still in the tent. I couldn't shake it out of that dang pole. And I don't think I'll tell you anything more 'til I get a lawyer."

"Suit yourself. Let's take a hike to my car so I can radio the sheriff. I'm a little out of my jurisdiction. Lucky you! The county jail's a bit newer than ours. But I suspect you'll have a lot of time to compare jails over the next few years."

By the time Sergeant Tolna returned, we heard sirens heading our way from the sheriff's office. "Before the sheriff arrives, I want to take a look at those tent poles." He pulled up the front of the tent and extracted both poles from under the collapsed canvas. He held one up and peeked through it, as if it were a telescope. "Nothing inside of that one. Must be in this one." He peered through the second one. "Darn this one's clear too. Must be in the tent. Can I borrow your flashlight, Jase?"

Before he searched the interior of our tent, we helped Sergeant Tolna replace the tent poles and stakes and reerect our tent. After a thorough search, the sergeant came up empty-handed. "It's not there. I wonder if Smith lied to us. But wait a minute. If it wasn't on him — and it wasn't in the tent, why was he in the tent in the first place? This is not making any sense."

"Sergeant Tolna, I'm a little confused myself. What're you looking for?"

"A diamond bracelet, Jase."

"Why didn't you say that in the first place? I've got that in my backpack," Danny stated matter-of-factly. He ducked into the tent and came out with a handkerchief wrapped around an object. "This fell out of the pole when we were putting up our tent. I recognized it and was going to return it to the owner when we got home after the Camporee. You want to take it back to her, Sergeant Tolna?" Danny handed the hankie-wrapped bundle to him.

The sergeant unwrapped the bracelet and held it up for all to see. In the campfire light, the many facets of the bracelet's eight carat-sized diamonds sparkled and glittered.

"Danny, you know the person who owns this bracelet?"

"Sure! Mrs. Singleton."

"You're right. Mrs. Martha Singleton. I don't know how you do it, Danny. But you seem to always have the right answers."

After Sheriff Connors and Sergeant Tolna congratulated us once again for cracking another case, we sat at the picnic table nibbling on a roasted marshmallow and sipping our hot chocolate, a reward from Scoutmaster Mel.

"Danny, how did you know that Mrs. Singleton owned that bracelet?"

"She was wearing it when I met her."

"Where was that?"

"At Dad's garage, when she brought in her car to have the brakes repaired."

"I don't know that name. Does she belong to the First Methodist Church?"

"Nope. But she did bid on my bicycle. You remember — *MS.*"

20 DECORATION DAY

WHEN WE SAT DOWN FOR BREAKFAST TOGETHER ON Tuesday morning, my head was still spinning from all that had happened in the previous few days. The bicycle auction had produced two positive outcomes. First, the bicycle had been presented to BBB, making us fully capable of transporting sizeable quantities of live bait quickly to Homer One's tanks. Second, the generosity of the last two bidders netted $200 for the troop's camp-scholarship fund.

In addition, because we scouts had captured the thief and recovered her bracelet, Mrs. Singleton was so thrilled that she magnanimously matched the $100 donation of the other donors. With $300 added to the fund, no Troop 46 member wanting to attend Camp Moon Lake that summer would miss out.

The Camporee had been an unqualified success. We flawlessly executed our duties as host troop. The events we facilitated were professional and informative, ranking right up there with *International Morse Code*. Naturally our exemplary campsite had won high praise from everyone. Because it was the scene of Conroy's capture, it garnered even more attention than we had anticipated.

Danny and I made the newspaper again for having subdued yet another nasty piece of work. As usual, Chuck Nichols spared no flattering adjectives in his two-part series, appearing in the Sunday and Monday editions of the *Riverton Daily Press*.

Unfortunately no mention was made of JB's contribution, which we put right at our scout meeting on Monday night.

To my surprise, Scoutmaster Mel announced that I had been selected by Riverton's VFW Post to deliver *General Logan's Order* at Wednesday's Decoration Day opening ceremony at Addison Square. Wearing my scout uniform adorned with my new First Class badge and Merit Badges, I would be the program's first speaker. Following my presentation, military officers, veterans, and city officials would speak for a total of an hour or so before the VFW master of ceremonies launched the annual parade to the Forest Hill Cemetery where the memorial ceremony would conclude the Decoration Day celebration.

Today this holiday is known by another name. Referring to Decoration Day as *Memorial Day* first occurred in 1882, but this name did not come into common usage until after World War II. In 1967, a Federal law officially changed the name to Memorial Day. On June 28, 1968, the Uniform Holidays Bill moved the celebration from May 30 to the last Monday of May. This change created a three-day weekend for Americans.

My being selected for this honor on this particular occasion was very special. We'd just learned on Monday that the army was sending Uncle Van back to Riverton to participate in the Decoration Day ceremony as well. I would be sharing the stage with my favorite uncle who just happened to be a genuine war hero. Aunt Maude and Johnnie were also coming to see the family and to attend the Libby-Comstock wedding. They would be staying with Grandma and Grandpa.

For all these reasons, we eagerly awaited their arrival that Tuesday night on the 10:05 train from Washington, D.C., by way of Detroit. Since all of us wanted to meet their train, we had arranged to borrow the Tucker station wagon to pick them up and transport them to the farm. Because of the holiday, there was no work or school the next day. Therefore, none of us minded staying up late to welcome the Harrison family back home again.

Having missed his weekly in-depth reading of the Sunday paper, Dad was trying to catch up before he headed off to work. "Wow, the Japs have begun their withdrawal from China. That's great! On the other hand, those Japs from China will be available to defend their home islands against our invasion of Japan when it comes." At that time, we had no way of knowing the U.S. Joint Chiefs of Staff had just approved *Operation Olympic*, the invasion of Japan. Amphibious landings had been scheduled to begin on November 1, 1945.

"What a *coward!*"

"Who's that, Dad?"

"Oh — I was just reading —. The German High Command and the Provisional Government have been imprisoned by the Allies. They'll be put on trial for war crimes. But one of Hitler's top henchmen chose not to face the music. SS Reichsfuhrer Heinrich Himmler committed suicide. He was the one responsible for the concentration and death camps. Nazi supermen? More like yellow-bellied bullies, if you ask me."

"John, what's the latest news on the bracelet thief?"

"Gee, Marie, I wish you'd been at the scout meeting last night. Jeff gave us an update on *John Smith*. Seems he's wanted by the Ohio State Police for grand larceny. Stole the car of a farm family he worked for down there. But more importantly, he's a navy deserter. They say he walked away from the hospital when he was going through boot camp at Great Lakes. FBI's been looking for him for some time. One of the Ohio state troopers told Jeff that this guy's served time for stealing jewelry before. What else did Sergeant Tolna say, boys?"

"His real name's Eddie Conroy. After he stole the bracelet, he realized he'd be a suspect and didn't want to be caught with the loot on him. That's why he opened our tent carton, stuck the bracelet inside the pole, and made his mark on the carton. Later, Mr. Tucker caught him in the garage looking for that carton."

"And it just so happened to be the carton containing *your* pup tent. You boys always seem to be in the right place at the right time."

"Then I'll bet this is the right place and time to ask for some more eggs — if you please, Mrs. A."

While Mom gave everybody seconds, she informed us, "When you get home from work and school today, I won't be here. We've formed a committee to plan Louise and Jim's wedding reception on Saturday. We're meeting at four o'clock at the Reilly's. With all the stores closed tomorrow for Decoration Day, we wanted to get our arrangements down to a tee so we can make our purchases on Thursday — then do our baking and other preparations on Friday."

"Who's on the committee, Marie?"

"We have Miss Bundy. She'll be in charge of the church kitchen. And Rose Bradford and Mary Reilly. There's Louise — and me. Who am I forgetting? Oh, of course, Christine Tucker."

"How many people are coming?"

"This is the list of those who've responded. Let me see. Two, four, six —," she counted. "Forty-three in all. And only one of them is a *maybe*. Governor Dewey."

"Don't worry, Mrs. A. He'll be there," Danny assured her.

When Mom erased the question mark next to the governor's name, Danny nodded his approval.

BY TUESDAY MORNING, WE had hoped our weekend skirmish with Conroy would have become old news at Hamilton School. While I didn't mind a bit of attention, excessive adulation expressed by some Hamiltonians was downright cloying. Our experience told us that these excesses would soon burn themselves out and everything would be back to normal.

Upon entering the schoolyard, we passed several students who simply nodded hello. Gradually the weight of anticipatory anxiety lifted from my chest. My step lightened and my mood changed for the better. By the time the bell rang, I was almost giddy with relief. When we reached the entrance, suddenly the door burst open. Standing there and grinning like a Cheshire Cat was Mr. Lund, who seemed unfocused and out of breath. For an instant, I wondered if Governor Dewey were making a return visit.

"Look! Look!" Mr. Lund shoved a piece of yellow paper onto my chest. I snatched it out of his hand and took a step backwards. But Mr. Lund kept coming toward me. "Look! Look!"

I clutched the paper against my chest with one hand and attempted to fend him off with the other. But he kept pushing and pushing at the paper until I'd skidded backwards to the edge of the concrete porch. To escape, I turned around and ran down the steps. When I reached the sidewalk, I looked back to see if he had followed me. Mercifully he had not.

Danny and JB were still standing at the door, watching me with their mouths agape. Sensing that Mr. Lund had relaxed a trifle, I opened the wrinkled wad of yellow paper.

It was a brief telegram from Governor Kelly.

0705 EWT, Tuesday, May 29, 1945

From: Honorable Harry F. Kelly
      Governor's Mansion
      Lansing, Michigan

To: Jase Addison, Danny Tucker, and Johnson Bradford
      C/O George Lund, Principal
      Hamilton School
      Riverton, Michigan

Greetings and congratulations to Jase, Danny, and JB:
Boy Scouts   100%
Bad Guys   0%
Keep up the good work!

Your friend,
Governor Kelly

Without warning, Mr. Lund ran down the steps, snatched the telegram from my hand, and screamed, "This is unbelievable. Isn't it, Jase? Unbelievable! Governor Kelly has sent *me* a telegram! Isn't this unbelievable?"

Frankly I was at a loss for words. First, I thought the telegram was addressed to the three of us. But even if it were addressed to him, I wasn't sure what was so *unbelievable* about it. Second, I was beginning to feel stressed again. The weight that had recently lifted from my chest crashed back into place, driving me like a nail about two feet into the sidewalk.

Confused by all of this, I looked at Danny. He sensed my need and came to my rescue. Calmly he walked down the steps and gently removed the telegram from Mr. Lund's hand.

After reading it quickly, he advised, "Mr. Lund, you should call
the *Riverton Daily Press* about this. Yes, sir! Call our friend, Chuck
Nichols. Tell him you're having a press conference to announce
something *very special.* We'll go to Miss Sparks' classroom now and
wait until he comes. When he gets here, please send your secretary
to get us. We want to be there when you show Mr. Nichols this
telegram. I guarantee his reaction will be *unbelievable.*"

"You think so, Danny."

"Mr. Lund, would I kid you about anything this — this
unbelievable?"

As usual, Danny's methods were a bit unconventional, but
they did the trick. While Mr. Lund rushed back to his office to call
the press, the three of us sought the protection of Miss Sparks'
classroom. When we arrived there, a situation requiring Danny's
immediate attention presented itself at the door. Having just seen
Danny manage Mr. Lund with ease, I was curious to see how he
would handle this dewy-eyed fifth grader who was obviously
smitten with him.

"Hi, Judie. How's everything?"

"Thank you, Jase," she cooed softly.

Not wanting to be impolite, I responded, "You're welcome,
Judie. It was nothing."

As I opened the door, I whispered to Danny, "When you're
finished talking to Judie, we'll see you inside."

Danny's face turned red. He sputtered something about a press
conference.

"Right. We'll see you there too."

JB and I walked in and took our seats. In need of a brief rest
before class started, I lowered my head into the circle of my arms
on my desk and closed my eyes. When the last bell rang, I raised
my head and looked around. Danny wasn't there. I glanced at JB,
who shot me a shrug.

After the opening formalities, Miss Sparks called the roll.
Danny was the only person absent. She looked at me. "I believe I
saw Danny before school, Jase. What happened to him?"

"I don't know, Miss Sparks. He was standing just outside the
door when JB and I came in. He was talking to Judie Matlock.
I —."

At that very instant, the door banged open. Danny entered the room, followed closely by Miss Banks, one of the two fifth-grade teachers. She made a beeline for Miss Sparks' desk. Bending over, she whispered. Miss Sparks nodded her head slowly. "That'd be fine, Danny. See you when you return."

Danny waved to us and then followed Miss Banks out of the room. I looked at JB, who shrugged again. During morning recess, Danny was nowhere to be found. At lunch hour, it was the same story. No Danny! Afternoon recess produced the same result.

"JB, this is very mysterious. Let's go inside and ask Miss Banks what happened to him."

But Miss Banks' room was empty. So was that of the other fifth-grade teacher. We considered asking Mr. Lund, but we ruled that out, owing to his agitated state of mind that day. Before class began, we decided to seek our teacher's help.

"Miss Sparks, where did Danny go?"

"He accompanied the fifth graders on a field trip. Miss Banks claimed he possessed special insider knowledge of the place they're visiting today."

"Where is that, Miss Sparks?"

"She didn't say."

We were skunked.

The rest of the afternoon plodded along very slowly. When the last bell finally sounded, JB and I scurried out of the classroom, down the hall, and out the door. When we reached the sidewalk, we heard the *beep* of a car horn. I glanced up to see Danny climbing out of a familiar car. JB and I wandered over and poked our heads through the car window.

"Hello, fellows! I'm returning your partner-in-crime. I need to get back to the office. See you guys later."

I looked at Danny, who had a funny grin on his face. "You have some explaining to do."

"I do?" he replied in his overly innocent voice.

"Talk!"

"Okay! I'll confess. When Judie told me the fifth graders were going on a field trip to the *Riverton Daily Press,* I told Miss Banks, because of our notoriety, I had some insider pull with the paper. I offered to go along to show them the ropes. She thought it was a great idea. And the field trip actually was fantastic. That's all there was to it."

When Danny said *that's all there was to it,* I immediately started looking for *what else* there was to it.

"Not good enough. Why'd you really go? Was it Judie?"

"Nope!"

"What then, Danny?"

"I went to warn Chuck Nichols not to take any phone calls from Mr. Lund."

THE TUCKERS WERE ONLY too happy to lend us their station wagon to pick up the Harrison family at the Grand Trunk station. "There's plenty of gas. No need to worry, John."

"Thanks, Sam. Nothing will be open that late so I appreciate it."

We said our goodbyes and left for the station.

When we arrived, we found the platform crowded with people. Those meeting arriving passengers carried *Welcome Home* signs and bouquets of irises, peonies, and roses. Others were catching trains to destinations all over the country. Among them, civilians like us had suitcases and hat boxes. Those in uniform had duffel bags, slung over their shoulders. Since most people were smokers, the smell of burning tobacco mixed with coal smoke from train engines and filled the air. Many impatient and weary travelers spoke loudly and acrimoniously, causing tension to fill the air as well.

"We're plenty early. Why don't we go into the depot and sit down? That way I can check with the stationmaster to see if their train's on time," Dad suggested.

As Dad made a path through the crowd, we dutifully followed single file behind him. When we entered the depot, I heard a familiar voice. "Hello, John. I see you're not wearing a poppy yet."

I looked up and saw Mr. Hornbeck from Hornbeck Shoes. In his crisp VFW uniform, including his official fore-and-aft cap, he looked like a soldier on a mission. In each hand, he held a bunch of red crêpe-paper poppies with wire stems wrapped in green tape.

I hadn't seen him since Danny and I had last stopped in at his store to look at our feet through his new fluoroscope machine. For the record, we saw the same skeletal image that we'd seen the time before. Our foot bones still radiated that eerie yellow-green color.

"Hello, Armand. You're on duty pretty late this evening."

"You're right, John. I'm pulling eleventh-hour duty tonight. Tomorrow's Decoration Day, and we still have red beauties to bestow on folks like you."

"Armand, you're in luck. We're in the market for four poppies."

"Here they are! Pick out the ones you want. Course they're all identical, you know."

Dad plucked four poppies from a bouquet and handed one to each of us. He reached in his wallet and removed a bill. "Where do you want me to put this, Armand?"

"Just drop it into my apron pocket, John. Thank you very much. It's going to a good cause this year, believe you me."

After pushing the stem of my paper poppy through a buttonhole in my shirt, I wondered where and when this unusual Decoration Day tradition had begun. "Dad, why do veterans always sell red poppies this time of year?"

"Jase, I know enough to answer your question adequately, but we have in our midst a real authority on the subject. Mr. Hornbeck is the VFW Post historian. Last year he spoke at great length about Decoration Day to Burke's employee-management council. He's the ideal person to ask."

"Mr. Hornbeck, could you tell me?"

"You bet, Jase. As this year's presenter of *General Logan's Order,* I know you're trying to learn as much as you can about Decoration Day. I'd be delighted to answer your question. But first, how much time do you have? I've got a two-hour answer — and a bunch of answers shorter than that."

The heat of my impending red face began creeping up my neck. I had momentarily forgotten that the VFW Post had selected me to make the presentation. As the post historian, Mr. Hornbeck undoubtedly had a say in my selection. I was embarrassed.

But I decided to forgive myself and try my best to move forward. "Uncle Van's train arrives at 10:05."

"I'll make it my two-minute answer. And please forgive me if I have to stop to make a poppy sale."

"Certainly, Mr. Hornbeck."

"As you know, the observance of Decoration Day was inaugurated by General Logan in 1868. But the poppy didn't emerge as the symbol of remembrance until World War I. It started when Lieutenant Colonel John McCrae, a Canadian doctor, wrote his celebrated poem, *In Flanders Fields,* about the fields of poppies in the Ypres salient near Flanders, Belgium. On that site, dreadful losses were suffered by both sides. Yet, the poppy seems to have prevailed. The poem, published in 1915, challenges us not to forget those who died there, even though beautiful poppies now cover the battlefield.

"In 1918, after hearing of McCrae's death in France, a patriotic American named Moira Michaels penned her reply to him in a poem entitled *We Shall Keep the Faith.* There she promised him that red poppies will always remind us of the blood of those who died in battle. Next she conceived the idea of wearing a red poppy on Decoration Day to honor those who had died serving our nation in war.

"In 1924, the Veterans of Foreign Wars was given a trademark for the *Buddy Poppy,* the designation of artificial red poppies that are the genuine products crafted by disabled and needy veterans. Since that time, we've sold our poppies all over the country, especially around Decoration Day.

"And that's not the long but it's the short of it, Jase. Any questions?"

"I do have one, Mr. *Hornshoe.* What's a —?"

"Jase, it's not *Shoehorn,* it's Hornbeck," Danny advised.

"Sorry, Mr. Hornbeck. I was going to ask you, what's a *salient?*"

Before he could answer, Danny informed everyone, "It's a part of a military front, line, or fortification that juts outward into enemy-held territory."

"Thank you, Danny. I was going to ask that myself," Dad admitted, glancing at his watch. "The train should arrive any moment. Nice job, Armand. Thank you again."

"That's Mr. Shoehorn to you," Mr. Hornbeck chuckled.

Everyone chuckled back except Danny. He simply mumbled, "Huh?"

When we returned to the platform, I saw the stationmaster looking at his pocket watch that was attached to a tooled-leather fob secured to the tooled-leather belt around his waist. Quickly he pivoted and nearly bumped into Dad. "Excuse me, sir. Are you waiting for the 10:05 from Detroit?"

"Yes, we are. Any news?"

"Nothing serious, but the train hit a cow on the track. The engineer had to stop. He estimates they'll be about 15 minutes late. Sorry about that, folks. It's the last train until the milk run at 3:19 a.m. There should be plenty of seats in the depot. I recommend you go inside and relax."

We all traipsed back into the depot. When Mr. Hornbeck saw us, he frowned. "What's up, John?"

"Van and Maude's train will be 15 minutes late. It's now due at 10:20."

"Boy, I didn't know you were waiting for Van Harrison. I was on my way home but I think I'll wait around. I'd like to shake that man's hand. Do you mind?"

"Heavens, no! Can't say I blame you. Please stay with us."

After we all sat down, I decided to use my time productively. I pulled my copy of *General Logan's Order* out of my back pocket. When Mr. Hornbeck saw what I had done, his eyes opened wide. He was obviously impressed. I read through the document one more time. Because it was not very long, I realized I was beginning to memorize it. I remember wondering whether that was a good or a bad sign.

When I finished, I folded the document and was about to return it to my pocket when Danny expressed an interest. "May I take a look at it?"

He unfolded the document and slowly read its contents.

General Order No. 11
Headquarters, Grand Army of the Republic
Washington, D.C., May 5, 1868

The 30th day of May, 1868, is designated for the purpose of strewing with flowers or otherwise decorating the graves of comrades who died in defense of their country during the late rebellion, and whose bodies now lie in almost every city, village, and hamlet churchyard in the land. In this observance no form or ceremony is prescribed, but posts and comrades will in their own way arrange such fitting services and testimonials of respect as circumstances may permit.

We are organized, comrades, as our regulations tell us, for the purpose, among other things, "of preserving and strengthening those kind and fraternal feelings which have bound together the soldiers, sailors, and marines who united to suppress the late rebellion." What can aid more to assure this result than by cherishing tenderly the memory of our heroic dead, who made their breasts a barricade between our country and its foe? Their soldier lives were the reveille of freedom to a race in chains, and their death a tattoo of rebellious tyranny in arms. We should guard their graves with sacred vigilance. All that the consecrated wealth and taste of the Nation can add to their adornment and security is but a fitting tribute to the memory of her slain defenders. Let no wanton foot tread rudely on such hallowed grounds. Let pleasant paths invite the coming and going of reverent visitors and found mourners. Let no vandalism of avarice or neglect, no ravages of time, testify to the present or to the coming generations that we have forgotten, as a people, the cost of free and undivided republic.

If other eyes grow dull and other hands slack, and other hearts cold in the solemn trust, ours shall keep it well, as long as the light and warmth of life remain in us.

Let us, then, at the time appointed, gather around their sacred remains and garland the passionless mounds above them with choicest flowers of springtime; let us raise above them the dear old flag they saved from dishonor; let us in this solemn presence renew our pledges to aid and assist those whom they have left among us as sacred charges upon the Nation's gratitude, the soldier's and sailor's widow and orphan.

JOHN A. LOGAN
Commander-in-Chief.

When he finished reading, he refolded it and handed it back to me.

"What did you think, Danny?"

"I think you'll do a terrific job tomorrow, Jase."

I just smiled at him.

MY PULSE STARTED TO race when the stationmaster announced the train would arrive shortly. From past experience, I knew once the incoming train passed the city limits, the number of street crossings would increase. Accordingly, the closer the train came to the station, the more warning whistles we would hear. When the predictable series of in-town whistles started, I began bouncing on the balls of my feet. My excitement was nearly unbearable. When the sleek, black steam engine rounded the bend west of the station, my breathing became irregular. I needed to cheer. Or perhaps scream.

"They're coming, Mom! They're coming!"

"I know, Jase. Isn't it exciting?"

"Wow! Look at that engine!" Danny yelped.

By then, the locomotive's engineer had reduced the train's speed to a crawl. On cue, the station's only redcap pushed his four-wheel, flatbed wagon to his luggage off-loading position on the platform. On both of its black-enameled side panels, bold gold lettering proclaimed it to be the property of the *Grand Trunk Western Railway Company*. The presence of the redcap, preparing to retrieve the Harrison family's luggage from the baggage car, was exhilarating. They were really arriving. This wasn't just a dream.

When the engine hissed to a stop, there was a frenzied movement of people both on the platform and within the train. The unloading process had begun. The conductor jumped down onto the platform to communicate with the stationmaster. Eager to depart, passengers pushed each other toward the exits located at each end of their cars. Those waiting on the platform pushed each other toward these same exits without really knowing from which their returning family member or friend would emerge. To give them room to perform their duties, railroad personnel pushed us back, away from these exits.

Mom spotted them first. "There's Aunt Maude — down there. Two cars down. Come on!" Mom propelled us toward her sister. I had yet to see them, but I moved as Mom directed. "Maude! Here we are. Yoo-hoo! Welcome home!"

Standing on the steps of their car, they waited for the people ahead of them to finish hugging and kissing. More handsome than ever in his smartly tailored uniform, Uncle Van was holding Johnnie in his left arm and waving with his right. When I saw Aunt Maude blot her eyes with her hankie, it surprised me. I couldn't remember ever seeing her weep, either in sadness or in joy. Perhaps when she was my roommate while Uncle Van was fighting in Europe, she couldn't allow herself to feel either emotion. But we were all together again in Riverton. This time, we were all safe.

Finally we had our chance to do the hugging and kissing, and we exercised our right enthusiastically. We shook hands, kissed cheeks, patted backs, smiled, and sniffled until we were nearly exhausted. While Dad and Uncle Van claimed the luggage from the redcap's wagon, the rest of us filled the time with small talk.

In the excitement of the homecoming, I had nearly failed to observe another person at the off-loading position. Dressed entirely in black with his hands folded behind his back, Mr. Edward Draper waited patiently. The passenger luggage would have to be off-loaded first. Next to him stood his black-enameled gurney whose subtle gold lettering proclaimed it to be the property of the *Draper Funeral Home.* His presence was an ominous reminder that not all young soldiers returned from the war to joyful families. Some returned in wooden boxes. On Decoration Day, these were the men we would honor, on that next day and every year to come.

Danny seemed to read my mind. "It's sad. Huh, Jase?"

"Yes, but this isn't a sad time for us. Is it?"

Danny shook his head and grinned. We quickly forgot Mr. Draper and his reason for being there that night.

Uncle Van turned his attention to the two of us. "Now then I've been hearing some good things about your latest crime-busting successes. You'll have to give me the complete lowdown of your recent heroics."

It was ironic that Uncle Van wanted to hear about *our* heroics. In Washington, when he was awarded the *Congressional Medal of Honor,* I hadn't heard him regaling people with stories about his gallantry.

"We'll be happy to give you all the nitty-gritty, Uncle Van. Until then, visualize four Ps," Danny instructed.

"Four Ps?"

"You got it, Your Uncleship!"

Uncle Van looked at me. I shrugged my shoulders and shook my head. Once again, I had no idea what Danny was talking about.

Although I wasn't sure this was the appropriate place or time, I broached a sensitive subject with Uncle Van. "Did you have an opportunity to spend much time with President Roosevelt before he passed away?"

"Funny you should ask that, Jase. Your Aunt Maude and I were discussing that on the way here. We feel privileged to have gotten to know both President and Mrs. Roosevelt. His passing has been difficult for us to accept. But there's one thing you should know. We're sure our friendship with them evolved quickly because of you and Danny. The President enjoyed you boys immensely. He dearly loved bragging about how he'd beaten Governor Dewey in a *partisan struggle* to win your loyalty. When I worked with him at the White House, I heard him say this time and time again.

"Your Aunt Maude and Mrs. Roosevelt have also developed a very fine friendship. Even though they only met a few months ago, I believe they're close friends, more so since the President died."

"Where's your *Medal of Honor,* Uncle Van?" Danny asked boldly.

"Oh, I only wear the medal itself on formal occasions."

Danny looked crushed. Uncle Van took note and tried another tack. "But I always wear this *Medal of Honor* service ribbon on my uniform along with these others," he explained, pointing at the blue ribbon containing an array of white stars in an M-shaped arrangement.

Hoping to continue on this tack, I added, "I'll bet that's the service ribbon for the *Victoria Cross.* Isn't it?" I pointed at a crimson ribbon containing a miniature gold replica of the medal itself.

"Yes, it is."

Danny still looked despondent. I didn't quite understand. "What's up, Danny?"

"I wanted to see Uncle Van's *Medal of Honor.*"

Uncle Van gave it another try. "You'll see it tomorrow. I'll be wearing it at the Decoration Day ceremony. Will that be soon enough?"

Danny didn't answer. Something was still troubling him. I pressed him further. "Danny, will you please tell us what's bothering you?"

"Oh, all right. I wore all of my medals and scout badges," he explained, unzipping his jacket. "I wanted to show them to Uncle Van. But it's not fair."

"Why not?"

"I'm wearing six and he's not wearing any. I didn't want to hurt his feelings."

AFTER WE LOADED OURSELVES and the Harrison luggage into the Tucker station wagon, we were *quite cozy* as Mom put it. Danny offered to help by holding little Johnnie, who hadn't opened his eyes since Uncle Van carried him off the train. I was amused to see my slightly egocentric best friend devoting his full attention to Johnnie, whose only expression of gratitude was to drool on Danny's jacket sleeve.

Perhaps in hopes of improving the cramped conditions, Mom offered a suggestion. "With the delayed arrival and extra time for getting the luggage, we're running awfully late. Jase, you have a big day tomorrow. Before we take Uncle Van and Aunt Maude out to Grandma's, perhaps we should drop you boys at the house so you can go to bed."

In a heartbeat, Danny squelched that idea. "We'll be perfectly fine, Mrs. A. No one has ever died of lack of sleep. Besides Grandma's expecting us. Wouldn't want to disappoint her. Now, would we?"

I didn't need my handy *Captain Midnight* decoder ring to decipher Danny's words. By saying *Grandma's expecting us,* Danny really meant Grandma's expecting *me*. Knowing Grandma well, Danny was expecting *her* to prepare a small feast for his arrival.

Sometimes, Danny did the right thing for the wrong reasons. This was one of those times. I really wasn't sleepy. On the contrary, I was eager to see Grandma and Grandpa's reaction when we arrived with the Harrison family. My presentation on the next afternoon was the least of my concerns. Besides I had rehearsed until I was blue in the face.

"Look! Every light in the house is on. That means they're expecting you, Maude. Maybe it's a surprise party. Sure, that's it. Old Nate Craddock and the Craddock sisters will be here. And Ma's invited the lovely Gypsy family, the Nyaris. And maybe the Donaldsons. And Homer Hagan. And the Henrys. Probably they'll all pop out of a cake at midnight," Mom teased.

"Do you really think Grandma will have a cake, Mrs. A?" Danny wondered hopefully.

Grandma and Grandpa came out of the house to meet us. I feared they would squeeze every last Harrison to death before we made it to the porch. Poor Grandma was suffering from broken-record syndrome, causing her to repeat the same words over and over. "Oh, for crying all night, just look at you. Oh, for crying all night, just look at you. Oh, for crying —."

When we entered the kitchen, secretly I felt completely validated. There was a feast all right, but it was no small one. Grandma's kitchen looked like it did on Christmas afternoon with all the family there for dinner. In the bright light, I noticed that Uncle Van had gained considerable weight since we had seen him last in Washington. Of course on that occasion, he was very thin since it had only been days since his escape from the German prisoner of war camp in Belgium.

"Danny, let me take the baby so you can have a little bite of something," Grandma suggested, confidently reaching for Johnnie. Oddly Danny stepped back and wrapped his arms more tightly around the still-sleeping baby, causing Johnnie to omit a mini-noise, consisting of half-sneeze and half-sigh. Choosing Johnnie instead of a table covered with Grandma's scrumptious offerings was strictly out of character for Danny.

Grandma was taken aback. She was also clearly exasperated with Danny, who normally could do no wrong in her eyes. It was time to roll out the big guns. In terms of influence over Danny, there was no weapon more lethal than Aunt Maude. You should have seen her. Like Delilah setting her trap for Sampson, Aunt Maude stared into Danny's eyes and tousled his hair, completely melting his resistance. Gently she lifted Johnnie out of his arms. "He needs to be changed. While I'm doing that, why don't you have something to eat? If you want, you can have him back after you finish."

Aunt Maude knew Danny well. Once he started nibbling, he was a goner. Johnnie would require a new holder, and I believed Grandma just might volunteer. I also believed that Danny wouldn't mind.

After Aunt Maude had left the room, Mom asked, "Ma, did you get over to Granville today?"

"Of course! Don't worry. Everything's taken care of."

Most of Grandma's family, including her parents and both sets of grandparents, had been members of the Church of Christ in the small village of Granville, some 10 miles from the Compton farm. For that reason, the Hope family was heavily represented in the peaceful cemetery, a rolling parcel of sparse woods and prairie adjacent to the church parking lot. Grandma made a point to attend church services there often, especially during the summer. After the service, she would retrieve her gardening gloves and tools from the trunk of her Terraplane and head for the cemetery. While caring for their gravesites, she shared old family stories with her ancestors, who in turn rewarded her with fresh memories of events she had nearly forgotten.

Following decades of tradition, families in and around Riverton spent the morning of each Decoration Day preparing family gravesites for the summer visiting season. This involved reseeding patches of missing grass, trimming shrubs or perennials, and planting annuals. The Hope family favorite was the red geranium.

While Grandma didn't mind this annual chore, her pride simply wouldn't allow her to permit others to see the Hope gravesites *under construction*. Bucking tradition, Grandma made an effort to ensure her family's graves were in tip-top shape before the other families arrived to do their spring work. Each year, on the day *before* Decoration Day, Grandma headed to Granville armed with three dozen geranium plants and her gardening tools. Her plants were in the ground and her gravesites manicured hours ahead of the other families.

With Johnnie out of the room, Grandma swooped in for the kill. "Danny, why don't you sit right here? If you'll take off your jacket, I'll hang it by the door. Just go ahead and help yourself. What would you like to drink?"

Without Johnnie in his arms and with food completely surrounding him, Danny became downright compliant. This was the old Danny we all knew and loved.

"I see you're wearing your medals and Boy Scout badges. They're very impressive pinned on your sweater. Did you show Uncle Van?"

"Hamshuf adshap boofed aram!" Danny refused to recognize normal proscriptions against talking with your mouth full. He rationalized thusly, "After all, which's more important? *Talk* or *nourishment?* Ask yourself this, when's the last time you heard of somebody dying from lack of talk?"

Who could disagree with that?

When Aunt Maude returned with Johnnie, he was wide awake and ready to play. He grinned, gurgled, and thrashed his arms. She took him directly to Grandma, who also grinned and gurgled as she wrapped her arms around him.

In an effort to move our midnight snack along, Mom handed out plates and silverware and put the coffeepot back on the cookstove. After I served myself, I sat down across the table from Danny.

I noticed he was wearing his *New York Medal of Recognition.*

That surprised me because his lease arrangement with his brother Chub had proved so profitable. Not only was Chub obsessed with wearing Danny's medal to school, but he still had no sense of the true value of small coins, namely dimes.

"So, Danny, how come Chub gave you back your *Medal of Recognition?* Did he run out of dimes?"

"He didn't give it back."

At first, I was confused. It must have been the late hour. Finally it dawned on me. I move to revise and extend my comments above to read as follows:

"I noticed he was wearing *my New York Medal of Recognition.*"

Without objection, my motion was unanimously accepted.

BY THE TIME WE returned the Tucker station wagon and walked home, it was after one o'clock in the morning. While none of us would have missed the Harrisons' homecoming or feasting at the Compton farm, we agreed it would be wise to sleep in for as long as we could the next morning. Therefore, our normal breakfast meeting didn't occur until eight o'clock.

"Boy, I don't know about the rest of you, but I slept like a log," Mom proclaimed. "I hope Maude and Van caught up on their sleep. I guess we don't have to worry about Johnnie. He appears to get plenty of sleep — anytime he wants."

"Marie, what's today's timetable? We need to work on the graves at Forest Hill sometime before the Decoration Day ceremonies begin, but I don't want to miss seeing Van and Maude."

"This morning, Van's meeting with Colonel Butler at the camp to plan their presentation. Then Maude and Van are coming here for a sandwich before we leave for Addison Square. Jase's presentation begins promptly at one o'clock. There'll be about an hour of speeches including Colonel Butler's and Van's. Then the parade to the cemetery will last about an hour. The Soldiers Monument ceremony will end with the 21-gun salute followed by taps at three o'clock."

"In that case, we better go to the cemetery right after breakfast."

Before the war, Dad had erected a white wooden trellis behind his parents' tombstones and planted a *New Dawn* rose. Because it bloomed all summer, this light pink rambler was popular for cemetery use in Riverton. Between the tombstones, he had planted a white peony bush and blue iris bulbs beside it. Each year, the peony and the iris bloomed around Decoration Day, and the rose followed shortly thereafter.

Following Grandma's example, Mom had purchased four red geraniums to place in front of the tombstones. Even though she would have to replant them next year, Mom knew her geraniums would bloom until fall. We helped Dad load the hoe, rake, watering can, pruning scissors, grass shears, trowel, weeding claw, and the flowers into the Chevy's trunk. We were prepared for anything.

When we arrived, the cemetery was crawling with cars and busy gardeners. Members of the American Legion were dutifully filling brass flag holders with miniature American flags at the graves of all war veterans. The emblem on the holder symbolized the military unit or the campaign in which the veteran had fought. In the light breeze, American flags fluttered proudly throughout the cemetery.

We unloaded the trunk and carried the tools and plants about a hundred yards to the Addison plot, containing six gravesites. Dad's parents occupied two of them. Two others were reserved for Mom and Dad. The last two were earmarked for me and some future sibling or spouse if either of these eventualities occurred.

Dad trimmed the grass, growing out-of-control around the tombstones, and cut away the deadwood from the rose, retying its vines to the trellis where necessary. Mom loosened the earth around the peony and the iris, snipped the dead stems from those perennials, and prepared her geranium beds.

Danny and I volunteered to be water boys. After a two-block hike to the nearest water pump, we waited in line for our turn behind a dozen other water boys and girls. When topped off with water, our 12-quart galvanized watering can was a heavy load. Danny and I took turns carrying it back to the Addison plot.

After admiring our work, we loaded the car and headed for home. When we turned onto Forrest Street, Grandma's Terraplane was parked in front of our house.

"What's Grandma Compton doing here, Mom?"

"That'll be Aunt Maude and Uncle Van. They used Grandma's car to go to the meeting at the POW camp."

"Great! I can't wait to see them."

While Aunt Maude and Mom assembled the sandwich makings in the kitchen, we men sat in the front room, chatting about manly topics like the war, baseball, and fishing. Suddenly it dawned on me. "Where's Johnnie, Uncle Van?"

"Oh, Grandma Compton's keeping him. She'll bring him with her to the Addison Square ceremony. She and Grandpa are catching a ride to and from the festivities with their neighbors, the Henrys."

While we were finishing lunch, Uncle Van confronted Danny on some unfinished business. "Danny, you promised to give me the nitty-gritty on your latest crime-busting successes. What did you mean when you told me to visualize the four Ps?"

"All right. Here goes. We've solved three cases since we saw Aunt Maude and you at the White House," Danny stated. "The first was the Conrad Hoffman case. He was one of the leaders of the German American Bund and the former husband of Mrs. Libby. We flushed him out of the Libby house using Sergeant Tolna's police car.

"The second was the Sergeant Shane case. He was the POW guard who went berserk and shot three people in the German restaurant. After his escape, he came after Mrs. A because he hated her teaching sewing classes to the German POWs. He was on his way to hurt her when I knocked him out with my perfect pitch."

Danny's latest characterization of the errant toss surprised me. A *perfect* pitch? All along I had been thinking it was a *wild* one. *What did I know?*

Without missing a beat, Danny continued, "Our third was the Eddie Conroy case. He was the navy deserter and jewel thief. He stashed his loot in, what later did him in, our pup tent.

"And there you have it! Any questions?"

"Just one, Danny. Where do the four Ps come in?"

"I just told you — *police* car, *perfect pitch,* and *pup* tent. Three cases solved by four Ps."

Turning to me, Danny confirmed, "Right, Jase?"

"Precisely put, pal!" I professed.

ALTHOUGH ADDISON SQUARE WAS used by the City of Riverton for official functions, technically it was not the town square. Situated at the far north end of Addison Street, it was some distance from the center of town. This block-square parcel was owned by Christ Episcopal Church which, having been built largely with donations from my great-grandfather, occupied the far eastern portion of the fully landscaped property.

Wide sidewalks from the four corners of the square intersected at its center where a cobblestone circle with a 70-foot diameter was embedded in the lawn. In the center of the circle stood a large bronze cross. Lining the sidewalks and circle itself were handsome lampposts, festooned with red, white, and blue bunting to celebrate Decoration Day.

To one side of the cross, a substantial oak podium was positioned in front of an array of flag stands, containing the American, the State of Michigan, and VFW flags. To provide the audience with a view of the elegant fieldstone church, rows of chairs were positioned to the west of the podium.

The last row was reserved for a dozen members of the Riverton High School band who would play for the singing of the National Anthem. Because the city had a limited number of wooden folding chairs, Rivertonians typically arrived early to ensure they had a seat. Others, arriving later, carried their own chairs. Standing through an hour's worth of speechmaking in the midday sun was to be avoided, if at all possible. Of course, in those days, both the gentlemen and ladies wore hats, which offered some protection.

The invocation, delivered by Father Hardy from Christ Episcopal Church, would be followed by the National Anthem, and the Pledge of Allegiance. Then Mr. Hornbeck, the master of ceremonies, would introduce me as the first speaker. When I finished, he would introduce Colonel Butler, who would make some brief remarks relating to the importance of recognizing our fallen heroes. In turn, the Colonel would introduce Uncle Van, the returning hometown hero and the main speaker of the day.

The first row of chairs was reserved for us speakers. I sat between Mr. Hornbeck and Colonel Butler. Danny sat directly behind me in the second row. While I was in my scout uniform, he had worn his blue blazer, white shirt, and Michigan tie. Emulating those in military uniform, he had pinned every one of his medals over his left breast pocket. Of course on this day, Uncle Van wore his *Medal of Honor,* which hung from the blue ribbon circling his neck.

My mind scrolled backwards to the White House and President Roosevelt's presentation of that award to Uncle Van. After smiling at all of us, the President began reading the citation that declared Uncle Van had distinguished himself by demonstrating gallantry and intrepidity above and beyond the call of duty while engaged in operations against the enemy. Because I was overcome by feelings of pride, joy, and admiration, I have difficulty remembering the rest. Fortunately for the family, the citation is enshrined at the Pentagon where it will honor Uncle Van in perpetuity.

During the week before Decoration Day, Danny had heard me rehearse my reading of *General Logan's Order* so many times, he became bored. As a diversion, he decided to time me, using the kitchen clock. He did this twenty-three times. On average, my delivery time was three minutes and 14 seconds. On a whim, he counted the number of words in the order. There were 486. Finally he calculated the words-per-minute.

"Amazing! It came out exactly 150! Did you realize you talked 150 words a minute, Jase?"

That's how bad it got.

On the other hand, because I was so familiar with the content, I was relaxed and confident of doing a good job. That was before Mr. Hornbeck started to get nervous on my behalf.

"Jase, we don't have a public-address system. You'll have to speak **very loudly** to be heard in the back rows — especially when the wind's gusty like it's been off and on all day."

"I'll do my **very best**, Mr. Hornbeck."

Until his admonishment, my only concern was my reading. But he had added the loudness of my voice and possible gusts of wind to my list. Just what I needed, right before my presentation.

When he finally took the podium, Mr. Hornbeck looked impressive in his neatly pressed VFW uniform. In his flattering introduction, he summarized my acts of courage with Danny over the previous year and the widespread recognition we had received from the press, world leaders, and the public at large.

"For the reading of *General Logan's Order,* please welcome Jase Addison." After shaking my hand, he turned the podium over to me. I laid down my copy of the order and turned my attention to the audience.

That's when it hit me.

Hundreds of people were staring right at me. Suddenly I felt a tremendous pressure on my temples. My chest and my throat simultaneously tightened. Panic-stricken, I looked down at Danny who evidently sensed what was happening. Without missing a beat, he shot me a wink and a grin.

Instantly the spell was broken.

I took a deep breath, looked down at my paper, and began reading. "General Order No. 11 — Headquarters, Grand Army of the Republic — Washington, D.C. — May 5, 1868.

"Article One. The 30th day of May, 1868, is —."

In response to Mr. Hornbeck's distracting motions, I stopped. With his mouth wide open, he was frantically waving his hand between his chest and his chin. Having gotten my attention, he ceased gesturing and whispered, "Louder!"

I turned up the volume.

" — designated for the purpose of strewing with flowers or otherwise decorating the graves of comrades who died in defense of their country during the late rebellion, and whose bodies now lie in almost every city, village, and hamlet churchyard in the land.

He seemed satisfied.

In this observance no form or ceremony is prescribed, but posts and comrades will in their own way arrange such fitting services and testimonials of respect as circumstances may permit."

Suddenly a powerful gust of wind struck me in the chest. Its force pushed me a step backwards. The only copy of *General Logan's Order* shot over my head on its way skyward. I watched as the paper disappeared beyond the row of tall elm trees, lining the perimeter of the square.

When l turned back to my audience, every face wore an expression of sympathy and concern. In desperation, I looked at Danny, who rescued me again.

"We are organized, **comrades, as our regulations tell us, for the purpose, among other things, 'of preserving and strengthening those kind and fraternal feelings which have** bound together the soldiers, sailors, and marines who united to suppress the late rebellion.' What can aid more to assure —."

By his fourth memorized word, I had joined him. Together we recited the remaining words of *General Logan's Order*.

The applause was deafening. Of course, Danny stood and bowed from the waist.

21 WEDDING BELLS

"THE WEDDING RECEPTION WAS PERFECT IN EVERY respect," Reverend Noble proclaimed to the members of the committee, all of whom purred in response to the handsome young minister's flattery. "You're all to be complimented," he added, before leaving the ladies and us boys to finish our cleanup chores in the First Methodist Church basement.

"It's too bad Louise missed hearing that comment. She worked harder than any of us. Don't you think so, Marie?"

"Oh, she did that all right, Miss Bundy. But we could have never accomplished this without your help in the kitchen. Your ability to operate all that equipment so every food item came out on time and perfectly cooked was nothing short of a miracle. How can you do that so effectively?"

"Practice, my dear. Practice. I've been doing that ever since the church was built. I even worked with the architect to design this kitchen. Frankly I think of it as my own."

"Louise and Jim were lucky to have you in charge down here. Believe me."

"Speaking of the newlyweds, do you know where they're honeymooning, Marie?"

"I know they're going by train because Governor Dewey mentioned he'd be taking them to the station after the reception. But I don't know where they're heading. Does anyone know?"

After emptying the huge trash barrel, Danny reentered the basement just in time to hear Mom's question. "Know what?"

"Where the newlyweds are going for their honeymoon."

"Sure. Chicago. They're going to take in the Don McNeil *Breakfast Club* radio show. Just like Grandma Compton, Jase, and I did last fall when we got our first *Medals of Courage* from President Roosevelt and J. Herbert Hoover. Right, Jase?"

"How do you know that, Danny?" his mother pressed him skeptically.

"I suggested it to Coach Jim a few weeks back. He made me promise to keep it a secret until they left town. Is there any cake left, Mrs. A?"

While Mom served Danny his sixth piece of cake, JB and I continued to dry the silverware.

"There were a couple of people I didn't know," Mrs. Bradford admitted. "Who was that strange-looking man wearing that old tuxedo?"

"Oh, that's Buddy Roe Bibs. Since last summer, he's been a permanent resident and trustee of the Good Mission Church."

"What an odd name."

"Oh, that's just his nickname. Whenever Reverend Squires addresses a Mission resident whose name he doesn't know, he calls him *Buddy Roe*. Then he tacks on something about the man to make it more personal. Bibs always wears bib overalls. So he became Buddy Roe Bibs."

"Where did he get that ratty old tuxedo?"

"That was Gentleman Jim's old uniform."

"Who's that?"

We all snickered.

"You may not believe this, but until this past summer, Gentleman Jim was one of our two neighborhood bums. The other one's Bohunk Joe."

"What happened last summer?"

"For one thing, Gentleman Jim took a bath, shaved, and put on a suit and tie. Then he testified in court as a character witness for the two Libby sisters. Without his testimony, their prison sentences would have been much longer."

"Have they thanked him since their parole?"

"If they haven't, they'll have to wait a week or so."

"Why's that?"

"He and Louise have just left for their honeymoon."

"Oh, my gosh! Jim Comstock was Gentleman Jim? You've got to be kidding me! Am I the only one here who didn't know that?"

We all laughed, including Mrs. Bradford.

"Mom, just so you don't feel alone. I saw three people I didn't recognize either," JB admitted. "There was an older man with two women who looked and dressed exactly alike."

"That was Nate Craddock and his cousins, Abigail and Lucille Craddock. They live on the farm adjacent to the Compton farm. This past fall, Mr. Craddock was held hostage by two escaped German POWs, who had also kidnapped Danny. After he was rescued, Nate was so ill the Craddock sisters moved here from Ohio to take care of him. They're honest-to-goodness miracle workers. They've completely refurbished the Craddock farmhouse and even Mr. Craddock himself. To top it off, they've generously established a college-scholarship fund for the children of families in our neighborhood. We'll have to check with them, but I believe you might be eligible, JB."

"Really? That would be great, Mrs. Addison."

"The ceremony was absolutely lovely!" Mrs. Reilly exclaimed. "Didn't everyone look beautiful? Barb and Anne in their identical peach-colored dresses were stunning. I've never been to a wedding with two maids of honor. And Jim and his best man, Harry Chambers, looked as handsome as all get out."

On that point, the ladies all agreed.

"I thought the most touching part of the wedding was when we lined the sidewalk to see the couple off."

"That's when I caught Mrs. Libby — er — Comstock's flowers," Danny reminded us.

"When the billowy cloud of pure white fluff from the cottonwood tree swirled above and finally came floating softly down on the wedding party, it was simply — magical."

"Mom, this entire spring's been magical."

"You're exactly right, Jase, old pal," Danny declared. "In fact, every season of this year has been magical!"

And so it had!

AUTHOR'S NOTES

THE HISTORICAL SETTING

The four Cottonwood books, *Cottonwood Summer,* *Cottonwood Fall, Cottonwood Winter: A Christmas Story,* and *Cottonwood Spring,* span the four seasons of the last year of World War II. This year-long story begins with the D-Day invasion in June of 1944 and ends shortly after V.E. Day, the surrender of Germany, in May of 1945.

That single year impacted America and the rest of the world like few other years in history. And the larger-than-life events of that year provided a dramatic historical setting for these books. Moreover, the world leaders who orchestrated these events, including Franklin Roosevelt, Winston Churchill, J. Edgar Hoover, and Thomas Dewey, are also characters in the Cottonwood story. They serve as role models for the eleven-year-old home-front heroes, Jase Addison and Danny Tucker, who emulate, astound, and ultimately befriend these four giants of history.

According to reviewers, the Cottonwood books are entertaining, comedic, heartwarming, gripping, and loyal to small-town values of mid-20th century America. But perhaps more importantly they also remind readers of the enormous sacrifices made by Americans, as well as other peoples of the world, during the war.

To provide a perspective, estimates of worldwide civilian and military deaths, resulting directly from the war, range from 50 to 70 million. As a nation, the Soviet Union suffered the most with 27 million deaths. The total number of men and women serving in the armed forces of the combatants was over 85 million.

Of those, 16 million were Americans. Our country's population at the start of the war was 131 million. Therefore, one out of every eight Americans was in uniform, including well over half of all Americans between the ages of 18 and 40. During the war, it was extremely difficult to find an American family without a father, uncle, son, brother, or sister in the service. In contrast, today we are a country of over 300 million people with only 1.5 million of our citizens serving in the armed forces. Instead of one out of eight, the proportion serving today is one out of 200.

Between 1941 and 1945, American losses were staggering, especially when compared to our nation's more recent military conflicts. The number of American aircraft lost in operations against the enemy was 45 thousand. We also lost 157 major warships and submarines. Not counting hundreds of thousands of wounded, America suffered 405 thousand killed in action, 79 thousand missing in action and still unaccounted for, and 130 thousand captured by the enemy. Of those captured, 14 thousand died in captivity before they could be rescued. Today, over 93 thousand Americans, who were killed in action in World War II, are buried, not here at home, but in military cemeteries in Europe, Africa, and the Far East.

WORLD WAR II AND THE COTTONWOOD STORY

For readers, who have traveled with us on this Cottonwood journey, we offer the following inventory of the major milestones of World War II addressed in the four Cottonwood books:

Prior to *Cottonwood Summer*

1939
September 1 -   Germany invades Poland to start World War II.
September 3 -   Britain, France, Australia, and New Zealand declare war on Germany.

1940
June 14 -   Germany launches Blitz against England.
September 27 - Axis pact signed by Germany, Japan, and Italy.
November 5 -   Franklin D. Roosevelt reelected President.

1941
December 7 -   Japan bombs Pearl Harbor.
December 8 -   America declares war on Japan and enters World War II.
December 10 -   Japan invades Philippines.
December 11 -   Germany declares war on America.

1942
February 22 -   President Roosevelt orders General MacArthur out of Philippines.
March 11 -   MacArthur leaves Corregidor, pledging to return.
April 1 -   Japanese-Americans sent to relocation centers in U.S.
April 18 -   Doolittle conducts surprise B-25 raid on Tokyo.
May 8 -   American carrier forces defeat Japanese carrier forces in Battle of Coral Sea.
June 5 -   American carrier forces defeat Japanese in Battle of Midway.
August 7 -   Americans make first amphibious landing on Guadalcanal in the Solomons.
November 8 -   Americans invade North Africa.

Prior to Cottonwood Summer (continued)

1943

May 13 -   German and Italian troops surrender in
                  North Africa.
July 9 -   Allies land in Sicily.

1944

January 22 -   Allies land at Anzio in Italy.
May 19 -   Allies capture Monte Cassino in Italy.

During *Cottonwood Summer*

1944

June 6 -   D-Day: Allies land at Normandy in
                  Northern France.
June 13 -   First German V-1 attack on Britain.
June 19 -   Americans shoot down 220 Japanese planes at
                  "Marianas Turkey Shoot."
July 3 -   Battle of the Hedgerows in Normandy continues.
July 20 -   ssassination attempt on Hitler fails.
August 25 -   Allies liberate Paris.

During *Cottonwood Fall*

1944

September 4 -   Allies liberate Antwerp and Brussels.
September 13 -   U.S. troops reach Siegfried Line.
October 20 -   U.S. Sixth Army invades Leyte in the Philippines.
October 21 -   Germans surrender at Aachen in Germany.
October 25 -   First Kamikaze attack in Leyte Gulf in
                  the Philippines.
November 7 -   Roosevelt defeats Dewey in Presidential election.

During *Cottonwood Winter*

1944

December 16 - Germans launch Ardennes counteroffensive (Battle of the Bulge).

December 17 - Waffen SS murder 81 U.S. POWs at Malmedy in Belgium.

December 26 - Patton relieves Bastogne in Belgium.

1945

January 17 - German withdrawal from Ardennes complete.

January 17 - Soviets capture Warsaw.

January 26 - Soviets liberate Auschwitz.

February 4 - Roosevelt, Churchill, and Stalin meet at Yalta.

February 19 - U.S. marines invade Iwo Jima, an island 650 miles south of Tokyo.

During *Cottonwood Spring*

1945

March 2 - U.S. airborne troops recapture Corregidor, a fortified island in Manila Bay.

March 9 - Tokyo firebombed by 279 B-29s.

April 1 - Allies discover stolen Nazi art and wealth in salt mines.

April 1 - U.S. Tenth Army invades Okinawa, a Japanese prefecture (state).

April 12 - Allies liberate Buchenwald and Bergen-Belsen concentration camps.

April 12 - President Roosevelt dies; Truman becomes President.

April 21 - Soviets reach Berlin.

April 28 - Italian partisans capture and hang Mussolini.

April 30 - Adolph Hitler commits suicide.

May 7 - German forces surrender unconditionally to Allies.

May 8 - Victory in Europe Day (V.E. Day).

May 9 - SS Reichsfuhrer Heinrich Himmler commits suicide.

May 20 - Japanese begin withdrawing troops from China.

May 25 - Joint Chiefs approve Operation Olympic, the invasion of Japan.

After *Cottonwood Spring*

1945

July 5 -	Liberation of Philippines declared.
August 6 -	First atomic bomb dropped on Hiroshima, Japan.
August 9 -	Second atomic bomb dropped on Nagasaki, Japan.
August 14 -	Japanese agree to unconditional surrender.
September 2 -	Japanese sign unconditional surrender; Victory over Japan (V.J. Day)
October 24 -	UN charter ratified by England, France, China, Soviet Union, and United States.

ACKNOWLEDGEMENTS

In 1999 when I began to write fiction, I never dreamed that ten years later the result would be four successful *Cottonwood* novels. Dozens of people have played indispensible roles in this decade-long effort. Here in *Cottonwood Spring*, the last book of the series, I would like to acknowledge just a few of them.

The inspiration for *Danny* was Billy Curtis, my very best friend growing up on Frazier Street in Owosso, Michigan. Our childhood adventures formed the basis for many of the *Cottonwood* stories. Other storylines are pure fiction, created solely from my *active* imagination. Only Billy and I know the difference, and that knowledge shall always remain our secret — and ours alone.

My young and enthusiastic seventh-grade teacher, Mrs. Pat Vaughn, rescued me from academic oblivion by cleverly daring me to live up to my potential. Owing to her care and concern, my lust for learning was launched at precisely the right moment in my life. I will be forever in her debt.

Many *Cottonwood* storylines involved characters based on friends from families who lived in my old Frazier Street neighborhood: the Curtises, Worthingtons, Farleys, and Hildebrants. No author could find more loyal and dedicated fans. I greatly appreciate their continuing friendship and support.

The *Addison, Harrison,* and the *Compton* characters were based on members of my own family. My parents Charles and Mildred

Slaughter were accurately portrayed as *John* and *Marie Addison*. My uncle, James Waters, served bravely in World War II and provided a credible basis for the *Cottonwood* character, *Van Harrison*. His wife and my childhood roommate, Aunt Dee, was *Aunt Maude*. My cousin, Jimmy Waters, was *Little Johnnie*. My maternal grandparents, Grover and Lavina Mitchell lived the life of *Grandpa and Grandma Compton*, Terraplane and all.

Over the course of the Cottonwood series, my older cousin, Leonard Mitchell, graciously provided fact after fact about the early years on the Mitchell family farm. And during the writing of *Cottonwood Spring*, I relied heavily on refresher training in the subjects of fishing, catching bait, and mushrooming from my old school friends Bill Walters and Jim Bishop.

Here in Nashville, I was indeed fortunate to receive the continuing support and encouragement from our friends at Ingram Books, Tennessee Humanities, and the Nashville chapter of the Women's National Book Association.

Finally I could have never mustered the staying power to complete the *Cottonwood* series without being fueled by the thousands of thoughtful and generous telephone calls, e-mails, and letters from fans all over the world.

Thank you all.

Gary Slaughter
Nashville
March 2009